DIANA

Book Three
The Sacred Women's Circle

Judith Ashley

Windtree Press
PORTLAND, OREGON

Windtree Press
818 SW 3ʳᵈ Avenue #221-2218
Portland, OR 97204-2405
www.windtreepress.com

Cover Design: Christy Caughie @GildedHeartDesigns.com
Book Layout ©2013 BookDesignTemplates.com
Editing: Kelly Schaub
http://www.the-efa.org/dir/memberinfo. php?mid=8345

Ordering Information:
Quantity sales. Special discounts are available on quantity purchases by corporations, associations, and others. For details, contact the "Special Sales Department" at the address above.

Diana/Judith Ashley -- 1st ed.
ISBN 9781940064550

Dedication
To Kris, Heather and Michele: my own sacred women's circle.

Acknowledgements

Every book requires a village of people to bring it to you, the reader. My village is extensive and for *Diana* starts with my best friend, Michele, who listened to me read each days words and gave me feedback. Lois stepped up next and read the entire manuscript. Long phone conversations ensued with discussions on how to not only make this story better but what to include or hint at for the books to come. A final edit was done by Kelly Schaub.

Along the way, I had amazing support from Maggie Lynch, Terrel Hoffman, Sarah Raplee, and the #RCRWFTB folks. And not to be forgotten, Mariah endured many "in just a minute", "let me finish this paragraph, page, chapter". The reality that you are proud of me gladdens my heart.

Authors note: Again there are aspects of international travel that may not be accurate but are included as they are for the story. This is fiction, after all.

1   THE TRUTH

Kinslow, Ireland
Winter Solstice

Diana Pettybone sank onto the wide stone window sill at The Manor, the castle-like home of her friend and circle sister, Elizabeth. Outside the winter sun shone brightly, its rays streaming in the mullioned glass. It was a beautiful day for a wedding, but a disastrous day for her marriage. Her tears drenched the silk robe pulled tight. She shook with silent sobs, her broken breathing the only sound. Shivering, she shifted, set her feet on the sill, her arms clutched her knees as she rocked slowly like a winding down pendulum, lost in a world of darkness. The clock on the mantle chimed the hour, the sun's rays flashed through the window like shafts of lightning.

Her rocking eased, her tears slowed. Diana leaned her forehead against the glass, her gaze unseeing. She was hollow inside but not empty. The echoes of her envious, jealous, covetous thoughts feeding the self-loathing oozed into every cell as she searching for answers.

There were none.

Or perhaps she was blind.

Emotional exhaustion did that; immobilized the brain. Hers seemed unable to quit its painful thoughts, unable to give her any peace.

She hated the words that flashed through her mind, the envy that ate at her heart, the jealousy that sucked up her energy, the covetousness that stabbed at her soul. What else could she do other than what she'd been doing?

Every alternative had its own pain.

She rubbed her forehead against the cool glass, trying to ease the pounding in her head, to wipe the jealousy from her mind.

It did not work.

Instead she found shivers of emotion striking like lightning; the hated words an endless tape in her mind.

The clock on the mantle chimed the half hour. Diana sat on the stone sill, in this small sitting room in her friend's home, her head bowed in futile repentance. A knock on the door, a voice calling to her; in her misery she did not answer. *How can I face the woman on the other side of the door?*

The clock on the mantle chimed the hour. Too exhausted to cry or rock, Diana stilled, leaned back against the window's casing, prepared to face her personal nightmare; she'd be left with nothing if she didn't find a way out of this morass. *I'll lose my best friends, my sacred women's circle, if I don't find the way out of my loveless, toxic marriage.*

The idea of leaving had been on her mind a dozen maybe even a hundred times—but she stayed. It was her choice, therefore her fault she remained with Dennis. A dark, humorless chuckle escaped as she reviewed the remnants of her reasoning.

No one in my family ever divorced. What a scandal that would be, especially when my parents had warned Dennis was not worthy of me. How ironic since I was and still am the daughter who never did anything right. And Bill? He needed - still needs a father, doesn't he? Lastly I was raised in the Catholic Church and taught divorce was not an option.

Diana sat, her arms now wrapped around her knees, her eyes gritty from tears. Although bathed in the rays of the sun, her desolation wrapped her in darkness. Her head thundered, sparks of a sharper pain skittered across her scalp. Bands of steel in her shoulders and neck spasms added their unrelenting hold to her suffering.

She rolled her neck and shoulders, willing the stiffness away. *I have to find a way, a way past this all-encompassing despair, this resentment so strong it's only a matter of time before it consumes me and everything, everyone I love is lost.*

It wasn't just her circle sister Elizabeth's wedding this morning that sparked her misery. Lily, the first in The Circle to marry, and her husband Jackson were celebrating their six-month anniversary today. Even after six months, their joy easily matched that of the newly-weds, Elizabeth and Michael. Since her arrival ten days ago and especially since Dennis's three days ago, she'd had no relief. No relief from seeing their joy, no place to evade their happiness. Day in and day out she'd been faced with the reality of her marriage: empty, loveless, painful and more than that, toxic.

Once again she asked the questions that seemed to have no answer.

"What's wrong with me? Why can't I have a loving marriage?"

Diana slowed her breathing and consciously challenged her physical and emotional exhaustion. *I want to move past this debilitating pain and incapacitating fear.* She breathed deeply, a cleansing breath, breathed a second and yet a third time. *If I want my life different, I must act and act now while I have this window of time to think, to choose, to plan.* Her heart raced. Anticipation? Dread? She didn't know.

Slipping off the sill, she braced her arms on the stone ledge and waited for her legs to stiffen. Her attention focused on the small sitting room that had become her sanctuary, her haven. Restless, she paced around the room, blew out a guttering candle, and watched the thin spiral of smoke from the wick as it disappeared into the air leaving behind a trace of bayberry. Calmer now, she turned, taking in the details of the room. Her gaze paused on her Winter Solstice altar, on a stack of three books she was reading, and on the low table in front of the fireplace where her women's circle's Solstice gift lay: a starter set of Tarot cards.

Diana crossed the room to the chair by the fireplace, lifted the multi-hued green wool throw off the back and wrapped herself in its warmth in an effort to chase away the bone-deep cold, a residue from her storming emotions. Easing down to sit cross-legged on the rug in front of the hearth, she took the poker from the rack and stirred the embers. Bit-by-bit she added small pieces of kindling, blowing softly on the glowing light until the fire came back to life. Between the wool and the blaze the marrow of her bones warmed. She stared into the flames, blanking her mind in a short reprieve.

I have this small window of time to sort things out. Once home in Fremont my daily life, responsibilities, expectations, and Dennis will impinge upon my time. It was dramatic to think now or never but those words rang clear, like a bell ringing in a pristine-dark night one can hear for long moments after it stops.

Diana

What do I want? A loving, respectful marriage, a husband who is faithful to me, the passion Lily and Elizabeth have in their marriages, someone to look at me as if I am his world. I know what I want. So, what must change for me to have a loving, respectful, safe relationship in my life?

That was her question. Simple. Clearly stated.

The answer obvious.

Her husband, Dennis, was the main stumbling block to having the marriage she wanted. Yes, there were other issues: she just turned forty and finding someone else was daunting in and of itself; there were Bill and her parents; there was her Catholic upbringing. But in the end, being married to Dennis was the biggest obstacle.

Diana sat and watched the flames dance, their red, orange, and blue colors melding, flowing together.

One truth: *Bill is gone.* A sophomore in college he was building a life on the East Coast and it was time to let him go.

A second truth: *I'm no longer Catholic.* Over eight years ago she'd joined this women's circle. Together they had crafted a spirituality with a foundation built on the "old ways" of earth-based religions. Their ceremonies brought peace and joy to her heart. Lily, a member of her women's circle and one of her closest friends, saw today as the beginning of a new year. As a rule in pagan traditions, it was Samhain. *I haven't really thought about it, even after all this time, but maybe Winter Solstice is a new beginning for me, too.*

A third truth: *My parents, even now in their seventies, will surely criticize me if I leave Dennis whether by separation or divorce.* But it would be nothing new. *When have they ever praised me, been please with me, approved? I can't remember a time.* Her posture slumped. *Their disapproval is still painful.*

Determination straightened her spine. *While their disapproval is still painful, Dennis's on-going infidelities are intolerable.*

Diana stood and looked around the room seeing the light from the sun make mullioned window patterns on the dark carpet, seeing the flickering from the fire dance on the walls, seeing The Tarot cards beckon to her.

In her circle, Hunter, Sophia, and Gabriella used The Tarot cards regularly and even Lily, Elizabeth, and Ashley used other kinds of divination cards. She participated in group readings but had never attempted her own reading. Until this gift she'd not even owned a deck. As a beginner, she appreciated the meanings were printed on each card to help a novice discern more easily what the cards were saying.

I know the basics: have a question in mind and concentrate on it as I shuffle the deck, and lay out the cards. What would it hurt? It would be doing something different. Actually for me it would be doing something very different. She smiled as tingles of excitement skittered across her skin.

Diana padded to the table and sat facing the fire. The cards like a siren, called her to take a chance, to dash herself on the rocks in order to break free, to find a new way forward. She reached behind her for a pillow off the couch and tucked it under her. Her fingers slipped around the box drawing it closer. As she opened it and took out the deck, wisps of anticipation snaked up her spine.

I have to have a question. Her brow furrowed in thought. The feelings of anticipation evaporated; hopelessness slithered in. *This is so dumb. What am I doing?* She started to put the cards back in the box.

A knock on the door.

Dennis's voice snarled, "I know you're in there, Diana. What the hell are you doing?"

The door knob rattled as he tried to push his way in. She sat in silence unwilling to acknowledge him. Her heart pounded, her hands dampened, her breath locked in her lungs.

"You'll pay for this little escapade! Oh, hi there, Montgomery."

Diana marveled at how quickly Dennis could flip the switch and change. His bonhomie was evident in his tone as he engaged Jackson. She heard Jackson's deep voice but he was too far away from the door to make out his words.

"Just checking on Diana. Nothing to worry about, I can assure you."

She listened as Dennis's now jovial voice dimmed, signaling he was moving away. Her heart slowed, she wiped her hands on the throw, her lungs gasped for air.

Her hands shook as she put the cards back on the table and took a deep breath.

I want my life to be different, to have a man who loves me, respects me, and is faithful. Show me the way.

Her hands grappled with shuffling the new deck of cards. *Show me the way.*

Her hands grasped the cards more confidently as she shuffled them a second time. *Show me the way.*

Her hands easily shuffled them a third time as she chanted under her breath, "Show me the way."

2   THE TAROT

Diana's breathing slowed, as she followed the directions for the ten card Celtic Cross spread. Her damp fingers stuck to the cards and she wiped them again on the wool throw. Her mouth dry, her throat scratchy, she pushed those symptoms out of her awareness, ignored her body in favor of the more compelling promise of guidance out of her dilemma.

The first card represented Present Position. She laid down the Eight of Wands.

The second card, Immediate Influences. She laid down the Four of Pentacles.

Next, was the Goal or Destiny card: The Tower.

The fourth card, Distant Past: The Magician.

The fifth card, Recent Past Events: Three of Cups.

The sixth card would tell her about Future Influences: The Page of Wands.

Her directions suggested that she "read" the first six cards before looking at seven through ten. As she started to study the cards more closely, she stopped. *If I'm going to do this, I might as well do it right and keep a record so I can go back and see what the cards have told me; the direction they send me.*

Standing, Diana strode to the high boy against the wall opposite the fireplace and opened the bottom drawer. Under a sweater she found what she wanted: her Journal and pen. After closing the drawer, she returned to her place at the low table.

She reviewed the Present Position card: The Eight of Wands and wrote.

I'm at a crossroads in my life and if I don't take action, nothing will be resolved. I need to let go of my need for money if I'm going to move on with my life.

Diana stopped and considered what she had written; the tension in her body gone, her mind fully engaged.

I don't know that I need money per se but it's true I enjoy many aspects of my current life-style. So, I must be prepared to change if I separate from or divorce Dennis. I won't have the house, car, clothing budget I have now but I also won't have a husband who cheats on me.

Thoughts flowed through her mind as she assessed the Four of Pentacles.

I have many skills. I'm organized, creative, and flexible. My business is growing and I love what I do. I have a strong circle of women to support me no matter my direction.

She continued journaling as she read and pondered the meaning of The Tower: the card of chaos and change; The Magician: the card of personal power; the Three of Cups: the card of abundance. She studied the next card and wrote.

Future influences: The Page of Wands. A young man, under the age of thirty? That's a surprise. I'm forty now - a young man in my life? Well, the card is future influence not future husband or lover. I don't think I know a young man who "encourages and inspires others to be their best". The Page of Wands also represents a young man who is "outgoing, gregarious, active and involved, self-confident and charming". It sort of fits Bill, but he's my son. How can he influence my future?

When she stopped to review this first reading, because she wrote not only what the cards said but also her thoughts and impressions, her interpretation was richer. Her body confirmed that taking action was a way out of despair: her hands were no longer damp, saliva soothed her once dry mouth.

Diana looked into the flames absorbing the meaning of the words she'd read and written: the cards supported her intuition. It was time to make a change, to move forward. She had a strong foundation and people to support her. *There will be sacrifices but ones I can more easily live with than the slow death of my soul.*

From the depths of her being the message, I don't want to live the rest of my life in a marriage so devoid of love, of caring, of compassion, of respect, rang true. Being brutally honest with herself, she also didn't like the fact she now mirrored Dennis in so many ways. *I may not have affairs with other men, but I no longer care about or respect him.* A sardonic smile replaced her serious expression as she picked up her Journal and wrote:

It is all about appearances. He didn't even question my sleeping in another bedroom once Bill moved out. After all, who would know? He must know I'm too ashamed of our marriage to tell anyone. I've not even been totally honest with The Circle.

Diana took a deep breath and turned over the seventh card: The Questioner, the Queen of Swords. She looked at the words printed on the card, her brows furrowed in confusion. She read the words again. Then stopped and wrote in her Journal.

I've gained wisdom from life's experiences. I've had lots of conflict and sorrow in my life. I've an intelligent, analytical mind. I'm logical and have common sense. I'm emotionally balanced.

That last point stopped her. The Journal clutched in her hands, she sat her gaze intent on the flames as her mind struggled with the words on the cards. In that moment she transcended this place and was connected to a universal source of knowledge: a source that knew her inner thoughts; that knew her heart; that knew her soul.

She wrote:

Right now I don't feel balanced emotionally. I feel as if I'm standing on a precipice surrounded by dangers, by challenges. The ground is shaking as if an earthquake rumbles deep below me. There is no safety. My choices are to jump and hope I land on the other side in one piece or to remain where I am and take my chances that I won't be swallowed up when the earth splits apart.

She looked back at the Queen of Swords digesting another one of its meanings.

I value my honesty. I've developed a popular course on how to be honest and talk to people about unpleasant or painful situations in the workplace. I've tried to talk to Dennis, to use the skills I teach with him. But they haven't worked.

Diana turned the eighth card over: the King of Pentacles. She reviewed her chart and jotted in her Journal that this card represented her Influence On Others and vice versa. As she read the writing on the card, she was struck with how many of the attributes reminded her of Dennis. She hurriedly wrote her impressions from reading the card.

He's over forty, a hard worker, smooth talker, a deal-maker, risk taker, successful. He is also affectionate but with other women. He's generous with them too, buying gifts, taking them on business trips, giving them his time and attention.

Her breath caught as she read the words and realized some of what was on this card applied to her; some of the blame for the rot at the core of their marriage hers.

The lifestyle we live, the big house, the nice furnishings, the social standing - the trappings of success. I've let those things pay me to look the other way, to settle for a loveless marriage. Dennis may chase those trappings, seeing them as a measure of his success, but I've sold my soul for a generous clothing allowance.

Reflecting on the King of Pentacles, Diana let her gaze rest on the flames. Thoughts flickered through her mind like the dancing colors in the fire. She turned the card around and read the 'reverse' attributes seeing two that fit Dennis and other than repressed anger, none of them seemed to fit her. She wrote:

Puts his needs first and hurts other's (mine and Bill's) feelings without thinking.

As she wrote the words on the page, she realized again that he didn't hurt them on purpose that would mean he was thinking about them when he made his choice. He wasn't—but knowing that didn't diminish her pain.

She put her pen down, closed the Journal and held herself. *What have I done wrong? Why do I stay? Why do I accept his treatment of me? What is wrong with me? Why can't he love me? Why can't my own parents love me?*

Her breathing came in soft gasps as she struggled with the onslaught of her own accusations. Her stomach clenched with pain, her mind whirled with confusion as she sought answers to unanswerable questions. She searched for and found the mantra, the saying that allowed her to take control of her unruly mind, quiet it into submission, and find her way to the calm needed to finish this task.

I am a beloved child of The Universe and The Universe lovingly takes care of me, now and forever more. I am a beloved child of The Universe and The Universe protects me, now and forever more. I am a beloved child of The Universe. I am safe, I am loved now and forever more.

As she repeated the prayer over and over, the tension ebbed from her body, her breathing deepened, her stomach calmed, the unanswerable questions faded. She picked up the ninth card— The Lovers. This card represented her Inner Emotions. As she read the words two lines leaped from the page. "In order for a relationship to work you must leave your parents. An important decision must be made." More than one interpretation came to her as she pondered those statements.

The realization was painful but true. She still made decisions based on whether her parents would approve or not. Case in point, she had remained in a marriage bearing no resemblance to what she wanted. *The truth is they will find something to criticize regardless of what I do.* A marrow-deep sorrow overwhelmed her as she faced the reality: never would they approve of her, never would they be proud of her, never would they really love her for herself. Wishing and hoping they would change were just that – wishes and hopes. They were not her reality.

The important decision? She wrote:

I think this card is telling me if I want that loving relationship, I have to make a decision to seek it. And, I need to take a look at how my need to have my parents' approval keeps me locked into a loveless and unhappy marriage. In order to have the relationship I want, I must decide to leave Dennis physically. We've each left the marriage emotionally but as long as I live in that house I'm implying the marriage is important to me and may have a chance of succeeding. I don't believe that. It takes two people working together to have a loving marriage. That isn't and won't happen. I need to leave.

The tenth card, representing the Final Result, lay on the table in front of her. She reached out, picked up the card, and turned it over. The Ten of Wands. She scanned the words searching for the answer.

Show me the way.

What she saw was not a clear answer. "My heart is heavy; I doubt my own worth". Those words rang true. Her heart was heavy and she did doubt her own worth. She doubted whether she was worthy enough to have the loving marriage she wanted. The Ten of Wands told her to make changes in her life by looking for creative solutions to her problem.

Her Journal open and pen poised, Diana took stock of her thoughts and feelings.

My first reading and I'm frightened and exhilarated at the same time. I can see more clearly that I need to leave Dennis if I'm ever to have what I want, what I covet in Lily and Elizabeth's marriages. I need to make a plan, use my creativity to find a way. I'm good at making plans - and I've got the support of Lily and Sophia as well as the younger women in my circle. I know they will all stand with me.

I don't have an answer to my question, but I do have a direction. There are things that will be lost to me - my home, my standard of living, my social status, my parents, and maybe even Bill. I don't know how he will react to my divorcing his father. I do know I need to make a clean break - divorce not separation.

What do I need to do first? I'm not sure I know right now but I have faith that the right plan will come to me because this is the right time.

Diana marked her place in her Journal, capped the pen, and settled back to watch the flames entertain. *I'm not so naïve to think it will be easy, be painless but I already feel different— more settled, more self-assured.*

The clock chimed, the toll telling her it was six o'clock. Over the past four hours, she'd faced her demons, stated her truth, and felt freer and more courageous because of it. *Lily once shared that true courage was facing your demons in spite of the fear. I think she's right.*

Gathering the cards, she tapped them together, and slid them back in their box. She stood and picked up her Journal and cards, crossed the room to the high boy and tucked them in the bottom drawer.

Diana padded to the window and looked out into the darkness. The rain caressed the window panes. She sighed. Shoulders back, spine straight, chin high, she strode across the room and looked in a mirror, a mirror that showed her red-rimmed lavender-blue eyes and makeup beyond repair. With quick movements she removed the smeared mascara and pressed a cool, wet cloth to her eyes.

The redness faded.

With precise movements from years of practice, she swiped on her mascara and blush. Slipping out of the robe, she pulled on her signature black slacks paired with a ruby red silk blouse and brushed her dark brown hair into its formal shoulder-length pageboy. Last, she dabbed her scent, a subtle blend of darker tones, at the base of her throat and her wrists.

At the door, she paused and wrapped in her newfound courage, stepped into her future.

3 THE DECISION

When Diana entered the front parlor, everyone was already there having a drink before dinner. She returned Sophia and Lily's worried, questioning glances with a slight nod and smile. Dennis's glower was muted because he was cornered by Jackson and his architect friend from Italy, Giovanni Migliori.

Seamus, Michael's house man, walked by with glasses of wine and champagne. She was the crystal champagne glasses—brilliant, clear, and fragile. She declined.

Later, Seamus called them in to dinner. As she passed through the dining room door, Sophia and Lily reached her side. The three of them found places at the table next to Michael's neighbor and friend, Paddy. She noticed Giovanni, Gabriella and Daniel, Jackson's friend, provided a similar band of protection for Ashley. Michael seated Elizabeth next to him and Eleanor, Jackson's mother, and Shannon at the opposite end. Dennis and Ashley's husband, Art, sat side-by-side and seemed to be at least one sheet to the wind. As early as it was, they'd certainly reach the 'three sheets' level before midnight. Michael's free Irish whiskey was too good a deal for either of them to pass up.

Individual words were often indistinct as conversation flowed around the table. Ashley's Southern accent was a clear contrast to Eleanor's British one, Michael, Paddy and Shannon's Irish lilt and Giovanni's Italian accented words. The various cadences of voices were comforting although Diana's contributions took the form of a nod or shake of her head when a question was directed to her.

Elizabeth's and Michael's happiness wreathed around the table. Lily and Jackson shared secret glances. Dennis glared communicating his displeasure at her absence this afternoon, absence that made him look bad in the eyes of the other men. *But did it? Did they even notice I wasn't there?*

Finally dinner was over. She'd picked at her food, eaten enough to avert suspicion, but couldn't describe even one of the multiple courses Seamus had prepared. Her preoccupation with her decision to leave Dennis meant, for all intents and purposes, she'd missed Elizabeth's and Michael's wedding dinner.

"I'd love it if the seven of us could meet for a few minutes," Elizabeth gestured around the room to indicate her circle sisters. "Those who are joining us for our Winter Solstice Ceremony may want to rest for the next couple of hours. We'll gather at half-past-eleven in the back hall."

"We can use my sitting room," Diana heard herself offer as she stood to leave the dining table. "I'll go ahead and build up the fire." Hurrying to avoid a confrontation with Dennis, she started up the stairs. Male voices floated to the first landing from the foyer.

"I own the pub in town," Michael said, his Irish brogue strong. "I could have one of the lads take you two there. There's a small apartment above, in case you decide to spend the night instead of coming all the way back here. The women'll be busy until sun-up at least."

She'd stopped on the landing, just out of sight, and waited to hear the answer. Her hands were damp and her heart pounded as if she'd just exerted great effort instead of scurrying up fourteen steps.

"As my guests, drinks'll be on the house," Michael added.

"And we sure do appreciate your hospitality and all," Dennis replied, a slight slur to his words.

Hidden on the stairs, she waited until Michael led them out the front door before she dashed the rest of the way to her room, her body weak with relief.

Readying the room, Diana stirred the embers and added a log to the fire before pushing the low table and couch to the side so they could sit on the floor in a semi-circle before the fire. A large white handkerchief created the foundation for an impromptu altar. As the women entered they placed rings, bracelets, earrings, necklaces, and rocks from pockets on the white cloth.

Elizabeth opened the circle and called upon The Lady, the spirit of The Sacred Grove, to provide protection while they immersed themselves in the Ceremony to come.

"This is a busy night so I won't take long but there is something I want to discuss with you before we turn our attention to tonight's Ceremony." Elizabeth's smile grew more radiant as she looked at each of them.

"You all know that Michael has agreed to open the old wing of the house as a retreat center." She saw everyone nod as she looked around the circle. "To start, I am thinking of monthly weekend retreats. Topics? Sacred space, personal totems, house totems, you know, that kind of thing. You all met Shannon who will help me but she also has things of her own to do."

Diana remembered the vibrant redhead, at one time Michael's live-in girlfriend. Elizabeth had moved past that history and now counted Shannon a friend.

"What I want to discuss is, what I want you to know is I see this mirroring what Lily started with the house totems; something our business, The Golden Cauldron, will be doing. I want to find out what your ideas are; what your involvement might be. Like the house totems, The Retreat Center will need everyone's involvement to be successful."

"I'd love to help out in whatever way I can." Diana embraced the chance to physically distance herself from Dennis. "I can certainly spend more time in the summer and then on school breaks—March and December." *Should I share my decision about my marriage? No, now isn't the time.*

"I can write here as well as anywhere else with my laptop," Gabby offered. "Now that I can work off-site I have more flexibility. Just let me know when and where and I'll be there." She laughed. "That may have rhymed but only by accident."

"If you can come, Ashley, the children can come, too," Elizabeth reached out to pat her friend's knee. "They've taken to the horses. The lads in the stable would keep an eye on them as would Seamus."

"Thanks, E," Ashley's soft drawl reflected her Southern roots. "They love it here, ya know. They've got school. But, like the others, y'all can count on me when school's out."

Sophia and Hunter exchanged a look. It was Sophia who spoke up. "I can come when school isn't in session. And I can bring Logan with me, if that's okay with you, Hunter. I know with Twinkle Toes, your ability to be here is more limited. I don't know if I can be gone all summer as much as I'd love to. I have my garden and then the ill friend I'm helping."

"I'd love it if Logan could spend the summer here. She'd love to come with you or Ashley and the kids," Hunter spoke. "You all know I want her to be more involved. So if she can come with any of you, I'd be delighted."

Diana glanced over at Hunter. *She looks sad, a bit left out. Perhaps not. I shouldn't project my feelings onto others.*

"With my clients and husband," Lily smiled and Diana thought she saw her shoulders relax, "my visits will most likely be more frequent but shorter. The weekend retreats will work out well. And since I have more flexibility, I can come during school sessions."

"Thank you," Elizabeth's excitement was contagious. "I feel so blessed to have you all in my life, supporting these new directions: Michael, The Lady and the spirit of The Sacred Grove, and The Golden Cauldron Retreat Center. The English language doesn't have a word to express all of my feelings. I think "ecstatic" comes close but still doesn't capture the whole of it.

"We've two hours to prepare ourselves for our Winter Solstice Ceremony. I think we've talked enough about the future of the Retreat Center. It's time to move forward with tonight's activities. Any questions?"

Silence.

Elizabeth stood and said prayers to close the circle.

As the women gathered their things from the altar and prepared to leave, Sophia and Lily lagged behind. Diana watched Sophia close the door and knew the two women were staying for her. She walked to the window and looked out into the night. The stars flickered in the velvet dark of the sky reminding her of a woven material with silver and gold threads that caught the light, creating patterns that shimmered and glowed.

A log shifted, the fire crackled. She waited. *Will they speak first? Will I?*

She turned from the window. Sophia and Lily sat in front of the fire, looking into the flames, their backs to her. Her options?

I can ask them to leave and they will.

I can join them, sit in silence and they will also.

I can stay where I am and they will honor that also.

She sought her newly found courage, reminding herself of her new truth, and made her decision.

As she crossed the room, she rechecked her decision from every angle. Once the words were spoken, she wouldn't renege. Settling between her circle sisters, she stared at the colors of the flames as they blended, merged, and flowed from yellow, to orange, to red and then the shimmering blue.

"I've decided to divorce Dennis."

There, the words were out. Funny how they sounded when said aloud. She'd expected noise, a gasp from the universe, gulping sobs, something to symbolize this was a momentous occasion. Instead—silence.

Lily took her hand and held it firmly but not hard. Sophia put her arm around her shoulder and squeezed.

No words, just silent comfort.

The three women sat, silence surrounding them. The clock struck the hour. As one they stood arms locked around each other. For a time, they remained as one.

"Remember you are never alone." Lily's hand touched her face, held her chin as she looked her in the eyes. "You do not have to do any of this alone unless you decide you must."

"Remember you are loved by many." Sophia's gentle smile filled her vision as Lily stepped aside. "I expect phone calls in the middle of the night from you. Having those who love you by your side will get you through this. Being stoic will not."

"I don't have it all sorted out yet," Diana whispered. "I have to think it through, make a plan." She gulped air to stem the flooding anguish, wrapped her arms tightly around her waist. Tears slipped down her cheeks; the ruby red silk now blotched with her torment.

"It's time to get ready for Ceremony," Sophia said her voice soft.

A reminder it was time to put away the pain, time to draw on her courage, time to embrace her future. "One more hug before we go?"

She nodded and the arms of her friends enveloped her.

4   WINTER SOLSTICE

The air in the back hall crackled with excitement, the hum from The Sacred Grove a subtle under-layer to the subdued excitement of voices. While Logan, at sixteen, had been invited, she'd chosen to remain with Ashley's children. They were going to have their own Winter Solstice ceremony and ask the Goddess to bring them good dreams. Seamus was also missing. He was remaining in the house with Logan and the children, promising to have one of his lavish breakfasts for them at sunrise.

Diana was thankful Dennis and Art had chosen to spend the night at the pub. Their ridicule would have dampened the mood, the ambiance, the power of the Ceremony. Moving into the back parlor, the heightened energy swirled through the small room. Realization struck: she was relaxed, loose limbed, and easily slipped into an altered state where a bubbling inhabited her core. A calmness, a peacefulness, a rightness penetrated her body much like she experienced when watching a bubbling spring. Bubbling springs sent water gurgling out, away from their center. Bubbling spring, gurgling stream, deep-flowing river, endless ocean—all a part of the Universe as was she. *Where will this energy bubbling in my core take me tonight?*

As this was now Elizabeth's home and she was familiar with the energy in The Sacred Grove and with The Lady, she had the role of Intercessor, The High Priestess, the leader. Briefly she explained that Sacred Groves were made up of trees not indigenous to the area and were believed to have been planted by Goddesses or Spirits. The Lady was the personification of the spirit or energy of this place. If they were quiet within themselves they would feel, hear, sense the energy as it was particularly strong here. She also warned that The Lady often came to people in visions and she expected many if not all to see her this night.

"Winter Solstice," she reminded everyone, "is about the fight between light and dark, life and death. In the old days, on the longest night and shortest day, it seemed that dark and death would win and light and life would lose. Our role tonight is to challenge the darkness and call back the light. We'll meditate, sing, chant, dance, tell stories, and pray until the sun rises and we can welcome the light back into our lives. As the night sky lightens, we'll leave The Sacred Grove, get the children, and gather on the front lawn to see the sun climb over the hills; to bear witness to the sun's return: the victory of light and life."

Diana watched as the nine women and five men readied themselves to leave the small parlor. Shannon, also familiar with the energy of this place, stepped outside first. She lit a torch and a wand made of cedar, sage, and lavender from a small cauldron on the stone terrace before starting down the path. Each person followed Shannon's lead. She saw Lily helping Eleanor, Jackson's mother, onto the path before following close behind. They moved single file, holding torches high to light the path. At the bottom of the hill, Elizabeth led them clock-wise along the path encircling The Sacred Grove. They trod the path three times in honor of maiden, matron, and crone, stopping when they reached the North entrance for the third time.

Shannon stepped forward. She raised her arms in prayer and Diana and her circle sisters did the same.

"We come in peace,

"We come in gratitude,

"We come to welcome the light."

"Blessed Be." Everyone's voice spoke these last words before following Shannon into The Sacred Grove where the women and men arranged themselves in a circle around a shimmering pool and burning fire. Earlier Elizabeth had suggested if they wanted to release any fears into the darkness, there would be time and space to do so. *I shuddered as if a bone-deep internal earthquake had struck at E's announcement.*

During the quiet times, Diana prayed and meditated in an effort to rid herself of her fears of the future when she left Dennis. The fear of his anger, the fear of her son turning his back on her, the fear she wasn't strong enough to stand against the criticism from her parents and others who believed the façade of her life, the fear she would be left alone, the fear she would fail in this effort to grasp the life she wanted for herself.

When she had mentally rolled her fears into a tight ball and visualized them imbedded in her torch, she approached the center of the circle. She held her torch in the fire, mesmerized as the flames flew high into the night sky. A shudder passed through her as she shifted and plunged the conflagration into the water. Steam billowed. A ssiss in the darkness. Silence returned.

A thin thread of light announced their time in The Sacred Grove was over. Hunter and Ashley in the lead, they made their way up the hill.

Gathered on the front lawn, everyone watched the horizon, seeing the blue sky lighten with colors from pastel pink to vibrant red, soft lavender to rich purple, palest peach to deep orange—the colors streaking the horizon, a glorious backdrop to the still blackened hills. And then wonder of wonders, a thin slice of brilliant gold broke over the crest illuminating the world with light. Ashley's children danced in a circle, Logan clapping the beat. The adults stood with indulgent looks on their faces, watching the children dip and weave.

"It's a spiral dance." Diana recognized the movements and stepped forward. "May I join you?"

Small hands reached to draw her into the dance. Her heart light, her feet fleet, she joined the children and dipped and weaved going round and round. One by one the adults approached, asked permission, and gained entrance to the circle. Couples formed: Daniel maneuvered to be with Ashley, Giovanni with Gabriella. Jackson was with Lily, Michael with Elizabeth. She noted that Paddy was with Shannon which left Hunter, Sophia, and her without partners. *Is this a foretelling of my future? It doesn't matter. I've made my choice.*

In and out, round and round, dipping and weaving they danced until the sun had fully risen.

"Logan taught them the dance last night," Hunter volunteered as the dance came to an end.

"What a wonderful gift for us all," Sophia exclaimed as she continued to sway to an inner music, "a perfect ending to our Winter Solstice Ceremony."

Elizabeth and Michael walked toward them, her arm around his waist. "We'll have to add the Spiral Dance next year with the children leading it. That was inspired, Hunter."

"It wasn't me." Hunter's pride in Logan was evident as she looked at her daughter now congratulating the children with high fives all around. She gestured widely. "This was all Logan's idea."

Ashley and Daniel were now with the children. As Daniel took the time to talk to each child individually, they seemed to stand taller, their children-chests puffed out, broad grins on their faces.

Sophia leaned toward her. "I'd never really noticed how well Daniel got along with Ashley's children until this trip. He'd be a wonderful father. I do sometimes wonder why a kind, likeable man like him isn't married. And seeing him with these children, why doesn't he have a bunch of them himself?"

Sophia's questions went unanswered as Seamus came to the door, ringing the bell that signaled breakfast was ready and getting cold.

Diana remained in the yard, watching the sun climb inexorably into the clear blue sky. She was aware she wasn't alone but took her time, grounding herself and finding her center before turning.

Sophia was waiting for her, holding out her hand. Diana took it and arm-in-arm they went into the manor house.

If Dennis was there, she could handle whatever he did. She wasn't alone. At some level her instincts told her Jackson would step in and if he did, so would Michael and Daniel; maybe even Giovanni and Paddy. She suspected, because she hadn't asked her not to, Lily had told Jackson of her decision to divorce Dennis. More than once she'd caught Jackson's considering gaze on her during the Solstice Ceremony. And it was Jackson's voice she'd heard in the hall outside the sitting room door when Dennis was threatening her. There was comfort along with embarrassment in knowing that Jackson knew about Dennis's private behavior toward her.

Life held good secrets and bad secrets. Good secrets sustained love and laughter, brought joy and happiness, created anticipation of something marvelous. Bad secrets festered, contaminated everything around them; even good things were damaged by bad secrets. Bad secrets also created anticipation; anticipation with the elements of fear, humiliation, and embarrassment. To curb bad secrets, light had to shine upon them.

Winter Solstice was the time to call forth the light into the world. This Winter Solstice they had called forth the light for the outer world and in so doing, the darkness of her inner world was illuminated.

The irony did not escape her as she entered the breakfast room. The dawn after Winter Solstice, the return of the light, and one of her darkest secrets had been exposed to others. Her circle sisters knew some of it, but no one knew it all. Jackson knowing a piece of her darkness; and the others' guessing added another ring of nakedness, of vulnerability. But today, at this hour, she welcomed the vulnerability, reveled in others' knowing about the darkness pervading her life.

On another level in her mind, she knew the time would come when the reality of other people knowing her truth would lay her open to the devastating possibility of their scorn. Mentally she added "scorn" to her list of feelings awaiting her on her new path. *Can I remain on my path when feelings of embarrassment, exposure, humiliation, vulnerability and now scorn overwhelmed me? Can I face the censure, criticism, the cancerous barbs? Can I survive it all?* The thought of being so stripped, laid bare and unprotected had her heart racing, her lungs seizing, her entire body engulfed in fear.

Fear immobilized her, challenges energized her. Somewhere she'd heard the Chinese symbol for crisis was also their sign for opportunity.

Can it be as simple as that? Can I simply change my perspective? Can I see these fears as challenges, challenges I'm strong enough to face, to meet, to overcome? I know what I want. I can ignore—no, not ignore them but focus on what I want instead of what I don't want. Setting her mind on creating the image of what she wanted, her mood lifted, her body softened, her lips curved into a smile as the light of a true loving relationship with a faithful man filled her heart.

.

5 FREMONT

She managed to keep Dennis at arm's length during the remaining days in Ireland. She managed to never be alone with him. She managed until they were back in Fremont and walked in their own front door.

The door slammed shut behind her. "Bitch," he shouted, grabbing her arm and swinging her around. "Making me look bad in front of everyone there! What did you say to Montgomery?

"I'm talking to you!" Spittle from his vehement words struck her face, and telegraphed his fury. He cursed, pushed, shoving her into the wall. His chest bellowed, his hands fisted, he loomed over her.

Her calm, remote demeanor surprised him and most likely saved her from a more lethal physical assault. She managed to step away from the wall, away from Dennis, to pick up her luggage and cross the foyer to the stairs. She walked deliberately, somehow knowing that if she appeared to flee, it would feed his anger. In her own room, she locked the door, braced a chair beneath the knob, and began to unpack.

Even while he pummeled the door, she remained almost—serene. It wasn't that she didn't hear him. It wasn't that she didn't feel the brunt of his anger. It was simply that this part of her life was coming to an end. His vile words strengthened her foundation; nails in the structure that supported her decision to divorce him, to leave him, to be rid of him forever.

She'd had the presence of mind to have a solid core door and a heavy duty lock installed when she moved to this room.

He hadn't noticed.

He did now. The door didn't rattle, didn't shake, and didn't budge as he beat on it.

Humming one of her favorite songs about the old women who weaved the night sky changing everything she touched, Diana shifted to an altered state, a place to escape from Dennis's battering on the door. She was like that woman right now. Everything she touched, everything she did, changed something in her life. Here in her room, she was powerful, safe, in control. *I am a beloved child of The Universe and The Universe is watching over me; guiding and protecting me now and forever.*

Ready to integrate Ireland into her sacred space, she removed the red embroidered scarf covering her altar and added a nugget of stone from the dance Elizabeth took them to; a cone from one of the trees in The Sacred Grove; a piece of Connemara marble she'd bought in a small shop in the village. Lighting the candle, she held the smudge wand to it. As the smoke rose she waved it over her body and swirled it around the room.

Dennis stomped off slamming doors along the way. The garage door opened, a car drove away, the door closed.

The energy in the air shifted.

Removing the chair from under the doorknob, she unlocked the door and smudged the doorway. *More, I want to do more.* Composed, she walked into the hallway, waving the wand of sage and cedar. She wandered through the house until all was cleansed. *Interesting—not my house but "the house".*

When the smudge wand burned down, she was finished. Back in her room, she closed and locked the door before standing in front of her altar. Arms raised in gratitude, the words flowed.

"I give thanks to The Universe for being with me, for holding me in its arms, for keeping me safe, for giving me strength and guidance as I move forward with my life."

White light surrounded her, flowed through her and she softly sang the words to The Sacred Grove's prayer.

"I am the light

"I am the source

"Through me love flows to all the world.

"I am the light

"I am the source

"Through me love flows to all the world.

"I am the light

"I am the source

"Through me love flows to all the world."

6 MATTHEW

Monday Diana prepared for her class on employer and employee relationships at Fremont Community College. The series was popular with small business owners and people thinking of starting their own business. Having a mix of ages, backgrounds and experience added a diversity she valued. A real high was hearing students' reports of business growth after implementing a strategy they'd discussed. Seeing an idea click and thinking take a new path was another thing she loved about teaching this class. And a third benefit was a small yet growing consulting business from previous students or because of their referral.

In addition to prepping for the class, she'd made an appointment to talk with the attorney and accountant who'd helped Lily and Jackson sort things out before they married and had helped set up The Golden Cauldron, The Circle's business. She left early for her class to make sure she missed Dennis. Avoiding him had become imperative as his continued physical threats and verbal abuse was taking a toll. *I know I need to move out but until I've things worked out I have to stay.*

The quiet of the empty classroom contrasted with the noise in the halls as students chattered on their way to class. The stress of living with the constant threat of seeing Dennis had her heart beating a rapid tattoo, her breathing stutter and her palms dampen. *I've an hour to pull myself together.*

First she sprayed the room with an aromatherapy blend Sophia made—a blend of calm and energy with lavender, peppermint, and bergamot. As she walked the perimeter of the room, misting the air, she whispered a prayer of gratitude. *I am a beloved child of The Universe. I give heartfelt thanks to The Universe for being with me this day. While aspects of my life may be difficult, may present me with challenges, I am grateful for The Universe watching over, guiding, and protecting me now and forever more.*

Next she arranged the tables and chairs in a U-shape. In this configuration people could easily take notes and spread things out if they desired. In addition, they could see and interact with each other as well as with her. This methodology added value by providing them with a way to network and build the relationships vital to growing a business.

Someone knocked on the classroom door. Diana turned to see one of her students through the door's window. She waved, motioning him to enter.

"Hi there, Ms. Pettybone," Matthew Houston's tall, lanky body filled the doorway. "Good to see you." His gaze never left her as he sauntered into the room and collapsed in the chair at the end of the left table closest to where she still stood.

"It's good to see you too, Mr. Houston." Diana finished sorting her handouts as she engaged in small talk.

"Saw a couple of the others in the parking lot. Should be along soon."

"I'm glad to hear that. I think most of last term's students will be back." She shifted to face him, to make eye contact. A shiver flickered through her veins when she looked into his emerald green eyes.

"Harrison won't be. Arrested for driving drunk over the holidays. Big accident. You remember that don't you?"

"I wasn't in town over the holidays. So, no, I didn't hear about it. I hope no one was hurt." She sent a simple prayer to whoever was involved.

"No one dead. At least not yet. Couple of people hurt pretty bad. Still in the hospital."

Diana smiled distractedly to herself as he continued, in his short-choppy-sentenced way to fill her in on what had happened. There were times he was eloquent. His presentation last term on his construction business had been excellent. But in informal conversation, this was quintessential Matthew Houston.

Before he'd finished speaking, the noise outside the door announced other students arriving. They called out greetings, found seats, and settled in. Taking her place at the opening of the "U", she noted Mr. Houston moved his chair in such a way as to discourage anyone from sitting to close to him. *I wonder why?*

"Welcome everyone. It's good to see you." Diana addressed the group of nineteen, her best "welcome-to-my-class smile" on her face. "I hope you all had a successful and fun-filled break. While I know most of you from last term, I do see two new faces. Let's start by going around and introducing ourselves."

"Ms. Pettybone?"

"Yes, Mr. Houston?"

"Last term. You asked how we thought this class could help us. You want that too?"

"Thank you for that reminder Mr. Houston. Yes, that would be helpful for each of you to include how you think what you will learn in this class will help you with your business."

Perched on the edge of a table, Diana attempted to relieve the pain in her feet from standing for over three hours. The class had run long, the discussion intense between Mr. Houston and another student, Mary Duncan, about how to discipline an employee. Mr. Houston, who'd taken two previous classes, advocated working things out with the employee, giving an example from his own business experience.

Ms. Duncan, who was new to the class and recently been promoted to a supervisory position, stated it was a waste of time when you could just fire the person and hire someone new.

"There's always someone out there who needs work," she'd countered.

The other class members, who looked up to Mr. Houston, watched the interplay between the two. She had purposely stayed out of the discussion, privately pleased that the young man had such a solid grasp on the fundamentals she'd taught.

The class finally over, students milled around, gathering papers, stuffing them in backpacks, briefcases or like Mr. Houston, a zippered portfolio. While everyone was busy, she took a minute to study the young man in his early thirties: dark brown hair with hints of red, emerald green eyes, tall, lanky and yet muscular. She knew he had a small construction business which would account for the muscles, the darkened skin even in winter, and the calloused hands. Her impression of him was he was 'lanky' but as she surreptitiously observed him she realized his shoulders were broad, his hips narrow. He dropped his pen. A flush crept up her neck as she continued to look as he bent to retrieve it.

What are you doing? She screamed in her mind. *He's a student, you're married.* Hastily looking away, she hoped her embarrassment was concealed from the others.

"Ms. Pettybone?"

Diana turned away from the view of Mr. Houston's well-formed butt and hoped no one noticed her flushed face. Margaret Hurst, a returning student, her brows scrunched in thought stood waiting for her acknowledgement.

"Yes, Ms. Hurst?"

"Are we going to the coffee shop tonight? We did that after most classes last term and, well, we were wondering if we could do that tonight?"

"Of course you can," Diana said.

"Great." Ms. Hurst turned to the class. "Ms. Pettybone said we can all go to the coffee shop. We'll see you there." She waved to Diana on her way out the door.

Before she could decline, the class poured out the door. Diana gathered her papers, tapping them into submission before putting them in her briefcase. *How did I let that happen?* She picked up her coat; felt it lifted from her grasp. Turning, she saw Mr. Houston, her coat in his rough-hewn hands, watching her. An involuntary quiver traced through her at the hungry look in his eyes.

"Let me help you with this," Matthew's polite tone of voice matched his posture as he held her coat open for her.

She slipped her arms in the sleeves and he settled it around her shoulders. Did she imagine it or did his hands linger a moment longer? Was that a stroke or was he just smoothing out a wrinkle?

"Thank you, Mr. Houston," she spoke in a formal tone. Picking up her briefcase, she started toward the door only to find his long strides had him already in front of her, opening it and standing aside to let her pass.

"Thank you again."

The coffee shop was crowded with the addition of her class. Diana was unsettled. They sat around small café tables, knees touching and bumping underneath the surface. Matthew Houston sat on her left, his knee rubbed against her thigh as he sat down and then rested almost casually against hers. It was difficult to keep her attention on the conversation; to keep it focused on anything other than the lime-scented heat to her left, the weight of his leg on her thigh, the brush of his arm when he took a drink of his coffee.

The enterprising Margaret Hurst claimed the seat to his left. Diana could see Margaret diligently working to engage Matthew in conversation. He seemed adept at avoiding anything other than a superficial answer.

A half hour later, her tea finished, she raised her voice to be heard above the chatter.

"I'll see you all next week." She reached down between the chairs to grab her briefcase as she stood. Another hand intercepted hers.

"I'll walk you out," Matthew said, standing, her briefcase in his hand. When they'd first sat down, he'd stuck his portfolio at the back of his chair. He quickly grabbed it and tucked it in the same hand carrying her briefcase before gesturing for her to precede him.

Outside the air was crisp, cold, a hint of snow in the air. Once clear of the doorway, she turned. "I can make it from here, Mr. Houston. You don't need to bother yourself."

In the light from the coffee shop window and street lamp, she watched as his mouth quirked in a lop-sided grin.

"I'm parked next to you. No bother at all."

She saw a sense of satisfaction flash in his eyes. He had her trapped. The sense of being prey to his predator flickered. *Nonsense, D. Utter nonsense. You're imaging things.* Turning toward the campus parking lot, she started walking. He ambled beside her. Their breath made clouds in the air. Fascinated, she watched as the individual puffs blended into one wispy cloud before slowly fading away.

"We're here," Matthew said stopping next to her car. "Keys?"

She reached in her pocket and pulled them out. He took them from her hand, clicked to disable the alarm, opened the door and waited as she got in. He passed her briefcase to her and then her keys.

"Thank you, Mr. Houston." Diana gazed up at his strong jaw, firm mouth and straight nose. She stopped short of looking at his eyes.

"You're welcome, Ms. Pettybone." He closed the door and stood watching as she started the car. Once it purred to life, he turned to his own vehicle, a well-used late-model pickup with Houston Construction painted on the side.

Backing out of her parking space, she paused, waiting for him to start his truck before driving on.

She told herself it was the polite thing to do. Batteries died in the cold, damp weather. That felt like a lie.

She wanted to make sure he was safely on his way before she left. That was a half-truth.

Where was her new courage? Courage to face the truth, at least in her private thoughts? The truth? She was attracted to him. The slight shiver when he looked at her, the comfort of his knee resting against hers, the heat of his hand taking her briefcase—reminders she wasn't dead.

But nothing could happen with Matthew Houston. He was a student of hers and he was at least eight years younger than she was. *I just turned forty and am still married.* Another part of her conscience rallied. *He isn't that young. And he won't always be a student. And you won't always be married.*

The slice of parking lot her headlights illuminated: a miniscule piece of the world around her. It was strange in some ways to know what lay deep in the darkness; things she couldn't see now but were still there. She was tired, so very tired. His truck's engine caught. Rruummed as he gave it gas. His lights were now on. There was no reason to stay here, lost in her rambling thoughts.

As she approached her house, lights shone through all the windows. Dennis was home and waiting for her. She didn't feel fear and maybe that was stupid of her. But she did feel a weariness that came from deep in her bones. She drove on past the house. *My meeting with the attorney and accountant is set for ten a.m. I don't want to face Dennis or survive another night of his intimidating manner, his mental brutality.*

Tears blurred her vision; she gripped the steering wheel tighter and kept driving. Ten minutes later she pulled into another driveway, swiped at her tear-stained face, gave up in frustration that she would look all right. She wasn't all right. That was why she was here. By rote, she grabbed her briefcase when she got out of the car, set the alarm, and made her way to the front door.

Only then did she notice the darkness.

Desperation drove her on.

Ringing the bell and knocking on the door, she waited.

The sound of the lock turning, the door opening. Sophia reached out and pulled her into the house, into her arms. "I'm so glad you came to me," she whispered as she held Diana close. "So very, very glad."

Taking her hand, Sophia led her to the family room at the back of the house. "Sit here," she pushed an unresisting Diana onto the couch. "I'll put water on for tea."

Diana heard her running water and setting the kettle on the stove. She was so very tired, so very numb. She wanted to help but couldn't seem to move. Tired, numb, paralyzed.

Sophia padded back to her. "Where are your car keys?"

With effort Diana pulled them from her coat pocket.

Sophia took them from her hand. "I'll be right back. I'm going to pull your car into the garage."

The tears renewed their onslaught as she held herself close and rocked. Sobs tore from her throat. Her breathing was fractured, her stomach nauseous, her head throbbed; the numbness and paralysis gone.

Arms close around her, held her, rocked her.

The two women sat on the couch, one holding the other. The tea kettle sang and still they sat. The shrill whistle cut through the air, jarring, bringing the sobs and tears to hiccups and sighs. Sophia rose, went to the kitchen, took the kettle off the stove and fixed their tea. Returning with steaming mugs and a plate of cookies, she set them on the coffee table. *Just what I need tonight. Chamomile tea, my favorite peanut butter cookies, and a good friend.*

"May I stay the night?" she whispered, her voice shaking, a few new tears slipping down her face.

"You may stay for as many nights as you need." Sophia reached out to touch Diana's arm. "May I call Lily and see what her plans are for tomorrow?"

Diana's forehead wrinkled in confusion.

"You'll need some clothes and other items. You wouldn't be here if you felt safe at home so I don't think it wise for you to go to the house alone," Sophia explained. "I'm not out of school until four. I thought Lily might be able to go with you in the morning to get the necessities."

"I see the attorney and accountant at ten." Diana looked at herself. She'd worn this outfit all day and it showed. She nodded as she fought to calm her fears and find her inner strength. "Yes, if Lily or someone else can come with me that would be best."

Sophia stood. "Rest here and try to relax. Drink your tea and eat your cookies."

Diana's watery smile reflected the tears shimmering again in her eyes. "Yes, mother Sophia," she whispered.

7   DECISIONS, DECISIONS

The smell of cinnamon, the feel of a strange bed, the steady sound of footsteps, the soft knock on the door; Diana's foggy brain registered what her senses communicated about the world she was about to enter before opening her eyes, eyes still gritty from too many tears and too little sleep.

"Come in Sophia," she pushed back the covers, swung her legs over the bed's edge, and stood. The door opened but it was Lily not Sophia on the other side.

"Sophia's already gone. You remember she likes to get there a little early." Lily reached out, took her hand, and squeezed. "I've got a fresh pot of tea brewing and as you can smell, hot cinnamon buns on the counter."

"Thank you for coming," she said. Tears welled without her noticing, until they teetered on the rims of her eyes. *How can there be any left?* Tears trickled down her face, curved under her jaw, trailed down her neck, disappeared in the neckline of her borrowed nightgown. Eyes closed, she willed them away—to no avail. Arms held her, their touch telling her it would be all right, she would be all right, she was not alone. She allowed herself a few minutes of comforting before pulling away.

"If crying was the cure for my problems, all would be solved," Diana said a weak smile on her face. She bent to pick up her clothes from the chair by the bed.

"Let's get that tea and cinnamon buns and make our plans for the morning. I am yours to command," Lily quipped.

A simple plan was hatched. Lily would call the house to see if Dennis answered and then call again when they were a few blocks away. With Dennis out of the house, they'd go in and pack Diana's essentials. Lily would pack the clothes and make-up; Diana the business papers and other things she wanted with her. By dividing the tasks and focusing only on bare essentials, they estimated they'd be through in no more than thirty minutes. Next, Lily would take Diana to her appointment with the attorney and accountant before they went back to Sophia's.

By noon the two women sat in a small restaurant having lunch. The morning's adventures had gone smoothly so they'd stopped to celebrate. Since they both loved the curries of India, choosing a top-rated restaurant with a lunch buffet was easy.

The attorney had given Diana tasks to complete before the end of the day to protect herself: opening her own savings account with half of their joint assets; closing her personal credit card accounts and opening a business one. No need for a credit card account for personal items, she was embarrassed by the amount of clothing, shoes, make-up she already owned. Years would pass before she needed anything more than stockings and underwear. As she and Lily ate, Diana found herself smiling, a feeling of lightness and hope infusing her body.

An additional task was to make a list of items in the house she wanted. Surprisingly the list was short—a dozen objects if you didn't count the books. She had a small box of her favorites already in the car but shelves of them were left behind.

The attorney and accountant encouraged her to ask for health insurance coverage and financial support. They also counseled she suggest mediation as the way to divide assets because they knew Dennis would fight her on everything. It put her in a more positive light and would make the process easier. Dennis was very aware of appearances and this was one way they hoped to use that propensity against him.

She took a sip of her lemon water and glanced across the table to find Lily watching her, wearing her professional-case-management-expression.

"I'm doing okay," she assured her friend, "much better with your car full of my things and the appointment behind me. It was easier to do it all with you there." The tears threatened, she blinked rapidly and beat them back. Her smile was tremulous but the tears remained unshed.

"Can you stay in the rest of the day or do you have appointments?" Lily's brow was furrowed with concern.

"I can stay in."

"I think that's a good idea, D. We know Dennis is going to have an extremely difficult time dealing with your decision." She paused.

Diana saw the frown and her friend start to say something and then stop herself.

"Just say it, Lily. It's all right. You don't have to tiptoe around me."

"I'd like you to come and stay with us, D." Lily spoke rapidly, urgency in her tone. "You could have the whole lower level to yourself. Our security system is top notch." Her forehead furrowed with worry, she reached across the table and rested her hand on Diana's. "I'm sure Dennis will come looking for you, try to force you to change your mind, to go home with him."

"I know." Diana gave her friend what she hoped was a reassuring smile. Lily's frown deepened. "I took that into consideration when I decided to leave. I'm strong enough to stand up for myself in this." She took another sip of lemon water and ran her fingers up and down through the condensation on the glass. "I don't want to bring Dennis' nastiness into your home or Sophia's. We both know he'll check your houses first before going on to the others." She sighed, "I'd better call everyone and let them know what's going on."

"Leave it for another day," Lily counseled. "It'll sound more genuine if they deny knowing where you are when he calls looking for you."

"You may be right. Yes, I think you are right." A calm determination infused her words. "He is good at detecting nuances in voices. But you and Sophia?"

"We'll be screening our calls and if he gets through, we'll deal with it. Neither of us is afraid of him and we wouldn't hesitate for a second to call 911 if he tried to threaten us."

"He might, you know. He was threatening me, physically intimidating me and sometimes pushing and shoving. Before, he'd always been more indirect: denigrating names, criticizing my appearance, blaming me for the problems in our marriage. Something has happened. It's like the ante's been raised."

"The good thing is you are out of there," Lily's voice rang with conviction.

"Yes, that is a good thing." Diana reached for the check the waitress had just put on the table. "This is my treat. Maybe I could have done this morning without you, but I am ever so grateful I didn't have to."

As the two women left the restaurant and walked to the car, Lily stopped her hand on Diana's arm.

"I've another idea," Lily offered. "You could move into my little house. It would be very easy for me to move my office to the big house. Think about that, D. The house has an alarm system. It would be a place of your own until you decide what you want to do.

"I realized when we got back from Ireland that I don't want to drive across town to work. I like sitting in my robe working on a report. And, yes, I could get a laptop but I'm used to my own computer system and don't want to learn something new right now." She patted Diana's arm before starting toward the car. "At least think about it."

Diana stood stunned, watching Lily stride to her car. She'd expected the invitation to move in with Jackson, Eleanor and Lily as well as Sophia's offer—but the little house? Amazed and humbled, she knew how much the house meant to her friend. Reaching the car she slid into the passenger seat.

"Thank you, Lily. That's most generous of you." She put her hand out to stop her friend from speaking. "No, don't deny it. I know what your house means to you: that you'd entrust it to me is a precious gift." She gazed out the window, took a deep breath to stem the once again threatening tears, and turned back to her friend. "I seem to be making a lot of decisions quickly these days." Her laugh sounded shaky and her breathing matched. "Thank you, Lily. I'd love to live in your home. But first, I want to see what Dennis does. I plan to keep my car in Sophia's garage so it won't be easy for him to find me. Let's see what he does when he gets the divorce papers before we make a final decision."

"I'll bring the key and alarm pad over this evening. That way you can move in whenever you want." Lily's solemn face was transformed with her grin; the solemn mood in the car lighter with her chuckle of delight. "Jackson will be eager to help me move my computer, printer, and files to the house. I'm sure he'll have everything cleared out of the office by tomorrow evening."

"I don't … "

Lily placed her hand on Diana's arm. "You are giving Jackson a gift, D." Her look was serious, earnest. "Just remember that when you think you're imposing. He'll be grateful to you for showing me how much I see "his" house as "our" house. I actually feel a sense of relief knowing my house will be in good hands. Another gift."

"One gesture turns into three gifts. It's meant to be." Diana settled back in her seat her mind already mulling, musing over the day's events as Lily started the car and maneuvered through Fremont's traffic. It felt so right: divorcing Dennis, turning to Sophia and Lily for support and moving into a place she could make her own.

I am a beloved child of The Universe and The Universe lovingly takes care of me, now and forever more. I am a beloved child of The Universe and The Universe protects me, now and forever more. I am a beloved child of The Universe. I am safe, I am loved now and forever more.

8 THE ATTACK

Diana scurried into the classroom minutes before class began. She'd had a challenging week and a particularly exhausting day: Dennis calling her cell phone every few minutes; banging on Sophia's door, threatening to break it down. No television or radio on—she didn't dare use her computer because the screen gave off light and it made noise when booting up and shutting down. The curtains drawn, she sat in the quiet waiting for him to leave.

Should she call the police? If she did it would confirm she was there. So she waited, waited for him to leave. *When will he get discouraged and stop looking for me?*

Students were chatting amongst themselves when she entered, full of apologies. Her imagination played havoc with her senses— Mr. Houston's eyes following her as she prepared for class? *I'm just stressed.*

Another lively class followed with Ms. Hurst obvious in her efforts to gain Mr. Houston's attention.

When class was over, she joined her students as they walked to the café near campus. Surprised arched her brow, when the place began to close. Two hours had passed. This casual atmosphere and involvement with students was a bonus she enjoyed—a nice contract to the more formal classroom setting and a way for her to strengthen her relationships with them. It was from these casual after-class discussions she gleaned ideas for other classes to develop.

Walking with several of the students back to the parking lot, she said her good-byes as each one reached their cars. Mr. Houston was not parked next to her tonight and although he offered to walk her to her car, she politely declined, walking on alone. She clicked her car alarm off, unlocking the doors with her key fob.

Like a snake striking its prey, an arm shot out of the dark, wrenching her head back. *Dennis!* His arm, wedged against her throat, tightened, he yanked her around, shoved her against the car, his hand caging her neck. Starved for air, unable to scream, unable to speak, unable to make a sound, the cold metal of the car door handle gouged her back. Seeing the rage in his eyes, she was for the first time truly afraid of him.

The piercing shriek of the car alarm punctuated the night.

"You bitch!" Dennis's guttered growl ground in her face as he released her.

Air! She gasped and sucked the life-giving oxygen deep in her lung. Her brain sharpened, searched for an escape. As if in slow motion he raised his hand. It moved inexorably toward her. Her head snapped with the force of the blow and she staggered to the side. Before she evaded him, he grabbed hold and held her firm; his hand coming back, aimed at the other side of her face.

And then he was gone.

With Dennis no longer holding her up and dazed from his blow, Diana slid down the side of the car, crumpled on the ground, curled into a ball, her arms protecting her head.

The key fob tugged from her clenched hand, the shrieking alarm silenced. She shifted her arms, opened her eyes and stared into the worried face of Matthew Houston. Large, rough hands cradled her head; calloused fingers traced her chin and raised it.

"Are you okay?"

His mouth moved but his voice was soft and far away.

Movement caught her eye: Dennis.

Did she say something?

Matthew moved swiftly and smoothly upward, his arm warding off Dennis's blow.

Her eyes closed but not her ears. Sounds of fists hitting flesh; grunts, curses, mutters—silence.

"What's going on there?" a voice shouted.

Someone else here to help? Peeking out to see who else had responded to the sound of the panic alarm, Diana immediately closed her eyes against the searing pain. Campus security had arrived.

Matthew was back at her side, kneeling in front of her, shielding her from something.

The security guard strode toward them; flashlight and nightstick at the ready. "I told you to stay… ," his harsh shouted words died on his lips. "What happened here?" The flashlight illuminated her face. "Ms. Pettybone? Is that you? What the hell happened?" He reached out to pull Matthew away. "I've seen you before, you're one of the students right?"

Matthew nodded.

"Then who's over there?" he gestured behind them both.

"He hit her," Matthews said his voice grim.

The guard's flashlight shone on her face, the blinding light stabbed her brain. Her head pounded, her ears rang, and she shivered with cold. Even though her mind told her legs to stand up, told her she had to get warm, her body remained motionless.

Something blocked the worst of the piercing lights and she dared to open her eyes. Matthew bent over her, watching her. The security guard had moved away to talk to the police officers who had just arrived and were getting out of their patrol car.

"Thank you for alerting me," he whispered.

She nodded and a surge of triumph swelled at that small movement. He seemed to notice because he smiled.

"Can you move your arms?"

She could.

"Can you move your legs?"

No, but then they were trapped beneath her body. She tried to shift, to move her legs but the effort brought those wrenching spasms.

She stopped.

"Can you move your head?"

Pain seared behind her eyes as she turned her head slightly to the left and to the right. Tears that had been teetering on the rim of her eyes fell, creating slippery tracks down her face.

A police woman came into her view and bent down. "Did this man hit you?"

"No," she whispered, her voice cracking. The officer was gone talking into her shoulder mic before she could say more.

"I'll be right back," Matthew said before standing and striding to where the officer and security guard stood over a supine body. He exchanged a few words, everyone looked back at her. He came back to her in a path that block the view from her vision. "I know you're cold, but it's best to have the EMTs check you out before you move."

"Thank you," she whispered the two words, unable to think of something more adequate to say, to tell him what his being there meant to her. She had no doubt that Dennis could have killed her in his rage. In her worst imaginings about what might happen when she left him, it never occurred to her that he would attack her especially in public.

Crumpled on the cold pavement, her insides trembled, her muscles seized with any movement; her mind fractured with jumbled thoughts. Somewhere from the turmoil emerged a truth: *after twenty years of marriage I don't know him.*

An officer stood before her. "The EMTs are on their way. Should be here in a few minutes. While we wait, I want to check a couple of things with you if you're up to it."

Diana nodded her head, closing her eyes in an effort to block the pain that jigged like lightning through her neck, up her scalp, to thunder in her temples.

The officer confirmed her name and that she taught at the community college, that she had a class tonight and had accompanied the students to the nearby coffee shop after class. She'd whispered "yes" after each question rather than move her head again. "Mr. Houston here was the last to see you. Is that correct?"

"Yes."

"What happened next?" the officer asked.

What had happened? Her memory fragmented. Dennis was there, he hit her, she fell. Oh, yes, he yelled at her. She could feel the tears start again.

The officer spoke again, her voice gentle. "Mr. Houston stated that when he came on the scene, a man had his hand raised and it looked like he was going to hit you. From the looks of you, Mrs. Pettybone, he already had. Is that right? Mr. Houston also stated that he pulled the man off you. Is that right?"

Diana nodded, even knowing the pain would strike like knives in her neck, like thunderbolts in her head. She couldn't say the word out loud. *How could I have been so stupid not to know he would do this? How could I have refused someone escorting me to my car?* She knew the answer to that—another student perhaps but not Matthew Houston with the concerned, worried emerald green eyes, who watched her with such intensity.

The officer was talking, the words flowing over her. A hand on her shoulder, new faces surrounded her—the EMTs. They were efficient: neck brace quickly in place, quiet voices asking questions, fingers taking her pulse.

"Help me," she whispered. "Help me stand up." She shifted again and this time moved first one and then the other leg free. Her legs tingled, her back muscles complained. "Please help me." Struggling to stand on her own, her knees buckled before she could lock them.

Two EMTs caught her, steadied her. At her insistence they allowed her to walk to the back of their vehicle to be checked out further. Flashlights flickered in her eyes, her vital signs were checked, experienced hands ran over her limbs.

Matthew never left her, staying as close as the EMTs allowed. It shouldn't be comforting to have him close, but it was both comforting and embarrassing. Talking was hard, but the ringing in her ears had eased. Listening and storing the words away to be taken out and examined in another place and time. Dennis had hit her. What she hadn't realized was the damaged he'd done. As if from outside herself, she watched the EMT wipe blood from her chin and describe her injuries: "hand print left side of face, localized swelling, internal cut on left side of mouth, appears disoriented."

She didn't like that word and struggled to focus on where she was and what was happening. And that's when she saw Dennis being hauled to his feet, handcuffed, and escorted to the police car.

"No," she croaked, all confusion gone. "No," her voice was louder now.

The police officer looked over at her, motioned her partner to go on, and strode over to her. "Mrs. Pettybone," she stood with feet apart, her hands on her hips. "He hit you. That's assault. We're taking him downtown where he'll be booked. Things being as they are, most likely he'll be released before morning." She paused, her face hardened. "What he did to you is not just wrong, Mrs. Pettybone, it's a crime. He needs to be held accountable for his actions."

She stopped again, took a few steps closer, her features relaxed. "I know it's a difficult and scary time for you right now. But believe me when I saw you do him no favor by brushing this off as "nothing". It is "something", and as hard as it is to face that, if you don't press charges, you give him permission to do it again." With those final words, the officer turned on her heels and strode off.

Tears streamed down her face. She didn't want to be hit ever again by anyone. They didn't understand what was behind her reluctance. Everyone would know what happened. The sordidness of her marriage would be public knowledge. No one really knew it all: not her parents, her women's circle, or her son. *Now they would, they'd know I'd been hit by my husband. And some of them will wonder what I'd done to deserve it. How can I face anyone?* She buried her face in her hands as the nightmare her life had become inundated her.

The EMTs were talking to her again. She forced herself to focus on their words.

"We'd like to take you to the ER to be checked."

"No." She fought to contain her rabid emotions, her own traitorous thoughts. Her voice was stronger now, the tears stopped. "No, I want to go home."

"We strongly encourage you to go to the ER to make sure there aren't other injuries … ,"

"Good," she interrupted, her voice firm. "I just want to go home. Where are my car keys?"

"Ms. Pettybone, it isn't advisable for you to drive right now," one of the EMTs started.

"She won't need to drive." Matthew came into her view. "If you can stay for five more minutes, I'll have her car secured and then take her home."

Diana opened her mouth to refuse him but he'd already turned away. He got in her car and drove away.

True to his word, he was back in five minutes without her car. One of the EMTs commented on it. Matthew patted his coat pocket. She heard a clink, her car keys. "I'll get it. In the morning."

The conundrum that was Matthew Houston continued as he helped her to his truck, assisted her into the seat, and buckled her in. He got in, turned the key, and off they went.

"How do you know where to take me?" She knew she sounded defensive, edgy.

"Cell phone. Called the number you'd dialed the most. A Lily Montgomery answered. Gave me Sophia's address. It's closer. Said she'd call ahead."

The lime-scented heat from the man beside her along with the truck's heater filled the small space. The bone-deep chill, the shivering eased. Eyes closed, she breathed deeply, wincing as muscles complained, and sought the peace in her center.

I am a beloved child of The Universe and The Universe lovingly takes care of me, now and forever more. I am a beloved child of The Universe and The Universe protects me, now and forever more. I am a beloved child of The Universe. I am safe, I am loved now and forever more.

"We're here." The words were spoken in a soft masculine voice. A large hand rested on her shoulder, her seat belt unbuckled and gently slid from her body.

The passenger door opened. Sophia took her hand. Matthew's door opened, closed, his steps coming around to her side. Sophia let go.

Matthew picked her up from the seat. He didn't set her on the ground but held her close as he walked to Sophia's front door. Her cheek rested against his broad, muscled chest, the texture of his wool coat rough beneath her skin. His scent, fresh air and lime, enveloped her. His strong arms held her as if she were a small, fragile child. She was safe, protected. Nothing bad could happen to her when she was in his arms. A new sensation, something precious, something she couldn't have. Matthew with the emerald green eyes that drank her in, could see her soul. He was something she couldn't have.

She slipped down his body; heat flickered from her core outward. Her feet finally touched the floor; she wavered, wobbled, then got her bearings.

"Okay?" he asked.

His worried face, the concern etched in the frown on his forehead reflected in his eyes was for her.

She nodded and stepped to the side, out of the haven his arms provided her and staggered.

He caught her.

Sophia came to her side. "Let's get you out of your things and into the family room." She bustled taking Diana's coat, gloves, and scarf.

A soft knock on the door.

"Just go straight ahead with her," Sophia's voice.

Large hands held her up, guided her down the hall to the couch in the family room.

"Sit," he ordered gruffly, "before you fall."

Diana tried to look up but her neck spasmed. He was too tall. She rested her head on the back of the couch and tried again. Her gaze moved slowly over him, noting his grim expression, an expression now changing from a bruise forming on his cheek. His hands were scuffed like the toes of a boot: reddened, roughened, bleeding—hurt. Stunned anew it registered, he'd stood up for her, protected her, was hurt because of her.

Frowning, she reached up to touch his hand but he was too far away. Seeming to know what she wanted, he sat beside her. Diana reached again, took his hand in hers, and raised it to her face, to inspect it. Her fingers skimmed across the furrows on his wounded skin.

"Did you have your hands looked at?" she said her voice a concerned whisper.

"No. Nothing to look at. Just hands." The rumble of his voice, his heat, his scent, his closeness was a balm to her damaged heart. He'd stood up for her, protected her, was still with her.

She held Matthew's hand, her hazy mind in a state of limbo. Nearing voices from the hallway pricked her consciousness. *I know that voice. Lily's come.* She'd lost track of time, but knew it must be well after midnight. *Such dear friends.* Her mind dimmed, her vision fogged.

She was warming up, whirling in a spiral of dizziness.

She vomited.

9 AFTERMATH

Bright streaks of sunlight slipped through the cracks in the shades creating their own shifting masterpiece on the walls. Bright streaks of pain shot through her body creating their own frenetic dance through her muscles. Muscles that spasmed as she tried to shift on the bed; her head pounded with sledgehammer precision; her eyeballs hurt; her mouth tasted sour; her throat rasped raw.

Diana pushed the memories of last night and their attendant feelings of embarrassment, humiliation, and shock away. Images of Matthew hovering as she emptied her stomach into a pan, of Sophia and Lily tending her with cold cloths and soothing words, of him carrying her effortlessly to this room; the care with which he'd laid her on this bed as if she was valued, special, precious.

She wanted a little more time to just be. To not have to do anything, be anywhere, or decide anything. Just be.

A soft tap on the door; it opened a crack. Lily peeked in. "I have a cup of tea if you're up to it," she said her worried look in contrast to her calm voice.

"Wonderful," Diana croaked.

"Something to drink will fix your voice right up," Lily added and approached the bed, a steaming cup in hand.

Diana struggled, wincing as her muscles fought her intention to move into a sitting position.

Lily set the cup of tea on the dresser, moved to the bed, and began to arrange pillows to better support her. "How's that?" she asked.

"Much better, thank you." Diana leaned back and willed her body to relax against the pillows.

Lily handed her the cup of tea and perched on the bed.

Diana sniffed, chamomile. It was hot and the heat from the cup felt good in her hands. "What time is it?"

"Eleven."

Diana grimaced as she shoved the cup at Lily and struggled to push back the covers. Lily gently restrained her. "You need to rest, D."

"But—" Diana stilled and sank back against the pillows, her breathing shallow from the pain of exertion.

"There's nothing for you to do right now." Lily's voice was calm, reassuring. "I took the liberty of calling your attorney's office this morning and informing him of the events of last night. He will pass it on to Ms. Lawford, the divorce attorney he'd mentioned. He was quite adamant you need an attorney who specializes in divorce. Also I called your doctor and we have an appointment at 4:45 this afternoon. In the meantime, you need to rest."

"I know I should be grateful, Lily, but right now I feel embarrassed, humiliated. Why didn't I see this coming?" Tears welled, waiting to plunge over the edge, slide down her face, dampen her nightgown. She fought to contain them and won— this round.

"The reality, D," Lily held her hand, "is that you are human." She patted it and smiled. "I know, I know it is a shock to learn that you are just like the rest of us," she quipped. Her voice and manner once again serious, she said, "I like to think of myself as an astute observer of others, and I didn't see it either. I knew Dennis would be furious, that he'd yell, threaten, and try all manner of things to coerce, to get you to change your mind. I thought he might hit you because he had shoved you against the wall; but to accost you in a public parking lot? No, I didn't see that coming at all. I'm still saying prayers of gratitude for Matt."

"Matt?" Diana interrupted.

"Yes, Matt. The man who brought you home? He seems very nice—said he's taking your class this term. Thank the Goddess he heard your panic alarm and came to check on you. I don't know what Dennis would have done. Oh, D," Lily said and gently squeezed her hand, "I want to hold you, to hug you, to tell you everything will be all right. But, if you feel anything like I did after my accident, you'd hurt worse."

"I am so blessed to have you here now." Diana closed her eyes and sought the courage to ask the questions that tumbled through her mind and her stomach. "Of everyone in our circle, you are the one who best understands what I'm going through right now. It was so hard for you to have us "hover"." She opened her eyes, chuckled, took a deep breath, and winced as her chest muscles spasmed, and sighed. "And I know your ex, Paul, was abusive." Diana looked down at the cup still held in her hand. "Did you feel this way? That you should have known, should have been able to figure this out, should have been able to protect yourself?" She looked up into Lily's dark blue eyes. "I feel so ashamed," she whispered. "As if it is my entire fault; I should have done something?"

"Hold those thoughts, I'll be right back." Lily scrambled off the bed and dashed out of the room.

When she returned she carried a tray with a box of tissues, napkins, a pot of tea, plate of cookies, and her cell phone. She put the tray on one side of the bed and climbed on the other, her back to the footboard.

"If we're going to have a serious discussion, I want to be prepared." She poured more tea in their cups, gave Diana two cookies on a napkin, and placed the tissues within easy reach. "To answer your questions, "yes", I felt all those things when I was married to Paul. The humiliation, the embarrassment, the questions I asked myself always put me in the place of blame. It was always my fault; I should have done or not done something; if I just figured it out everything would be okay.

"That is crazy-making, D. When we are clear in our thinking, we know it's crazy. We married men who are adept at creating an environment that supports that crazy thinking and discourages clear thinking." Reaching out, Lily patted Diana's foot. "It will sort itself out, D. It will take some time, but it will sort itself out."

They sat in silence, nibbling their cookies, sipping their tea. Lily broke the silence.

"By the way, the divorce attorney you were referred to, Ms. Lawford? She called while I was gathering these things," Lily gestured toward the tray, "and asked if you could meet with her today. She's already received copies of the police report, the security guard report, pictures—you are definitely in good hands with her. Dennis will rue the day he laid a hand on you."

"Do I have to see her today?" She hoped she didn't—knew she did.

"If you are up to it, D. You need to talk to her about a restraining order. I know it won't keep him from attacking you, but it will up the consequences for him. My hope is he'll think twice knowing he'll be arrested for violating a restraining order. You also need some protection when you get the rest of your things from the house. Sophia and I thought maybe this weekend we could get what you want and store them at my house until things are more settled."

"First things first, Lily. I have to get out of this bed and I must say my body is not happy about that."

"How does it feel about a nice hot soothing soak in Sophia's jetted tub?"

Diana smiled her first genuine smile since she'd left the coffee house. "It likes that idea a lot." Handing Lily her cup, she pushed back the covers and with some effort swung her legs over the side of the bed.

With Lily's help, Diana bathed, dressed, and ate lunch. The two women stopped by Ms. Lawford's office on their way to the doctor. Against her attorney's advice, she didn't sign the papers for a restraining order. *I can't believe he'd try anything like this again. The humiliation of Matthew punching him, the police hauling him off. There's no way he'll risk something like that again.*

It was after six when they pulled into Sophia's driveway because she'd had to wait to see the doctor. Diagnosis? Mild concussion, bruises on her face, cut inside her mouth. Treatment? Rest, ice packs on the bruised swelling, rest, gentle rinse with salt water for the cut, rest. Prescriptions? Anti-inflammatory, pain, muscle relaxants.

Exhausted, Diana sat for a minute her hand on the armrest gathering her strength before opening the door and going to the house. She heard Lily's voice from a distance.

"I'm calling 911, Dennis. Get away from that door!" Lily ordered.

Her door jerked open and Dennis' angry face filled her vision. He was furious, much as he'd been last night. In her peripheral vision she saw the door to the house open and Sophia rush out, carrying a baseball bat.

All traces of exhaustion fled.

She was vitally alive, alert, aware of every nuance.

Lily gave Dennis one more warning to back away.

Instead, he reached in and grabbed her arm.

In the background, brakes screeched, a door slammed.

Dennis tightened his grip trying to pull her out of the car. Her seatbelt held and Dennis shouted in frustration.

A part of her went someplace safe and watched the scene before her as if in a movie.

Matthew's strong hand clamped over Dennis's wrist and squeezed, his voice ordered Dennis to let her go.

The hand on her arm loosened.

Dennis threw his elbow into Matthew's stomach. Matthew used Dennis's momentum to bring his arm behind his back, twisting it high. Dennis howled in frustration and pain.

Sirens, once distant were here. Flashing lights surrounded her. The police had responded quickly to Lily's call. Dennis flailed, trying to wrench away from Matthew's hold, to escape but Matthew's grip was firm, his muscles flexed as he ratcheted Dennis's arm another notch.

And then it was over.

She was in the house. The alarm set. And, Dennis, again handcuffed, was driven off in the back of a police car.

Diana stared at Matthew's broad back. He turned toward her and smiled and she smiled back. Today was the second time in as many days he'd come to her aid. No one had ever stepped in as her protector before; of course she'd never needed protecting like she had last night and today. It felt good to have him here.

Although Lily and Sophia would have done everything they could to protect her and they were a formidable pair, her brow furrowed in thought, an unease sitting between her shoulder blades; a supremely uncomfortable feeling slithered through her. In his rage, Dennis would have hurt one or both of them before the police arrived. Matthew, in protecting her, had also made sure Lily and Sophia were safe.

As if drawn by her thoughts, he was beside her on the couch, shoulder, hip, thighs touching. Sophia and Lily were busy in the kitchen.

He took her hand in his and said, "I don't think he'll be bothering you any time soon." His breath caressed her cheek. "I'll come by and check on you tomorrow." He put his free hand out to stave off her objections. "Don't Diana. I need to see. For myself. Know you're okay. And, so you know. I'll be around this weekend. For the move."

His hand held hers, his knuckles still roughened from defending her last night. *Cherished. Safe.* His heat seep into her knee, thigh, hip, shoulder, his lime scented freshness a fragrant cocoon. She rested her head against the back of the couch, closed her eyes. When he left her side, left the house, she shivered from the loss of his heat and so much more.

10   THE PROCESS OF HEALING

"Your body can't heal as fast when it's contorted in pain," was the crux of Lily's stern lecture. A message Lily had learned firsthand in her recovery from a serious accident. Could she emulate her friend and deal with this with the same grace and gratitude? She scrapped her initial plan to not take the anti-inflammatory and pain pills, hating the hazy brain feeling of the pain pills and the stomach upset of the anti-inflammatory ones.

It was embarrassing and humiliating—daunting to go out in public, her face still swollen and bruised.

She didn't. Instead hiding indoors and experimenting with make-up in an attempt to hide the bruising.

She gave up. When Sophia came home Friday night with special make-up used to cover scars, she cried.

Saturday arrived. There were no secrets. Her body gave her away: her jaw still puffy, the handprint on her cheek in blues and greens, her neck stiff. No one asked how she was doing.

They knew she'd say she was "fine", "okay", "all right". One look and they knew better.

Ms. Lawford asked Diana to make out a list of what she wanted from the house. The list was a simple one: the rest of her clothing; the rest of her office including furniture, equipment, a collage of pictures of Bill she the wall, business books, file cabinets; the rest of her selection of tonics and various crystals, rocks, and other spiritual objects scattered around the house.

Everyone showed up.

Matthew and Jackson shook hands and exchanged words that, from their expressions, were serious. As the two men parted, Jackson glanced over at her, smiled, and waved.

Even Logan and Ashley's children had a job—that of opening and closing the screen and front doors. Her great organizational skills included her list, a map of the house and the room where the object was located. Her job? Sit by the front door and check items off her list. In less than two hours they were done.

Twenty years of her life filled the bed of Matthew's pickup truck, plus Sophia and Hunter's vans. Free—a terrifying and yet, exhilarating sensation. She'd followed The Tarot, made her decision, drawn upon her own courage, asked for support from her friends. And now—now she was free. A sense of euphoria swept through her leaving her light-headed, floating as if the ground under her feet were pillows, not dirt.

Still on a euphoric high, she was shuffled into Gabriella's car and back to Sophia's. Lily led the entourage to the little house, overseeing the unloading. Ashley and her children, Logan, and Gabriella were in charge of the food. Diana had no job; unless you counted resting and staying out of the way as "a job". A year ago Lily had personified graciousness in the face of their efforts to help her as she recovered from the accident. Diana plastered a smile on her face, hoped it showed her in a good light, sat in the family room, and waited for the day to end.

It was well after dark before everyone left. Diana, on the couch, her feet tucked under her, rested her head on the back. This was actually one of the hardest and longest days of her life. Everyone worked so hard trying to be upbeat, cheerfulness oozing from their eyes, mouth, pores; the energy of their compassion smothering her.

In the midst of it all, Matthew: Ashley's kids adored him; Logan had a crush on him or at least the beginnings of one. From the looks of things, he and Jackson seemed to get along well. He was relaxed, comfortable with them all. He didn't bat an eye when they prepared a "spirit plate", an offering of bits of all the food they would consume to the spirits. Nor did he blink when blessings were said.

He'd asked Sophia about her living room but Diana hadn't heard the answer. Even though she didn't hear the words, she knew Sophia told him about her sacred space, probably pointed out the altar there and in the family room. *I will admit I was surprised when she showed him her fallow, January garden.*

"I can get a tiller, if you want." Diana heard his offer and Sophia's enthusiastic acceptance.

It seemed from that exchange he planned on being around or at least hoped to be. *How can I discourage him without being cruel? I've no idea why he is here, why he insists on being a part of all of this, why he hasn't gone away. I certainly can't be the reason, I'm forty, bruised, used, a mess.*

Observing his interaction with the younger women, Gabriella, and Hunter, Diana guessed he was drawn to Gabby. She'd seen him laugh, noticed his straight white teeth, his mouth open, his head thrown back.

Memories of his mouth on the back of her hand flashed and she shivered as warmth started in her core and crept outward. She reminded herself she was forty. He was too young. Her mind locked on those words. Her body ignored them. The back of her hand tingled where he'd kissed it on Tuesday.

It was Saturday.

What is wrong with my body? I've had my hand kissed before. The courage she'd found in Ireland whispered in her ear. "It's never felt like this time. It's never lasted so long." A breath of pent-up air escaped when those unsettling thoughts finally drifted away.

She untucked her legs, yawned, started to stretch, thought better of it, and stood. In the kitchen, Sophia was wiping down the counters.

"You look like you're moving better."

"I am, Sophia. I can actually pick up my feet instead of shuffling."

"You also look tired, D. A cup of tea before bed?"

"No, I think I'll skip the tea."

"See you in the morning then." She turned to get a bowl from the lower cupboard and ingredients from the upper ones. "We'll have fresh homemade bread and maybe some sticky buns in the morning." She measured water and yeast into the bowl.

Diana yawned, her jaw cracked. It hurt but not as much. She tentatively massaged the bruised side of her face grateful it was healing. The herbal remedy and arnica gel she applied morning and night were helping. Giving Sophia a hug, she wished her sweet dreams.

In the bedroom she readied herself for bed, slipped under the covers, and turned off the light. Darkness was unnerving and had been since the attack. Getting up, Diana opened the curtains, letting in any ambient light before returning to bed, snuggling under the covers and watching the night sky. The lights of Fremont dulled the stars, the moon wasn't visible, but in her mind's eye she pictured Grandmother Moon and thanked her for being with her. As her eyes began to close she whispered the words that brought her comfort.

I am a beloved child of The Universe and The Universe lovingly takes care of me, now and forever more.

I am a beloved child of The Universe and The Universe protects me, now and forever more.

I am a beloved child of The Universe. I am safe, I am loved now and forever more.

11 TO TEACH OR NOT

The next Monday morning dawned cold, the bright sunshine a counterpoint to the brisk wind. After a week of hibernating, it was time to get back to work. Word of "the incident" was all over campus. She'd received a call from Administration. "Could she continue with her class this term?" She'd given them an emphatic "yes". Now, with the class a few hours away, doubts crawled through her stomach leaving nausea in their wake.

Standing in front of the bathroom mirror, she fussed with make-up that failed to conceal the slight swelling. She stared at herself in the mirror, took inventory of the face that stared back: aloof, cool, hair the color of aged whiskey worn in a formal shoulder-length pageboy; eyes the color of lavender; fine lines at the corners of her eyes, the corners of her mouth. Her gaze traveled down to capture as much of her as showed in the mirror: a neat trim figure, size eight.

Time would pass and the swelling and bruising fade and disappear. *There won't be any physical traces of the attack in another week but how long the emotional remnants will remain? No one can tell me.* She frowned and moved her jaw, contorting her face to stretch muscles that were stiff from non-use. *What to do about my class tonight is the question.*

My options are to teach the class as usual, take Sophia and Lily up on their offer to be guest instructors, or be sick and cancel the class.

The questions with which she wrestled:

Could she hold her head high for two-and-a-half hours?

Could she deliver the lesson and leave?

Could she walk to her car after the class and not panic?

She knew students and faculty had talked about her, about what had happened. *Will my being there create more discussion?* She sighed and looked deep into the eyes in the mirror. *There is no option I embrace, much less like. I've relied on Lily and Sophia so much this past week. Without them, I don't know where I'd be.*

But, she did know. She'd be lost, very, very lost.

The clock was ticking, time was passing. Cliché but also true. A decision needed to be made. Sophia would be home in two hours, Lily right behind her. *My class starts in five hours.* She stepped back from the mirror. After all she'd done to look presentable, her face still looked out of alignment.

Diana wandered through the house seeking a sign, an answer she trusted. The confusion cleared. *I know where to find the answer.* In the bedroom in the bedside table drawer, she found what she wanted. Taking her Journal and the deck of cards along with a smudge wand, she returned to the family room. The smudge wand lit, she cleansed herself, her Journal, and the deck of cards.

The Tarot had shown her the way out of her marriage to Dennis. She would trust the cards to show her the way through the tangle of thoughts and feelings strangling her ability to decide. Perched on the edge of the couch, the deck in her hand, a flash of light caught her eye.

Glancing down Diana saw her wedding ring. Holding her hand up, she admired the rainbow streaks flaring from the stone. *I love this ring.* She sighed. *Maybe I can wear it a while longer.* The thought was seduction incarnate. *Didn't the cards say I have to give up things in order to have the happiness I want?* She shook her head, disgusted with herself. *You'd rather be tied to Dennis and wear this ring than be done with him?*

On the couch, memories flooded her mind, their feelings her body. Dennis, Diana and Bill—D.D.B. She caught herself smiling at early memories of the three of them as a family. *There really had been good times.*

She stood and paced around the room. *It isn't fair. No, it isn't fair. But fair or not I have a decision to make.* It was important to cut all ties with Dennis; in her soul she knew that. *My wedding ring has to go.*

Tears threatened as she returned to the couch ready to wrestle the ring she'd worn for twenty years from her finger. It slid off without a hitch, landed in her lap. She held it to the light taking comfort in the flash of rainbow-colored flames before tucking it into the pocket of her blouse and turning back to the cards.

I'm taking steps to manifest my goal of a loving respectful marriage. You've shown me the way to this point. I need more direction. What should I do about teaching my class tonight? She picked up the cards and started the ritual to find her answer. "Show me the way," she whispered the mantra as she shuffled and dealt, as she focused, concentrating on her question, willing the cards to answer her; to light her path; to show her the way.

12   THE STAR SPREAD

The Star spread, the instructions suggested, worked best for emotional issues. Using the included diagram Diana laid the cards out in the shape of a five pointed star. The top point: Feelings: the Eight of Wands; to the right, the second point: Influences: the Ten of Pentacles. The third point: Emotional blocks: The Fool. Point four: Expectations: the Six of Swords. The fifth point: Most likely outcome: the Ten of Cups.

Instead of immediately reading the meaning on each card, Diana looked at the overall spread. *I wonder if I can sense or see the message on my own.* Quieting her mind, she sat her gaze on the cards. *I see each suit and the major arcana in the layout. That must be a good sign because my answer has come from all The Tarot's resources. And I remember the Eight of Wands from my first spread in Ireland. Something hasn't changed.*

Sitting in silence, Diana prepared to read the cards; committing herself to follow their message. *Why do this if I don't plan to do as they suggested?* On the brink of another leap of faith she still had options. Push them together and put them back in the box, or take a deep breath and plunge into the mystery.

She opened her Journal, took that deep breath and began.

The Eight of Wands: Another crossroads. The first crossroads led to my leaving Dennis. But that is not the only decision I must make. This card says I must take action, or miss out on an opportunity. Too much planning can slow me down. Clarify new goals, set new priorities, look for important news/information. Will my fears of other people's opinions hold me back? That is the crux of the matter. I can teach tonight. I'm physically able to. But what will happen/how can I face them?

Uncomfortable, her stomach unsettled, tension stiffened her spine. With a death grip on her pen she wrote about facing others and what their opinion might be.

A message is in these words for me, a truth is buried in those words.

Mentally she noted to spend some time thinking about it later.

The Ten of Pentacles: Material success equals security~or does it? This card is about the influences affecting my answer. Will my contract not be renewed? Will students drop out of my class if they see me like this? I need to stop asking myself these questions. They don't help me make a decision at all.

The Fool: My emotional block. An interesting card. Letting my inner self free? Being open and spontaneous? I can't remember the last time I was truly spontaneous. I'm sure I have an inner self, we all do, but I'm not sure I know her. I can be free of responsibility by choice ~ I've the soul of an entrepreneur. I like that - a new phase in my life. I like that, too. Trust my own ideas no matter what others say.

The idea to trust herself, to not pay attention to what others thought of her; she was familiar with it intellectually but on a practical level it was an unknown and the concept was disquieting. *I can't remember a time in my life when I didn't take into account at least one other person's opinion when I've had a decision to make.* Her stomach slightly nauseous, her spine rigid, her fingers gripped the pen.

Six of Swords: Expectations. Problems, overwhelmed by crisis. I feel unable to cope with day-to-day problems; doing so drains my energy. My future will be better than my present (I certainly pray that is true).Things sort themselves out. Travel or journey may be in my future. I used to have a more positive outlook on life but I am more pessimistic now.

Ten of Cups: Most Likely Outcome. I'm entering a period of peace and contentment; a special love relationship; supportive family; great friends; commitments made and kept. Joy, happiness; forgiveness, reconciliation. I have all the material possessions I need.

The message from The Fool is I can choose to stay home tonight, to have others' teach this class or I can choose to go. It's my decision. However, it goes much deeper than the question about the class. The underlying question: What will people think of me (how I look, that I didn't come, that I'm in such a disastrous marriage)? Am I good enough to teach this class?

In some ways I'm caught up in that sticky web as much as Dennis. I can't say I like that thought but it's true. I may handle it differently, but what other people think does matter to me. Should it?

Can I change? If I can, how would my life be different? What immediately comes to mind is I'd have more spontaneity in my life. And perhaps more happiness, more joy.

But there is another half to the argument: it does matter what other people think. Why? Why do other people's opinions of me matter more than my own? Why am I always trying to gain people's approval? That is certainly a life pattern, a pattern for which I'm paying a high price: less joy, more worry, more pressure, and no spontaneity in my own life. The cards say I'm at a turning point. Perhaps this is it - making a choice to put my opinions first.

What do I want? A little more time to just be. A little more time to take care of me. I don't have to go tonight. I can let myself be free of the responsibility this once. I can take a little more time for my body and my soul to heal before I go forth. It isn't that my students don't or won't know what happened next Monday. They know now. But I'll have had a chance to rebuild my reserves so I can more easily manage whatever happens.

I can stay here. I can take the time to call Bill and tell him I've left his father. One more thing done; one more load lifted. At least I'll know whether I've lost him for good, if my relationship with him will be even more superficial than it is now.

Interesting both times the cards say forgiveness is needed. Is it possible after all that has happened to forgive and reconcile with Dennis? No, I may find a way to forgive him, but reconcile? Return to that marriage? Never! I'm done with it.

Diana sat, Journal in hand, pen still poised. Her mind whirled with thoughts. Taking a deep breath, she stopped, calmed her mind, tuned into her body. Breathing deeply, she checked herself: heart rate steady slightly elevated; pulse to match; breathing purposefully deep and regular; stomach settling down; knees a bit shaky; spine stiff with tension. Focused on her hand, she willed its death grip on the pen to ease, focused on her body until the tension was gone. Only then did she resume her Journal writing.

Maybe the forgiveness isn't about Dennis. Maybe it's about me. Maybe I need to forgive myself; reconcile with that inner self; find the joy and happiness I want. And, in the process, become more spontaneous, live more in the present, see more of what is around me. I am not alone, thankfully. I have a choice about tonight. As soon as I wrote that I'd have Lily and Sophia teach the class, I felt such a sense of relief. I know this is the right answer for me.

Her place marked, she closed the Journal, gathered the cards, returned them to the box and put them away.

Sophia and Lily will be here shortly. She puttered around the kitchen, setting the tea kettle on to boil, wiping down the counters, getting mugs out. Sophia had an intricately carved chest containing a variety of teas and she placed that next to the stove.

Restlessness kept her pacing. *What else is there for me to do?* A smile bloomed on her face as she padded to her room, rummaged through a box until she found her stash of chocolates. Pulling them out of their hiding place she tucked them under her arm as she searched for the tin of shortbread. Back in the kitchen, she got a plate from the cupboard and began to create a pattern of chocolates and shortbread. Just as she finished putting the last piece in place, she heard the alarm click off, the door open, and Sophia's cheerful voice called out a greeting.

"I'm in the kitchen," Diana shouted over the tea kettle's piercing whistle.

"How wonderful to come home to tea," Sophia started. "Oh my," she said to Lily right behind her. "Look what Diana has for us."

Diana laughed as both women made a big to-do over the sweets.

They made their tea and, adding a plate of cheese, crackers and a bowl of hummus to Diana's chocolates and cookies, took their feast to the family room. Diana listened as her two friends recounted the adventures of their day. Lily's included three hours in the emergency department with a client before the decision was made to release him to go home. A satisfied smile on her face, she explained how she'd engaged a neighbor to check on him, fix his dinner, and remind him to take his evening meds.

Sophia had helped diffuse a potentially difficult situation at school. Two students had been arguing, their voices growing louder. While disappointed that some of the other students were egging them on, she was glad to have been able to intercede before it got out-of-hand. Both boys had come into her classroom and talked things out. The problem? Both wanted to ask the same girl to the school dance.

"You look as if you've solved a world problem." Diana commented.

"It's very rewarding to have two students sit down, talk something out, and in this case see that the only thing that really mattered was what the girl wanted." Sophia chuckled. "At this age, hormones are often in charge. Whenever I can nudge a young person's brain to control the hormones, I'm ecstatic."

"After anguishing over my class tonight I decided to ask The Tarot," Diana said in a straight-forward tone, a smile on her face. "So, if the offer is still there, I'd be very appreciative if one or both of you taught the class tonight."

Lily smiled over at Sophia. "Of course we'll teach your class, won't we, Soph?"

"Indeed we will." Sophia reached over and patted Diana's hand. "Very smart of you to consult the cards."

A layer of tension Diana wasn't aware of eased. "I think I may call Bill tonight. I haven't told him I've left Dennis and I don't think Dennis has either. I can't imagine Bill wouldn't at least call or email me if he'd heard that news."

The three women drank their tea while Diana shared tonight's class outline. Sophia and Lily talked about scenarios that supported the concepts and looked forward to the class. As plans were finalized, there was a knock on the door.

"Come in, come in," Sophia said welcoming someone.

Diana turned toward the hall to see who had arrived, expecting Hunter or maybe Gabriella. Instead the doorway filled with a masculine form: Matthew Houston.

"Just stopped by. Make sure Ms. Pettybone got to class safely." His intense gaze pinned her in place, pierced by his green gaze much like a butterfly under glass.

Sophia's voice penetrated her fog thickened brain. "...not going. Lily and I will be taking her place."

Diana shook her head to dispel his effect.

"Oh, unless she's changed her mind." Lily's voice.

Her brain scrambled to make sense of the fragments of conversation that registered. Matthew Houston here to see her safely to class? Her eyes flitted around the room, her hands twisted in her lap. *I have to stop this from happening.* She wasn't sure what "this" was but the pull felt as if she was a fish on a hook and he was reeling her in. Something was happening between them; something she wasn't ready for; something that frightened her.

Three pairs of eyes watched her, waiting for her to speak, to clarify what the plans were for tonight. It felt like minutes passed before she found her voice.

"Thank you for the offer of an escort, Mr. Houston. Sophia is right though. I've decided she and Lily will teach the class tonight. I'll be back next week."

His eyes raked over her body. Her heartbeat quickened; her breathing stuttered. Warmth enveloped her body, a blush spread across her face.

The silence was broken by Sophia inviting Matthew to have something to eat. He accepted and Lily fixed him a plate of crackers, cheese, and hummus. Sophia got him a tall glass of ice water. Diana sat, as if in a trance, barely hearing the words, unable to track the conversation.

And then they were standing to leave. Lily and Sophia gave her hugs, Matthew just watched. He said a polite "good bye" and stated firmly that he'd be back next week to see her safely to school. By the time she'd opened her mouth to protest, he'd turned his back on her and was striding to the door. It was unsettling to hear Lily and Sophia thank him for his kindness; tell him they would feel much better knowing he was watching out for her. Following them to the door, she set the alarm as soon as they were out. She was alone.

Eight-thirty on the East Coast.

She got her phone, fixed another cup of tea, and curled up on the couch pulling the warm navy blue throw over her legs. A sip of tea from the cup in one hand, she inserted her Bluetooth with the other, reached for the phone, speed dialed '2' for Bill, and listened to the phone ring.

13 BILL

Bill's familiar voice came through loud and clear. "Hi, Mom. What's up?"

"Are you busy?" she asked in a voice tinged with hesitation hoping he didn't notice.

"What's going on, Mom?"

She pictured him sitting a little straighter, listening more closely.

"Mom?" he asked, worry resonating in his voice.

"I'm okay, Bill," she said in as calm a voice as she could muster. *Maybe calling him wasn't a good idea.* A deep breath to calm her racing heart, a swipe of her damp palms on the navy throw and she forged on. "I have some news and wanted to tell you instead of writing it in an email. Do you have a moment now?" The words rushed out, tumbled over one another; not as she'd planned.

"Mom, whatever it is, just tell me," he said, his voice rising with concern, with anxiety.

She steeled herself, took a deep breath, and blurted, "I've left your father. I've moved out. I've filed for a divorce."

There, she'd said the words, told her son she'd failed in her marriage. A sharp pain lanced through her clenched jaw, her nails dug into her fisted hands. The pain helped her focus, focus on relaxing her jaw, unfisting her hands and wait for Bill to speak.

"When?"

Just the one word. Not enough to telegraph his feelings about her decision.

"I moved out two weeks ago, filed for the divorce last week," she said in a voice laden with defeat—not defiance, not confidence, but defeat.

"Why haven't you called before now?" he asked in a neutral tone that surprised her.

"I needed some time to sort things out. This was not something your father and I agreed upon. I had to make sure this was the direction I wanted to take, that I needed to take."

"And are you sure?" he asked, his voice softened.

"Yes," she said with the confidence she lacked a moment ago. "Yes, I am sure."

There was silence on the line. Silence she was compelled to fill.

"I know I'm forty and it may not happen, but I want, someday, to have a loving marriage with someone who respects me."

"Thank God," Bill interrupted her. "Mom, if you are calling to ask if I'm okay with it, I am." She heard his deep, harsh breathing over the phone line a sign he struggled with emotions.

Tears slipped down her face, her chest constricted, her breathing labored. *I'm not going to lose my son.* Putting down her cup of tea, she reached for the tissues and blew her nose—quietly.

"Don't cry, Mom. Don't cry. Geez, please don't cry," he said, panic in his voice.

"It's all right, Bill. I've got an unlimited supply of them. I won't run out," she joked.

"It's fine with me if you do run out," he grumbled.

"Actually it would be fine with me too, but that doesn't seem to be the case." She sighed. "I was so worried you would judge me wrong for leaving," she whispered her deepest fear.

"How long have you known Dennis cheated on you?" he asked in a calm, professional tone.

"You knew?" Diana's eyes widened, her mouth gaped. Nausea, lightheadedness, and clamminess inundated her body at her son's question.

"Of course I knew. He didn't exactly try to keep it from me. Took one of the bimbos to that playoff game you couldn't make. Remember? The one when you were sick?" Bill continued in his fake nonchalant tone.

Her lungs constricted and she struggled to breathe. *I remember. That bastard!* "I'm so sorry, Bill. If I'd known—"

"What, Mom? What would you have done? Would you have left him? Or forgiven him when he lied?" he asked, anger and a hint of frustration infused his voice. And then he sighed, a sigh so deep it must have come from the depths of his soul.

To her he sounded so very old. Not the carefree nineteen-year-old with a life ahead of him. "Honestly, Bill, I don't know what I would have done. I like to think I'd have left him then." She paused, sorting through her feelings, putting her thoughts in order. "It's been difficult enough now. Your father isn't taking it well."

"Mom, can we just refer to him as "Dennis"? I'd rather not be reminded right now that he is my father."

Diana was stunned at the vehemence in her son's voice. Her decision to stay because Bill needed a father had hurt him. *I've failed.* Overwhelmed by feelings of despair, her chin sank to her chest.

"I'm sorry I didn't leave Dennis earlier. You are one of the reasons I stayed. I-I-I believed a son needed a father. I-I-I thought—well, it doesn't matter. I'm truly sorry you and Dennis don't have the relationship—" she stumbled over the words.

"I'd like to know why you stayed, Mom. It never made sense to me. Dennis treated you like crap," he interrupted, his anger back.

"I was afraid. Pure and simple I was afraid. No one in my family has ever divorced. My parents would disapprove. They'd never support us separating, much less a divorce. I'd married Dennis and I was expected to make the best of it. You know the adage, "you've made your bed, now lie in it." I was raised and married in the Catholic Church."

Tired, so very tired—the weight of being wrong heavy. Even though she'd tried to do the right thing: what a good daughter, good wife, good mother should do, in the end, it didn't matter; she was wrong, she'd failed.

What could she salvage from the mess she'd made of her life? Give her son the gift of the truth, at least the truth as she saw it.

"What would people think? My entire teaching experience at Fremont Community College has focused on interpersonal relationships in one form or another. Why would anyone take a class on relationships from someone who can't keep her marriage together? And then I wanted to preserve our family for you. As I say the words now, they seem stupid or ridiculous but at the time, that's what I believed or at least told myself."

"What changed?" Bill's voice had changed again, the tired-old-man-voice back. "What's different?"

"It struck me when we were in Ireland for Elizabeth's wedding how happy she and Lily were in their marriages. I found myself so jealous, wanting what they had. Dennis was trying to put on the appearance that our marriage was as wonderful but seeing truly happy couples; well, it put a very different perspective on things. I decided then I had to take a chance if I wanted love, respect, joy for myself. I knew it wouldn't happen with Dennis, so if I wanted it, I had to leave.

"I wasn't going to be gone this soon. I thought it would take at least a couple of months, maybe even a year to put things in place. But, Dennis and I had a fight and I knew I couldn't stay. I'm at Sophia's for now. Lily has offered to let me use her house and some of my things are already moved in there. But, ... ," Diana stopped. *How much should I tell him? I've already said more than I intended.*

"But, Dennis was a butt wasn't he. Did he threaten you?" Bill asked, filling the silence.

Her mind scrambled, she struggled to find the words to answer him, to keep that truth from him.

"Mom, did Dennis hit you?" Bill challenged in a growled angry voice.

Even this truth had to come out. Bill wouldn't let it rest. He'd start calling around until he eventually found out. He'd always been good at ferreting out secrets when he really wanted to know something.

"Only once."

"Before or after you left?"

"After. He's extremely upset. I don't think he ever thought I'd leave," she said with a sigh of relief that Bill knew it all.

"It's Monday evening; don't you have a class to teach?"

Diana smiled, a sad, lopsided one. *That's my Bill, my ferret. Sniffing, searching, finding.* "Yes, it's Monday and Sophia and Lily are teaching my class tonight."

"That fucking bastard. He hurt you didn't he?" His cold fury rolled through the phone line.

How could I have done this to my son? Asked, answered—I didn't do this to Bill. My efforts to protect him by my silence did exacerbate the problem but I'm not the one who cheated in the marriage and I'm not the one who turned violent. Reminded of what she'd accomplished since Winter Solstice, she made a decision. *It's time to speak up and tell him the whole story.* Tears did not threaten, her heart did not race, her lungs did not seize, instead she felt calm, controlled, confident.

"Let's start at the beginning," she spoke with quiet determination. She'd tell him all of it, her part in the fraudulent marriage as well. He deserved to know. If he was ever to have a happy, healthy marriage maybe he could learn from her mistakes. "When I first met Dennis, he was full of bright energy, intelligent, handsome and very popular on campus. I was flattered he wanted to go out with me. I was rather mousy in those days with no real fashion sense or style.

"It was thrilling to be *special*. I couldn't remember a time when my parents had praised me, been proud of me or anything I'd done. Being special was new and very exciting, and I didn't want to lose that feeling. I looked at what the popular girls were wearing and emulated them. Dennis always noticed and complimented me when I got it right. And, no, I didn't realize then that I scurried around to change or fix things until I did get it "right" according to him. I'd tried all my life to change, to get it "right" for my parents and never succeeded. This was heady stuff, being able to change enough so I was "right" and one of the most popular men on campus wanted me."

Diana and Bill talked for an hour longer as she told him about her marriage, his birth and the joy he brought to both of them. "Don't ever think that Dennis didn't want you. He was so proud, always carrying pictures of you," she laughed, "and no one could escape seeing them." Her voice softened, "He still does, you know, carry pictures in his wallet and his favorite ones are on his desk."

She answered all of Bill's questions honestly, swallowing her pride, her embarrassment. He deserved to know for sure he was not responsible for any of the bad times and was, in fact, responsible for so many of the good times. That wasn't quite right either—*I don't want him to feel responsible for any part of the marriage.*

"Dennis and I did the best we could, being who we were. I truly believe that. We are the ones who are responsible for what our marriage was and how it turned out. Your role was and is as our child, our son. That will never change. I know you are building a life for yourself on the East Coast and I know it's time for me to let go. I'm working on it. I'll always be your Mom and support you as best I can. I'll always love you and I hope you know to the bottom of your heart and deep in your soul that is the truth."

"Thank you, Mom. I know you love me. And, I love you." He sighed before inhaling deeply. "I know Dennis loves me too. But, I can't forgive him for what he's done to you."

"Maybe in time we can forgive him because that is the best thing we can do for ourselves; what we need to do in order to move on with our lives." Diana hoped that was true.

"What are you doing Spring Break?" A change in subject, a new direction, positive energy in Bill's voice.

"I think I'll be in Italy? Why?"

"Italy?"

"Yes, one of Jackson's architect friends has some clients who would like someone to identify house totems for them. I've volunteered to go."

"I'm going to email you." She could almost hear the gears whirring in his head. "Check your Spring Break dates. Our school schedules don't always match. You see, Mom, I miss you and was thinking of coming home, to Fremont."

"I miss you, too." Tears stung her eyes, her heart hurt. "I'll look forward to the email."

Silence hung in the air.

"Love you, Mom."

"I love you, too."

Diana pressed the red key to disconnect from what had been a difficult yet healing conversation. Her knees to her chest, she rocked. Owning her part in everything had vanquished her worst fear. Bill had not turned against her. In fact she felt closer to him than she had in a long time. There was a saying, something about the truth setting you free. She didn't remember where it was from—a very wise person obviously—but it was true, she felt freer.

No longer rocking, she rested her chin on her knees and contemplated the last few weeks. *I made the decision to leave Dennis on December 21 and today is January 19—amazing how quickly things moved once I made a decision.* Lost in her thoughts, she snuggled into the corner of the couch. Her dreams of a man who would love her and be faithful to her seemed more possible now.

14 IMBOLC

The next day she and Bill exchanged emails confirming Spring Break dates. His Break was the week after her time in Italy. He called her on Thursday just to check up on her. During their conversation, he confided that he'd stayed away because Dennis treated her so badly. *The gift from leaving Dennis is a closer relationship with my son.*

Saturday she moved the last of her things into Lily's house. There really wasn't that much but everyone showed up to help. The potluck salad they'd put together as well as the extra hands and feet to move things around really were a blessing.

Monday night Matthew Houston showed up to escort her to class. She refused to ride with him, taking her own car. He followed her through the streets, catching up to her outside the classroom door.

"Why did you just drive off when I had to stop for the red light?" he said, his face serious, his jaw tight.

"You're being too protective," she challenged him.

"Really?" He flicked his cell phone open, holding it to show her a picture of her face the night of the attack.

She glared at him and managed to smooth her face into neutral if not welcoming lines, before striding in to teach her class.

Sunday she arrived at Sophia's tingling with anticipation; the promise of the bright energy they created when they were all physically together strong. Elizabeth had flown in from Ireland on Friday. Today the seven of them would be together for Ceremony for the first time since Winter Solstice.

Elizabeth carefully opened a package on the counter in Sophia's kitchen. After unwinding yards of bubble-wrap, a dark blue bottle was finally exposed. Lifting the bottle out, she uncovered a silver bowl with Celtic designs engraved on the outside.

"The centerpiece of our altar," Elizabeth exclaimed and Diana saw joy bubbling in her younger circle sister. "I brought water from the well in the Sacred Grove. And this bowl has been in Michael's family for generations. I found it in the back of a lower cupboard in The Manor's still room."

As one, the seven women walked to Sophia's living room, her sacred space, where they held their ceremonies. On the carpet was a peach-colored silk cloth. Elizabeth set the silver bowl in the center and carefully poured the water. Finished, she stood in the West. One by one they came to the altar, set their offerings on the silk and stood. Diana placed her small selenite wand in the East, a piece of moonstone in the north, a piece of pale yellow calcite in the south, and an opalescent stone in the west. Her last offering a candle added, as was everyone else's, to the circle surrounding the silver bowl.

Sophia handed her a tall white taper. Lighting it from the lone lit candle just inside the living room opening, Diana held the taper high, "I am the light, I am the source, Through me love flows throughout the world." Repeating the words, her steps measured, the light of optimism glowed within her as she walked the room's perimeter lighting the plethora of candles and leaving the room aglow in candlelight. At the altar, she bent and lit her candle before handing the taper to Sophia and taking her place in the East.

One by one her circle sisters took the taper and lit a candle on the altar. Someone had set a candle holder inside the silver bowl and Elizabeth placed the taper there.

Hands held high over their heads, they said prayers to open the circle, calling the energy of light and love and whatever animals and ancestors needed to come to them. This was Imbolc, Candlemas, a time to support the return of light and to honor the pagan Celtic Goddess Brigit, who later became the Christian Saint Brigit. They called on the light, encouraged its return, and the energy of white light encircled them. Opening prayers finished, they sat. A piece of rainbow obsidian was their talking stone and they used it much like the Native American did a talking stick.

Elizabeth began. "I know I emailed you all about our first weekend retreat. It was more than I'd hoped for. Do any of you remember my talking about those young women I'd met at New Grange last summer? Well, I'd sent them a notice about the Retreat Center."

Diana inwardly smiled, drinking in the joy and energy from Elizabeth's ecstasy. *She just might levitate right in front of us.*

"They wanted to come right away so I quickly put something together and they brought two friends and Shannon knew of two young women who were interested so there were seven of them and Shannon and me. It was amazing. I am so very blessed to have such a solid start. Seamus, of course, made fantastic, wholesome, simple meals.

"We did opening and closing ceremonies, had time for them to mediate, journal, or just sit and reflect. We also identified totem animals for those who wanted that." She grinned and added, "I was exhausted, am still exhausted so not at my best. This energy you see comes from the buzz of adrenaline-soaked exhaustion." She passed the stone to Ashley.

Diana loved the sound of Ashley's soft Southern drawl. She understood much better what Ashley endured. Everyone knew there were times when Art was more physical, shoving and pushing her, maybe even slapping at her. *Does she ever think about leaving him? Does she know we'd all be there to support her?*

Something was different tonight. A different energy mixed with the calm certainty she experienced when they were in ceremony. *Change is in the air. What is in store for us?* Her mind had wandered; she returned her focus to what Ashley was saying.

"...feel so much stronger. The time in Ireland was so healing, Elizabeth. I'm so blessed having y'all in my life. And, I'm so proud of you, Elizabeth. What a great thing ya have going on over there, yer such an inspiration to us."

I've done Ashley a disservice drifting off like that. I'll find a way to spend extra time with her later. She turned to listen intently to Gabriella.

"Not much new. Day job's still okay because it gives me time to work on my novel. I've finished the first draft and am into editing," she said before turning toward Elizabeth. "Being able to write in peace at the place you and Michael have provided me is a wonderful gift. There's absolutely no way I can ever repay you."

"Of course there is." Elizabeth reached across Ashley and patted Gabby's arm. "Just write that best seller and keep our place safe." Her gaze drifted around to each of the other women. "Sometime I think we don't appreciate the gifts we give one another," Elizabeth said. "Without Gabby in our house, Michael and I would have to hire a property manager to keep an eye on it; and we would still worry; and then we'd have to hire someone to come and clean when we wanted to be here. Gabby is saving us all of that expense and worry and she thinks she owes us!"

The two friends held hands a moment longer before Gabby passed the stone to Hunter.

"I know what you mean, Elizabeth. The love and support I receive from each of you sustains me when doubts arise. And they do. Twinkle Toes may be operating in the black but not by much. Logan will be off to college in a couple of years and I'm not sure how I can swing it right now." She shook her head and rested her chin on her chest before straightening, a determined look on her face. "If I have to, I'll go to the trust for the money for her education. I won't allow my pride to interfere with her being able to go to the college of her choice."

She handed the stone to Lily. "This time last year I was ensconced in Jackson's house, dreading being in such close proximity to him and hating the dependence the accident had forced upon me. Without your love and support, as well as all those hours of listening to my fears with such understanding, I don't know how I could have made it through to find the happiness I experience every hour of every day. I am so blessed to have Jackson in my life, to have each and every one of you in my life. To think what can happen in a year? For me, it's a miracle."

Sophia was the next to receive the stone. Her gaze wandered the room, resting on the silver bowl, the water shimmering from the reflection of the candle. "In olden times, Imbolc was the beginning of spring—the time when light finally overcomes dark, the days becoming longer. By the end of this month bulbs will be blooming, early camellias and other shrubs will show signs of color or be in full bloom. Hope that spring is on its way, hope that light overcomes the darkness, hope that life surpasses death—Brigit was a goddess of fertility. My wish for us all is that we have an abundance of peace and health in our lives."

Diana took the stone, now warm from so many hands and prayers. She held it close, covered with both hands.

"You all know about Dennis' attacks on me and that I've filed for a divorce. I just haven't been able to make myself petition for the restraining order. It may seem strange to you, but a part of me can't believe any of this has even happened and the part that knows what happened can't believe he'd do anything more." Staring at the stone, she searched for the words. "I couldn't have made it this far without each of you." She glanced up, caught Elizabeth's gaze. "You gave me the time, the space to make this decision in Ireland." She spied Lily, smiled. "You and Elizabeth are shining with the light of love. Sophia," she gestured in her direction, "harbored me. And Lily? Well, Lily gave me her little house, a place of my own. Each of you," she fought back the tears, her smile quivering, "each of you has contributed to my peace of mind, to my well-being with your prayers and actions." She chuckled. "You stocked my kitchen and I'm still feasting on the wealth of food you all brought." She sighed and looked around. "It may not seem like much to any of you, but to me, overwhelmed as I am right now with my life, it has been priceless."

Monday when Matthew knocked on her door, she invited him in, offering him an herbal tonic, knowing he didn't care for tea. She finished gathering her things, turning off the computer and checking the back door to confirm it was locked before joining him in the living room. He'd finished his tonic and had rinsed the glass and put it in the dishwasher. He certainly was thoughtful—thoughtful and protective.

After class they went to the coffee shop with the others before he walked her back to her car and followed her home. He waited in his truck until she was in the house, lights on, alarm set.

While Diana preferred he just drive on, he wouldn't agree to that. Reluctantly she'd agreed she would call his cell phone and let him know everything was okay. She was more comfortable with that than his coming inside and he wouldn't settle for her flashing the porch light. "Too much like a parent signaling date's over," he'd told her. She'd laughed, he'd smiled and that tug between them deepened another notch.

At times she was uneasy. Even though she never actually saw anyone, it felt like someone was watching her. While it occurred to her to check it out with Matthew, she never did. Instead, she either brushed such uncomfortable thoughts aside or buried them deeper and went on with her life.

15   PICTURES

A week later, as Diana prepared for the evening's class, her phone rang.

"Diana, Carol Lawford. We need to talk. Dennis is counter-suing for divorce. I've made time in my schedule to see you at 5:15," she said, her tone brisk.

"But," Diana's mind whirled with confusion.

"He says he has pictures of proof of your infidelity."

"But I haven't. There isn't anyone."

"My class begins—."

"I know. This won't take long."

Early for her appointment, her stomach in knots, Diana paced the small waiting room, sat and squirmed in the chair before standing again. Her restlessness prevented her from looking at the magazines on the small side table or enjoying the fish tank against the wall. She recognized the efforts to create a calm, serene environment but while her head noted them, her body churned with the stress of waiting, of wondering. *Pictures? Of whom? I can't think of anyone. Ms. Lawford expressed how important it was to be beyond reproach. I have been. I know I have been!*

Ms. Lawford opened her door at 5:30, invited her in and gestured her toward a table with chairs set under the window. Diana crossed the cluttered room and waited. The view of the river bisecting Fremont was spectacular in the waning light and she distracted herself by admiring it in an attempt to keep herself calm. *Screaming at Ms. Lawford to hurry won't help.* Finally she was motioned to one of the chairs and sat. A folder appeared on the table in front of her. She took a deep breath, opened the folder and stared.

A black and white picture of her with Matthew. *I'm taking my car keys from his hand. But,* she tipped it slightly, *it looks like we might be holding hands.* In the next photograph he was standing in her dining room. She was handing him a glass. All together there were a dozen pictures of her with Matthew Houston: his hand on her elbow, his bending to hear something she was saying, and one where it looked like his hand was on the small of her back.

She looked up at Ms. Lawford, confusion and despair in her eyes.

"What is this all about?" her voice trembled.

"Dennis is suing you for a divorce. His attorney also said they are contemplating suing this young man for alienation of affections." Her tone was formal, business-like; her facial features a neutral mask.

"Dennis can't be serious?" Diana sputtered in incredulous outrage.

"I'm afraid he is serious." Ms. Lawford went back through the photographs and put three of them aside. She tapped the others together and placed them back in the folder. "These are the most damaging."

Diana looked at the pictures. One was of Matthew accepting a glass of tonic. One was of him holding her car keys out to her as she sat in her car. One was of him bending to hear something she was saying, and it looked like his hand was resting on the small of her back. In each of them she was looking up at him. "Is that it? Is that the problem? I'm looking up at him?"

"No, Diana, it isn't you. Look at the pictures again," Ms. Lawford encouraged.

Diana studied the pictures. *It can't be the scenario: handing someone a glass, car keys. Ms. Lawford said it wasn't me.* She looked more closely at Matthew.

His bending to hear something she was saying and it looked like his hand was on the small of her back—intimate, two people comfortable with each other, sharing secrets. The fact she was telling him something about a book she'd just read wasn't relevant. *It's how we look together?*

"Mr. Houston is the man who pulled Dennis off me. He's a student in my class who's taken it upon himself to escort me to and from class. He's concerned Dennis may attack me again. There isn't anything between us," this last came out as a whisper.

"From the looks of things, I'd say Mr. Houston would like something to be between you."

"I'm forty," Diana protested. "He's almost ten years younger and, rather like a son to his mother, he's being protective."

Ms. Lawford shook her head, a rueful smile on her lips. "If you believe that then you are blind to the reality of things. This Mr. Houston does not look at you as if you were his mother."

She sat down beside Diana, her voice now stern. "Wake up here, Diana. Look again at his face. He is interested in you, interested in you as a woman—not as a mother. It's written on his face for the world to see." She shifted in her chair to better look Diana in the eyes. "And you, in your blind denial, are smiling at him."

Nausea rolled through her. She was going to be sick. Wrapping her arms tightly around her middle, she rocked, hoping to ease the chaos engulfing her body. Tears and worse, a moan, escaped. Ms. Lawford picked up the photos and added them to the folder.

"What does he want?" Diana whispered. The feelings of confidence and freedom evaporated in the few minutes it took to look at twelve pictures. She was smart enough, savvy enough to know these photographs could be damaging if their divorce went to court. *And a lawsuit against Matthew?*

"He wants you to call the divorce off and return to the house. He doesn't care if you two resume marital relationships. He wants your word you'll never see this man again. If you don't agree, he'll file the lawsuit against Mr. Houston. And, yes, he does know who he is. He'll do whatever he can to ruin him."

The sound of her cell phone interrupted. Her first impulse was to ignore it. But she glanced at the time and knew who it was.

Matthew was at her house.

She wasn't home.

He was worried.

She slipped her phone out of the pocket of her coat. It stopped ringing as she did so. A glance at the screen confirmed it was Matthew. Less than a minute passed when it rang again.

"Are you okay?" his first words and before she could reply. "Where the hell are you?"

She heard his distress. *He isn't angry, just concerned. What do I say? I have to tell him about the pictures, warn him in some way.*

"Diana? Are you there?"

"Yes, Matthew, I'm here." She glanced at Ms. Lawford who nodded before standing and crossing the room. She stared at the folder of pictures left in front of her. "I'm at my attorney's office. There have been some… ," she paused seeking the right word, "…developments I'd guess you'd call them. I may be a little late to class. Perhaps you could go ahead and let them know I'll be right along?"

"That's not an option."

She heard the determination in his voice. *Was a troubled frown on his face? Was he pacing, working off the energy built up from his concern for her?*

"Your choices," he was telling her, "come home first and we'll go from here; or I'll come there and get you. Which do you prefer, Diana?"

"Actually, Matthew, you've left out a third option. I can go to the school on my own and meet you there. I can assure you Dennis will not physically attack me tonight."

"How can you be sure?"

She heard a challenge but not a threat. He was determined to see her safe and she was equally determined to see him safe. There could be no more opportunities for pictures of them together. She sighed.

"Because he's just attacked me in a different way, he'll wait to see what I do. I'm positive I'm safe from any physical attack tonight." She paused. "Please, Matthew. Please, just meet me at school. You can wait in the parking lot if that will ease your mind. If I don't hang up now I'll be really late."

"I'll let campus security know you're coming. Park next to their building and they'll see you get safely to class."

"I can do that. That's actually a great idea," she tried to sound upbeat.

"This isn't over, Diana. We'll talk later." The phone went dead.

She turned and saw Ms. Lawford watching her from across her office.

"Take the pictures, Diana. I've another set in your file." Ms. Lawford gestured to the table. "I will be surprised if Mr. Houston doesn't have more questions for you later."

Diana stood and picked up the folder. With a weary sigh, she dropped it in her briefcase. Standing, she crossed the room, shook hands with her attorney, and left the office. Exhaustion dragged her footsteps as she walked down the hall to the elevator and on out to her car.

Will it never end? Will I never be free of Dennis? Will I have to move back with him to protect Matthew? Serial questions in a continuous loop through her mind, questions with no easy answers.

16   HOW CAN I BE SO WRONG?.

The class over, Diana dashed to the parking lot only to remember her car was at campus security. Matthew had waited for her arrival from the classroom door, kept his steady gaze on her throughout the session, and with measured steps, followed her in her mad dash to escape him. Retracing her steps to the campus security building and her car, her mind whirled. *I know I have to talk to him, to warn him—please just not right now.*

Time was what she needed.

Time to wrap her mind around what Ms. Lawford had pointed out to her.

Time to figure out what to say and how to say it. She trotted to her car, slipped behind the wheel, started the engine and looked in her mirrors. He wasn't there. Was she relieved? Yes and no – relief tinged with regret.

Fifteen minutes later, Diana pulled into her driveway. A car parked across the street caught her eye but she dismissed it—it wasn't Dennis's. She relaxed as she put her car in park and turned off the key. *I'm home. I made it home.*

When she got out of her car, a shadow detached itself from the neighbor's shrubs. Sidling along the side of the car, she shifted to get into the open, to escape her stalker—Dennis.

"I'll help you pack," he snarled, a cruel smile on his face. "You're coming home with me now." He reached for her.

She pushed her briefcase into his chest and tried to dodge under his arm.

His hand clutched her scarf.

The front door opened.

"Is that you, Diana?" Lily's voice. "Diana?"

"Let me go now, Dennis!" Diana shouted, dropping her briefcase and tugging on her scarf in an attempt to free herself from his grasp.

He twisted the cloth around his fisted hand and pulled her closer.

"Pettybone? What's going on here?"

Diana glanced to her left and saw Jackson.

"Just collecting my wife, Montgomery. Nothing for you to concern yourself with. Right Diana?" he said in a cruel, demeaning tone.

Before she could answer, the trio was illuminated in headlights. She turned her head to shield her eyes from the glare, instinctively knowing who'd arrived, who was checking to make sure she'd gotten home all right. The tall figure of Matthew Houston was silhouetted by one of his truck's headlights.

"Montgomery."

"Houston."

The two men nodded to each other and stood side-by-side.

Dennis tightened his grip.

Her breathing stuttered as the scarf dug into her throat. Her hands clawed at the constriction in an effort to prevent suffocating.

"Pettybone," Jackson said reasonably, "why don't you let Diana go into the house with my wife? I think we men can settle things, don't you?"

"She's coming with me now," Dennis countered glaring at Jackson. He turned, tugging the scarf, forcing her to take a few steps or lose consciousness. "I'll bring you back tomorrow to pack up your things," his voice slimed over her.

Diana heard the threat beneath. If she went with him, he would beat her. If she refused, he'd accuse Matthew right here and now.

Lily came out of nowhere, slipped in next to her and raised her hand, a butcher knife clutched in her fist.

"Your choice Dennis," her voice sticky sweet as she glared at him, "is to let Diana go or I'll have to cut the scarf. Between the dark and the glare of the headlights, you never know what I might cut in the process."

She watched Dennis consider his options and saw the moment he realized his disadvantage. The tension on the scarf eased as he unwrapped it from his hand.

"This isn't over, Diana. You will come home. I will not tolerate your fucking this bastard." He gestured toward Matthew. "I'll destroy him. You know I can and will do it." He stalked off, down the sidewalk, and turned the corner.

Lily took her arm. "You're okay, D. He's gone. Come. Let's get you into the house."

A sense of relief flooded her body as Diana gulped in air, stiffened her spine and looked around her. Jackson and Matthew stood to the side, allowing Lily to help her. One shaky breath, one foot moved forward, then another and another.

With Lily's encouragement she made it into the house and took off her outerwear before collapsing on the couch. Jackson dropped her briefcase on a chair while Matthew closed the door. Lily bustled around fixing tea and cookies.

"You may wonder why we're here," Lily began sitting on the couch beside her.

Diana nodded.

"Matthew called to say something had happened and he didn't know what. He just wanted someone to know, D. He was worried and concerned, that's all," she said draping her arm around Diana's shoulders.

"I talked it over with Jackson and we decided to come over to make sure you were okay. We decided to wait inside because we felt too conspicuous sitting in the car." Lily gently squeezed her shoulder and added, "I hope you don't mind. This is your house now.

"You must tell us what this is all about," she encouraged as she handed some tissues to Diana and waited, an arm now stretched along the back of the couch, the other resting lightly on Diana's arm.

Lily's comforting presence helped. The two men across from her, their posture identical: slouched in chairs, long legs stretched in front, gray and emerald green eyes watching her intently, didn't.

Where was her courage? Where was her determination to have a new life? What were the answers that would keep her from returning to Dennis? Or would she return to him to keep him from destroying an innocent?

"I can take care of myself, Montgomery," she heard Matthew say.

She glared at Matthew, her expression severe. "You have no idea what he is capable of, Matthew."

"Some," he replied. "I know what he's capable of with you. Hitting, threatening, intimidating."

"Are you seriously considering going back to him, D? Seriously? Knowing he'll beat you?"

The concern in Lily's voice echoed her own. She knew what Dennis would do if she returned. She also knew what he'd do if she didn't.

"I don't see a way through this mess that doesn't have dire consequences." Diana sat up now, bent over, and spoke to her knees, unable to look anyone in the face. Each of them had stood up for her, stood by her, supported her in reaching out for her dream.

"Something happened. Her attorney's office." Matthew's voice pierced the silence. "Won't talk about it."

"Perhaps we should go upstairs where we can talk in private," Lily offered.

Diana shook her head. "It's just so embarrassing. Nothing happened but it looks as if something did." She stood and crossed to her briefcase, plucked out the folder of pictures and handed it to Lily. She remained standing in front of her friend, her head bowed in defeat.

Lily opened the folder and looked at the pictures. One by one she handed them across to Jackson, who had stood to receive them.

"Pictures of us." Matthew's voice was barely audible. "The bastard had you followed," he said in a voice with a steely edge to it. He stood, his hand jabbed out to take the pictures from Jackson who looked to Diana for direction. With her acquiescence, he passed them to Matthew.

"Hell," he muttered softly as he sifted through the photographs.

"He said he'd ruin you, Matthew. File an alienation of affection lawsuit." Tears slipped down her cheeks, dabbing at them did not stem the tide. "You've been kind, Matthew. I don't want you dragged into this."

"I'm already "into this," he growled. "What?" he glared at her. "You think I can't protect myself?"

"This isn't about a fist fight, Matthew." Diana planted her hands on her hips.

"That's it? I only hit? Can't talk?" he said his voice deadly calm.

She'd crossed a boundary but wasn't sure what it was. Her gaze sought Jackson's seeking his help but he was staring at Lily, some unspoken communication flowing between them. When she looked back at Matthew, he'd regained his seat, and eyes averted, looked out the window.

"Sit, D." Lily patted the place beside her on the couch and Diana did. Grateful that Lily was going to take charge, she sank to the cushions and sighed.

Jackson spoke up. "As I understand it, Pettybone plans to sue Houston here for alienation of affection and then do something to ruin his business unless you return to him. Do I have it right?"

Diana looked over at Lily's husband, sprawled again in the chair, elbows planted on the armrests, fingers tented; his gray eyes watchful.

"Yes, that sums it up," she said in a quavering voice as another wave of nausea hit.

Lily rubbed her back whispering, "You can do this D. You are one of the strongest women I know."

"I don't feel very strong, but I am eternally grateful you are here," Diana said as tears traced their way down her face. As she swiped them away, realization stunned her. Her breathing hitched, and the nausea weakened its hold. *The Tarot said I have decisions to make, it wouldn't be easy, but if I follow through, I can have what I want.* Tonight, symbolically, she stood at one of those crossroads.

Shifting on the couch, she held Lily's hand, looking first at Jackson and then at Matthew. Her gaze rested on his.

"I owe you an apology, Matthew. You are much more than your fists." She paused, took a deep breath before plunging in, infusing her voice with a confidence she had yet to feel. "I know you are building your business. I also know Dennis has contacts and will do anything he can to get his way including telling outright lies if he thinks he can get away with it. Usually he doesn't have to go that far because he's a master at innuendo. These pictures are evidence of that. We both know there is nothing between us," her brows furrowed at Matthew's grimace.

He raised his hand to stop her. "Montgomery, what do you see when you look at them?" He gestured toward the folder. "Honest, candid answer, please."

Jackson shifted to look directly at Matthew. "Are you sure you want my honest, candid answer?"

"Yes." Matthew nodded.

Jackson looked at Lily who shrugged, leaving the decision up to Jackson.

Diana grabbed the folder of pictures and looked through them again now knowing what everyone saw because of a trick of the camera lens. "Is it a crime to look happy?" She battled an impulse to tear the pictures, rend them into confetti.

"You know it's more than looking happy," Lily's soft voice comforted her. "These are pictures of two people who enjoy each other's company, who like each other, are comfortable with each other. I think the two of you have things to talk over; if not tonight, then soon. I doubt that Dennis will wait long, D." Lily leaned over and hugged her.

Diana relaxed for a moment in her friend's embrace. Lily was right; she and Matthew did need to talk.

Jackson rose as did Matthew.

"Lunch tomorrow, Houston?" Jackson invited.

Lily said, "I have another idea, Jackson. Why don't we have Diana and Matthew to dinner? They could talk downstairs in private."

"I'll leave that up to you, love. My plan is to find out more about Houston's construction company. Never know when I'll have a job come up and Daniel'll be busy." He turned back to Matthew. "Dennis may have contacts but so do I. He may be able to dent your business but I can guarantee he won't ruin you."

Hope swelled in her chest. Jackson had never offered that kind of support before. He stood in front of her, his arms out for a hug. Without waiting for her, he stepped forward and wrapped his arms around her in a fond hug.

His hands firmly on her shoulders, he stepped back. "I don't expect my wife to learn of your problems from Houston or anyone else ever again. For crissake, Diana, how many times did you listen to her when we were finding our way?" He gave her a gentle shake before letting her go. His finger came up and he shook it in her face. "No more of this crap, do you understand me? I'll not have my wife in a tizzy because of your pride," he huffed.

Lily, an amused look on her face, stepped to his side, rose on her toes, and kissed his cheek. "Well said, Jackson. Very well said."

Lily turned and took Diana's hands in hers. "Always know you can call me, D."

"I know, Lily. I know I can call any of you. I just … ," her words trailed off. "I was so stunned by the pictures and his demands; I just lost myself for a bit."

"Have you found yourself?" Lily queried.

"Yes, I think I have. I knew this would be a journey filled with challenges that would demand I make hard decisions. It never occurred to me other people would be so directly affected." She turned to face Matthew. "I don't think Dennis will be back tonight. I think it best if you leave with Lily and Jackson." She raised her hand to ward off the comment she could see on his lips. "We do need to talk, Matthew. I think in the daylight, in a public place would be best."

"What about Lily's suggestion of dinner at their place?" He looked determined to talk to her sooner rather than later.

"I still have to travel back here in the dark. And if you follow me Dennis has another opportunity."

Matthew ran his hand through his hair; rubbed the back of his neck in a gesture that was becoming familiar.

"You can spend the night with us, D." Lily paused a moment before adding, "Yes, that will work. You and Matthew can come to dinner." She looked at Jackson before turning to Matthew. "My husband is an excellent cook," she bragged. "Diana and I can entertain ourselves while you two talk and Jackson fixes dinner. Then, you two," she gestured to Matthew and her, "can go down to the family room to talk for as long as you need."

Jackson pulled Lily against his side, leaned over and kissed the top of her head. "You are amazing, Lily-love."

"Thank you, Jackson." Lily snuggled closer to him. She gave him a brilliant smile and then turned to Diana and Matthew. "How about tomorrow night? Can you both make it?"

Diana looked at Matthew. He nodded and so did she.

Lily leaned into her husband; his arm wrapped around her shoulder and pulled her close.

She wanted that for herself: the special connection Lily and Jackson had. She turned to Matthew who also observed the couple.

"Tomorrow night then," she confirmed.

"Yes. Tomorrow night." Matthew stopped in front of her. "I'll see you then, Diana." He paused a moment more, his gaze searching her face, before turning and following Jackson out.

Lily rushed to her, gave her a quick hug, and out the door she went catching up with Jackson and Matthew before they were off the porch. As a unit they turned and stared at her, stern expressions on their faces.

"All right. I'm closing the doors and locking them," she called out following her words with action. Through the front door glass she saw the three figures stop, speak a few words, and then move on to their respective vehicles.

Turning back to the living room, she picked things up and put them away. Exhaustion claimed her and her legs trembled as she finished her nightly routine. Overlaying the exhaustion a calm certainty had settled and all tension was gone—unless her thoughts strayed to Matthew.

The last few weeks of denying there was an attraction had a major flaw. Awareness of where he was in a room and his proximity to her was telegraphed by her lungs breathing a little deeper to pick up his fresh lime scent, her heart beating a little faster, her steps a little lighter when walking with him to her car. And then there was the way his eyes followed her; the way he seemed to know what she needed.

So this is how far Dennis will go to maintain the illusion of the perfect couple in a perfect marriage living a perfect life. It is all about appearances. Another thought surfaced. *And he sees me as "his" as in he owns me in some way. Hmm, I hadn't seen that before.*

With Lily, Jackson, and Matthew's help she'd faced them all. It eased her mind to know whatever challenges were before her, she did not have to deal with them alone. With the guidance of The Tarot and the support of her friends, she was at another crossroads. *Will I return to Dennis to protect Matthew? Will Dennis keep his word about Matthew even if I do? I'll see what the cards say in the morning.*

17   Temperance

Diana snuggled deeper under the covers. Daylight streamed through the small window, the bare branches of the tree created lacy patterns on the deep crimson comforter. This morning was different; she was more alive in some yet-to-be-discerned way. Without actually moving from her cocoon, she squirmed and squinted to see the time.

Nine o'clock and I'm still in bed. How decadent. Vaguely she remembered hitting the snooze button, wanting a little more sleep after a restless night: waking, drifting off, dreams just outside her consciousness. As she considered the day before her and her long "to do list" with both household and work tasks, dinner with Lily, Jackson and Matthew, and then talking with Matthew, she knew she'd keep busy. *But first on my agenda: The Tarot. My question? What do I need to know and remember to make it through my day?*

Tossing back the covers, she reached for her robe and slipped it on before sliding her feet into cold slippers. She grabbed a clean bra, deciding against panties. Not wearing them every day was a small sign of the rebellion spreading throughout her life. In the closet she rummaged around for a pair of black gabardine slacks and an emerald green silk blouse. The matching jacket of black wool with an emerald green lining had cutouts on the pockets that let the green silk shimmer through.

After her shower, she dressed but chose to wear no make-up, another little piece of rebellion. Tucking the blouse into the waist of her slacks, she put her slippers on and padded to the kitchen to make herself a glass of herbal tonic before moving on to the living room.

Sitting on the couch, she took a moment and sipped her tonic before picking up her Journal, reaching for a pen and opening the book to a new page.

Today I face my future. Will I return to Dennis? Can I talk to Matthew? What do I need to remember, to know as I go through my day?

Using the pen to hold her place in the Journal, the calm certainty similar to what she experienced during Ceremony infused her body. When she picked up the cards and slid them from their box, it intensified. Concentrating on her question, she held the cards loose in her hands before shuffling three times. Cutting the cards into three piles she restacked them preparing for the reading. *My pattern is different. I've put the middle pile on top and the bottom pile remains on the bottom.*

Diana placed the cards back on the table and focused on her question. Anticipation sang and confidence infused her posture. Fortifying that confidence with a deep breath, she turned over the top card: *Temperance.*

The card's message? Flexibility, change and adaptation. She thought about these words before reading the rest of the card's message and noting it in her Journal.

I will need flexibility, be able to change and adapt today. I think these are three traits I'll need in order to move forward, today and beyond. I can achieve balance and control over my life. Part of my task is to take ideas and life experiences and synthesize them to form new ideas. I may have to compromise in order to gain cooperation.

She looked at the last phrase on the card: *Possible reconciliation.* Her brows furrowed as she sat in pensive silence, her mind whirling. Standing, she strode to her office, and pulled a dictionary from the bookcase. Back on the couch, she leafed through the pages until she found 'reconcile', 'reconciliation'. Some form of that word had appeared in each of her spreads. She believed in coincidence, synchronicity, serendipity. It followed that she needed to deepen her knowledge of this word.

Make peace or adjust.
Resign oneself to something.

Which definition do I want to hold in my heart? I think it is a combination— resigning myself to the ugliness I'm facing. Whether I return to Dennis or not, there is ugliness. It's more a matter of whether I want to be with him in ugliness, with no hope of things getting better or face the ugliness without him. I don't think there is an option of no ugliness and if I'm honest with myself, there probably never was. I've the skills I need to counter-balance the ugliness. I need to remember to do that – to find the beauty, the goodness that is always there.

Do I trust that even if I return to him, Dennis won't attempt to ruin Matthew? _No_. I don't trust Dennis at all. What's worse is I don't even know this Dennis. It's as if a stranger has taken over his body. He may look like Dennis, and even sound like him, but he isn't the Dennis I married.

The idea of him touching me, claiming his marital rights as my husband is repulsive. He may say he wants nothing to do with me, but once I've moved back no one, nothing will stop him from raping me. Even though my body feels more awake and more alive sexually, I'd rather remain celibate than be intimate with him.

What's left is to adjust, to make peace with what will come.

Temperance, the card of flexibility, change, and adaptation, is telling me to use my people and management skills to find a new way using bits and pieces of the old. I need to go forward protecting those around me as best I can. I've resisted getting a restraining order thinking whatever he's done is the last of it. I just can't seem to wrap my mind around Dennis being so physical. Perhaps Temperance is telling me I do have the people and management skills to keep myself and those around me safe.

If Matthew is willing to undergo the scrutiny, the innuendo, and the questions that Dennis' current path will demand, then I will be on that path also. It's my choice to move forward toward my dream of a loving relationship. I'm not alone. Every one of my women's circle stands with me.

Friday when we come together I'll share this with them. It's been hard for me to tell them everything and no one knows my whole history. Now feels like the time to open up. Who knows who may have another point of view, an idea, a suggestion that will help me stay the course, calm the stormy waters.

Capping the pen, she closed the Journal, slid the cards back into their box and sat for a time pondering the Temperance card's message. *My feet are firmly on the ground, on the path I'm meant to take. I'm no longer fearful or anxious about talking with Matthew. In fact I'm not sure we even need a private talk. I'll ask him straight out "Are you willing to endure Dennis' tricks?" If his answer is "Yes", well, what else is there to say?*

Diana pulled into the Montgomery's driveway. Her earlier resolve lost. Resting her head against the back of the seat, she sat with a damp palm on her queasy stomach, the other on her thigh. Not for the first time today she took three deep breaths to settle her body's unease. *Where is Matthew's truck? I don't recognize the one already here.*

The door to Jackson's mother's apartment opened and Eleanor called to her. "Come in Diana. I am so glad you could come and visit me."

Confusion sparked quickly smothered with a realization that if someone was watching, the opportunity to catch her going in the same door as Matthew was lost.

"It's good to see you, too," Diana called out in greeting, a warm smile on her face as she got out of her car, set the alarm and crossed the short distance to Eleanor's front door.

Once inside, Eleanor closed and locked the door. With a gesture towards the French doors into the main house she said "Go on in. Everyone is there."

"Are you joining us for dinner," Diana asked.

Eleanor shook her head. "You need your privacy, D."

"But you are more than welcome to join us for dinner," Diana encouraged. "Nothing secretive will be discussed. I don't want to come between you and one of Jackson's home-cooked meals."

"It is quite all right. He will bring me a plate with enough food for two," she said a fond smile on her face.

"Just so you know then," Diana leaned down and whispered conspiratorially in Eleanor's ear. "I've decided that if Mr. Houston is willing to endure Dennis' shenanigans, I will go forward with the divorce."

"I cannot imagine that young man will not stand by you, D. He seems very determined right now."

Diana smiled at the older woman, reached out and gently squeezed her hands. "The road will be very rocky. Thank you for your support."

"You are welcome, my dear. Now go on through before they think something is wrong. They've all been waiting for you since your young man and Daniel arrived a bit early," Eleanor said nudging her toward the French doors.

Straightening to her full height, she marched through the doors and ran head-long into Lily.

"We heard you set your car alarm and wondered what was keeping you," Lily said. "Come and join us. We are having a glass of wine before dinner."

"I'll pass." Diana followed Lily into the room. Her eyes collided with Matthew's and her body grew warm, softened in response. Reminding herself of tonight's mission, she strode forward, her hand outstretched to greet Daniel, who she hadn't seen since the wedding in Ireland.

Daniel took her hand and pulled her to him, giving her a hug of welcome while whispering in her ear. "Shall I make him a little jealous?"

She schooled her features to a blank façade before stepping back. "I have no idea what you're talking about." Smoothly she disengaged from Daniel's grasp and turned to greet Jackson. Beyond him stood Matthew, his generous mouth set in a grim line. The thought to call him Mr. Houston flitted through her mind. She quashed it, stepped in front of him and offered her hand in greeting while she stared into his emerald green eyes.

"Good evening, Matthew," she said her voice surprisingly calm to her ears. Mentally she was sure of her direction, but physically her body had doubts. Or maybe it was excitement, anticipation, rather like getting ready for battle.

Her thoughts scattered the instant he touched her and shook her hand. Their hands told a story, his large, browned and slightly reddened from working outside, hers small, pale, blue veins tracing the back.

He didn't let her go.

Surreptitiously she tried to pull her hand away, to restore order to her wits. For another moment, he held her firmly. When he let her go, Diana leaned against the slate counter to anchor herself to something solid.

"I've a question for Matthew," she said, thinking her voice fairly steady. Her hand on the counter, she turned to look at him. "Having had some time to think things over, are you still willing to put up with, to endure whatever Dennis tries? Are you still willing to risk all that you've built to this point?" She fixed her gaze on his, watched his emerald green eyes darken, a slight smile form on his lips.

"Yes."

His deep voice echoed in her mind, filled her with its rich texture, tears teetered, a tremor rippled through her. She fought to still herself. He was standing in front of her now, his hands cupping her shoulders.

"I can handle it, Diana," Matthew said in a decisive tone followed with a light squeeze of support. He stepped away, his arms dropping to his sides.

"I wasn't sure what your decision would be." Jackson's comment caught her off-guard. She turned away from Matthew. *Of course they'd all been listening.*

"What helped you decide this direction?" Jackson added.

"I'm sure regardless of my decision there will be ugliness. I'm sure Dennis is just as likely to attempt to ruin Matthew if I return to him or stay away. I'm sure going back to Dennis will be the death of what's left of my soul." Her hands rubbed her arms, a shiver trembled through her.

Lily came to stand beside her, an arm around her waist. "You are not alone in this fight, D."

"I know. That's one of the reasons I'm able to go through with this." A part of her was amazed she was still on her feet, still able to converse despite the battle going on in her body.

"The guys have come up with some ideas," Lily continued. "Let's sit and let them tell us what they've planned." Lily handed Diana a glass of tonic.

Diana sipped the ice cold drink, fixed just the way she liked it, as she and Lily listened to Daniel explain that Jackson had mentioned Matthew as a possible back-up for future work. Earlier today he'd visited a couple of Matthew's projects and was impressed with the quality of work.

"I've bid on a couple of contracts and know of another two coming up within the next week," Daniel commented. "I wasn't going to, but I'll bid now. I can sub them out to Matthew if I get something."

"Tell them the other part, Daniel," Jackson encouraged.

"Oh, you mean that Houston and I share a love of old Victorians?" Daniel said with a wink at Matthew.

Jackson raised an eyebrow.

Daniel shrugged but continued. "I love old houses, restoring, refurbishing, you know, bringing them back to their glory days," he paused. "I've thought of specializing in restoration work, even teaching homeowners how to do some of the work themselves."

"Daniel, that's a wonderful idea," Lily chimed in. "Your own house is a perfect example of the work you can do. I think you could easily restructure things so the converted carriage house could serve as a workshop with four to six people there at a time."

Jackson chuckled and turned to Matthew. "My wife has more ideas of how things could be done than anyone I know."

"That's because you haven't seen Diana at work," Lily chided. "She's my equal in every way when it comes to ideas, plans, and implementation. Right, D?" Lily turned to her and winked.

"I can hold my own," Diana said and smiled. "But Lily has an advantage knowing Daniel's house. My best advice is to follow your dream. Do what brings you the greatest joy. Then whatever the outcome, you will always be happy."

"Dinner's ready and will be ruined if I can't get you all to sit down," Jackson threatened good-naturedly, setting bowls on the counter. Everyone helped themselves to his special spaghetti and homemade red sauce; salad with his secret dressing; and warm garlic bread oozing with butter.

Diana relaxed in good company and great food. As dinner progressed and conversations veered between Daniel's dream of restoring old homes and various ways of supporting Matthew through the rough road ahead, Diana let her mind drift.

The five of them sitting together, eating, talking, laughing—it felt right, comfortable. *I remember Lily talking about having a sense of belonging when she first drove up to this house; but for me it isn't the house, it's this group of friends.* Matthew laughed a deep masculine sound that caught at her, pulled her in, brought her back to the table surrounded by smiling faces.

After eating their fill, they decided to hold off on dessert— Jackson's homemade ice cream for an hour. Matthew commented that would give them enough time to talk privately. Diana's head snapped up, her stomach instantly in turmoil.

"I don't think we have anything to discuss privately, Matthew." She hated her voice sounded so prim, so proper. "You said you could handle anything Dennis did, what else is there?"

He stood from the table, stepped to her side, and leaning over whispered in her ear, "How I feel about you? Public? Private? Choose."

The blush rose from her toes to the roots of her hair. She'd not prepared for this conversation here or in private. *Temperance: flexibility, change, adaptation; compromise to secure cooperation.* The words came readily. She laid her napkin on the table. Matthew held her chair as she rose.

"If you insist, Matthew." Without looking back, she strode to the stairs and descended to the family room below. There were no doors separating this large room from the upstairs. But she knew in the right place, they wouldn't be overheard. She strode to the far wall, stopped and abruptly turned.

He was right behind her. If she stepped forward, she would press against him. She had more of his attention than she was comfortable with, more than she wanted, more than she deserved. Matthew Houston needed a younger woman, not a forty-year-old, still-married woman. *I'm not old enough to be his mother, but I'm too old. He needs a younger woman, someone to build a family with because he'd be a wonderful father. I had Bill, then a miscarriage, and Dennis was cheating on me, more children weren't wise.*

She must have frowned because his calloused fingers traced circles over her forehead. His free arm circled her back pulling her closer while his fingers continued their magic on her brow. Her mind emptied of thought, her body drained of resolve, her knees buckled. She shuddered and sagged.

He caught her and held her close. The scent of him: outdoors, fresh air and lime enveloped her, his strength comforted. Fingers no longer touched her brow but slipped along the side of her face to cup her chin. Acceding to the pressure of his hand, she raised her face to his.

Stormy emerald green eyes bore into her. Her eyes widened and her mouth parted as his head slowly lowered to hers.

He was going to kiss her. She should struggle, say "no", push him away, remind him of the pictures and all the other reasons this was a bad idea. Instead she quieted, waited for the inevitable—his kiss. Her eyelids fluttered shut; her body relax into his hardness.

His lips brushed hers. Sensations thundered through her. Every cell in her body danced a jig, laughed, reached out for more. *When was the last time?* His, in that moment she was completely and utterly his. Reveling in the awareness of her feminine self, she opened and gave him access when his tongue probed. *It has been so very, very long.* She entwined her arms around his neck, pulled him closer; dared to dart her tongue to tangle with his. He groaned, his breathing broke, but was the thundering beat coursing through her from his heart or her own.

He shuddered, took her hands and disentangled them from his neck. He stepped back, creating space between them. And she, she swayed, leaned toward him, sought his heat, his strength.

Cool air swirled.

He was gone.

Diana opened her eyes startled to see him standing in front of her, desire darkening his irises, fighting for control. Amazing heady stuff to think she was the reason he fought to control his passion.

"I've dreamed of this moment," his forceful gaze locked with hers, "dreamed of holding you, kissing you, touching you."

Her face blushed a fiery red. In her wildest dreams she'd never imagined much less thought this could happen. It was mind-boggling.

A look of dismay on his face, he started to turn away.

Reaching up, she stroked his cheek, the warm skin smooth beneath her fingers. *He shaved for me.* Bemused, she shook her head, still seeking to understand how this could have happened.

He stepped away, looked away, dropped her hand.

"Sorry," he pushed his hands in his pockets. "Got out of hand." He reached up and ran his hands through his hair, rubbed the back of his neck.

"Don't be, Matthew. Please, don't be sorry. I don't think I could bear it right now," she said, turning from him and pacing once around the room. When she stopped in front of him, confusion furrowed his brow, registered in his eyes.

"I know I'm much older than you. You've been so kind to me, and now are risking a lot to help me. I know I shouldn't have responded to you like that when you were, you were just being kind." She was babbling, not making any sense, the words just pouring out. "It's, it's been so long since anyone has held me like that." She hugged herself and stared at the Berber carpet beneath her feet. "It-I-I know I'm too old for you."

His hand caressed her face with a tender touch. She looked up and saw kindness in his eyes. For her.

"Kind? I'm not being kind. What I feel for you goes far beyond that." He bent down, brushed kissed in her hair. "You are not too old nor am I too young." He kissed her forehead, cheek, and chin. "Do I confuse you?"

She nodded.

"Good. I want you that way—confused, bewildered, muddled. I want you—soft, pliant, responsive. God, Diana. I haven't wanted anyone the way I want you."

Who moved first? Who knew but more important, she didn't care. Somehow she was in his arms, her mouth eagerly meeting his, her body reveling in the arousal raging through her. He kissed her fully, deeply, thoroughly. And, again, it was Matthew who pulled back and set her aside, who shook his head, a rueful smile on his face.

"What I want—. Not here. Not yet."

He struggled to compose himself, tuck his shirt back into his pants. *Did I pull it free?* Her fingers brushed over her kiss swollen lips before her hands patted her hair in place and checked her own clothing.

"We'd better get out of here while I still have some brain cells working." He claimed her with his eyes. "I don't think I could stop next time. I want… ." Stopping, he turned away. His shoulders heaved, his breathing slowed.

She reached out and touched his shoulder.

He reached up and took her hand. Turning back to face her, a smile lit his face. "Now are you glad we had a private talk?" His hand stroked through her hair, tucked it behind her ear.

"Very glad." She smiled back. "Are we presentable?"

"Barely," he grinned and pulled her toward the stairs, "but there are no promises about next time."

18   SECURITY?

Two days later Diana woke with a start.

Banging.

She struggled from bed, glanced at the clock as she grabbed her robe. Nine o'clock. Shaking her head, she shoved her feet into her slippers, and rushed down the stairs to find Jackson and a service truck in the driveway. Stifling a yawn, she opened the door and gestured him in.

"I didn't mean to wake you, Diana," he said looking at his watch, his demeanor serious. "Are you okay? I really didn't think you'd still be asleep at this hour."

"I'm fine," she said turning away to hide another yawn. "I wasn't expecting anyone so I indulged myself by turning the alarm off."

"You may not want to go back to bed just yet because there'll be men on the roof." At her quizzical look, he continued. "Lily decided to upgrade this security system by installing cameras. We talked it over yesterday and decided to do it now.

She won't be moving her office back here." He grinned and rocked back on his heels.

She touched his arm a smile playing around her mouth. "I believe you have fully captured her." Emotions tightened her throat; she gave his arm a quick squeeze. "I'll never be able to thank you both for what you're doing for me now." She noticed the crew unloading boxes from the truck. "Is there time for me to dress upstairs before the work begins?"

"I'll make sure of it."

After dressing, Diana fixed a pot of tea for herself and nuked muffins for the four workers and Jackson.

Feeling restless and at loose ends, not wanting to start a project while the men worked, Diana announced she was going for a walk around the block.

"I'll be back shortly." She'd taken but a few steps before Jackson appeared by her side. They walked in silence part of the way before she stopped.

He'd walked a couple of steps further before realizing she wasn't beside him. She closed the distance.

"Don't I go anywhere now without an escort?" she said in a tired, resigned voice.

"For now. It won't be forever. But until this nastiness runs its course, I think it best you not go anywhere without someone with you. And, to be perfectly honest, that someone should not be Matthew Houston."

"Not even around the block?" Her shoulders slumped, any spring gone from her step.

"I don't trust Pettybone, especially not right now. He's acting rather crazed if you ask me. So, to answer your question, Diana, no," he looked her straight in the eyes, "I don't think you should even go for a walk around the block alone. If you need to walk, ask someone to go with you." He raised a hand. "It won't be forever. It's one of the prices you're paying now for that future you want."

"You mean part of the ugliness I must face because of my decision to leave Dennis." Looking at this inconvenience from that perspective helped. Her commitment to see the beauty around her brought her balance.

He nodded.

She sighed and started walking, her pace brisk. "I've not been able to convince Matthew to stay away."

"He'll still follow you to school and home on Monday nights, but that's all. He knows now is not the time to try and see you. Talk to your attorney, Diana. I think you can make a case for him following you on Monday night given Dennis' attacks have both been on Monday nights after your class."

"I have a telephone conference with her later today. I'll add that to my list." They turned the last corner, the house in sight. Jackson accompanied her on a longer walk around several blocks in the neighborhood but the crew was still working when they returned. Even though she'd told him to go on, he insisted on staying until the work was completed.

The installation of cameras and upgrades to the existing system complete, the security team leader explained the protective membrane they'd adhered to the large window off the kitchen deck as well as the two picture windows in front would prevent that glass from ever breaking which would prevent entrance. The new cameras meant anyone attempting to break in would be recorded. Also they'd double checked the range of the motion sensors and assured her that no one could get through a smaller window without an alarm sounding.

Diana paid close attention as the lead man explained and demonstrated the system. It was complicated in some ways and easy in others. The fob with buttons to turn the system on and off helped. "Away" armed everything "stay" only the perimeter.

"Thanks, Liam."

Diana watched Jackson shake the lead man's hand, clap him on the back and walk him toward the truck. Liam didn't get in the truck but continued on across the street to a sleek BMW parked in front of a neighbor's house. He waved, got in and drove off. The crew loaded the last of their equipment as she and Jackson walked into the house. Standing in the dining room, she looked out the window as Liam and the crew drove away.

"You called in a favor." It wasn't a question, just a statement of fact. "Thank you."

Jackson strode to her side, put an arm around her shoulders and squeezed. "You're special, Diana; special to Lily and the other women, and because of that, special to Daniel and me. It wasn't my favor that was called. Liam's company works with Daniel on different projects." He dropped his arm.

"It seems as if I owe everyone more than I can even imagine repaying." Her voice trembled and she swiped at tears escaping her eyes.

Jackson stepped in front of her and tipped her face. "Look at me, Diana," he said, his voice gruff.

She opened her eyes and saw stormy gray eyes boring into her.

"Stop that nonsense. You don't "owe" anyone anything. Have you no idea how much you give to others? How important you are to your friends? What it would do to them if anything more happened to you?" He dropped his hand, shoved it in his pocket and sighed. "When I first met Lily, she confronted me about my mother. I'm going to tell you what she told me because I think it's applicable."

Diana nodded. She remained still and silent, waiting for him to go on, for it to be over.

"At one point we were discussing Mother's care and I was bemoaning the fact that I wasn't there doing all the things for her that Lily was. She turned into her prim and prissy self," he said then laughed. "I love that side of her, you know."

He paused, his demeanor serious as he continued. "She told me that if I wanted to feel guilty, to just go ahead. She challenged me to make sure what I was complaining about was really about mother and not about me. Afterward," a soft smile tipped the corners of his mouth, "well, afterward I did think about what she'd said. I felt guilty I wasn't there but mother was extremely happy with things the way they were. She'd already fallen in love with Lily." He chuckled and turned to Diana. "Probably already making plans to bring us together. You know she always saw Lily and me as a couple, even in the beginning when we spit nails at each other.

"And just so you know, Lily sees you and Matthew as a couple." His hand shot out to curtail any rebuttal. "As does Dennis, and what's more important, as does Matthew."

"And you?" Diana was the regal ice queen, her posture erect, her jaw set, her knees locked, her voice frosty.

Jackson smiled, not at all put off. "If you find the happiness with Matthew that I've found with Lily, then I wish that for you with all my heart." He turned and strode to the door. "I've appointments to get to. Be sure to set the alarm when I leave."

After he was gone, Diana stood in the dining room fob in hand. She pressed the button to turn the alarm on; the mechanical voice announced it was set. On numb legs she walked to the couch, perched on the edge, her mind whirling with his words. *How to make sense of it all. How to—.* Pacing through the house—kitchen, dining room, living room, office back and forth, back and forth, her mind raced, thoughts tumbled over themselves. The need to move eased; she slowed then stopped. In the kitchen she fixed an icy tonic. As she sipped the calming drink, an idea emerged from the chaos of her mind.

Asking for and accepting help is a gift. That's what Sophia and I told Lily when she called me at three in the morning when she and Jackson were having their problems. I never felt she owed me anything for coming to her that night. Why is it so hard for me to accept her help? To accept anyone's?

Back in the living room, she relaxed into the cushions on the couch. *I loved that movie **Pay It Forward**. I know there will be a time when I can pass on to another the gifts I'm receiving from everyone now. In some ways, Lily is passing on the help I gave her.*

She sat and sipped, pondering recent events and making a mental "to do" list. Her tonic half finished, she rose and went into the office to get her cell phone. Her phone showed she had a voice message. She put in her earpiece and listened. *Matthew, checking in to see how I am just like he said – every day at nine a.m. and again at nine p.m. – just to make sure everything is okay.*

She pressed the key that automatically dialed his number. It rang once before she got his voice mail.

"Thank you for checking on me, Matthew. Jackson came by with a crew and the security system on the house has been upgraded with cameras. And, I have a key fob that makes having the system on when I'm home easy. Don't worry about me, Matthew. I'm fine." She pressed the red button to disconnect.

She sighed and shook her head as a mild sense of unease floated through her body. *It's strange to have people check on me, to care so much about what happens. I know the others in The Circle and those who care about them will stand by me. But that's quite different from experiencing it physically. I feel it in my gut when they put that caring into action. It's a heady yet troubling feeling to know I matter that much.*

She pressed the key that dialed Lily's number and settled back on the couch.

"Hi D," Lily's chipper voice came clearly through the line.

"Thank you, Lily. Thank you ever so much. I appreciate the extra security more than I can express." She rushed on, "But I'm calling about tomorrow night. I was hoping you could swing by and pick me up so we could go to Sophia's together. Would that work?"

"I'll be there at six and you can show me the new gadgets." She paused before adding, "Did Jackson tell you Daniel set this up? He'd made a phone call earlier yesterday when he found out about Dennis's antics Monday night."

"I think the owner of the company was here."

"Liam?"

"Yes. He drives a silver BMW so I figured he was the owner."

"Liam is the owner and a longtime friend of Daniel's. And it didn't hurt that he knows Jackson and me. I've helped him out with some ideas for his mother's care. I'd love to talk more, D, but I've got an appointment to get to. I'll check in with you later."

"I'm just fine, Lily. I've got my list and am ready to get to work and start checking things off. If you have time, okay; but please don't think you have to. I'm actually doing much better than I thought I would given the events of the last couple of days."

"I'll talk to you later, D. In love and light."

"In grace and gratitude."

"Blessed Be." They said in unison.

19   Confession

Diana wished every day was like today: anticipation of being with her women's circle, celebrating the love and joy of the divine feminine, singing, sharing their lives and food. The relationships with each of these women sustained her in bold and subtle ways both now and over the past eight years. The love Lily and Elizabeth found with Jackson and Michael gave her the push she needed to seek her own loving relationship. *No, we aren't blood relations but we are closer than many families.*

Lily picked her up on schedule and they arrived at Sophia's, dishes and ceremonial items in hand. Tonight was a special night because Elizabeth was leaving on the red-eye to return to Michael and her home in Ireland.

Somewhere during the day Diana had decided she needed to tell the others about Dennis' latest shenanigans. She listened to the sharing of her circle sisters, concentrating on each as she spoke. When the warm stone came to her, she held it close, covering it with both hands. Now was the time for her to reach deep inside herself for the courage to speak her truth. *I want them to know everything. To move forward, the time for secrets, for false pride must be behind me.* As she looked around the room, she knew with certainty they would understand. Her heart beating a rapid tattoo, her breathing shallow, her stomach churning, she began.

"You know I've left Dennis, have filed for a divorce, and about his assault on me last month. What you don't know is Monday night, he confronted me, attacked me again. He grabbed my scarf, I couldn't breathe." Her breathing hitched as she slid into the darkness of consuming terror that had devoured her that night.

A gentle pressure, Sophia's hand on her knee, brought her back to this place.

"I'm so blessed Jackson and Lily were there." Calm enveloped her. "Matthew Houston was also there. Even though I'd told him not to, he'd followed me home from class to make sure I was safe." The calmness faded, replaced by an overwhelming sense of shame.

"Dennis has had me followed and there are pictures of Matthew and me. Talking, walking together, nothing in particular, just everyday things except in these pictures we look—intimate." She looked desperately around the circle, willing them to understand.

"You've all met Matthew. He's honest and hard-working. I know he needs a woman more his age, someone who can be what he needs. I'm forty now, not ancient, nowhere near being a crone, but I'm much older than he." Tears coursed down her cheeks. Tissues lay now on hands clutching the stone but she couldn't let go of the stone, couldn't wipe them away. Shaking with sobs, her voice cracking, she forced herself to go on.

"I wa-wa-want someone to l-l-love me. Someone to hold me," she choked out. "I wa-wa-want to be s-s-special to one man who will remain f-f-f-faithful to me. I can't go back to Dennis. T-T-There'll be n-n-nothing left of me if I d-d-do," she gulped air, struggled to finish her confession.

"H-He's threatening t-to destroy M-Mathew's business; t-to expose m-me in such a w-way I'll n-never be able to t-teach or c-consult with a anyone again; to f-force me b-back to him b-b-because I-I-I'll have n-no way to s-support myself." Rocking she held herself tight, the tears soaking her blouse.

"He's had affairs ever since we were first married and I've stayed with him all this time. What's wrong with me? Why wasn't he faithful? Why... ?" She curled into herself unable to continue.

"May we speak, Diana?" Sophia's gentle voice penetrated her sobs.

She nodded.

"You're asking the wrong question, Diana. The question is "What is wrong with Dennis that he does not honor and respect the loving, wonderful woman you are?" That is the question. It isn't about you, it's about him."

"But I stayed with him all those years," she moaned, the sound coming from deep within her soul.

"Yes, you did." Lily spoke in a firm yet gentle voice. "You stayed for Bill and for any number of reasons. But, you've left now. You'll make yourself crazy, D, if you ask yourself unanswerable questions. Believe me I know, having tortured you for hours and hours over my indecision about Jackson."

"But Matthew... ," gulping, she raised her head.

"One more thing," Lily interrupted. "Matthew is an intelligent, strong man who knows the risks and is willing to take them. He's a man of integrity who is willing to protect you however he can, in this place and in this time. Don't diminish him because of his age, D."

"The truth is, I don't feel worthy of his protection, Lily. He's young, handsome, strong and could have more than me in his life right now."

"All that may or may not be true, but right now you are the one he wants to protect." Lily's tone was severe as she went on. "I don't ever want to hear you say you are not worthy of being protected again. That's the most ridiculous thing I've ever heard and goes against our beliefs. You are alive, D. Alive."

Diana looked up into the furious face of her friend.

Sophia put her hand up cutting off anything else Lily might say. "I want you to sit here and listen to the words of the women in this circle, Diana." Sophia gestured around the circle. "There are messages you need to hear from us tonight: messages that will illuminate the darkness that surrounds you. Imbolc is a time of encouraging the light, supporting its triumph over the darkness and while it isn't the first of February, another tradition is to celebrate it on the new moon. Elizabeth, would you be willing to go first?"

"I would be honored." Elizabeth said, her hand rubbing Diana's back. "You are a woman of strength. As I listened to you talk, I knew I would not be an intact, functioning person if I'd been in your marriage. And, Bill? He's a wonderful young man. And, you've your consulting business you're growing. Dennis was abusive as well as adulterous but you've more than just survived it."

"Thank you for showing me your courage, D." Ashley's quiet voice spoke now. "I see your courage and know my time'll come. Yer a guiding light for me and I'm blessed to have ya in my life."

"And through it all you're still concerned about others." Gabriella's face frowned with concern. "That's a sign of deep compassion. More compassion for others than for yourself, I think. Perhaps you can create a Kwan Yin altar for guidance, to give some of that compassion to yourself."

Hunter spoke up. "I believe it's impossible to go through life without dark moments. I'm grateful I have all of you in my life when the darkness comes. You've been with me at those times, Diana, and I am here for you in this, your time of darkness."

She looked at Lily, saw her glance at Sophia. A sob broke forth as she heard the words softly sung by the two women and quickly joined by the others.

" beautiful

" whole

" soul

Her sobs muffled the words but she knew this song. They invited her to see herself as beautiful, as whole, and to acknowledge the soul connections in this sacred circle. She collapsed into Sophia's arms, the pain of the years of Dennis' infidelity washing from her body through her tears.

20 UGLINESS AND VALENTINE'S

They had put her to bed at Sophia's in the same room she'd stayed in when she'd first left Dennis. It was eleven the next morning when she awakened, a little later when she got up. Saturday: a quiet day of reflection except she spent hours sitting in silence: not thinking, not meditating; just resting her mind and her body. Sophia was there, puttering in the kitchen, talking quietly on the phone, offering her tea, toast, cookies. Diana accepted the tea but it sat growing cold in the cup with only a few sips taken.

The doorbell rang at six. Sophia turned off the alarm and let in Lily, Hunter, Logan and Gabriella. Art was home so Ashley and the children didn't come. Diana dimly remembered hugging Elizabeth good-bye when Gabby and Hunter took E. to catch the plane. *When I'm better,* somewhere deep inside a kernel of hope told her it would be better, *I'll make it up to her.*

At times they gathered in the family room chatting about this and that. No one expected her to contribute at all which was a good thing because tracking the conversations was difficult. Her circle sisters came, to show her in a concrete manner, she wasn't alone. Somehow they knew she was at the point where she needed something concrete in her life, something solid, something that didn't shift.

At nine, she excused herself, going to bed, and sleeping twelve hours straight.

During the night something had happened. She didn't know what but upon waking groggy and stiff, the sense of unease was strong.

Sophia drove her home at one because Diana had things to do to get ready for the week ahead. Grocery shopping was on both of their lists, so they stopped along the way to pick up the few items each needed.

The feeling of unease she'd awaken to had continued, becoming more intense as Sophia drove down the slightly curving road to the house.

Her car sat at a strange angle, the rear window shattered the glass crazed and opaque.

Sophia slowed and parked across the street. First she called the police and then Lily.

Rocking, hugging herself, a keening cry escaped from Diana's soul. *Cold, I'm so very, very cold.* Sophia reached over, placed her hand on her thigh: the warmth from her hand a small comfort. They remained in the car until the police cruiser pulled up behind them. A burly-looking officer got out and approached as Sophia lowered her window.

Sophia quickly explained the situation to the officer including she didn't notice any damage to the house. She added that there were security cameras and the owner of the house was on her way. Leaning her head against the car's headrest, Diana closed her eyes, and wished it all away. Of course that didn't work.

"I'm taking your house keys," Sophia said before she got out of the car.

The voices dimmed so she knew they'd crossed the street to look more closely at her car. Another car door slammed. *Lily? No, a masculine voice spoke.* Hazarding a peek, she saw Jackson talking to the officer and then leading the way into the house. *Probably to get the camera's recording.* At that point she didn't care. It was hard enough to open her eyes, to raise her head—the bone-deep exhaustion of dealing with another attack consumed.

In her mind the list grew: *call a tow truck, find a body shop, arrange for her car to be repaired, deal with the insurance company, police report, rent another vehicle, clean up the broken glass.* A numbing paralysis claimed her. *Right now I don't have the energy to move my little finger.* As if in another world, she watched Sophia write down whatever the officer and Jackson were saying.

Dispassionately she watched Sophia go back into the house.

Another vehicle arrived. Lily got out of her car and ran up to Jackson. He hugged her, said something, and she dashed into the house.

Jackson and the police officer approached. *Should I get out of the car?* She couldn't summon the will to do so.

The officer leaned into Sophia's still-open window.

"Mrs. Pettybone?"

She nodded.

"I've seen the surveillance camera's recording. Mr. Montgomery viewed it with me and identified the person damaging your vehicle as Dennis Pettybone. You don't have to view the video now if you can assure me that Mr. Montgomery knows what Mr. Pettybone looks like."

Her eyes squeezed shut, she nodded. Shivering uncontrollably, her hands clamped over her ears to block out any more unwanted words, a moan escaped. Her door opened, her seatbelt unbuckled, Jackson's arms came around her and steadied her as he helped her out of the car.

"Don't let him do this to you, Diana. He isn't worth it."

While she knew Jackson's words were true, it took strength and courage to fight through the fear. She didn't have any more—she was exhausted. After sleeping soundly for twelve hours she was still exhausted. If she could, she'd curl into a ball, go to sleep, to make this all go away. She looked up at Jackson; saw the concern on his face.

"He's winning, isn't he?" she whispered.

Jackson nodded. "Right now? Yes, he is. But it doesn't have to be that way. Remember, you aren't alone, you can fight him. You are strong enough to withstand his crap. Always remember, Diana, you don't have to do this alone."

She nodded. *I need to pull myself together.* Efforts to stiffen her body and lock her knees failed. Her body did not cooperate. She leaned against the car.

A tow truck appeared. Jackson stepped away to talk to the driver.

There was more to it than her car being destroyed. Friday night's confession had taken a lot out of her. *I'd said I wanted it all out in the open. To tell them the whole truth but then I was only going to tell them about Dennis' most recent attack and my decision to resist his efforts to force me back into the marriage. When I talked about the scarf, I couldn't breathe and everything came tumbling out.* She'd been shaken to her core and kept talking: talking about her dreams, about Matthew, about being unworthy.

Jackson returned to her side, concern still etched on his face.

"I've got AAA." Her voice was steadier now. "My card is in the car."

"All taken care of," he said. "Do you have your car keys with you?"

"No, they're inside on the small table by the door."

"Let's go get them and get what you want out of the car." Jackson's hand cupped her elbow in support. She took a few steps holding on to the fender. Her legs felt shaky but held her upright.

They crossed the street and into the house.

Jackson called out as they entered.

Sophia and Lily answered from upstairs.

Diana settled on the couch while Jackson grabbed the keys and went out to get her things from the car. A few minutes later Lily and Sophia appeared, each with a suitcase in hand.

Both women raised their hands, palm out to forestall any words she might think to say.

"You're coming back with me," Sophia started. "It isn't safe for you to be here right now."

"D, I know you've resisted having a restraining order but I'm asking you to reconsider. Please talk to your attorney about it. If you refuse to get one, you know you aren't safe here or anywhere." Lily's brow furrowed, her hands waved in the air before settling on her hips. "I know they aren't foolproof," she added. "But the consequences to Dennis will be increased and that may be a deterrent."

"We've packed several changes of clothing," Sophia talking again. "We can also pack some things from the office on our own, or you can supervise. Which do you prefer?"

Hearing her friends, understanding what they were saying was one thing—responding right now was more than she could manage. Lily sat beside her, her arm around her shoulder, and hugged. "It'll be all right in time, D. Let us support you in this, okay?"

She nodded. Her mind numb.

Lily and Sophia consulted with her about what to pack from her office and she nodded or shook her head depending on the item. Progress.

Eyes open, no tears fell. A T-bar of steel kept her spine straight and shoulders back. She was too rigid to rock and too exhausted to moan. The sound of the tow truck winching her car onto the truck bed signaled her car being taken away. To where? She didn't even know. *I ought to get up, talk to the driver, see where it's going, make sure everything is taken care of. Can you be too cold to shiver? No, I'm not cold, I'm numb.*

"What the hell?! Montgomery what's going on here? Diana, is she okay?" Matthew's voice. He knelt in front of her, rubbing her cold, cold hands, his green eyes piercing, seeing into her soul. "God, Diana." Abruptly he stood, pulling her with him, into his arms. He held her close, pressed her head to his chest, his heart beat in her ear. Nothing more than his arms around her, rubbing her back, holding her.

Her arms wrapped around him, and she hung on to his strength.

"Glad you weren't here. Bastard. He'll pay." The words muffled in her hair as he quietly cursed. His soft voice did not lessen the threat in his words.

She didn't want Matthew touched any more than he already was by this ugliness. "No," she shook her head and whispered, "no," as she tried to look up, look Matthew in the eye. His strong arms held her close, too close to do so. Shifting, she tried to gain purchase so she could see his face. His grip loosened.

"No, Matthew," she looked directly into his eyes. "You mustn't do anything to him. You'll be the one who pays. It will hurt me if you do."

She saw confusion first and then his face hardened with anger. "You reconciling?"

"Absolutely not! If you go after him, Matthew, it will only support his accusations that there is something between us," she said. Pleading, she added, "Please don't do anything."

He smiled and lowered his head. His forehead rested on hers and then he dipped closer and touched his lips to her. "I believe there is something between us," he whispered before he brushed his lips over hers. "Something I like a lot."

As he pulled her tightly against him, she imagined a long missing piece slipping in to finish the puzzle. Eight years difference in their ages. Enough that the idea they'd ever be together, ever have a "happily-ever-after" was dismissed. But for this one moment in time, she relish a few minutes of being held.

Throats cleared. She startled and tried to pull away but Matthew's arms only flexed to keep her in place. "Yes?" his voice rumbled through his chest and reverberated to her toes. "I know."

He sighed; his arms slackened and then slid to her upper arms. He stepped back and her body, bereft, shuddered. She looked up into his eyes, noting how dark they were. A tremulous smile played on her lips, her eyes bright with unshed tears.

Things moved quickly then. While Matthew had held her, the tow truck had left with her car, someone had swept up the broken glass, Jackson had reset the surveillance cameras, and Sophia and Lily had put her belongings in Sophia's car. *Nothing to do but lock up the house.*

Jackson and Matthew spoke and shook hands, serious expressions on their faces. Without looking back, Matthew strode to his truck, got in and drove off. As they walked to Sophia's car, Jackson took her arm.

"First thing is to let your attorney know what's happened. Call and leave a message as soon as you get back to Sophia's. And call again in the morning. You need to be proactive and get a restraining order in place. You need to be firm on this, Diana. You need to press charges. The police officer is filing a report. You need to let your insurance company know it was vandalism. Your attorney can advise you better than I. Call her." He gave her a hug and stepped aside.

Next Lily held her close, sharing one of her excellent hugs, the kind that warmed the recipient's heart.

Lily stepped back and with a contemplative look said, "This is a small glitch, D. Not the end of the world, just a small glitch. We'll have you back in the house in no time." She hugged her again before letting her go. "Did you hear the invitation to dinner tonight?" she called out as she started to her car. "Jackson's cooking again and there's homemade ice cream for dessert."

"We'll bring brownies," Sophia responded. "Tell him to make an extra batch of vanilla ice cream and his decadent chocolate sauce."

Diana got in the car, pulled her seat belt on. *I'm going to survive this.* Breathing deeply, she looked out at the bleak February landscape: the grey sky laced by stark branches on overhanging trees.

Sophia started the car and pulled away from the curb.

Diana's vision filled with the dark green of the Douglas firs, a smattering of blue spruce and long needle pines. She leaned back against the headrest and closed her eyes, humming and then softly singing one of her favorite songs, one she learned at a Women of the Fourteenth Moon Ceremony about walking in beauty. There was a stark beauty in the bleak winter landscape. There was beauty in the love and support of her friends. *In order* to counter the ugliness in my life, I need to keep my eyes open and focus on the beauty around me.

21   WHAT HAPPENS NOW?

She had expected Matthew to be there.

He wasn't.

It was better this way, she told herself but still wondered if he'd declined an invitation or hadn't been invited in the first place.

Good friends, good food, good conversation. Conversation centering on the mundane: the weather, Sophia's garden, Eleanor's trip to see her daughters and their families in March. This year she planned on spending three months back east.

"My fall fifteen or was it sixteen months ago was a blessing in disguise. I am so much stronger now and look forward to this trip and all it entails," Eleanor shared.

"Your hard work in physical therapy has paid off, mother," Jackson added. "You're positively "sprightly".

Maybe this ugliness will turn out to be a blessing in disguise. Maybe in a year I'll be glad all this had happened because I'll be delighted with where my life is. Maybe... . She drifted off until she was called back to the present by Lily's voice.

House totems. Was she still open to going to Italy in March to work with Giovanni? She nodded. A spark of pleasure popped at the idea. I'm looking forward to leaving the ugliness—at least for a week.

"Bill is coming home for his Spring Break. I hope we can schedule the Italy trip so I don't lose any time seeing him because the weekends overlap."

"What about seeing if he can go with you?" Jackson asked.

Her hand flew to her chest and tears filled her eyes.

"What a great idea," Lily chimed in.

Sophia nodded.

"I'm not sure," she began, her mind flying through all the challenges the additional cost would bring. *I may need those funds for legal and living expenses depending on what Dennis does; depending on the divorce settlement; depending on so many things.*

"Our treat," Jackson grinned. "We've enough frequent flyer miles to easily cover Bill's ticket and there won't be expenses once you're there because you'll stay at Migliori's villa. So, you see, Diana, it isn't an expense to us at all."

"What a wonderful idea." Sophia chimed in. "Bill may be able to get extra credit for one of his classes with this trip; seeing a famous architect in Italy. I imagine Giovanni could show Bill some sights that the average tourist would miss."

"Great idea," Jackson agreed. "I'll email him tonight and see what he says. Let me know if Bill can get permission to go with you, Diana. And, be sure to have him ask about the extra credit. I know Migliori would be more than happy to help him out."

The evening ended on a high note with everyone excitedly talking about house totems and Italy. Back at Sophia's, she readied herself for bed. The Tarot said to focus on the positive things in her life. Her prayers? *May The Universe open my eyes to the beauty around me so I see beauty in spite of all the ugliness.*

Monday she talked to Ms. Lawford. The restraining order was quickly in place once she finally agreed to it.

Sophia's doorbell rang. Her exclamation of surprised delight summoned Diana to the front door.

Two boxes delivered by the flower shop were in Sophia's arms. Two boxes: one of roses and one with the paperweight. No note, no card, no hint but she knew.

Sophia put the roses in a beautiful cut crystal vase.

"We can move them from spot to spot so we can always see them," she said moving them into their view when they sat down to dinner.

The roses and the paperweight—beauty in an ugly day.

The next Saturday she moved back to the little house. Even with the additional safeguard of the restraining order she kept the alarm on at all times. No one trusted Dennis wouldn't try something.

Other safety precautions: park close to the store when shopping, park in front of campus security and have one of the guards escort her to class, and leave with a group of students from the coffee shop.

One thing was different now. She welcomed Matthew checking on her, making sure she got safely to her car and home. *Has my life changed forever? Will I always have to be so cautious? Will I always worry about being safe?* Questions that had no answers right now but were even harder not to ask herself.

Back in the little house (she thought of it as 'her' house now), she adjusted to living alone. Progress.

Compulsively she checked the alarm system and surveillance cameras were on every time she heard noises outside.

Finally it was March: a new month, a new beginning for her life, a trip to Italy, and time with Bill. The tightness that had enveloped her body since early January eased. Hope that she was firmly on her new path fueled a sense of waiting opportunities in this new month.

Typing a report, Diana moved the paperweight to shift the papers underneath so she could continue. The swirling greens distracted her from her work.

A frown replaced the smile as memories of Valentine's Day and Dennis emerged. *He always got me something: usually an expensive box of chocolates and a piece of jewelry. I don't wear any of the things: too many dark memories. If worse came to worse, I could sell or pawn them.* Another idea brought joy to her heart. *I could have the stones reset. I do love sparkly jewelry and Dennis always gave me pieces that refracted the light into a million rainbows. There, a picture of beauty from the ugliness.*

These days she was much better at seeing the beauty around her. Sometimes, like now, it just came to her, dropping into her mind like a prism catching a ray, sending a beacon of radiant light, showing her a different side of things: the beautiful side.

Her fingers skimmed over the cool glass that warmed from her touch. And, within the myriad greens of the orb was the emerald green of Matthew's eyes. Her body softened, her senses heightened—she rubbed her arms longing for a human's touch.

Shaking off the memories and longing, Diana looked at the wall calendar. Red stars marked the two weeks she'd spend with

Bill. Pride in her son straightened her posture. He was majoring in international business but missing a week of class during finals meant this trip hadn't been a sure thing. He'd checked with his professors, had permission to miss classes for the week, and arranged to take the finals either before he left or upon return. He was thrilled he would get extra credit for the week in Italy with Giovanni Migliori. For her, the bonus was Bill would spend his Spring Break in Fremont with her.

The dark cloud that memories of Dennis evoked swirled as what he'd done to discredit Matthew in the last three weeks surfaced. His efforts to tie up his financing failed because Jackson and Daniel stood beside him; co-signed on loans, and made sure he had work for his crews. The bond between the three men grew stronger. Daniel was helping Matthew with renovations on his house and Jackson now invited both Daniel and Matthew to Sunday night spaghetti feeds.

How is Dennis dealing with this? He's never done well with failure before. I've no doubt he sees his efforts to discredit Matthew being thwarted as a major failure.

She saved her report and turned to look out the window. Monday night's class and the weekly dinners at the Montgomery house were her chances to see Matthew. They were never alone which was a good thing because it would be so easy to let him take care of her, take care of everything, knowing, trusting implicitly that he could.

I can't allow that to happen. I must not allow that to happen. Matthew deserves so much more than I have to offer. A cat stalked the playing squirrels as the litany of her failures, her short-comings scrolled through her mind.

22 THE MEETING

The next day was the day Dennis and she had agreed to talk; to see if they could come to some agreement without mediation. Not mediation to reconcile but mediation over the terms of the divorce. It would be the first time she'd seen him since the incident outside the house—the one with the scarf. Her hand unconsciously went to her throat and rubbed. A shiver shuddered through her and she breathed deeply to steady herself.

Dinner with Lily and Sophia this evening was something she looked forward to. Her friends had arranged everything including who would take her to the appointment and who would pick her up. She didn't have to drive, didn't have to be alone, everything would be just fine. Glancing at the clock, she knew it was time to get ready.

In the bathroom she checked her make-up and hair and waffled on whether to change into something else. The cobalt blue silk blouse was one of her favorites. A hint of blue eye shadow and bronze blush on her high cheek bones added subtle layers of color to her face. For whimsy she dotted gold glitter, fairy dust on her throat chakra, blending it in to her skin. Turning this way and that, she smiled as she appraised her reflection in the mirror. The fairy dust glinted. Doubt changed her smile to a frown. *This is a serious meeting. I should take it off but I love sparkly things.* The glitter gleamed when the light caught it just right.

She left the fairy dust in place.

Dennis glared as she and Ms. Lawford entered the room. Mr. Harris, his attorney, stood and extended his hand. Both she and her attorney shook it. Dennis reluctantly got to his feet, nodded in their direction, before returning to his rigid position in the chair. Her insides were in revolt. *Can they see how shaky I am?*

The attorneys began with their introductory statements, the reporter typing away to preserve these words for posterity.

They'd reached this point because when Dennis had filed a counter-divorce suit and named Matthew Houston in an alienation of affection suit, Ms. Lawford stated that unless they dropped the suit against Mr. Houston Mrs. Pettybone would amend her petition for divorce and name all of Mr. Pettybone's paramours. It had worked and the suit against Matthew had been dropped.

I remember barely making it to the bathroom when I heard that. I clung to the toilet for an hour. Ugliness had a habit of driving her to her knees in front of the porcelain throne.

Of all the things she wished were happening right now, being here in Dennis' attorney's office was not one of them. *Ms. Lawford assured me that it will be easier to pick our things up and leave than to order Dennis and his attorney to do so if things become too fractious.*

The attorneys continued to talk.

As requested, Diana had completed the list of the few things she still wanted from the house. For the most part he could have it all: the silver service, china, and art work.

Drifting off, she visualized the items on her list. The sculpture of dancers for Hunter's dance studio; another sculpture of an elderly couple, looking tenderly at each other for Lily; starts from a couple of plants in the yard for Sophia; a box of romance novels from the 1980's for Gabriella; her high-end mixer for Ashley; and a painting that reminded her of the sacred grove for Elizabeth.

Her list had many more other things than she actually wanted because Ms. Lawford told her she needed to pad her list so there'd be something to negotiate with.

"Your job today," Ms. Lawford had said as they'd stepped out of the elevator, "is to keep your features schooled to as neutral a façade as you can manage. If anyone is going to look out-of-control, I want it to be Dennis not you."

A shout—her mind snapped back to the events happening around her.

Dennis rising, leaning across the table, shouting at her.

Mr. Harris grabbing Dennis's arm, shoving him back in his chair.

Ms. Lawford calmly gathering her papers.

"When your client is able to control himself, let us know." Ms. Lawford stood, everything tucked into her briefcase. "Come, Diana," her voice steel-like, "we are through here."

Diana automatically stood, picked up her note pad, and stuffed it in her briefcase. She grabbed her coat, hoped her gloves were still in the pockets, and followed her attorney out the door.

Dennis's voice carried through the quiet office, "Take your goddamn hands off me, Harris. I can always get another attorney. You're letting that bitch take everything. She shouldn't get a fucking cent."

The outer office door closed behind her. Ms. Lawford marched to the elevators, stabbed the down button. Diana caught up with her. Side-by-side they waited for the elevator. Ms. Lawford foot tapping.

The elevator arrived. They got in and quickly descended to the lobby. Still steaming, her attorney strode out to the sidewalk, where she stopped and dragged air into her lungs.

"Ah, some fresh air feels good," she said, letting the air out in a whoosh. "Well, that was interesting." She smiled at Diana. "I think overall that went well."

"I'm afraid I wasn't paying much attention," Diana confessed. "My mind wandered."

Her attorney grinned. "Dry attorney talk is all you missed until the very end. I started with a request that you be allowed to take starts from the plants on your list. Harris agreed and Dennis came across the table at you. That certainly allowed Harris to see the true colors of his client. Did you smile at that point?"

"If I did, it wasn't on purpose. I really wasn't paying attention," she said and worried her lower lip between her teeth.

"Don't worry about it." Ms. Lawford smiled. "If this were a fight, we won Round One." She looked up and down the street. "Do you have a ride?"

"We finished a little early. I'll just wait here until Sophia comes." She reached in her pocket for her cell phone. "I'll call her in case she can pick me up now."

The door opened and Dennis came barreling out. "Bitch," he hissed as he came toward her.

Ms. Lawford stepped into his path. "I'd be careful, Mr. Pettybone. There is a restraining order and I'll have no problem at all calling the police and watching them haul you away."

Dennis glared at her, fists clenched at his side.

The old saying "if looks could kill" came to mind. If it were true, she'd be very, very dead. The initial startle from seeing Dennis charge at her faded replaced by a dispassionate, cold numbness.

Dennis struggled for control and although rage still poured from every pore, he did gain a modicum of mastery over himself. "You'll be sorry you ever started this," he glared at her over Ms. Lawford's shoulder. "Very, very, very sorry, Diana." He turned on his heel and stomped down the street.

"Well, Diana. I think you need to come with me now. Call your friend and she can pick you up at my office. I don't want you alone."

They walked to Ms. Lawford's office in silence.

"Have a seat." Ms. Lawford gestured to a chair in her inner office. She strode behind her desk and sat, reaching for her phone as she did. She quickly dialed a number. Diana heard her ask for Mr. Harris and listened dispassionately as her attorney gave a barebones account of their side-walk encounter with Dennis. "Make no mistake, Harris, we will follow-up if Mr. Pettybone violates that restraining order by one inch." Her final warning stated, she hung up.

"Keep your cell phone handy, put 911 on your speed dial, make sure the alarm in the house is on the instant you get in the door, and the car door locks engaged the moment you close the door." Ms. Lawford's tone was brisk as she strode across her office to sit next to her. "He's a loose cannon right now. It may get worse before it gets better so be prepared at all times." She paused. "Take every precaution, Diana. You may want to consider moving back in with your friend. You're safer with people around you."

At those words, calm settled over her. With all Ms. Lawford's warnings, with all Dennis's threats, there was no fear. The serene sense of well-being cocooning her made no sense but that is how she felt.

Diana's call to Sophia ended with the plan that she'd call Ms. Lawford's office when she was outside and Ms. Lawford would escort Diana to the car.

Was that where the sense of well-being came from? Everyone watching out for her? She shook her head slightly. *No, that wasn't it. It was the finality of it—no going back.* Her feet were firmly on this path. There was no other alternative than leaving him if she wanted any kind of life at all. Knowing the decision was irrevocably made brought that sense of calm.

Her gaze focused on the African Violet profusely blooming on the window sill. There was beauty everywhere in the midst of ugliness if one only opened one's eyes and looked around. She was profoundly glad her eyes were open.

23   DISCUSSIONS AND DECISIONS

The plan had been for the three of them to have dinner at a favorite restaurant. With Dennis' latest outburst, that plan changed and instead Sophia drove Diana to Lily's house. Matthew would join them for Jackson's steak dinner as would Eleanor.

After dinner, they adjourned to the couch and chairs in the living area where the talk of what she should do continued. The calm sense of well-being hadn't lasted.

An urge to scream surged as they continued to talk over solutions as if she wasn't there. *Will they never stop their yammering about what I should do? Do they not understand I will never subject Sophia or for that matter Lily and Eleanor to Dennis' shit?*

Her hand involuntarily covered her mouth. *I swore! I never swear!* But that was her bottom-line. They'd already been drawn much further into the drama of her life than she ever intended. She was not going to continue in that direction. While a part of her knew they spoke from their concern for her, another part was tired of listening to them. She swiveled her chair so her back was to them.

The view out the Montgomery House windows was magnificent. The lights of Fremont below reflected off the dark ribbon of river, seeming to turn off and on as wisps of fog drifted by. The voices droned on behind her; she concentrated on the lights, letting her thoughts drift like the fingers of fog in the night.

Was this how Lily felt when we were all hovering around her after her accident? Most likely it was. While her situation was different, the dynamics were similar. Someone else knowing what was best, what was right for you. In her classes she taught that a key to feeling respected was someone listening and actually hearing what was being said. Their advice may all be well-intentioned but that didn't eliminate the frustration of not being listened to. She grimaced, tried to drift with the fog in the night, failed.

Jackson's approach was reflected in the window in front of her and she warily watched him come until he'd sat in the chair next to her, leaned over, and gently placed his hand on her arm.

"You do know we're all concerned about you." His grave voice and serious expression conveyed more than his words.

"I do know that," she smiled as she looked at him. "I just wish you'd all listen to me."

"Oh, I think we listened, we just don't agree."

"What do you think I've been saying?" Diana doubted that anyone really understood but asked her question anyway.

Jackson swiveled his chair so he faced her. Worry-lines bracketed his mouth, a frown creased his forehead. He reached out and took her hand, an earnest look on his features as he spoke.

"You are trying to protect all of us but especially Sophia, Lily and my mother from whatever Dennis does next. You are willing to take all the risks alone in order to do that. For some reason, you believe you can manage whatever is to happen on your own. Does that about cover it?"

She nodded and felt her shoulder muscles relax. *They do understand.*

"What you don't seem to understand, Diana, is that none of us are willing to let you face Dennis alone. That, my dear, is not an option for you."

An edict.

There was no other way of describing it. They were telling her that while they understood what she was saying, they would not allow it. That rankled and she could feel the anger beginning to boil.

"Not an option? You won't allow it?" she said in a loud and angry voice. Rising to her feet, she glared down at the messenger. She swung around to face the others. "This is my life! You have no right... !"

"That is so not true, D," Lily interrupted. "We have every right to make every effort to protect someone we love." She stood with her hands on her hips, her stance wide—a warrior woman. "How insulting to say we have no right. Really D." Shaking with indignation, she spat out the last words.

"Do you all think I should move back in with Sophia so Dennis can burn her house down or spray poison all over her garden?" Diana stalked to Lily. "Or perhaps I should move in here so he can terrorize Eleanor. Her apartment would be easy pickings for him."

Lily didn't back down and Diana realized she'd created a challenge as Sophia now stood before her with her palm face out to halt the torrent of words.

"Actually, Diana, we all believe you should stay with Matthew."

"What!" she shrieked. "You think what? Are you mad?"

"No, we are not insane."

Sophia is using her soothing voice and I'll be damned if I'll be soothed at this point!

Hands fisted on her hips, she glared piercing dagger looks at both of them. The urge to hit something, throw something, beat something was strong. If Dennis was this angry, she was surprised he hadn't done more. Someone's hands rested on her shoulders and in a knee-jerk reaction she threw her elbow back. The hands left.

"No one touch me!" Her shrill voice wavered. Perilously close to tears, she held her head high, arms rigid, hands fisted at her sides daring anyone to say or do anything more.

Eleanor moved into her line of sight, edged in front of Lily and Sophia and stood quietly. The other two women moved back. The tension in the air eased. She didn't want to spew her anger on Eleanor and with supreme effort managed to leash her temper.

"Come sit with me, Diana," Eleanor's British-accented voice invited. "We'll go into my apartment and leave these four people to themselves. Come along, dear." She took Diana's hand and led her across the room and into her apartment where she closed the door.

Diana looked back through the French doors to see four mouths hanging open, four faces reflecting astonishment.

"Now, sit where you will." Eleanor gestured around the room.

Diana chose the couch, her back to the main house.

A few minutes later Eleanor set a tea tray with a pot of tea, cream, sugar, and two cups on the table in front of them. She poured and handed Diana a cup. Diana doctored the tea with cream and sugar and sat back, sipping the hot brew. Neither of them spoke. The silence would not last forever but she welcomed the quiet respite.

"You are aware, Diana," Eleanor shifted toward her and began, "accepting help from someone is not the end of the world, nor does it make you a lesser person. And, I know you are aware it was a difficult lesson for Lily to learn. I believe it explains her fierceness in her fight with you over this."

"It may not be the end of the world. Oh, Eleanor," Diana swiped at her face as the tears began to fall. "I don't know how I'd survive if Dennis hurt any of you. I just want to protect you from him."

"How do you think any of us will feel if Dennis hurts you again? Do you know how hard it has been for Lily and, I believe Sophia, to see you hurt? The thought that Dennis will get to you again and this time hurt you more severely is more than they can bear." Eleanor sat back and sipped her tea.

Time, Eleanor was giving her quiet time to think about what she'd said—the truth. Eleanor spoke the truth. *I'm in one of those damnable true conflicts where no matter what my choice is; something is lost. If I go along with them, one of them might be physically hurt and I'd be devastated. If I refused, stand my ground and Dennis gets to me, they would be devastated.* A shaft of pain in her chest reminded her how her heart had ached to see Lily fight to regain her life after the accident last year. *And that was a random act, nothing I could have done to prevent it. The danger to me from Dennis is something everyone in the other room believes is preventable.*

When she'd finished her cup, she set it back on the tea tray and folded her hands in her lap mesmerized by how the fingers interlaced, the thumbs laying one way, and then the other as she shifted them. One way was more comfortable than the other but the other way was not wrong. *Perhaps this is the way to look at things? There may not be a "right" way but there also was not a "wrong" way.*

"What do you think is best?" she asked.

"Since you asked, I'll tell you," she said and patted Diana's her hand. Shifting, she looked squarely at Diana; her gray eyes seemed to understand how hard this was for her. "I think you need to move, at least for a while, from the little house. Even with the upgraded security system, you are not safe there.

"As I understand it, there is an opportunity for you to move into a three bedroom apartment in a high-rise, secure building. It is leased by a corporation and for whatever their reason, they want the space occupied until the lease is up the middle of April. An old friend of Matthew's works for the company and Matthew was asked to move in early this year. It comes with underground parking, security guards, and cameras; all the bells and whistles. Dennis may see you go into the parking garage but he cannot track you once you are past the security guards."

Panic surged, her heart rate increased, her breathing fractured. Desperate to look away, she stayed focused on the gray eyes, full of compassion and understanding, knowing the panic would win if she lost contact with Eleanor. Eventually, the panic receded, replaced by a growing sense of the inevitable.

"I see."

And actually she did see the logic. This plan provided her with a higher degree of physical safety. No vulnerability getting to and from the car; no one able to take pictures of her through her windows. What she understood was her body might be safe but not her heart.

"When is this move supposed to happen?" She swallowed hard, forcing the words over the lump in her throat.

"When do you think?" Eleanor said in her quiet voice as she squeezed her hand in a gesture of support.

Diana's attempt to laugh sounded more like a choke. "As soon as possible," she whispered and saw Eleanor nod.

Her third move in less than two months. Tears spilled down her cheeks. She'd lost so much in such a short time. Like a lifeline she clung to The Tarot's message as she struggled to rein in her emotions. *Look for the pleasant memories when things were bad; see the beauty when things were ugly; use my skills to find new and creative ways to deal with things.*

She took the tissue Eleanor pressed in her hand, dabbed her eyes, blew her nose, and sighed. "I should have packing down to a science by now," she said her smile watery, a few more tears slipped down her cheeks.

Eleanor slid closer, put her arm around Diana and gently guided her head to her shoulder. "It will all come out right in the end, Diana. You are a strong woman, with strong friends, supported by strong beliefs. It is time to rely on your friends and your beliefs to see you through this time."

"I know," Diana's voice was muffled against Eleanor's shoulder. Another deep sigh and she pulled away, sitting up, straightening her clothing, and patting her hair. "I must look a mess," she glanced at her reflection in Eleanor's window. "I do look a mess."

"And no one in the other room will think any less of you if you have a hair out of place."

"I know that too," she looked down; a slight blush tinged her cheeks. "I'm forty years old and I've just let myself be held as if I was a small child. It's rather humbling and embarrassing to know I've let things bring me to this point."

Eleanor stood. "Even at my advanced age, I still enjoy hugs and someone holding my hand. Don't ever lose the joy of experiencing another human's touch. It diminishes one's life tremendously." She reached out, gesturing Diana to rise and join her. "Let's go tell the others. They will be quite delighted."

24 THE APARTMENT

That night she stayed the night at the Montgomerys' house. After breakfast with Lily and Eleanor, she returned to the little house around eleven where Hunter was waiting for her. After a lengthy discussion about the pros and cons of what to take, she decided to move what she'd need for a month. In just over two weeks, she'd travel to Italy so she included items she wanted to take on that trip. The next few hours were spent sorting and packing. *One step at a time: move, settle, Italy, Bill. Deal with what happens after that when the time comes.*

During the day she was never alone. Hunter stayed until after lunch, Ashley and her youngest came by for a couple of hours before leaving to meet her oldest at the bus stop. Before they left, Gabriella arrived. Her younger circle sister regaled her with stories from different moves she'd made. Laughing felt good. At five o'clock Lily and Sophia arrived and she packed up the refrigerator and freezer.

Five-thirty sharp Matthew backed into the driveway with his truck. Jackson and Daniel followed. It took the three men less than twenty minutes to load what she'd decided to take onto the truck. A small box of personal items she kept with her—things for an altar and The Tarot cards.

Before six, the small caravan pulled away. She locked everything up tight, set the alarm, and prayed everything remained be safe.

A sigh of resignation escaped. This was an adventure, a trek into the unknown, but the sense of anticipation, of excitement that swelled when thinking of going to Italy wasn't there. *What worries me most? Will Matthew and I not get along or worse yet, will we get along too well. Regardless of how it goes, my time in the apartment is certainly going to be a test, a challenge, a— what else I'm not sure.*

Matthew led, she was next. Jackson's car with he and Daniel drove behind her and Sophia with Lily brought up the rear. At the parking garage's entrance, Matthew braked, she followed suit. Getting out, Matthew approached the guard house; motioning to the security guard they walked back toward her. She retracted her window and looked out at the two men.

"This is Diana Pettybone, Pete. This is a rental car so her vehicle will change."

"Just check in with me Ms. Pettybone when you get your car back. Someone's in the guard house 24/7. We don't expect to remember everyone's face but we have a list of car licenses. So, if you drive a car not on our list, we can't let you in."

"Thank you, Pete. When I leave with the rental car to pick up my own car, would that be the time to let whoever is on duty know?"

"Got a form for you to fill out. Stop by in the next day or so and I'll see that you've got it. I'm usually the swing guy, you know, working from 3 – 11."

"I'll do that," she gave Pete her brightest smile. *It won't hurt to make a friend and have him remember me. I wouldn't put it past Dennis to try bribes. There's no doubt in my mind we've been followed.* Realizing she trusted Dennis wouldn't be able to find out which apartment she was in, she acknowledged, at least to herself, she felt safer.

There was a special place to park when moving in and enough room for their three vehicles. With six of them working together along with the racks and dollies, her belongings were moved to the apartment in one trip.

The apartment was large. Master suites at each end with an open concept kitchen and great room separating them. A smaller bedroom was off the main area, the half-bath off the entry hall. Windows faced the mountains to the east; a small balcony provided a nice place to sit on a spring day or summer's eve. *No temptation to do that in early March.* She shivered and briskly rubbed her arms. At the window she looked out from the tenth floor. No tall buildings in front of them but there were to either side. *Could they see me from one of those building? I'll be careful not to stand too close.* The larger bedrooms were at either end of the apartment, the smaller bedroom opened off the living area; the smaller half-bath off the foyer.

Diana stood to the side of the windows and looked back on the room. *Everything is done in neutral colors and the décor is more modern than I like. It's only six weeks, and I'll be in Italy for two of them.* The coffee table in front of the large couch had a notebook she recognized as the one Matthew brought to class and a western paperback. Those were the only obvious signs Matthew even lived here.

The men had moved all her boxes into her bedroom.

She could hear Lily instructing them to remove the ones marked office.

"She needs room to unpack and put things away." Lily's laughter was a good sound. Her laugh brought a smile to even a stranger's face.

Sophia was in the kitchen area, unpacking the boxes from her refrigerator and freezer.

"I think I can make nachos?" she called out. "Would that suit everyone?"

A chorus of voices called out "yes". Sophia went to work browning the hamburger and ground chicken from Diana's freezer, opening cans of beans, chopping lettuce, tomato, onions, and avocado. That done she hunted for salsa and sour cream, opened a package of corn chips and piled them on a platter. As ingredients cooked or heated, she added them to the dish, piling ingredients on. The sour cream, salsa, and chopped avocado were in dishes to the side. Two more avocadoes were made into guacamole. In less than thirty minutes the feast was done and on the counter.

"It's ready," Sophia called out.

The others emerged from her bedroom and what was now being called "the office." The medium sized room had been empty and was certainly large enough for a desk. *Did Matthew run his business from his home or did he have an office?*

Wandering over to look in the room that would serve as her bedroom, she saw Sophia and Lily had already unpacked several boxes. Her suits, slacks, blouses, and jackets hung in the closet; an open box of under things on the bed for her to put away. *Now's a good time.*

A few minutes later that box was unpacked and broken down for recycling. Three more smaller boxes were stacked in the corner. *I think those are shoes and miscellaneous items.* Noting a good reading light over the bed, she moved the three books she was currently reading from the dresser to the nightstand.

Next on her list was to make the bed. *No bedding. I'll make do tonight. In the morning I'll go back to the little house and get my sheets and blankets.*

Returning to the family room, she lingered in the doorway and observed the others. Everyone seemed so happy right now: laughing, joking. Matthew was relaxed with Jackson and Daniel. The back-and-forth banter between them showed how easily they all got along. Matthew turned to get something from the refrigerator—a beer. As he turned to hand it to Daniel, he caught her eye and smiled.

Tentatively she smiled back. *Out of my element and in very deep water. When everyone leaves, I hope I don't drown.*

The others shifted to make room for her when she approached. A plate appeared in her hand along with a glass of tonic at her elbow. Helping herself to Sophia's creation, she added the salsa, sour cream, and guacamole. Because she loved avocado, she didn't stint on her serving.

She leaned over to Lily and whispered, "I forgot to bring bedding."

"Jackson and I can go get it and drop it off on our way home," she offered.

"I think I'll just make do tonight. I can go back to the house tomorrow and pick it up."

Diana's remark was received by a hard stare.

"I don't think so." The edge to Lily's voice stopped all conversation.

"What's the problem?" Jackson reached over and swiped a bit of sour cream from his wife's lower lip.

"Diana forgot to pack bedding and she wants to "make do" tonight and tomorrow go back to the house for it." Lily's tone and manner conveyed what she thought of that plan.

"Not a problem," Matthew said striding to his room. A minute later he appeared before her, a set of sheets in hand.

"I've a blanket in the car," Jackson added. "I keep it there for emergencies. I think I can get this crew home without it tonight. Where do you keep your extra bedding?"

"Sheets are in a storage bin under the bed and blankets in one of the bins along the wall."

"I'll stop by tomorrow and pick them up. I'm having lunch with Houston tomorrow, I'll pass them on to him and you'll have them by tomorrow night."

"Thank you, Jackson. That's really going out of your way."

"Actually it isn't. Daniel, Matthew or I will be driving by the house every day to check on things. I'll be reviewing the camera footage every couple of days." He came over and put his arm around her shoulder. "To be honest, I expect Dennis will do something. Just want to keep an eye on things."

The nachos had been decimated, the kitchen cleaned up, and everyone ready to leave. Matthew was to escort them down to the parking garage making sure they were able to leave. It was just eleven and the guards had changed. He'd bring the blanket back with him.

Diana walked about the now silent apartment resisting the impulse to peak into Matthew's room. The large flat screen TV in the great room had been left on, the sound low. She seldom watched television preferring to read or listen to music but the movie was an old one and a favorite. She sat down to watch *Come September* with Rock Hudson, Bobby Daren, Sandra Dee, and an Italian actress whose name she didn't remember.

So lost in the movie, she startled when Matthew came in the door. Diana hurried to straighten from her slouched position because she wanted him to see her as calm and serene. The fact she didn't feel that way wasn't important; she just wanted to faked it well enough to fool him.

Matthew's gaze concentrated on her, his eyes a dark green; his chest rising and falling as he breathed. He tossed the blanket on the back of a chair and started toward the couch. Running his hand through already rumpled hair, he stopped, rubbed the back of his neck, glanced at the TV before flopping in a chair his back to the set.

Diana fumbled with the remote, trying to figure out how to turn the TV off.

A smile curved his lips, amusement danced in his eyes as he watched her jab and punch buttons. "I thought there was nothing you couldn't do," he joked.

A picture of her throwing the remote at his head flashed, but she restrained herself. It was all about setting the right tone because they would be in close quarters for several weeks. Before she could speak, he held up his hands in surrender.

"There is a larger button. Yellow. Power. A very small button. Green. Mute."

She glared at him but with those simple directions located what she wanted. Stabbing the yellow button, the TV went dark.

"It's one of those universal remotes. Takes care of the TV, CD, DVD—the whole shebang." He grinned at her. "Tell you what, I'll help you get your bed made and we can call it a day."

"Thank you, Matthew, put I'm perfectly capable of making my own bed. I've actually done it by myself for years."

He was no longer amused. In one sentence, actually two, she'd quashed the light in his eyes. He pushed out of his chair, his gaze intent as he stared her down. She met his eyes but was the first to look away. As she struggled to find the words to apologize, he strode past her.

"Good night." The door to his room clicked shut. He was gone.

She was alone; more alone now than in the small house by herself; almost like living with Dennis; someone there but not. She'd done this: let her fear put sarcastic words in her mouth. *No, it wasn't the words. But I put "that tone" to my voice, "that look" on my face. In the end I'd done it enough with Dennis. Is that why he hated me enough to hit me?*

Rising from the couch, she made her way to her room and made the bed. As she did so, memories of when she and Dennis were first married surfaced. They'd make the bed together, sometimes not even finishing before they were making love. Tears stung the backs of her eyes. She blinked them back.

Changing into a nightgown, she brushed her teeth, washed her face, and took a good long look at herself in the mirror. *Tonight I look much older than forty. By the time this is over will I look even older?* Tightening and then relaxing her face muscles in an effort to relax her jaw, she shook her head. *I don't know what the end result will be. I can only trust my highest good is served by all of this.*

Before climbing into bed, she opened the small box she'd kept in her possession. Taking out the square of dark blue cloth, she placed it on the dresser. One-by-one she placed her treasurers on it. An open bright spring-green box was in the center. Because she didn't know the state of the smoke detectors, she decided to cleanse her new altar with light instead of a sage wand. Lighting a white candle, she waved it over the altar before walking around the room. First humming, then softly singing the song about walking in beauty. The song soothed her and reminded her that her task was to find beauty, joy and maybe have some fun every day. She blew out the candle, placed it in its holder, and slipped under the covers.

In the morning she'd consult the cards. As she started to drift toward sleep she pushed the vision of Matthew asleep in the bedroom at the other end of the apartment aside and focused on the idea of a daily practice of picking a card from her Tarot deck each morning. *I've thought of doing this before but haven't followed through. Tomorrow I will.*

Although the curtains were pulled, a sliver of light slipped through illuminating her altar. *A good sign.* Snuggling down in bed, she found a comfortable spot. As sleep claimed her, the prayer to The Universe cycled through her mind.

25 THE CHARIOT

Diana bolted awake. Heart pounding, muscles tense, she stared at the unfamiliar surroundings straining to hear any sound.

A noise: soft motor-like sound, a whishing of air moving.

Sitting upright in bed, a flood of memories of the last few days oriented her to the present. *First things first.* Diana tossed back the covers and headed into the bathroom. After her shower and dressing, she opened the curtain, letting the daylight stream in. Even though it was early March, the sun shone brightly. *A perfect day for a long walk.*

Her shoulders slumped. *I gave my word.* She sighed, the burst of energy the idea of going for a walk had produced, faded. *Unless I break my word, I won't be doing that. And, I won't inconvenience anyone more than I already have by asking someone to come walk with me. What can I do? Since I'm here, I'll finish unpacking and set up my office.*

When she opened her bedroom door, she found a boldly printed note taped to it.

Diana
Will call at 9 and noon. Dinner's taken care of. See you at
6.

> *Matt*

Her head cocked to the side, forehead furrowed, she thought of all they needed to work out between them: cooking, cleaning, taking out the trash? It would have to wait until tonight.

She padded into the kitchen, heated water in the microwave and found a pad of paper to start a list. *Tea Kettle.* She looked through the cupboards and located the tea. Something hot felt right this morning although she usually preferred something cold and fizzy which was why she enjoyed the tonics.

Checking out the office, she noted there was nothing to set her computer on. As she stood to the side of the living window sipping her tea, the rectangular table caught her eye. With three chairs set around it and the light fixture overhead, it was clearly identified as a small dining table. *I think it will work in the office. And we can eat at the bar or in front of the TV. Time to get to work!*

After rearranging the boxes of office supplies and equipment, she tugged and shoved until the table was in place. Her computer set up, she turned it on to check emails before tackling the rest of the unpacking.

Two from Bill.

Since telling him about the divorce, Bill had emailed her almost every day. Jackson had introduced him to Giovanni in an email and Bill was now in regular contact with the Italian architect. Hearing about Bill's excitement to meet Giovanni and tour Italian factories, Elizabeth had talked to Michael. Arrangements were already in the works for Bill to spend time in Ireland during the summer for another perspective on international business. *Grateful, I'm truly grateful for the support these men are giving my son. It never dawned on me my staying with Dennis had driven a wedge between Bill and me.*

"Great to hear from you. More news tomorrow." Clicking "send" she sent the brief reply and returned to the kitchen to make another cup of tea.

She jumped, tea sloshed onto her hand, when abrupt knocking on the door startled her. The sound was insistent and somehow sounded official. She marched to the door and looked out the security peephole. A man in uniform stood outside. *It looks like the same security uniform I saw on the guard last night.*

"Who is it?" she called out, hoping her voice sounded confident. "Who's there?"

A tap on the door and muffled words, she looked through the peephole again and saw a photo identification card. Nerves riffled, her knees weak, she braced herself and cracked opened the door.

The man on the other side deflated when he saw her.

"Is there a problem?" she asked.

"Mr. Houston called and asked me to check on you. I assured him no one could get to you but he was really upset. He's tried calling you and you didn't answer."

Diana looked at her watch: 9:45. *Matthew must be frantic. My phone? I think it's still in my purse. Is it even on?*

"I'll call him right now. Thank you for checking on me," she said as she closed and locked the door. Quickly she retrieved her phone from her purse on the closet shelf.

It was off.

She turned it on: Battery low.

I remember I turned it off because the battery was low and I couldn't find the charger.

As she searched for the charger, she called Matthew.

He answered on the first ring, his fear, frustration, and relief evident in how he said her name.

Putting manners aside, she interrupted him.

"I'm sorry to have caused you worry, Matthew. Now, please just hear me out. My battery is low and I have to find the charger. I won't leave the apartment today so if you can't reach me at noon, it's because my phone is dead."

"Just glad you're okay."

"I am very okay. I moved the small dining table into the third bedroom for a desk. I hope that's okay with you."

"Whatever is fine. My note?"

"Yes, and thank you for taking care of dinner for us. We can figure out how to handle these domestic chores tonight if you'd like."

"Fine."

Beep, beep, beep. "I've got to go." The screen on her phone blanked. *Did he even hear my last words?*

First she searched through boxes in the office for her cell phone charger. Not finding it, she returned to the bedroom and finished unpacking the three boxes stacked in the corner. Of course the charger was in the last one along with her shoes and slippers. *At the time it must have made sense but now? Well, I'm just going to chalk it up to creative thinking.*

Plugging her phone in and setting it on the dresser, she returned to the living room with her deck of cards in hand. First she retrieved her smudge wand of cedar and sage to cleanse and another of sweet grass to attract positive energy. Not wanting the smoke alarm to go off, she cracked the sliding door onto the small balcony. Second she lit the smudge bundles, and starting in her bedroom swirled the cleansing smoke around the room, including the bathroom and closet. Opening dresser drawers, she waved wafts of smoke inside.

The office and living areas came next. She stood at the front door, walked the few steps of the small foyer, and let the smoke infiltrate the half bath. More time was spent on the kitchen because she opened all the cupboards and drawers. Starting down the short hall to Matthew's room, she stopped outside his closed door.

Dithering whether to open it and continue the cleansing or not, she stilled. *He knows some things about our practice: spirit plates, smudging, and he's heard us talk about house totems and personal totems. He never seemed to mind—but that doesn't mean he wants me to smudge his space. I don't want to take the chance of upsetting him.* She turned from his door, crossed the common space to her room. *We'll be sharing this space for a month or so. I don't even know what he does when he's really mad.*

Decision made, she smudged The Tarot before getting the sweet grass. Once a thin stream of smoke rose from the braided grass, she started through the apartment calling in positive energy, making sure the smoke from the smudge wand reached every nook and cranny. Her work done, Diana stubbed out the wands, watching the wisps of smoke fade and disappear.

Smoke gone, she left the wands in the abalone shell she used instead of putting them away in the box holdling her altar cloths, various stones from around the world, figures of the Goddess and her power animal, fetishes, and incense. From the house she and Dennis had shared, she had cones from the eighty foot tall Douglas firs, dried berries from the pyracantha bush by the garage. Everything was wrapped in protective material or boxed, nestled in the drawer. As her fingers drifted over these treasures, she remembered others packed and stored until she had more room. These, her favorites, brought her the most joy, the most peace of mind. Her body relaxed, a calm serene sense claimed her. A smile on her face, she softly closed the drawer.

Back in the living room, she perched on the couch and looked at the cards and Journal. Taking a deep breath and relaxing on the exhale, she checked her body out from the tip of her toes to the top of her head. When the last vestiges of tension eased and she was centered within herself, she took the cards from their box. Going through the now familiar routine of shuffling and cutting the cards she focused on her question.

What do I need to know or remember this day?

The Chariot.

Her Journal open, Diana wrote down the meaning printed on the card and her thoughts as they related to her life.

The Chariot is the card of success, confidence, and determination. I need to be confident and determined today to ensure my success; victory over illness, enemies, and financial problems.

That is most heartening. While I don't know about the illness, at this point in time, Dennis has become my enemy. I'm worried about finances but maybe I need to draw on my confidence and know through my determination I'll be successful and therefore won't have financial problems. I can achieve my goals because I'm disciplined and have the will to do so.

I'm to focus on the battle at hand: divorcing Dennis. Hopefully that doesn't mean anything regarding Matthew. I'd prefer not to live in a battleground. Although I have years of practice, it isn't my present choice.

Be satisfied with my accomplishments but guard against arrogance. My reputation will be established; respect is earned.

She reread what she'd written before closing the Journal and putting the cards away. Crossing the room to the kitchen to reheat water for tea, another idea popped into her mind. She returned to the couch, picked up her Journal and wrote:

Another battle at hand is to organize this office so it is a functional workplace. With no desk, file cabinets or bookcase that is a challenge. But I'm up to it. I'm determined, confident, and creative and with that combination, I will be successful.

A surge of energy coursed through her as she returned to the kitchen, fixed her tea, and considered ways to manage the office. With several ideas in mind, she strode to the small room and started to work. Within an hour she'd brought order to chaos.

Books lined the far wall. A lamp on her desk, a burgundy glass from the kitchen held colorful pens and pencils, a few items from her sacred drawer created an altar on the right-rear corner of the desk—the one she gazed at when deep in thought. Cut down and taped boxes served as file cabinets, her hanging file folders easy to maneuver in her make-shift system.

A small clock she'd shoved in a box yesterday now sat on the left rear corner of the table. It was after twelve. She stopped working and checked her phone. It was charged now. She unplugged it, turned it on, a beep signaled a message.

12:01 p.m. Matthew. Even though she'd told him her phone would be off, he'd still called. He'd told her he would and he did. Tears trickled down her face.

Amazed she'd cry over something as simple as a voice mail message, she blotted the tears away with tissue and listened to his message. What she heard was more than the simple message: "Hi. Checking in. Call me back when phone is working."

He'd kept his word.

New tears spilled down her cheeks as a new awareness of what it meant to have a man keep his word struck her. Was Dennis telling the truth when he called to say he was working late? She never knew. Was he really coming home for dinner? Or would she know he wasn't when he didn't show up by eight o'clock. *I know I crave reliability right now because so much of my life is in chaos.*

When she called Matthew back, she left a message on his voice mail assuring him she was all right. It crossed her mind to ask about smudging his room but she decided against it. *If he said "yes" that's too much intimacy for me right now.*

Taking her cell phone with her, Diana returned to the office to go to work on creating a different lesson plan for her Monday night class. Almost all the students planned on continuing Spring Term. Her new idea: have them develop a project to improve their own business in some way based on what they'd learned so far. They'd work on it over the break and perhaps into the first week or two of the new term. Then she'd have them do twenty minute presentations to the group.

She heard the key in the front door and Matthew's "It's me."

The day had slipped by while she wrote, revised, and printed handouts and outlines. She stretched the kinks from her neck and back as she turned off her computer and straightened her work area.

She was being watched.

Matthew stood in the doorway, looking at her as if she were dinner.

She looked down hoping he hadn't seen the startled look in her eyes, how her body reacted to him: her face flushed, her breathing stuttered, and her knees wobbled. *It's so unnerving knowing he desires me.* Once again doubts about staying here rose, engulfing her with a sense of unease.

"Dinner. Counter. Shower. Be back."

In the doorway, she looked back at what she'd created today, pleased with her accomplishments both in setting things up and the work she'd done. Closing the door, she walked to the kitchen to see what he'd brought for dinner. She smelled it before she opened the sack: Mexican.

As she took out three large containers, two medium and one small, she studiously ignored the sound of his shower, pulling her attention back to dinner. The larger containers held burritos, nachos, and salad. The medium: salsa and guacamole and the smaller one sour cream. She busied herself getting plates and silverware out of the cupboards and drawers. The shower turned off as she pulled two bottles of beer from the refrigerator, she loved an ice cold beer with Mexican food.

Matthew's door opened, his fresh lime scent announced his arrival. He stood a few feet away, his hair slicked back, still damp from the shower, his face sporting the shadow of a day's worth of beard. Jeans fit his sculpted body like a glove but his plain white t-shirt was large. *Does he like his shirts loose or has he lost weight.* She frowned. *Why don't I know that? Shouldn't I know that?* A sane thought intruded. *I've never seen him dressed this way before. He's always worn a long sleeved, buttoned shirt over his t-shirt.*

His grin started with a quirk of his lips, spreading until his face crinkled and his eyes filled with amusement. "Like what you see?"

A bright red heat flashed from her toes to her ears. *OMG I'm staring at him.* To hide her embarrassment, she turned away picking up the serving utensils and putting them in the containers.

He'd stepped closer. His warmth encased her just before his hands gently grasped her shoulders and turned her around.

Glancing up, she saw his serious face. She lowered her eyes. With one finger he tipped her chin up. She didn't resist, couldn't resist. Her heart pounded so loud she knew he could hear it and therefore knew the effect he had on her. Lavender blue eyes met emerald green ones, emerald green eyes that were soft and searching her own.

What does he want? An apology?

He said nothing and words stuck in her throat. He dropped his hand to his side, seeming to come to some decision, about what she wasn't certain. Then he stepped back.

"Dinner."

The simple word unclogged her throat. "Everything is ready." She stopped herself before she wrung her hands. "Thank you, Matthew. I love Mexican and you got my favorites."

"Good to know. Mine too." He sat and helped himself to a burrito, a chunk from the nachos and some salad. "You eating?" He took a swig of beer and nodded toward the chair beside him.

Diana dished up her own plate of food and perched on the high chair. She reached across the counter and grabbed two napkins, handing one to him without thinking. "Oh, I'm sorry. I should have asked... ."

He laid his hand on her arm. "Don't Diana. Don't apologize or I'll think I have to also. We have to learn to trust that the other person is not trying to make things difficult or this will never work." He reached up and brushed her hair back, tucking it behind her ear.

She shivered under his caress.

"I want this to work for so many reasons." His voice was soft, he leaned closer, his breath a soft breeze against her cheek.

She was paralyzed but with what? Not fear, she knew it wasn't fear, except she was afraid to put a name to it. Picking up her beer, she took a swallow.

His hand dropped and he chuckled. The deep, rich sound reverberated through her. "I like seeing you drink beer from the bottle. Never thought to see it, but I like it."

Her spine stiffened a snappish reply on the tip of her tongue held back before the words escaped.

"You'll only see me drink beer from a bottle with Mexican food," she said in a voice tinged with frost.

"What about wine? I can pick up some wine if you'd prefer it," he said, his tone conciliatory.

I think he's teasing me, not ridiculing me. I need to trust him when he says he wants this to work.

"No, I usually drink my herbal tonics, tea, or water. A glass of champagne to celebrate something special and on rare occasions a cocktail. And you? Do you have a few beers when you come home from work every night?" Diana relaxed as she listened to Matthew talk about his routine. He was a bit grumpy in the morning until he had a cup of coffee. He drank two at the most three cups during the day and then generally had water. He also liked beer with his Mexican food, and in the summer when it was really hot, a cold beer after work hit the spot.

They talked through dinner getting to know each other's routines before cleaning up the kitchen. Matthew put the leftovers away while Diana loaded the dishwasher and wiped off the counter top. He commented on the list pinned to the refrigerator with a magnet and they made a plan to go shopping when he got home from work the next evening.

Diana took the lead in making up a grocery list. Matthew shopped for groceries by cruising the aisles and seeing what looked good to him at the time. To someone as organized as she, it seemed rather haphazard but certainly something she could deal with.

They moved to the couch and instead of watching TV, talked about other household duties. It really took no time at all for them to sort through the chores and decide who would do what. They'd share keeping the great room and kitchen picked up and each take responsibility for their own spaces as well as their breakfast and lunch. Dinner, they decided, would be shared, trading off nights. Matthew confessed she'd be eating more take-out than having a home-cooked meal on his days.

Diana was stunned to learn that a weekly cleaning service came with the apartment. Their day was Friday which worked out really well. If they wanted, the service would take care of any laundry and dry cleaning. Matthew used every benefit of the service. *The cleaning is one thing, but I'm very particular about my clothes—especially since I no longer have a clothing budget.*

When she remembered The Circle's meeting on Saturday, he'd already gone to bed. She didn't want to miss it but didn't know how to arrange to attend so she knocked on his door.

It opened.

He stood there, pants slung low on his hips, his chest bare, the rumpled bed behind him.

She'd gotten him up.

"I'm s... ."

His hand brushed her lips in a feather-light touch. "No apologies. Remember?"

He dropped his hand and she instantly felt the loss.

"The Circle meets Saturday. We didn't talk about how someone can come here or how I can go out." Even keeping her eyes on his face, she could see his bare chest in her peripheral vision. She flushed.

"If you can stay put tomorrow, I'll have a way rigged up for you by tomorrow night. You can let everyone know you'll be there."

"I can do that." As she turned to leave, her gaze lowered from his face to his chest. She quickly raised her eyes, a blush on her face. He grinned, amusement lit his eyes.

She glared.

His attempt to school his features to a more neutral mien failed.

"Good night, Matthew," she bit out as she spun on her heel and stalked across the apartment to her room. With care she closed the door because she would not give him the satisfaction of slamming it.

Less than a minute passed when a soft knock sounded. She threw open the door, standing with her feet planted wide, hands on her hips.

"God you're beautiful." Matthew stood in front of her, rubbing the back of his neck with one hand. "Not my best decision," he muttered as he looked at her, started to reach for her and pulled his hand back. "Don't be angry with me."

He looked like a little boy. Not quite sheepish, not quite guilty and very, very appealing.

"If you don't want me angry, then don't make fun of me or try to embarrass me," she ground out between clenched jaws.

"I like seeing you look at me. Is that a crime?" he asked in a soft voice.

She looked him full in the eye.

"And then you smile, like you won and I lost."

"No, and then I smile because the woman I want is looking at me. Seeing me. Hopefully wanting me." He held up his hand to stay her words. "I know now isn't the time for us to be lovers." His fingers touched her lips stopping her from speaking. "But it is my fervent hope when this is over, we will be."

"Matthew, I'm ... ."

His fingers were back.

"If you are going to tell me you're too old for me. That I'm too young. That I need someone younger. Don't. I happen to be an adult, old enough to know what I want." He took one step and leaned forward, resting his forehead against hers, his hands claimed hers, held them gently. "I don't see you as too old for me, Diana. I see you as just right," he whispered before stepping back. He squeezed her hands once before letting go.

The air around her cooled when he dropped her hands and turned. Standing in her doorway, she watched him stride to his room, shut the door behind him; watched as the sliver of light beneath his door went out; the pent-up air rushed from her lungs.

She shook her head hoping to make his words go away. They didn't.

The battle at hand The Chariot card spoke of was not just about Dennis but also about Matthew. *I don't know how to deal with this. He doesn't care what other people think? It doesn't bother him that people look, whisper behind our backs, comment about my being his older sister or worse, his mother. It might not be so bad now, but as I age? I don't want to be dependent on hair dye and plastic surgery to look young so people won't talk.*

But would he be worth it?

He might.

26   FREEDOM

What were the last few pages about? Diana put her book down and crossed the room to the windows. Careful to stand a few feet back just in case someone was looking for her, she gazed out. Another cold, bright day, stark shadows showcased on the streets, sidewalks, and buildings. *Will I ever be able to walk outside whenever the mood strikes me?* A walk outside, whether a brisk walk or a slow amble around the block or through the neighborhood, jump-started her brain. Somehow by the time she returned, her mind had created an idea, a possibility, a direction to take.

The sound of a key in the lock and the door opening brought her attention back to the room. Turning she saw Matthew standing in the doorway, watching her.

She smiled. No words, just a smile of welcome.

His chest deflated as he expelled a deep breath. Closing and locking the door behind him, he grinned and without taking his eyes off her, came into the apartment.

"I'll clean up. Be right back."

Water running—she tried not to imagine him naked, standing under the steaming, streaming water.

She failed.

He'd be magnificent. Lean muscles flexing as he moved his hands over his body: soap slipping, sliding everywhere. The heat rose in her own body as she allowed herself to picture him finishing his shower, toweling off. Somewhere in the back of her mind it registered the water no longer ran. A glance at her reflection in the window: wanton—an old-fashioned word, but one that seemed to apply to her. Face flushed, eyes dilated, her body thrummed with passion.

As she hurried toward her room to compose herself, his bedroom door opened. Panic threatened and she dashed toward her room. If he saw her, he would guess what she'd been doing and she'd see that grin, the knowing amusement in his eyes.

"I'll be right back, Matthew."

She splashed her face with cool water, freshened her make-up, and took several deep calming breaths. Under the circumstances, she looked as good as she was going to. Grabbing her coat, gloves, and purse, she went back to the living room.

Matthew was slouched on the couch, remote in hand, surfing through channels. He looked up, the now familiar grin on his face.

"Ready to go somewhere?"

"Yes." She stood quietly and waited for him to say something else.

He clicked the television off, stood, and stepped to her. He smelled of soap and aftershave, the fresh air and lime scent that fit him well. His heat beckoned. She locked her knees to keep from leaning into him.

"Got your car downstairs. Want to see?"

The spell gone.

Freedom awaited.

"Oh, yes. Can we go right now?" she asked, giddy with anticipation. Two full days in the apartment were coming to an end. *I'll be free again. Well, not as free as I once was but certainly able to come and go on her own.*

Matthew reached for her coat, holding it while she shrugged it on. She put gloves on and picked up her purse as he grabbed a jacket he'd slung over the back of the couch. He held the door open for her, gallantly gesturing her through.

She giggled with delight.

"Looks like you're ready to get some fresh air," he said as they walked down the hallway to the elevators.

She nodded. If she started talking, she'd babble and disgrace herself.

They reached the parking garage and Matthew directed her to a sleek, black Lexus. With the remote, he unlocked the doors and opened the passenger side for her. He quickly rounded the car and slid into the driver's seat.

"Jackson had a friend who was going to be out of town and agreed to let us use the car. What makes it ideal is that the windows are tinted. Outside you can see that someone's in the car but you can't make out who it is. And, if Dennis has anyone checking license plates, it will show it belongs to someone, not a rental car agency."

Diana settled back in the heated leather seat, taking in the instrument panel, and thanking The Universe for her friends. *I'd never have thought of anything like this. And grateful isn't a strong enough word for how I feel having friends who remain by her side through all this.*

They laughed together, pushing grocery carts through the aisles, learning subtle things about each other by the choices they made. Matthew waggled his eyebrows at her as he picked up a couple of cans of smoked oysters and watched as she pondered over which brand of canned peaches to put in her basket. He deferred to her in the produce department and she deferred to him in the meat department. By what he selected she figured he was definitely a meat and potatoes man. *Well, on the days I'm cooking, he'll also have a salad.*

It was heady to drive back to the high-rise, go through security and find their parking spot. Such simple things, things she'd taken for granted. *Never again.*

"Where are you parked?" she asked Matthew.

"Someone drops me off. Can't follow my truck. We'll have to figure something out on Monday because they can just sit at the school and watch for you."

"You're assuming someone is still watching or looking for me."

"Trust me. They are."

Her best prying techniques failed. Matthew remained silent getting out of the car, getting a cart to put their groceries on, unloading the trunk. Finally she gave up and just walked beside him as he pushed the laden cart to the elevator. *Maybe I'm better off not knowing why he's so certain.* It rankled but she decided to save her breath and wait for another time to bring it up.

After a concerted effort to engage Matthew in planning how to set up the kitchen, an effort he assiduously rejected, she sighed. "You aren't going to help with this are you?"

"Nope, told you, you'll have more "take out" than anything else on my nights," he said from his seat at the counter, a beer in hand.

"But on those nights when you do cook," she began.

He grinned. "I'll just ask you."

They had picked something up at the deli and once the groceries were put away, Matthew shooed her out of the kitchen. She went, curling up on the couch while he put their dinner together. *I could get used to having someone bring me dinner.* They spent a companionable evening watching television. He indulged her by watching Home and Garden Network. His comments on the prowess of the designers and carpenters had her laughing.

"I think I'll write the network about the "Get It Done With Matthew" show. I'll send in pictures of you working. Perhaps with your shirt off? That sort of cheesecake picture? I can ask Jackson and Daniel to write letters of reference." She was caught up in the moment, laughing, grabbing paper and pen, beginning to make a list.

What caught her attention? Perhaps the quiet, perhaps something more subtle. But she stopped and looked at him. Her breath caught in her throat at the naked desire flashing in his eyes. No one had ever looked at her with such longing, such wanting.

Never.

Giddy, she was giddy with the power of it.

She'd loved Dennis and believed they'd had a good sex life. *I'm not a stranger to orgasms and early in our marriage we were spontaneous in our love-making.* But what glittered in Matthew's darkened eyes was much more, so much more that her body began to respond to nothing more than his look.

What would it be like to have his hands touch me? She swayed toward him. With an effort she stopped, pulled back, and brought her unruly thoughts under control. *I will not spend another second thinking about his hands on me; his lips kissing me; his arms holding me.* Her legs shook when she stood.

"I'd better get to bed. I've a long day tomorrow," she said with false cheer in her voice as she started for her bedroom door. "We're meeting and having dinner at Gabriella's," she called over her shoulder. As she reached her bedroom door, she turned back to face him, saw he'd stood while she was crossing the room.

"Thank you for everything. I'll check in with you during the day so you know where I am," she said her voice serious, her eyes meeting his. When she entered her room and closed the door, she sagged against it. Her resolve was as weak right now as her knees.

What if I did allow myself to become involved with Matthew? Shaking her head, she grimaced. *What am I thinking? Other than sexually, I'm already involved with him on every other level. I've too much going on in my life right now and I'm still married. I can't add this, this sexual element to it.* Crossing the room she determinedly stared at her reflection. *No, I can't become lovers with him—no matter how much my body wants to.*

27 THE CIRCLE

A kind of euphoria enveloped Diana as she drove through the city. *I'm going toward something I want instead of backing away from something I don't want or almost worse, sitting, stagnating, hiding.* Pulling into the driveway of Elizabeth and Michael's house, she sat for a minute centering herself, taking inventory of how strong she felt. Before the evening was over and she was back in the apartment there'd be many questions, both obvious and subtle ones.

Should I just ignore them or answer them? That, of course, was her million dollar question. Her natural privacy said to ignore. The other women would persist in a kindly fashion to make sure there was nothing else to do for her rather than to intrude. They loved her, cared about her welfare, had stood by her through all this unpleasantness. *Don't I owe them something, some answers?*

I'll just see how things go, she decided as she got out of the car. Resting the bag of groceries she'd purchased at the deli on her hip, she locked the car before walking to the house.

The day flew by. She especially enjoyed the extra time with Gabby, listening to her friend's ideas on how to increase the conflict between her hero and heroine. *My life has had enough conflict during my forty years of living. And I don't see a Happily Ever After (or as Gabby calls it HEA) in my future. I'm not living in a romance novel.* Gabby smiled when she'd said that.

So everyone could easily read it, Gabby had printed off a long email from Elizabeth. Sitting with the others, it dawned on her that both Elizabeth and Gabby, whom she'd always thought of as her younger circle sisters, were older than Matthew. *I wonder when Matthew's birthday is? How close he is to turning thirty-three. I never pay attention to those things if it's even listed on the student roster I get.* She'd celebrated her fortieth birthday in December. *Maybe we're only seven plus years apart in age.* She pulled her errant thoughts to a halt and forced her mind back to Gabby's chattering.

In the kitchen, a pot of chicken stock on the stove, they worked together to finish the soup. Gabby chopped up the chicken and she the vegetables. The soup now simming, their conversation drifted to many subjects. Before they knew it, Ashley had arrived with the children followed an hour later by Lily, Sophia, Hunter and Logan. It was now expected that Ashley would bring her children and Hunter would bring Logan to look after them while the women talked.

The aroma of the homemade chicken vegetable soup filled the house along with the scent of chocolate and cinnamon from the two pies, chocolate cream and apple that they'd baked. The other women brought ingredients for a "potluck salad" and two loaves of crusty bread. As was their tradition, they made up a spirit plate, giving thanks to the plants and animals who gave of themselves for this meal.

After dinner, the food put away, the children settled; they smudged, said prayers and settled in a circle in the family room. Elizabeth's newsy letter was passed around with each of them reading a part of it aloud: four people were already signed up for the next Sacred Space weekend retreat set for the Spring Equinox, they'd cleared $1000.00 from the first one; she and Michael were doing well. Michael was busy with training and the beginning of racing season.

Diana felt blessed Gabby had not dogged her all day long with questions. When she'd first walked in the door, she was asked how she was and that was that. Now, however, she thought there would be questions stated silently and a few out loud. Deciding to grab the proverbial bull by the horns, she asked to go first. Picking up a piece of rose quartz they'd used on an altar in Ireland, Diana pictured Elizabeth in her mind before she spoke.

Letting her gaze roam around the circle, she took in the sight of these five women, so accepting, so forgiving of her missteps in life. Unshed tears glistened. Ruthlessly she quashed them and began.

"Thank you all for your help in my most recent move," she smiled hoping to lend an air of lightness to her words. "I've settled in. My computer is set up and books and files are unpacked. Last night Matthew and I went shopping so the cupboards are full. If you let me know ahead of time you are coming, I can make arrangements for you to use the secure parking garage. I just have to give the security guard your name, description of your car and license number." She paused, searching her mind for what to say next. The mundane.

"We have a chore list of sorts. Who will fix dinner on what days. It's simple actually. We just take care of ourselves. There isn't much to do because the building has a cleaning service that comes on Friday. We've agreed to pick things up each night before going to our own rooms. We haven't exactly figured out Monday nights because if Dennis is still trying to find me or follow me, he knows I'll be there, knows exactly where to find me." A shudder shivered through her at the flash of memories of his finding her before.

"I don't want to cancel the last classes but I'm not sure what to do to throw him off my trail. Matthew says he's still looking for me."

A glance passed between Lily and Sophia. *So Dennis is doing something to Matthew. I'll have a talk with him when I get home. Home, in just over forty-eight hours I'm calling the apartment home. I'm safe there. For the first time in a very long time I feel safe. Isn't it strange how Dennis having multiple affairs made me feel vulnerable?*

She'd drifted off. Drifted off into her thoughts. Looking around at the faces of her friends, her soul sisters, she saw their love, patience, acceptance, caring, compassion shining at her. Tears caught her by surprise, slipping down her face, dripping on her blouse. She handed the rose quartz to the one on her left.

Diana managed to pull herself back to the present as Gabriella finished. She promised herself to call and talk to her in the next day or so. Having spent most of the day with her, Diana knew how much Gabriella missed Elizabeth. She added to an internal list to call her in the next couple of days and invite her to come by.

Ashley shared her children's adventures. Nothing was said about Art. Diana knew if her marriage had been hellish, Ashley's was also. Another circle sister to reach out to. *Reaching out to others will be good for me. And, I love Ashley's children. Maybe they can all come to the apartment for an afternoon. I'll ask Matthew what he thinks.*

Hunter's dance studio was doing well and practice had started for their Spring Recital. She made a mental note to write the date in her planner so she wouldn't forget.

Lily was still thrilled with married life, with being Jackson's wife. She wasn't taking on new clients now, instead choosing to travel with him once a month when he was on longer trips and doing house totems for his out-of-town clients.

Sophia was already looking forward to Spring Break. "Just two more weeks," she said with a bright smile on her face. "My students this year are difficult to reach. I'm not giving up, but I am looking forward to a break and working in my garden".

The evening came to an end with their coming together, arms around each other, smiles gracing their faces, love shining in their eyes. When the younger ones appeared, they opened their arms and invited Logan and the younger children inside the circle.

"Elizabeth is with us," Gabriella whispered.

Light shimmered around them.

The jealousy and pain Diana'd felt so strongly on Winter Solstice was gone. Joy radiated from her. Gratitude that these women were her friends and she had a safe place to live humbled her. *Who knows what my future will hold?*

Diana walked out to the car, chatted with the other women; waited while Ashley got her children bundled and buckled in the car.

"Don't worry, Ash, I've plenty of time. Don't rush on my account." It didn't matter if she got home in thirty minutes or an hour.

She called out and waved as the women pulled out of the driveway and drove off. When she slipped into the driver's seat, she punched in Matthew's cell phone number.

He answered on the first ring.

"I'm on my way."

"Good."

"I'll see you soon."

"Okay."

That was all. No accusations. No threats. He just accepted her at her word. It had been a long time since a man had done that—just accepted she'd been with her friends and was now on her way home. *I like that feeling, like being trusted, like being seen as a woman who honors and values her word on things.*

In her heart she had to make sure she didn't like it too much.

28   Pre-Kisses to Post-Kisses

Due to single lane traffic as road crews worked on the main freeway, it took an hour to get home. Her earlier calm feelings gone, she wiped her damp hands on her slacks before, with studied stealth she opened and closed the door. Her goal was to slip into her room without him seeing her. She froze when the lock clicked into place. In the background, the quiet murmur of the television. Taking off her shoes, she padded across the hardwood floors intent on reaching her room without a scene.

She glanced toward the television, stopped, arrested by the sight of Matthew sprawled on the couch, one arm flung over his head, the other hanging over the edge, resting on the floor, the remote on his broad chest—asleep.

The tension in her body eased and she wobbled as muscles relaxed, her legs weren't working well. Her eyes? Her eyes devoured every inch of his masculine form now on display for her. *Where is my resolve to resist him?* Gone, replaced by an unrelenting draw to him in this most vulnerable pose. Crossing to the couch, she took the throw from the back intending to cover him.

As she removed the remote, his hand clamped hers against his chest. The heat from his body infused her own. Mesmerized, she watched his eyes open, catch her gaze, and hold it. Frightened? No, if she said he must let her go, he would.

The words didn't come. Instead she stood, half bent over the couch, her hand on the remote on his chest, staring into eyes she feared saw too much.

"Hi."

The sound rumbled in his chest, vibrated against her hand as her ears heard his voice.

He swung his legs to the side to sit up without letting go of her hand.

Pulled off balance, she tumbled over the back of the couch a squeak indicating her surprise.

He caught her, scooted to the side, and pulled her down next to him casually resting his arm along the back of the couch.

A deep breath to settle her jangled nerves still tingling from his touch and her fall calmed. They were both awake now and she had something to ask him. Turning to face him, Diana plunged in with the question uppermost on her mind.

"What is Dennis doing to you?" She watched his face closely, saw him shut down. "I know he's doing something, Matthew. I want to know what it is." She strove for a strong confident tone.

"Nothing," he muttered focusing on the television.

"That isn't true. Don't lie to me. You know I don't deserve it." Spurts of anger and frustration flashed through her. Struggling to keep them under control, she consciously relaxed her body, reached for the remote and turned the television off.

"We aren't discussing this, Diana." He reached for the remote.

She tossed it aside, out of his reach, saw his jaw tense.

"But we are." She spoke quietly committed to see this through to the end.

"Why do you even think anything is happening?" he challenged.

"Because you are so fervent in denying anything is and," she said and paused for effect, "I caught a glance between Lily and Sophia this evening that confirmed it." She remained calm composed on the outside and a quick check confirmed she was the same inside. *I really didn't have anything to be concerned about. Matthew is definitely not Dennis.*

They sat in silence, minutes passed, he sighed.

She smiled. *The power of silence is strong. Glad it worked with Matthew. Dennis just walked out.*

"Nothing big. Just little stuff." His voice was tired, his arms now rested on his legs, hands dangling between.

"For example?" Diana was thankful he was talking to her. *I need to know the repercussions of my decisions.*

"Spray painting equipment and job sites. Missing supplies. Cut sack of sand or concrete. Just minor irritating stuff." He shrugged as if to dismiss, to minimize his words.

"Things that cost you money and time."

"Yeah," he sighed and slumped back against the couch.

"What are you doing about it?"

He sat up at that, surprise on his face. "Doing?"

"Yes, what are you doing about it? Are you making police reports? Taking precautions to see your supplies and equipment are more secure?"

"Try to keep supplies in the truck until needed, installed cameras on the work site, hired a security company to do a drive by every couple of hours."

"Is it helping at all?"

"Got some pictures. Two people wearing ski masks. Can't see their faces. So far nothing to identify them other than I've got evidence for the police and insurance company."

"So you've filed a claim?"

"Nope. My premiums'll go up."

"So, you're just eating the loss." Diana contemplated what that might cost him in terms of his profit.

Before she could comment further, Matthew pulled her tight against his side.

"You're my profit," he whispered in her ear. "Money doesn't matter because I've got you here, with me. Dennis is just jealous. Dog-in-the-manger jealous. Nothing for you to be concerned about. It's covered."

She started to argue, to push away.

His arms tightened. "If you feel sorry for me, you can kiss me and make it well." The breath from his words feathered against her cheek.

Her will to pull away seeped from her bones and she melted into him.

"One kiss, Diana. That's all. Just one."

She heard the urgency, sensed his passion, but believed him when he said "just one." Foolish? Perhaps, but she believed he was a man of his word. *He has been so far.* "Just one." The words so simple, echoed in her heart. She wanted that one kiss. To be honest, she wanted much more. Tonight she'd settle for one kiss. She tipped her head, looked up into his eyes, whispered, "just one," saw the flash of astonishment followed immediately by one of satisfaction.

He lowered his mouth but didn't touch her lips. His lips caressed her cheeks, her forehead, nibbled down her neck, flicked across her ear, teased her chin, pecked her nose.

"These are pre-kisses," he whispered as his mouth meandered over her face. "Like in sports, there's the pre-game show." He continued his journey.

"Oh," she sighed savoring every touch. "How long are pre-kisses?" she managed to say, her voice deeper than its usual timbre.

"Until it's time to move on to the kiss itself," he murmured against her neck.

She softened, her body beginning to hum with desire. *Oh Goddess, if pre-kisses are this good...* . She wound her arms around his neck, pressed her body against him.

"Just to warn you," he nuzzled just below her ear. "Kisses are followed by post-kisses."

"Po-post-post-kisses?" she stammered as her mind began to fog.

"Hmm," his mouth nibbled a circuitous route to her mouth, claiming her lips in a devastating assault leaving her breathless and clinging to him as she surrendered.

Diana held on as he plundered her mouth, his tongue forging in and out, his mouth moving, slanting one way and the other as if seeking the perfect fit. She was lost in the heat, the scent, the passion, the excitement of kissing Matthew. She wanted to climb inside him, take him inside her—be closer, always closer. Her hands tangled in his hair, insistent, demanding.

He drew back, the ardent passion waning. The image of a drifting ship unmoored from its dock floated through her mind when he pulled his lips from hers.

He tucked her head under his chin, held her tight, and whispered.

"Now comes post-kissing."

"What do we do?" Her voice shook.

"Nothing. Just be with each other. Like this." His chin rested on her head, his hands stroke her arms, her back, his breathing slowed to normal.

She was wrapped in his arms; cherished. Her own breathing slowed to normal, the passion pounding in her core eased to a warm thrum. And still he held her. Time passed. She wasn't sure how much. *Had he fallen asleep?*

Held so close, Diana felt his sigh. He shifted and with his finger tipped her head up. His emerald green eyes showed his contentment; his mouth quirked up in a lop-sided grin.

"Beautiful. You."

Her heart sang with the truth of those words. Matthew's truth mirrored in his eyes: longing and a deeper emotion she didn't dare name. If these feelings were frightening, to name what she saw shining in his eyes would be terrifying. Words crowded her mind and her mouth. She stayed silent, basking in the appreciation in his eyes.

More moments passed. His arms loosened. She may not want to move away but to stay ensconced in his arms would send a signal she wasn't prepared to act upon. Reluctantly she pulled away, sat up, and sought to smooth her mussed hair. He smiled, reached for her and stilled her hands.

"Beautiful. Just the way you are. Mussed from my kisses. Don't." The command was gentle as was the touch of his hands to stay her own from fussing with her hair and her clothes. He stood then, reached down to help her to her feet, pulled her into a brief but hard embrace before he gathered the dishes on the coffee table and took them to the kitchen. Rinsing them off, he put them in the dishwasher and without a backward glance walked into his room and shut the door. For several moments she remained unmoving, digesting what had happened between them.

Trouble. Deep trouble, I'm in deep, deep trouble.

Gathering her coat from the back of the couch, she slowly walked to her room where she quickly readied herself for bed. Lighting the candle on her altar, she raised her arms and prayed asking The Universe to help her find her way; to guide and protect her; to keep her safe not only from Dennis but now clearly from losing her heart to Matthew.

I'd be devastated if I gave him my heart and he discarded it. Do I want to risk being set aside for a younger woman in two years or ten?

Tonight a comfortable spot eluded her. After an hour of tossing and turning, she got up, got The Tarot cards and sat cross-legged on the bed. The Universe always guided and protected her but in these circumstances she'd take all the help she could get. She began the now familiar ritual of shuffling and cutting the cards repeating her question as she did so. "Show me the way," she chanted under her breath as she dealt the spread.

29 ITALY

Spring Equinox
Rome, Italy

Every cell in Diana's body begged for sleep as she and Bill proceeded through Italian customs. In the end, The Circle hired a security company to escort her to and from her last two classes. The two brawny men sat in back of the class the first night but joined the group the second. She smiled remembering one of them said he'd like to sign up for her class and maybe something could be worked out if she still needed protection.

She glanced at her tall and handsome son, He caught her eye and smiled.

"We made it," he leaned toward her, whispering as if it were a secret.

She wouldn't cry, she told herself, and not for the first time, since meeting him at Logan Airport. It was enough they were in Italy together, although she was not naïve enough to think he'd spend much of it with her. From Giovanni's emails, she knew Bill's time was planned, committed. Days her committed to house totems, Bill's to factory tours. Other activities? Sightseeing or lazing by the pool at Migliori's villa high on a cliff overlooking the sea.

Passports stamped, they exited customs without incident, following the signs to exit this area of the airport. Bill spotted the sign with their name on it first.

"This way, Mom," he said and nudged her to the right toward the man with the sign that read "Pettybone." The man seemed to recognize them, waving the sign above his head while watching them. Bill nodded and headed in that direction, her carry-all bag as well as his own slung over one shoulder, his suitcase pulled behind. She lagged behind tugging her own suitcase in her wake.

The man bowed as they approached, reached out, took the bags off Bill's shoulder. With a gesture, no words, just a gesture, he took her suitcase handle from her hand started through the crowd.

Diana tried to take in her surroundings but the man moved too quickly for her to linger. One minute she was struggling to keep up and the next she was out a door and into a bright sunlit day. She stopped, needing a moment to catch her breath, to catch up with herself, to catch up with the reality of being here, in Italy, with Bill.

The man stepped to the curb and gesticulated wildly. Moments later a long, dark limousine pulled to the curb. The trunk opened and he efficiently stowed their bags. The driver exited the vehicle, striding around to open the door for them, motioning them inside.

Luxury: deep leather seats, the soft sound of classical music, an open bottle of champagne and two glasses, a small box of chocolates and an armful of flowers, their aroma scenting the car, a phone ringing.

The panel between driver and passenger slid open, an arm appeared snaking around to press open an almost hidden door. The phone. The arm disappeared, the panel slid shut.

Diana picked up the phone. "Hello?"

"Ahhh, you are here. Molto buono. I see you soon then." Giovanni's voice boomed, filling the back seat of the car with its welcome. "My driver brings you to my home. There I see you and we eat. You will be hungry, si?"

"How long will it take, Giovanni?"

"Two hours, maybe three."

"Bill and I may need to stop——"

"I tell them to stop at my home there in Roma so you can freshen up, si?"

"Grazie."

"Ciao."

Diana and Bill heard the ring of another phone mere moments later. The car changed course.

"Champagne?" her son asked.

"I think I will," she responded. "It seems the thing to do as it's open." She ignored the fact that Bill wasn't twenty-one and hoped they weren't breaking any Italian laws by him having a glass of the bubbly. Relaxing into the cushioning seats, her eyes closed, her breathing slowed. All she wanted was to sleep but she forced her eyes open and looked out the window. *Rome.* She spied a fountain's water high in the air, streets so narrow the limo couldn't pass through, people walking, on bicycles, scooters.

The limo stopped. The door to the building opened. A man in black pants and white shirt, with sleeves rolled up to his elbows and a woman dressed in black with a white apron stood in the doorway. The driver opened the limo's door and motioned for her to get out.

"You need to get out, Mom," Bill's voice was accompanied by a small nudge in her side.

She slid the few inches to the door, swung her legs out, and stood. Another person now stood at the door. A young woman with long dark hair and almond-shaped brown eyes smiled and extended her hands in welcome.

"Welcome, welcome," she said in a heavily accented voice. "I am Angelina. Giovanni asked me to make you welcome. Come in; come in," she said stepping aside and waving them into the cool interior of the house. A spate of Italian was directed to the two men and woman who quickly moved to do her biding. At least Diana thought that was what happened.

Bill had already followed the dark-haired beauty into the large open room beyond the foyer. Diana trailed a few feet behind. When in Ireland she hadn't understood everything being said due to the vernacular and at times the accent, but here? Here she was totally lost. Hearing Bill's voice, she tuned back in to her surroundings. He was speaking Italian. Slowly. Haltingly. But making an effort nonetheless.

Angelina laughed at something he said. Bill flushed with embarrassment and then laughed as Angelina told him what he'd said rather than what he'd meant to say while correcting his pronunciation. They turned toward her and Angelina walked back the few steps to direct her to the bathroom at the top of the stairs. Grateful to use the facilities, Diana hurried up the steps.

When she returned to the main floor, she followed the voices and found herself on a patio surrounded on four sides by the house. The foliage lush, the scent of flowers perfumed the air. A table was set and held large glasses of lemon water along with plates of small cakes and sandwiches. She sipped the lemon water, finding it refreshing after the hours on the plane. Bill ate enough of the sandwiches and cakes to make up for her lack of appetite.

Angelina traveled with them to Giovanni's. And, Diana thought, as the limo sped along the road, it was nice to have her with them because she talked about the history of the area. Bill seemed to be falling more and more under the young woman's spell. *That isn't right. Angelina isn't casting a spell. She's just being herself. Exuberant, intelligent, fresh—excited to show people her country.*

The sun was beginning its descent toward the sea when they pulled into the courtyard of Giovanni's villa. Set high on a cliff with spectacular views, it was surrounded by masses of tropical plants and flowers. They were met by staff and quickly ushered into the house, shown their rooms, and informed dinner was at eight.

Diana fell in love with her balcony. *To sleep out here, well, I won't but if I leave the doors and windows open—* A knock on the door announced a maid who helped her unpack, showed her how the faucets and shower worked, and left her to bathe and dress for dinner. While it was inviting to take a quick nap, Diana was concerned she'd sleep through dinner, so, instead of a nap, she showered, dressed, and went down to explore the gardens and perhaps find their host.

Giovanni lounged in a chair, his long legs stretched out before him, a glass of wine in his hand. Bill sat in front of him, leaning forward, elbows on knees wrapped up in whatever Giovanni was saying. She stood for some time, just inside the archway leading from the main room onto the veranda, watching her son and the handsome man with the dark flashing eyes, quick smile, and ready laugh. He really was the most sensuous man she knew.

Drawn to him as she was, she wondered what it would be like to have him hold her in his arms. *Would I feel as safe and cared for; as cherished as I do when Matthew holds me?*

She stepped through the archway, into their domain and cleared her throat to announce her presence. Both men started and turned to her, unaware of her until that moment.

Giovanni slowly rose, his warm, sexy, signature smile inviting as he bowed and gestured her forward. Bill jumped to his feet, kissing her on the cheek as she sat in the appointed chair. They were soon joined by Angelina and, promptly at eight called in to dinner.

Bill, Giovanni and Angelina talked about the appointments set up over the next four days. Angelina would accompany Bill and act as interpreter as needed. Over dessert, an exquisite tiramisu, Giovanni informed her that her first appointment was tomorrow morning. Four more clients were scheduled over the next three days. She and Bill would have their last three days in Italy for sightseeing or just relaxing at the villa or his home in Rome.

The sound of birds singing, the muffled sound of waves crashing on rocks and the scent of exotic flowers greeted Diana when she woke the next morning. She stretched and squelched the idea to turn over and go back to sleep. *I've a job to do and my first client is scheduled for this morning.* Even though she looked for one, she never found a clock in her room so she used her cell phone to tell her the time. It was after nine o'clock. She'd missed seeing Bill off for his first factory tour.

Getting up, Diana padded to the open doors and out onto the balcony. The cool tiles under her bare feet contrasted with the warm air; perhaps not warm for Italians, but certainly warm for someone from Fremont or Boston. Tempted to linger, she turned back into the room, reminding herself she'd come to do a job. After a quick shower, she dressed selecting her signature black slacks paired with a rose colored blouse. Her reflection in the mirror caught her eye and she smiled. She looked rested. Resisting the urge to remain barefoot, she checked hair and make-up were in place and slipped on a pair of sandals.

One of the staff directed her to Giovanni, who was sitting in the same chair on the veranda. The low table next to him held a pitcher of what looked like fresh-squeezed orange juice; a basket of bread, containers of butter and yoghurt, an assortment of fresh fruits in individual bowls, and a plate of pastries.

"Ahh, bello. You are here now." Giovanni smiled at her and gestured toward the table. "If this is not to your liking, they will get you something else."

"This looks wonderful, Giovanni." Diana poured herself a glass of the orange juice and sat as she sipped the golden liquid. She had fresh-squeezed orange juice at home, but this tasted different, richer, more golden. Unable to place what exactly was different, she stopped trying and just enjoyed. Starved, she sampled everything on the table, taking a few bites of the bread between courses to cleanse her palate.

Giovanni watched her.

It wasn't uncomfortable, more a knowing than anything else. But since he said nothing, neither did she. Sitting in silence, just being with him, reminded her of sitting with Matthew while he watched sports on television. *Stop, stop comparing them. You are here to work, not have an assignation with Giovanni.*

The last sip of orange juice slipped down her throat, her plate was clean. She sighed and turned toward Giovanni.

"That was wonderful. I was hungrier than I thought."

"I am glad you like. Ahh, and you sleep well?"

"Very well." Diana noticed that Giovanni appeared hesitant and his usual brash look was gone. Although it was a little awkward, she pressed on.

"You mentioned last night I would see someone this morning. Has there been a change in plans?" She flushed with awareness at the intensity of his gaze. *Does he see me as something more than a friend?* He blinked and it was gone.

"Ahh, si. Your first client in Italy." She thought his smile a bit sheepish as he stood and reached out his hand. She placed her hand in his and stood. He didn't pull her into his arms but did he hold her hand a little longer than normal? Turning, he gestured for her to follow him into the garden. At the fountain, he stopped and turned.

"My home. What do you see as the totem for my home?"

"But of course you would want to know the totem for your home."

He nodded once and stood, feet slightly apart, clearly uncomfortable.

The energy of the place had been in evidence from the moment she'd stepped inside the house. Here in the garden it was stronger. It wasn't a familiar energy so she'd yet to identify the totem. *I wonder if it is something I don't know or understand?* Sitting on the bench beside the fountain, she closed her eyes. *Spirit of this place, I ask you to reveal yourself to me. You have guarded this land for many years. Please show yourself and be honored for all your years of service.* A vague vision floated in her mind.

Diana flowed into a deeper relaxed state, let her mind open to possibilities; let an image appear. *A bird? A type of parrot? No, that didn't seem right A gull?* The image shimmered in her mind's eye. *Definitely a bird.*

She opened her eyes to see Giovanni's intense gaze on her. His brow rose in question.

"It's a bird but not one I'm familiar with. Do you have a book of pictures of native species of birds for this area? I can clearly see it."

"We get the book." He turned and strode toward the house.

Diana quickly followed him through the house and to his car. Giovanni drove down the winding road through several small villages to a town large enough for a book store. They shopped, and in addition to three books on birds and animals native to Italy, she bought gifts for her circle sisters: seven brightly colored paintings of local scenes and seven brightly colored scarves. Her bags stowed in the trunk of the car, they strolled through the town stopping for a light lunch of local cheese, bread, and wine.

Back at the villa, she excused herself, took the bags of books and gifts, and went to her room. Sitting on the balcony sipping a glass of lemon water just delivered by the maid, she held a book of native birds in one hand. She closed her eyes and brought the vision of the spirit to her mind. It flickered vividly behind her lids. Upon opening her eyes, she went into the room to get her notebook. She took a few minutes to sketch the bird and write as detailed a description as she could before picking up one of the books and leafing through it.

Diana closed the last book. *The vision is not in these books.* She picked up her sketch. *It will have to do. The spirit might be ancient or extinct—more like Lily's house totem, the dragon. That feels right.* She closed her eyes again and looked carefully at the vision rising in her mind. When she opened her eyes, she added some lines to the sketch and details to the description.

Her neck was stiff by the time she'd copied the bird and its description on a clean sheet of paper. She rubbed the back of her neck and rolled her shoulders to relieve it.

Putting her notebook away, she stacked the books on the bookshelf and freshened up. Giovanni was waiting. *I'm sure he wants a name, not a drawing and description. What if I can't do house totems here.*

Trepidation leadened her steps as she picked up the slip of paper and searched out her host. Her stomach rebelled, her shoulders tightened, and the urge to wring her hands signaled the level of her anxiety at the prospect. *How upset will Giovanni be? He can't be worse than Dennis.* She stiffened her spine, raised her chin, and descended the stairs.

30   GIOVANNI'S HOUSE TOTEM

Giovanni was on the veranda in his favorite chair with his eyes closed. *Is he asleep or deep in thought?* She stood quietly trying to decide what to do. Bill and Angelina had returned and were down by the pool. *I can join them or stay here.*

"You have come to me with my totem?"

The choice was gone. Her hands fisted and her knees locked. Initially unable to speak, she cleared her throat to dispel the nervousness and saw him open his eyes. She nodded instead of risking her voice failing.

A second later he was on his feet and striding toward her, his face split with a wide smile. He grabbed her in a huge hug, wrapping his arms around her, squeezing her, holding her tight. Overwhelmed by his masculine energy, so different from Matthew's, a measure of relief coursed through her when his arms dropped to his side and he stepped back.

"You tell me now who my totem is," he said. His eyes sparked with delight although his tone resembled an order.

She tried to smile as she looked him in the eyes.

"There is a slight problem," she began. As she saw his brows furrow, she hastened to add. "I have seen your house totem; I just don't know what it is."

"I don't understand," he said his brows quirked in confusion.

Diana thrust the drawing and description in his hands and took two steps back. Out of his reach, wary she observed him scrutinized the drawing.

"I know it isn't very good, but—"

"Come," he ordered, his voice full of excitement, a broad grin on his face. He grabbed her hand and with long, ground-eating strides towed her across the veranda.

To keep up, she ran.

He charged through the villa to a section she'd yet to see, through a conservatory to a small patio, beyond a wing of the main house. Continuing, he pulled her through the door of yet another building.

Catching her breathe, she glimpsed the ordered chaos of bits of plaster work, wood, tile and stone littering the floor and flat surfaces. Under large windows on walls shaped like the prow of ship, were work tables that showcased his designs. Leaving her no time to study anything, he tugged her to the middle of the room. He held her shoulders in his large hands and turned her to face the back wall.

The bird in her vision, a four foot by three foot mosaic, with iridescent tiles that mimicked the shimmer in her vision. Every detail she'd drawn or described was in the piece.

"I don't understand," she shook her head in disbelief. "I've never been to this part of your home before."

"When I build this studio, the workers find this buried in the ground. I have it restored and hang here." He walked to the mosaic, his fingers running over the surface. "It is bellisima, si?"

"Si, Giovanni. It is very beautiful." She stood transfixed by the ornate tile work that depicted the bird she'd envisioned. Giovanni nodded his head. "It is good that you find this," he said and gestured to the hanging, "to be my totem. It is very good I think." He grinned at her, swept his arm encompassing his studio. "Not many people invited to come here."

Diana turned away from the mosaic to inspect his studio. The room was shaped like a pentagon. Two walls glittered with windows overlooking the sky and sea. Two were floor to ceiling shelves filled with books, samples, and what looked to be souvenirs or knickknacks, most likely gifts from clients. The back wall was bare except for the bird, his house totem.

Giovanni slung his arm across her shoulders as they made their way back to the main house. He told her in more detail about the workmen finding the mosaic and the research he'd done trying to identify the artist and the subject. So far he'd found nothing solid.

Diana paid scant attention to what he was saying, lost as she was in her own thoughts and feelings. For a short period of time, she'd doubted her vision of the house totem. This was a lesson for her.

Trust The Universe will take care of me.

Trust there is a way forward.

Trust I can succeed and I am good enough to envision even difficult, hidden house totems.

The earlier doubts disappeared.

Having the books of birds and animals of Italy wasn't a waste. There were other clients to see and who knew what she'd find.

"Giovanni?" She knew she needed to bring the subject up before their appointment with clients tomorrow.

"Si?"

"We need to talk about what might happen tomorrow if I can see the spirit, the house totem but can't name it. You know, identify it like with yours."

"Not to worry. I be there and together we will know what to call it." He smiled his most charming smile and hugged her to his side as they reached the veranda. He slipped her hand in his as he bowed and gestured her into a chair. Raising her fingers to his lips, he kissed each one before gently resting it in her lap. He flashed a devastating grin and dropped into his favorite chair. Before he could raise his hand to gesture a servant forward, one was by his side. He spoke in rapid Italian; the maid curtsied in reply and left.

Diana shifted to tuck her feet under her and gazed out past the garden to the dark blue water, the white sails that glided on the surface. Closing her eyes, she let her mind wander. *My worries Giovanni would be angry with me for not knowing the name of his totem were for nothing. I won't deny I feel an attraction to him. Who wouldn't! He's tall, dark, handsome and very, very charming. And I do feel safe with him.*

Another tall, dark, handsome man's face appeared in her mind's eye—Matthew. *One of the bonuses of being here is being away from him. And yet he creeps into my mind when I don't expect it, like now—I'm comparing Giovanni and Matthew's hugs. This morning I wondered where he was and what he was doing. If I was home, it'd be my turn to fix dinner.*

Shaking her head to dispel these images, she sighed. *Italy, I'm in Italy! I've an amazing opportunity to see another part of the world, to spend some time with Bill and to earn extra money to tide me over while I get my life sorted out.*

The maid returned with fresh lemon water, and thin slices of bread layered with fresh mozzarella cheese, tomato and basil and drizzled with extra virgin olive oil: her favorite. *I could get used*

*to having someone wait on me; anticipate my wishes; lounge
around in the shade with a gorgeous view. I have a week to store
these memories. A week, I won't waste.*

Their last night in Italy was spent in Rome. She and Giovanni
dined at a small restaurant where he was a favorite patron. The
food was superb, the service divine.

"For you," he said as he presented her with a smaller version
of his house totem. "To remember your time in Italy."

*Such a kind, generous man. I'm looking forward to keeping in
touch.*

Diana relaxed into the aisle seat. Bill craned his neck looking
out the window for a glimpse of Angelina. Her son was really
quite smitten. Inwardly she smiled as vignettes flashed through
her mind of Bill and Angelina laughing, talking, sharing time
and space. Every day the two of them were off on some
adventure. He'd toured the factories Giovanni'd set up, adding a
day in Venice, one in Milan, and another one in Rome. Neither
Bill nor Angelina had spent much time at the villa. *I wonder if
Angelina is as taken with my son as he is with her?* Her mind
wandered into the future—Angelina as her daughter-in-law; Bill
living in Italy?

She reached over and patted Bill on the arm. He turned to
her, a broad grin on his face, delight in his eyes.

"It's been great being here with you; seeing everything. Just
great, Mom."

"It has been special, hasn't it," she said and searched his face
for signs of sadness. *Maybe I misjudged and he isn't as enamored
of Angelina as I'd thought.*

The plane took off and she and Bill settled back for the long
flight to Logan Airport.

31   THE PROMISE OF PEACE

Diana spoke briefly with Lily once they landed in Boston, confirming she and Jackson would meet their plane after meeting Charlie's a few hours earlier. Since Bill and Charlie were on Spring Break and she was in the apartment with Matthew, Bill staying with Charlie at Lily and Jackson's was an efficient plan.

They were soon on the last leg of their trip. In a few hours she'd be home and have her old life back. *I'll miss being fussed over, my every need anticipated and met often before I knew I wanted it.* A part of her looked forward to seeing everyone again, sharing stories, and catching up. Another part of her didn't. *Lots can happen in seven days and eight nights.*

Familiar faces lined the barrier as she and Bill made their way from customs to the airport lobby. She'd expected Lily and Jackson, also Charlie; but not everyone else. Hugs, excited voices and welcoming smiles greeted them. It was seven o'clock Fremont time and it seemed as though they'd traveled forever. *If*

I computed the time difference correctly, it is early morning in Italy.

Lily and Sophia tucked their arms through hers and they started toward the main lobby area. Hunter, Gabriella, and Ashley and her three children, Art Jr, Anthony, and Amanda trailed after. Logan was with Jackson, Charlie and Bill who were going to get the luggage.

Out of the corner of her eye she saw Dennis stalk toward them. He glared at her as he kept going until he stopped in front of Bill. Her heart stopped, she staggered and couldn't catch her breath. Only because Lily and Sophia had her arms in theirs did she remain upright.

"You're coming home with me!" Dennis ordered. "She," he pointed in her direction, "will not steal my son from me," he said, his face twisted, fury lashed out in his voice at her.

His outraged snapped her out of the shock of seeing him.

Bill ignored him and moved to step around his father.

Dennis blocked his path.

"You. Are. My. Son." He gritted out through clenched jaws, his finger jabbing the air.

This was not happening. Her eyes widened at the sight of her son now standing toe-to-toe with his father, curious on-lookers pausing, and then scurrying on.

"I'm not going with you, Dennis," Bill said in a clear, calm, controlled voice. "How you dare demand that is beyond me."

"That bitch is not going to take you away from me," Dennis shouted and glared at her.

Bill's eyes narrowed to slits, his mouth tightened into a grim line. "How you dare call Mom names, make demands after all you've done?" Remember Dennis you're the one whose cheated on her forever." Bill's accusation punctuated by his finger drilling into Dennis' chest. "You used me to cheat on her. And, you've threatened her and hit her."

She saw Dennis start to deny his son's words but Bill interrupted.

"Don't lie to me, Dennis," he sneered his father's name. "Remember, I was there when you brought some mistress or whatever you called her to one of my games when you knew Mom wouldn't be there. And, I have my ways of finding things out. I still know people here in Fremont."

"I'm your father," Dennis was protesting now.

"You are a sperm donor, Dennis. Nothing more. You can't keep your pants zipped. Dads keep their pants zipped and don't wave their cocks around at every female they see. Dads don't use their sons to cheat on their wives. Dads don't beat up their wives."

Lily's arm around her waist, Diana watched, mesmerized, as her son took his father to task for his treatment of his mother. Feelings like the ebbing and flowing of the ocean's waves rolled through her: pride and pain; sadness and relief; embarrassment and vulnerability. People stopped and watched and others steered clear of the drama unfolding in front of them.

"Your mother is just trying to drive a wedge between us. She's always tried to come between us. You know that. Remember—?" Dennis's hands were raised in supplication.

"Do you have any idea how many times Mom lied about you, Dennis. How many times she made excuses for why you weren't home for dinner, didn't show up for a game, couldn't help with a school project? Do you have any clue at all why she did that? Why she stayed with you when she should have left?

"She wanted me to see you in a good way; see you as the father you might have been. She lied to protect me from the reality of you."

Bill's shoulders slumped, the fight leeched from his body.

"Leave us. Just go," he said in a voice as old as the ages.

"But—" Dennis started to argue with Bill, and then stopped. His shoulders drooped and he bowed his head. "I don't want to lose you, son. I don't want it to be like this between us."

"Then you need to leave Mom alone. You need to stop tracking her, stop threatening her. You need to cooperate with the divorce. You need to give her everything she wants. You owe her more than you can ever pay.

"You need to leave, talk to your attorney, see a counselor, get a life of your own. Mom may not tell me if you continue to harass her, but believe me I'll find out. If you so much as raise a finger to her or deny her anything she asks for, that will be it. You'll find yourself divorced from me as well."

Diana saw airport security approach, the officer relaxed yet alert. "Problems?"

"No," Dennis shook his head. "No problems."

"There isn't anything else to be said, Dennis. You've some thinking to do and some decisions to make. Let your attorney know what they are." Bill picked up his carry-on bag and stepped around Dennis followed by Jackson, Charlie, and Logan.

Diana thought Dennis looked old—the grey at his temples aging him. The distinguished look she thought of as "him" gone.

Lily and Sophia stayed by her side as they left the airport for the parking garage. Driving across town to the Montgomerys' where a light snack awaited them, everyone was quiet.

Diana stood looking out at the fairy lights of Fremont twinkling in the night still stunned by what had happened. From his reflection in the glasses, she saw Bill being congratulated again by Jackson and looked upon with admiration by Charlie and

Logan. From time to time Charlie surreptitiously glanced at his mother and the thought flitted through her mind that maybe he'd speak up to his own father the next time he insulted Lily. She met Bill's eyes, saw him smile and give her the thumbs up sign. She smiled back.

She turned at the sound of a familiar voice.

Matthew.

They stood facing each other, an awkward moment passed, and then she was in his arms. Arms that closed around her, held her tight. The sense of being cherished, comforted, safe enveloped her. Everyone else faded into the background. Her head rested on his shoulder, a hand moved to the small of her back, his voice rumbled in his chest.

"You must be Bill."

Diana wrenched herself from Matthew's arms, her face burning with embarrassment. *What must Bill think of me?* She stumbled back, Bill caught one arm, Matthew the other. Together they steadied her. *What are they talking about?*

"... job there." Matthew's voice.

"Thanks, I needed to say something. Figured you and Jackson already had and this was my chance to stick up for Mom." Bill's voice.

"Appears you did." Matthew's voice.

Confused, she shook her head to clear her thinking. *It must be the exhaustion, the jet lag.* She'd missed Matthew coming in and now she couldn't keep track of the conversation.

"Diana?" Lily's voice.

She turned toward Lily's voice. Sophia appeared and took her arm, guiding her across the room to the kitchen bar. "Let them talk, Diana. It's a good bonding moment for the two of them."

Looking over her shoulder, she saw Matthew, thumbs tucked in his front pockets; Jackson one hand in his front pocket, the other around Charlie's shoulder; and Bill. They appeared to be deep in discussion about something.

The next thing that registered was her name in Matthew's voice. Turning she saw him gesturing to her. She really didn't want everyone to hear whatever it was he wanted to say so she walked across the room to where he now stood by the fireplace.

He put his hands on her shoulders and leaned toward her.

"Missed you," he brushed his lips across her forehead. "Really, really missed you." His hands had moved and his fingers now stroked her neck. He turned her so her back was to the fireplace, his body blocking her from most everyone's sight. She felt his thumb caress the hollow of her throat and slide upward, under her chin, a light pressure raising her head a little and then a little more until she was gazing into his darkened emerald green eyes before closing them as his mouth descended to hers in a gentle kiss. He pulled her tighter, his hands stroking her back.

Melting into him, Diana opened to him, welcomed him. She wanted this man, wanted him badly. She raised her arms, wound them around his neck, and deepened the kiss.

32   Facing A Truth

His mouth left hers first, his arms dropping away. Her lids fluttered open. He stood before her, eyes ablaze. Flushed, her knees weak, her own core burned with a passion she hadn't felt in a very long time.

"Let's go," he whispered, gesturing with his head toward the door.

She nodded.

The next few minutes passed in a blur as she said good-bye to Bill making plans to see him tomorrow while Matthew made their excuses to the others. He grabbed her suitcase and carry-on, herded her out the door and loaded the trunk of the Lexus with her luggage. When he pulled her across the console, she was glad the windows were tinted. Her body sought his, pressing as close as the confines of the car would allow.

Her breathing ragged, he set her back in her seat, turned the key in the ignition and backed out of the driveway.

"Get you home," he said his voice slurred with desire.

Diana relished the feeling she was the reason for his passion. She couldn't keep her eyes off him as he drove barely within the speed limit through the traffic to their apartment.

Grabbing the cart, he quickly unloaded the car. One hand firmly grasping her elbow, the other the cart; he strode toward the elevator. She jogged to keep pace and was breathless by the time the door slid shut.

They were alone.

Matthew kept the cart with her luggage between them, but his gaze devoured her. Her blood pumped faster and her breathing fractured by the time they reached the apartment. Anticipation thrummed through every cell of her body.

He flicked the lights on as he put her luggage in the foyer, leaving the cart in the hall. No hesitation on his part, no second thoughts as he shut and locked the door. She bent to pick up her carry-on intending to take her things into her bedroom.

"Leave it," he ordered.

She obeyed.

Her heart beat even faster as he reached for her, tugging her toward him.

He pulled her coat from her shoulders, draping it over the suitcase. Her scarf followed. She froze as Matthew began to unbutton her blouse, his touch reverent, gentle, caressing. *What will he think when he sees my forty-year old body?* Her mind raced with scenarios of his frown, his disgust, his rejection. The few times she'd allowed her imagination to get to this point, it was always dark, maybe a lit candle across the room, or the flickering flames of the fireplace. But not like this, with the light on—exposed.

She put her hands up to stay his, but he brushed them aside.

"Mine," he whispered and kissed her cheek. "Mine," his voice now like a prayer as he nuzzled her ear. "Mine." His arms wrapped around her and she swayed against him. Her feet left the floor as he picked her up, carried her into the living room and set her down on the back of the couch, his hands and mouth busy as they roved over her.

When he stepped back, his hands around her waist kept her from toppling backward.

"Champagne. I got champagne and stuff for us," he said his voice rough and gravelly.

Her eyebrows arched as she looked around. Fresh flowers, a box of her favorite chocolates, a bottle of champagne and two champagne flutes on the coffee table; more flowers and an ice bucket on the breakfast bar. The place was spotless. *He must have been very very careful since the cleaning people were here two days ago.*

"Matthew," she reached up and touched his smooth, clean-shaven face - just for her. His muscles tensed when she stroked his jaw. "I'm—" Where were the words to express how she was feeling? "Thank you," she whispered.

Still, alert, he waited for her signal, for her to let him know what she wanted.

Moments passed.

It was time for her to speak up.

"I'm not sure this is a very good idea," she paused, struggled for the right words; words that would sound sophisticated or at least smooth. She failed. "Matthew, I'm afraid you'll be disappointed in me. I'm not," she dared to look up and into his eyes. It was humbling to see such tenderness, such caring, such passion. *All for me.* It was heady to see how much he wanted her. *Just me.*

"Done? Or is there more?"

From the quiet of his voice, she knew he would wait until she said whatever it was she needed to say. From the look in his eyes, she knew it wouldn't matter. He wanted her.

And in the wake of that. Her own truth. She wanted him.

"Just so you know. I'm quite frightened. I'm not sure I can do this," she buried her face in his chest. Her face burned with embarrassment but her body burned with desire. If she was to slake her passion for Matthew, she had to face her embarrassment. She forced herself to look back at his handsome face, to step even closer, move her hands up his chest to his cheeks, to stand on her toes, to press a kiss to his mouth.

That was all the invitation he needed. His hands swept her up in his arms as he strode to his bedroom. He slid her down his body until her feet touched the floor. Hands flying over the buttons and zippers of her clothes, he pulled her gaping blouse from her slacks. With a gentle touch, he pushed the silk from her shoulders.

She stood, arms at her side, her eyes focused on the carpet, his shoes. He was still fully clothed and she was standing exposed. She shivered with awareness knowing he stared. *What did he see? Was he disgusted?* She stiffened her spine and looked up.

"Wondered when you'd look at me." He smiled and a calloused finger caressed her cheek.

She thought that was all he was going to say and started to protest that he was making fun of her.

"Beautiful. You are the most beautiful woman I've ever seen."

She saw his face, the look of adoration in his eyes.

Tears slipped and slid down her cheeks.

He raised his hands to cup her face, his thumbs swiping the tears away. "Shhh," he whispered as he leaned in to kiss her. "Shhh. Everything's going to be all right. I promise."

She relaxed into his hands, stepped into his heat. His hands meandered down to her shoulders, her arms, around to her back.

Her bra came undone.

The idea to cover herself lasted no more than a second before it burned to ash in the flames left by his hands continuing their journey to her waist. His thumbs in the waistband of her pants tugged the slacks and her panties over her hips. They slithered to the floor. Picking her up, he laid her on the bed.

The cool sheets on her bare back did nothing to cool her heated body. She held her breath, daring not to breathe and closed her eyes afraid of seeing the disappointment in his eyes as he assessed her body and found it lacking.

The bed sagged with his weight. Heat radiated from him; heat that smelled of clean lime and aroused male. Anticipating where his hand was and what he was doing consumed her. He was lying next to her, on his side facing her, his hand hovered over her stomach, now her breasts, now her arm. He touched her then. On her arm as she'd sensed. A gentle and caressing touch filled with heat, desire.

Themes from her Tarot reading urged her to act with confidence, to move forward, to trust her strengths.

He was waiting, waiting again, for some sign from her that she was ready. *Is he naked?* A stab of desire flashed from her toes to her head. Shifting towards him, she opened her eyes. Mere inches away his broad, naked chest: golden skin with coppery flat nipples; dark curly hair that spread across his chest and arrowed down toward his waist.

Her flat hand, fingers spread between his nipples, nipples that tighten in response, explored the texture of his body: crisp hair, smooth skin, calloused hands. One of the latter was stroking her side. The other propped his head up.

When brave enough to look at his face, instead of signs of disgust or disappointment, she encountered passion: controlled, smoldering passion. Her heart soared with the realization that he still wanted her: naked, trembling, uncertain her.

Her hand slid up his chest and disappeared behind his neck. At the light pressure she exerted his head lowered.

"You want me?" His hoarse whispered words excited her.

"Yes." She smiled at the heat burning in his emerald eyes.

"Good." He nibbled on her lower lip while his hand drew lazy circles on her abdomen. "I'm dying here while you debate your worth, Diana. Can't you tell you are more than I deserve?"

All she could manage was a shake of her head. Her body on fire, desire snaking through her, trembling.

"Cold?"

She shook her head.

He chuckled. "Must be doing something right." His lips sought her mouth, his tongue plundered.

She nodded as his hand found her breasts and played with her nipples. Arching, she wrapped her arms around him, pulling him tight. Her tongue danced with his, her fingers played in his hair, her body shifted to feel more of him.

His hands stroked, his mouth trailed behind his talented fingers, her body lifted, seeking more. Somehow he anticipated what she wanted, what would make her body sing with desire. His hands left her for a moment.

The sound of foil being torn.

He moved over her, nudged her thighs apart. His hard, thick arousal pressed against her core. She raised her hips in invitation; his answer a thrust that seated him deep. Her legs wrapped around his waist.

He went still.

She froze. *What was wrong? What have I done wrong?* Her legs slipped from his waist, her arms from his neck. The intense feelings of passion gone.

He rose up on his elbows and looked her in the eyes. "What happened?" His voice was strained.

"I'm sorry—." Diana turned her head away. "I-you—"

Matthew rested his full length on her. "What. Happened?" he asked. "You stopped."

"No, you stopped," she shouted. "It was you who stopped."

Her belly shook from Matthew who was still deep inside her. He was laughing.

Astonished, she glared. "What's so funny?" she snapped. Being on her back, she was at such a disadvantage, that and being connected with him in a most fundamental way. *I could just slap him!* She thwacked his shoulder with all her might.

No longer laughing but still grinning, Matthew said, "Ahhh, Diana. Do you know why I stopped?"

"Obviously not, as you seem to think it funny and I don't," she said surprised at the petulant tone in her voice, the pout on her lower lip.

"I just had to stop," he said his grin was gone. Resting his forehead against hers, he went on. "You know, get some control back. Didn't want to embarrass myself. You know, lose control?"

She shook her head, she didn't understand. She wasn't really experienced, only one other man when, in college, she and Dennis broke up, but she believed they'd had a satisfying love life. *Where did you get that idea? Having orgasms obviously wasn't enough to satisfy him.*

"Guess you're going to make this difficult for me."

She smiled.

He shifted, seating himself deeper, a self-satisfied grin on his lips.

She frowned.

"I haven't been with anyone in a year or so," he started.

"Dennis and I haven't shared a bedroom in over a year," she said. "I thought Dennis and I got along well but——"

"Shh. If you need to, we can talk about Dennis another time. Not now.

"I've dreamt of being with you, like this for a long, long time. The reality of you is a hundred times better than the dream. I don't want to disappoint you. I want our first time together to be one you remember for all the right reasons. Let me show you how much I want you."

33 THE STAR SPREAD – 2

Diana woke with an arm and a leg pinning her to the bed; her back nestled against a strong chest, her hair stirred by his breathing. Snippets of memory of their love-making flickered through her mind. He really was a thorough lover—very thorough, so thorough he was familiar with every inch of her body. She wriggled in an attempt to escape his grasp.

It tightened.

Not wanting to wake him, but needing to use the bathroom, she cautiously moved his arm aside. Sitting, she maneuvered out from under his leg. She spied his shirt, picked it up from the floor and pulled it on over her nakedness, buttoning the three middle buttons. The cotton soft against her body, she imagined it still warm from his body.

On naked feet Diana padded into the living area and on across to her bathroom where she took care of her personal needs. Everything took longer as she studiously avoided looking in the long mirror over the vanity.

Birth control was not something she easily talked about but knew if Matthew didn't bring it up, she'd have to. *I've been off the pill for over a year now.*

The altar on her dresser was bathed in shifting patterns of light and shadow from the moonlight streaming through the open curtains. She raised her arms in prayer, whispering the words that brought her comfort. *What am I going to do now?*

It occurred to her he'd expect them to continue as lovers. *Until when?* Until he grew tired of her? A deep pain lanced her heart. Remaining in front of her altar, arms at her side, her head bowed, her thoughts in turmoil. *He would grow tired of me. How could he not? What can I do now to protect myself? How am I going to go on living here with him, always knowing he will leave me?*

Her mind whirled with questions, possibilities; but no answers.

Diana padded back into the living room; saw her luggage just inside the door. *I'll unpack.* When she opened her carry-on bag, on top were her Tarot Cards. The mental whirling slowed as she picked up the box. Grabbing the Journal and pen she kept with it, she returned to the living room, turned on a lamp, sat on the couch and opened the deck. The Star spread was about emotions. *It's the right one for me.*

A glance showed her Matthew's bedroom door still open but all was quiet within.

Consciously she relaxed the death-grip on the cards and let the questions run through her mind, picking the critical one to focus on as she shuffled and cut the deck. *My feelings for him are frightening. How much I want him overwhelming. Is it even possible for anything to come of this? Is it possible to feel so beautiful, so cherished forever?*

Card 1 = Feelings: Two of Cups

Card 2 = Influences: Four of Wands
Card 3 = Emotional Block: Strength
Card 4 = Expectations: Three of Pentacles
Card 5 = Most Likely Outcome: Six of Wands
The cards were dealt before Diana read the words on each card and opened her Journal.

The cards are somewhat confusing – starting out with "a new love affair" and then turning more toward business – new projects, success, group ventures. When things get tough I need to remain calm, patient with other people's weaknesses. I have the ability to endure adversity. I have inner strength and can rely on support from a strong woman.

All of the women in my circle are strong but especially Lily. She's been through similar circumstances – not regarding Matthew – but certainly Dennis. She is so utterly happy and content now --- such a contrast to a year ago.

I wonder if I'll ever look back on this time of worry and doubt and be surprised I stewed so long over everything?
TIME WILL TELL!

She closed her Journal and gathered the cards together returning them to their box. Feet tucked under her, she sat pondering the confusing message in the cards. *Maybe more time to mull it over will help.*

Even with what she knew was several feet between them, his heat, his energy, his intensity surrounded her. Motionless she waited. Not certain exactly what for, but waiting nonetheless.

One finger stroked down the side of her neck, under the shirt collar, along her shoulder. Unable to breathe, she remained unmoving, wanting, straining for more.

"Missed you."

His breath sighed along the nape of her neck.

"Come back to bed, Diana," he nibbled on her earlobe as his finger kept stroking up and down, ear to shoulder, shoulder to ear.

His mouth curved into a smile, moved from her earlobe to her neck, his stubble sensitizing her skin to his touch when she shuddered.

"Diana?" He used his hands now, rubbing them over her shoulders, down her chest, towards breasts eager for his touch.

Her body blossomed with awareness of his every move; anticipated where he would touch her next. His fingers whispered across her skin. *More, I want more, need more, need him.* She arched back against the couch and gasped as he tumbled onto the cushion, pulling her into his arms and then onto his lap.

"Matthew?" her voice trembled.

He answered her question with a searing kiss. The three buttons on the shirt flicked open, her body caressed with long strokes of his hand. Her mind slowed, the question lost; lost in the haze of passion, her body eager, her hands on their own quest. *We're going to make love on the couch or maybe the floor.* Pressing herself against his erection, she wriggled. Her heart soared when he groaned. She wriggled again as much to tease him as to excite herself. *Wanton, I'm wanton, young and free and love it.*

Matthew, his hands on her waist, lifted and turned her. The thick, hard length of him slid along her inner thigh. She wrapped her arms around his neck, her legs around his waist and let him guide her down. He was breathing hard, as if he'd run a marathon.

He stopped.

An ache spread from her core outward until every cell in her body wanted him. Her nipples puckered, her lungs breathless, her hands itched to pull him closer. She was wet with wanting him. Inches, he was only inches away and he stopped. She kissed his neck, sucked his earlobe, rubbed her breasts against his chest, wriggled trying to lower herself another inch or two, to feel him inside her.

He held her still.

"Don't move. Please. Don't," he ground out.

Holding herself still, she rested her forehead on his shoulder, let herself relax against him and heard his groan.

"That didn't help."

The tension in his clenched jaw, in his steel beam neck, in his fisted hands did not ease as he held himself rigidly still until the condom was in place.

Diana matched her breathing to his as another way to melt, to merge with him.

All thought fractured as he thrust into her, touched her heart from the inside.

Her world spun out of control as she shattered into orgasm.

"Hold me, please hold me, Matthew. Don't let me go. Please. Please, hold me," she begged as her body soared into ecstasy.

As the splintered pieces of her body fused, tears threatened. Not the tears of pain or fear or sadness, but tears of great joy. Matthew held her. One arm was banded around her lower back, the other stroked her spine. *I never want to move again.*

She shifted ever so slightly; his body answered.

She moved; he responded.

She set the pace; he matched her. It was invigorating to be in charge. Leaning back and taking a good look at the man who'd enticed her to make love on the couch, she reveled in her power. Hair disheveled, face darkened with the stubble of beard, emerald green eyes mere slits as he looked at her through heavy lids. His bare chest with its dark hair rose and fell with the effort of his breathing. Most heady was the realization he fought to maintain control, to keep from his own climax, to give her another glimpse of the stars, of the galaxy contained in an orgasm.

His brows furrowed in concentration. She was close but so was he. Could she drive him over the top? Did she want to see him break?

She leaned back a fraction of an inch more.

There. She was on the cusp of her own glory and wanted him with her. Her release started deep within her.

"Matthew, come with me. Please, come with me. Now. Please." She could feel her inner muscle clutch, grasp, clench. She collapsed against him as he thrust up and up and up. He stiffened and groaned. The heat of his ejaculation spewed deep inside her. Arms banded around her, holding her so close it was as if they were glued together.

Too sated to move, they remained on the couch. Her head nestled under his chin, his heat warmed her front and where his arm and hand held her. Matthew's arm left her back returning moments later with the warm throw.

"Don't think I can move yet," he said his voice rumbling in his chest.

"I don't want to move yet," she whispered, nuzzling his neck, placing soft kisses along his jaw.

"What do you want?"

"Hold me, Matthew. Just hold me."

The condom broke. Does he realize? Do I need to say something? I suppose I do. Later. Right now all I want is to be held, to be cherished, to be loved by Matthew. The last words she'd written in her Journal floated through her mind. *Time Will Tell.*

34 THE MORNING AFTER

When she awoke, she was alone in her own bed. Her sheets, imprinted with his scent, were tangled. Wincing as she stretched; her body was a combination of pleasure and pain. Worries began to nibble; doubts began to rise. The broken condom? She quashed them, wanting the memories of an incredible night of loving to be hers for a while longer; unadulterated memories of being loved, of being cherished, of being wanted—no worries, no doubts.

I'm not going to worry about it. There's nothing I can do now and I don't want to worry Matthew. I'll make sure to get extra protection. Spermicide or something like that.

Her cell phone rang but before she tossed back the covers, it stopped. Yawning, she curled into the pillows, snuggled under the covers, closed her eyes, and drifted into the hazy non-sleep of visions.

A soft knock sounded on the bedroom door.

"Come in," she said, a smile on her face when Matthew stuck his head in, her cell phone in his hand.

"Bill."

His eyes darkened with desire, her face flushed. *How can we still want each other so intensely after last night?* She'd always thought, when she allowed herself a moment to wonder, that if she and Matthew became lovers he would turn away. It was the main reason she'd held off so long.

He chuckled. "Your mother slept in. Needs a little time to get herself together."

Diana threw the covers back as Matthew pulled the door closed. It didn't latch so she heard him talking to Bill as she moved to the bathroom. What she wanted was to linger and absorb the hot water beating from the massaging shower head before turning it to a warmer temperature and gentle spray. But she was in a hurry to talk to Bill hoping that would counter her embarrassment at facing Matthew.

No make-up, pair of black sweat pants and a cobalt blue scoop-necked top over her matching bra and she called it good. She shoved her feet into a pair of slippers as she ran a brush through her still wet hair. Looking at the clock, she chuckled to herself. A new record—from bed to now in ten minutes.

Matthew's voice drifted through the door as she opened it and walked into the living area. He was sprawled on the couch, still on her cell phone. Desire flashed in his eyes before he seemed to bank it. He held her phone out to her.

"Bill," he said as he stood and took the few steps to hand the phone to her.

Their hands brushed. A tingle and flash of heat arced between them.

"Thank you," she said in a voice even she thought a bit prim.

His mouth quirked into a grin as she took the phone from him.

"Hi, Bill. What are you doing?"

"Gosh, Mom, you never sleep in this late. It's almost ten o'clock."

"Must have been the long flight and a bit of jet lag." A glance at Matthew, his shoulders dancing with suppressed laughter, showed her he was enjoying this.

Distracted by the man in jeans and t-shirt, enjoying her discomfort, she had no idea what Bill was saying.

"I'm sorry," she interrupted. "I got distracted for a moment. Would you start again?"

"What are your plans today? Matt and I were talking about just hanging out today. He said he'd fix stew. Then Jackson thought it'd be better if the two of you came here because this place is bigger and everyone can stop by. Matt can still do the cooking if he wants."

"I see." But she didn't really. Of course she wanted to spend the day with Bill. Even though they'd been in Italy together, next weekend he'd be flying back to Boston and college. And, with his trip to Ireland and maybe back to Italy, who knew how much time she'd actually have with him this summer.

Could she spend the day with Bill at the Montgomery's with no one guessing she and Matthew had been lovers? *No, that isn't possible. First there was that kiss and the way we'd dashed out last night. Lily knows me far too well, and Bill? Well, at times he's more observant than I realize. And, he's calling Matthew, Matt, instead of Mr. Houston or the more formal Matthew. I need some time to sort things out but to do that I'll miss time with Bill.*

"Let me call you back in a few minutes. I need to talk this over with Matthew before we decide whether to have people here or go over there."

"Okay, Mom. Talk to you in a few."

She hung up and put the phone in her pants pocket.

Matthew was in the kitchen scrambling up some eggs. The smell of coffee brewing scented the air. A tall glass with ice, a can of seltzer water, and a long-handled spoon on the counter showed her he'd set things up for her morning tonic.

"Thank you." She poured the cold seltzer water into the glass, added two squirts of her herbal tonic and stirred. Fixing it gave her a few minutes to regroup, to compose herself, to think.

Matthew continued to fix breakfast for them, popping bread into the toaster, getting out the butter and jam, finishing the eggs, arranging everything on plates. She sat on the bar stool as he put her plate in front of her, followed immediately by silverware and a napkin.

He slid onto the chair next to hers and began to eat.

"Well," she started, and waited for him to respond.

He didn't.

"What's going on?" She tried again to draw him into talking to her, let the silence hang in the air. Out of the corner of her eye she saw Matthew's breakfast was almost gone and she hadn't taken a bite. *He must have been starving.*

Plate empty, he finished with a long swallow of coffee. Putting the cup down, he turned and looked at her. "What do you want to know?"

"I want to know what's going on."

"Bill called. I talked to him. He wants to see you today." He shifted on the stool so he was facing her. "Look, Diana. It was just a spur-of-the-moment kind of thing. Bill wants to see you but he also wants to spend time with Charlie, and Logan is coming by."

"How many people did you invite?" She was frowning, felt the pucker on her forehead between her eyes.

"Most everyone. You know, your circle women." He hastened to add. "I know it'd be a tight fit but there'd be room. Then I thought about feeding everyone. You know, making dinner. I make a pretty decent stew."

"You and Bill came up with all of this in ten minutes?" she said disbelief coloring her words.

"Yeah." His quirky grin gave him an appealing little boy look. "It'd be tight on the stew 'cause it needs a long time to cook, but if I get on it we'd at least be able to eat by six or seven."

"Do we even have any stew meat?"

"Nope, but I can get it. Here or at Montgomery's?" He stood and started toward the door.

"What do you mean? Where are you going? Matthew, wait." Diana's tone changed from confusion to an order.

Matthew stopped and strode back to the breakfast bar.

"What?"

"I'm sure your stew is delicious, Matthew, but—" A frown on her face she added, "I think I'd rather go to the Montgomery's than have everyone here." She fidgeted with her fork, finally taking her first bite of the breakfast he'd fixed. "This is very good." She stalled for time to marshal her thoughts. "I do want to see Bill and I do understand he wants to hang out with Charlie and Logan but I'm tired and would rather be able to come home when I want. It'd be easier to be there than to have everyone here."

"Not a problem," Matthew leaned toward her, his lips brushed her cheek. "Finish your breakfast before it's stone cold.

I'm off to pick up some snacks to take along. With three teens in the house, having snack food is good."

She took the time to eat her breakfast before calling Bill and checking on a few things. Everyone planned on stopping by except Ashley and the children. Art's parents were in town visiting.

"Matthew and I'll be there in a couple of hours. He's gone off to get snacks and I have to start unpacking. Tomorrow I'm back at work, you know."

"I'd like to come see you teach, if that's okay," she heard Bill's hesitation.

"And I'd love to have you come. We'll settle all of that when I see you this afternoon."

"Mom?"

"Yes?"

"Just want you to know I really like Matt."

She opened her mouth to say something, anything; but before words formed he added.

"I know it's your life and everything. I'm not telling you what to do or anything like that. I just want you to know I like him. A lot. I think he really cares about you. And, he'll stand up to Dennis if he tries anything else again."

Sometimes being tongue-tied was a good thing. She hadn't blurted something out. And she'd actually listened to and heard what Bill said. He accepted Matthew had a place in her life, she needed to move on with her life. And if Matthew was in it, she had his blessing.

"Thank you. It means a lot to me that you understand. It is a bit awkward living in the apartment with him. But it's a secure building and Dennis has been so unpredictable." She was babbling. She stopped, took a deep breath. "Thank you, Bill. If we're going to be there in a couple of hours, I need to go, get my things unpacked."

"I love you, Mom."

"I love you, too."

Diana sat for a few minutes digesting her conversation with Bill before she got up, cleared the dishes and put them in the dishwasher, wiped down the counter and stove, and put things away. In her bedroom she made the bed, suppressing the urge to hold the pillows to her chest, to breathe in his scent. She'd hoisted the suitcases onto her bed and started unpacking when she heard the front door open.

"I'm in here," she called as she lifted the blouses from the bag, carried them to the closet and hung them up. Turning back to the suitcase for more clothes, she saw Matthew in her doorway; his eyes darkened and she imagined he was remembering last night and what they'd done in her bed. As vignettes of their entwined bodies flitted through her own mind, her face heated and her body softened.

He stepped back, pulled his eyes from the bed to her face. Emerald green eyes dark with longing caught her gaze and held. In that minute she had no doubts he wanted her as much as he had at any point in time last night. Shivering with awareness, she clasped her clothes to her chest.

A couple of hours later they pulled into the driveway at the Montgomery's. In the interim, she finished unpacking. Matthew cleaned his room, changed the bed and remade it. Both did a load of laundry. When he'd gone to the store, he'd picked up a couple of cold cut and vegetable platters, chips and an assortment of dips. As soon as the food was set out, the young people immediately loaded plates.

Diana and Bill spent time playing checkers, hunched over the board in friendly competition. During the game, he confided that Dennis was calling him but he wasn't answering. One message he'd left Bill relayed to her. Dennis was calling his attorney in the morning and had already called off the investigator. If Diana wanted a divorce, he'd no longer fight her.

How many times in the past couple of month had she believed Dennis wouldn't do anything more? Too many. This ploy was to win Bill over and had nothing to do with a change of heart towards her. Bill sounded so hopeful. Unwilling to spoil his dream of them at least being an amiable family, she said nothing.

There were moments when she caught Lily or Sophia watching her or watching Matthew. Efforts to be nonchalant failed. She was excruciatingly aware they had their suspicions. And Matthew? Every time his eyes followed her around the room, her skin tingled and warmed. Once, when she looked at him, passion arced between them, enveloped her. To steady herself, she'd grabbed the back of a chair and tore her gaze from his. Surreptitiously she breathed deeply to calm her aroused body.

Lily turned on lamps as the daylight faded. *Time to go.*

"Diana?" Matthew was talking to her.

"I'm sorry. I drifted off."

"Dinner, Jackson asked about staying for dinner," he said. He stepped to stand directly in front of her, his brow furrowed.

What showed on my face to have him so worried? Her heart pounded, skipped a beat. The urge to take that last step, wrap her arms around him, let him hold her surged. She locked her knees, straightened her spine, and lifted her chin.

"I'm fine. I just got lost in my thoughts. That's all," she said failing to her own ears to sound brisk, business-like. Instead, she sounded out-of-sorts; not like herself at all. Shaking her head in an effort to dispel those troublesome thoughts, she added, "Staying for dinner is fine if it works for you. You're the one who has to get up in the morning to go to work."

He didn't move, just looked at her before stepping back and quickly striding across the room to Jackson.

"Let me help with something since we're staying."

"Thought we could treat the ladies to some real cooking," Jackson bantered. "You know, show them what real men can do in the kitchen. Have you guys ever done stir-fry?" he said gesturing toward Charlie and Bill.

"No," they chorused.

"Come on and I'll show you how."

With that the four males moved into the kitchen, banishing Sophia who was making tea.

"You go and sit, Soph," Charlie's voice. "We'll bring a couple of pots of tea in for all you ladies," he said and laughed before adding, "and a plate of your cookies. This is going to be fun, Jackson. I bet Mom will be surprised."

"She's used to my cooking, Charlie, but not yours. That's what will really be a surprise for her. And, your Mom, Bill. Have you cooked much for her?"

"Not really."

Diana laughed. "Bill, I remember a couple of breakfasts in bed on Mother's Day."

"Awww, Mom. Did you have to bring that up?"

She could hear Jackson and Matthew's good natured tone of voice as they joked around with Bill and Charlie. The low, masculine rumble was a pleasing backdrop to the familiar voices of her friends. *It's strange to think of Bill as a man, but at almost twenty he is a man in most people's eyes. Is Lily as surprised as she that her son is all grown up, off to college, making his own way in the world?*

Charlie and Bill arrived with the promised tray of cups and plates, tea pot and cookies. The women quickly made room on the table in front of the couch. Sophia took charge pouring tea for the five of them. Ashley and her children had gone home so she could make dinner for Art and get the children ready for school. Logan decided to sit where she could watch the guys cook and continued to talk to her friends. *She misses them a lot. Next year she'll be gone and everything will shift again.*

They each reached for a plate as they took their cup. When everyone had her tea, the plate of Sophia's delicious peanut butter, chocolate chip cookies were passed around.

Diana settled back in the chair, tucking her legs under her as she sipped her tea and listened to her friends chatter about the novelty of having men fixing dinner and waiting on them.

"Jackson fixes dinner most of the time, but to have Charlie help is amazing." Lily's face split with a huge smile.

"Are you surprised to see him all grown up?" Diana watched Lily closely, waiting for her answer.

"Yes. And this time last year I thought I'd lost him, that I'd never be close to him again. But, now he's back. Different, our relationship is very different, but I can talk to him. He even gives me a hug and a kiss on the cheek." She looked radiant.

Lily glanced over her shoulder at Jackson. Diana saw him look up and catch Lily's eye, saw the love flow between them. *Will I ever have that with anyone?*

Someone was watching her. Looking up, she met Matthew's eyes, his longing for her curled her toes. *It isn't love. It's infatuation, lust. I'm a novelty. He can't possible feel for me what I see, what I sense between Lily and Jackson.*

Hunter tapped her on the knee. "Come back, come back."

"I seem to be drifting off a lot today," she said without thinking. When she saw knowing smiles and nodding heads, she added, "Jet lag."

"Tell us more about your time in Italy?" Sophia leaned forward in anticipation. "Was Migliori a true Italian?"

"I'm not sure what you mean by "true Italian", Soph, but he was a perfect gentleman at all times." Gabriella's snort signaled her disbelief. Diana turned toward her friend and said, "True, true Gabby. He never tried to do more than kiss the back of my hand and that didn't even happen once a day."

"Only because he was worried that Matthew would show up and beat him to a pulp," Gabby rejoined.

Diana snapped her mouth closed. It was a good thing she'd lost her ability to talk. Her glare at Gabby was enforced by her brows scrunched in a frown.

"That's enough, Gabby," Lily cautioned. "I really don't think Matthew had anything to do with it. Giovanni likes to flirt and tease but I don't think he carries it much further than that." She turned to Diana, "Did you get the impression he has a string of lovers?"

"No." Grateful for the lifeline, Lily tossed to her; she took a sip of tea to order her thoughts before speaking. "No, I don't think he's as involved with women as you'd think. He enjoys them: talking, flirting, teasing in a sexual way but he seems very careful about whom he engages in those kinds of flirtations. And," she looked Gabby right in the eye, "how would he know anything about Matthew? Especially since there isn't anything to know."

"I didn't mean to upset you, D," Gabriella said, reaching over to pat her knee. "Really, whatever is between you and Matthew is—well, between you and Matthew."

In many ways it was an innocent remark not worthy of the flood of fears that inundated her. Could she drown in all those fears? Maybe not drown but certainly get swept off course. Dark emotions blacked out the light on her path. They weren't unexpected but they were unwelcomed.

Putting down her cup, she stood. "Excuse me." Unshed tears glistened, blurring her way to the staircase and up to the bathroom.

Taking her time, she used extra care splashing water on her face and patting it dry in an effort to keep her makeup in place. Deep calming breaths brought tears to her eyes. *If I had a magic wand, I'd go away somewhere, by myself, with no one around. No, no, that's not right.* She stomped her foot in frustration and bent forward to look in the mirror, look past the layer of confusion, look deep into her own eyes for the truth. *I'm afraid.*

Afraid her heart would be broken.

Afraid it was already too late.

Afraid the passion he felt for her now would die and there would be nothing between them, no heat, no warmth, only cold. *I'm cautious and careful, not a coward. I don't think of myself as a coward but I'm struggling here. I need some help to find my way along this twisted path. The Tarot. In the morning I'll ask The Tarot for direction. What to do. Right now what I need to do is pull myself together, go downstairs, and act normal. My son is waiting.*

For Bill she'd be the consummate actress through the remainder of the evening. It shouldn't be difficult. She'd stared in the "perfect marriage show" countless times over the years. Surely, for a couple of hours, she could muster an "everything is all right" performance. Pulling her shoulders back, she raised her chin, firmed her jaw, pasted a smile on her face, opened the door and stepped out. *I can do this. I can do this.* With those words playing in her mind, she strode to the top of the stairs. She stopped for a moment, taking in the sounds of women's voices below and male laughter from the kitchen.

Hand on the banister, she stepped down. *I can do this. I can do this. I can do this.*

35 Past, Present, Future Spread

Matthew and she made love last night, tearing their clothes off as they came through the door, tumbling first on the couch before making it to her bed. *He must have condoms stashed in the cushions.* When he got up to go to work, she'd snuggled down intending to get up as soon as she heard the front door close behind him. The distinctive tone of her cell phone woke her. Groggy, she fumbled around on the nightstand for her phone, answering it just before it went to voice mail.

"I've just hung up from talking to Dennis' attorney," Ms. Lawford said her tone brisk with an undercurrent of surprise. "They want to meet at our earliest convenience. Dennis is now agreeing to the divorce and to you having everything that was on your list."

"I see." And, she did. The loss of his son was the greater loss and he'd let her go in order to keep him. For that she was grateful because it meant this craziness was behind her now.

"What does your schedule look like, Diana?"

"I'm not sure but I have very few things that are locked in. You know my class tonight is one but I'm assuming they want to meet during the day. What about you?"

"I'm booked until Wednesday afternoon."

"I'm open all day so go ahead and negotiate a time with them. I'll be there."

"Consider it done." Ms. Lawford paused. "Do you know why the big turn around?"

"Our son. Bill let Dennis know he wanted nothing to do with him if he continued to treat me this way. I know Dennis told Bill he would be doing this but a part of me doesn't believe it's true. That it will last."

"Smart. Remain cautious. But there is reason to be optimistic. His attorney was very determined to convince me his client is serious about moving forward and ending the hostilities. I could tell he was speaking at his client's behest."

"If I don't answer when you call back, just leave a message. I'll confirm I got it and see you on Wednesday."

"I'll get right on it."

"Good-bye." Diana hung up. Somewhere during the conversation, she'd sat down on the edge of the bed, stunned, light-headed and a bit discombobulated. Every muscle sighed with relief, weak, rootless, and very aware of how much tension she'd held in her body. A new reality awaited and she sat absorbing it: move back into the little house; drive her own car; live without fear of being accosted by Dennis again. *I can start packing now.*

Catching her runaway thoughts, she paused and made a mental list. First, take a shower and get dressed. Second, consult the cards. Third, call Lily and see if she can have lunch with me. A plan in place, Diana padded into the bathroom for her shower, the first step in beginning the rest of her day.

The familiar pattern of contemplating her question, shuffling the cards and laying out the spread calmed her. This morning it took her several minutes of sorting through different words to find the ones for her question. In the end she settled on simple.

"What should I do about my relationship with Matthew?"

She chose the Past, Present, Future spread. With her question asked and the cards shuffled, she laid out the cards.

Past = Four of Wands

Present = The Fool

Future = The Hanged Man

Both The Fool and the Four of Wands had been in previous spreads but she knew she'd never drawn The Hanged Man. She picked up her Journal and pen.

According to the Past Card, I'm really alive and excited about the future. A period of freedom and new choices begin.

The Present Card, The Fool, says I'm unpredictable, open, spontaneous, and adventurous. I'm a free spirit and dreamer---but is this what I should be doing? This card also signifies a new phase in my life---lover? For how long? It's wonderful to feel my body so alive! The card also means I'm to trust in my own ideas and plans no matter what others say---easier if I didn't feel so confused about what is right...

The Hanged Man: the future. The card of contradictions. There are confusing times ahead—I'm to do the opposite of what my instincts tell me to do. My peace of mind will come from making the decision. Put aside selfish interests and be prepared to sacrifice in order to achieve success. I need to leave people and situations alone instead of trying to control them.

I was hoping for something more --- well, that's not true—the cards are specific—do the opposite of my instincts which are to hide from Matthew; to leave; to protect my heart.

I need some time to digest this reading, to sit and let it perk, sink in. I am dreaming now; I'm a free spirit but is this who I will always be or is this an anomaly and I'll revert to my former self. Would Matthew want me as I was rather than as I am?

Time Will Tell

Sit, mull, percolate, ponder, be with --- this I need to do first. Let the meaning from the cards settle in my mind.
In love and light

Diana sat with her thoughts about the message in this card layout. *The most difficult message? To go against my instincts.*

That means I'd stay with Matthew, open my heart, and hope for the best. After so many years of guarding her inner self from Dennis, to open herself to a man was a daunting idea.

Finally she gathered the cards together and returned them to their box, picked up her Journal and pen taking everything to her bedroom where she put them away. Her cell phone was still next to her bed.

Third task in her plan? Call Lily. When she didn't answer, Diana left a message about getting together for lunch or maybe a cup of tea in the afternoon. Since her class was tonight and she'd be picking up Bill and Charlie, her free time to talk with Lily was limited.

Restless from pent-up energy, she paced around the apartment and stopped to look out at the cityscape. While their view didn't come close to matching either the Montgomery or the Murphy houses, it was pleasant and calmed her. If she was home at the little house, she'd take a quick walk around the block. Here, however, the time and effort it took to get outside and then back in through security put a damper on one of her favorite ways to distract herself or sort thing through.

She turned away from the window and paced again. *I just need to keep busy. Work, there's always something to do. I can finish up my emails.* At her computer, deep in thought, by the time her cell phone ring pierced her consciousness, the caller had been transferred to voice mail. When she heard the beep that let her know a message awaited, she dialed in and listened.

Lily's message: *backed-up all day but could do lunch tomorrow. Leave a message if that works.*

Diana called her back and confirmed lunch tomorrow at eleven at their favorite Thai restaurant. At that hour it should be quiet and conducive to their talking about more personal matters. While she was retrieving Lily's message, another call came in; this one from Ms. Lawford. The meeting with Dennis and his attorney was set for four on Wednesday and she needed to block out at least an hour.

After noting these two appointments in her planner, she returned to the office to finish responding to the emails and confirm her preparations for class tonight.

It was almost five o'clock when Matthew's voice announced he was home. She stretched, rubbing the kinks out of the back of her neck as she stood. In addition to Matthew's voice, both Bill and Charlie's eager voices and the sound of pots and pans banging around in the kitchen drew her to the office door.

Bags of food littered the countertop, pans were on the stove. The refrigerator door hung open, one of her pet peeves.

"What's going on?" she asked her voice testy, most likely because that was how she was feeling.

"Hi, Mom," Bill crossed the space and gave her a hug. "Charlie and I are fixing dinner for you and Matt. Hamburgers. We brought everything; well, most everything. You know the meat, buns, onions—we've got this neat recipe we wanted to try out on you. Okay?"

He looked so earnest and hopeful, how could she stay in her curmudgeon role? Rising on her tiptoes, she kissed him on the cheek, "Of course it's okay."

He grinned and turned back to the kitchen area.

"We don't have much time, you know. Class starts at 6:30 and it takes a good thirty minutes to get there."

"We know," the two boys chorused.

Boys. What other word should she use when referring to them? They were not boys but it was hard to see them as men, even calling them "young men" felt awkward. Something she and Lily could talk about, or maybe Matthew would have an idea. *He seems to relate so easily to both Bill and Charlie. Jackson and Daniel have that same trait as does Giovanni. I'm sure Michael does because he gets along so well with Ashley's little ones.*

Back in the office, she packed her briefcase, and set it by the front door before going to her room and changing into her "uniform". Black slacks, a vivid aqua-colored blouse and black jacket. She seldom wore jewelry beyond a pair of stud earrings but decided to add a simple gold chain with a crane pendant she'd seen in Italy. A smile tugged at the memory of her dithering over whether to get it or not. She'd read up on the meaning of "crane" and learned it could reflect recovering something almost extinct in oneself as well as reflecting a sense of protectiveness or a need for secrecy; certainly apropos of her life.

"Dinner's ready."

A frown scrunched her face when she glanced at her watch; more time had passed than she'd planned. They were going to be late for the first class of Spring Term.

As it was they weren't late, rushing into the classroom with three minutes to spare. Introducing Bill and Charlie, having them see her teaching style brought her joy. *What would it be like to have them both living here, to have them take my classes?*

One of her security guards stopped by during the break.

"Just checking, Ms. P. You know, making sure you're okay," he said and asked for her card. "Got some really good people working for me. Hoped you'd have the time to help me put a plan together to keep them."

"Of course I can do that," she'd answered, handing him her card, wondering how she'd missed that he owned the small company.

After class they joined the others at the little coffee shop before she dropped them off at the Montgomerys'.

"Thanks for fixing dinner. The hamburgers were delicious," she told the boys as they left the car. Their hamburgers with Gorgonzola and Bleu Cheese worked into the meat before cooking and caramelized onions on top were huge. Half of her burger was in the refrigerator. *I should tell Matthew to take it for his lunch tomorrow.*

Matthew. He'd been on her mind all during class—he wasn't there. He wasn't enrolled in her class this term. Her mind drifted off. *Everything is different with him gone; different going to the café after class; different walking to my car without his unwavering support.* Of course she'd done a good job tonight. The fact was she'd taught these classes long before she even knew Matthew Houston.

In the parking garage, she gathered her briefcase from the trunk, and headed upstairs. The apartment was quiet: no television, no music—just silence. She put her briefcase in the office and went into the kitchen to get something to drink. A glass of ice water from the pitcher they kept in the refrigerator trailed down her throat. *We both like a glass of cold water. And other things?* Thai, Chinese, Indian foods; curling up on a rainy day with a book or watching television. Neither of them liked housekeeping but they managed to keep the place presentable from Friday to Friday when the service came. That was something she would miss when she moved out. It was amazing how comfortable they'd become with each other in so many little ways.

Matthew's door was ajar. Not open enough to see in, but not shut. Starting towards it, she stopped; she was not going to wake him. He must be tired because the last couple of nights he hadn't got much sleep. She smiled. Neither had she.

Turning, she headed toward her own room, pausing at the door before going inside; puzzled but not knowing why. Opening the door, her hand gripped the knob, her heart caught in her throat. Grandmother Moon was shining through the window, lighting his features with her soft light. He was so handsome, he took her breath away. A few tentative steps between the door and her bed—her knees touched the side of the mattress. The dark shadowed curve of his eyelashes against his cheeks, the rise and fall of his chest, the sound of his breathing mesmerized her.

Why he wanted her still made no sense. But what held her enthralled was her passion for him. She'd only been with Dennis and another guy in college when she and Dennis had broken up. But she'd thought she'd been satisfied by both men. Now she knew better.

Eyelashes fluttered open. Ensnared, no use struggling, caught as she was in Matthew's web: smoky emerald green eyes surrounded by thick black eyelashes, dark hair that curled beguilingly over his ears, soft lips that kissed her senseless, talented roughened hands that brought her to the peak of madness. One of those hands circled her wrist, gently tugged. She swiveled to sit on the edge of the bed rather than tumble on top of him.

He watched her with heavy-lidded eyes that bespoke of pleasure—exceptional pleasure just for her. While maintaining eye contact, she pulled her hand from his, stood, and moved back three steps. Slipping off her jacket, she let it drop to the floor behind her. Her eyes never leaving his, she started with the top button and slowly, one by one unfastened them until she reached the waist band of her slacks. She'd been careful and there were few hints of skin even though her blouse was undone except for the final two buttons. When she started to turn away, he rasped, "No."

A smile of seduction graced her face; power surged through her as she drew her blouse from the waist band. Her hands, covered by her blouse, undid the clasp and zipper of her slacks. She wriggled her hips until they slithered down her legs, pooling on the floor. Stepping out of them, she stood still.

The urge to turn away, to cover her body, her soul was immense. Unwilling to succumb to that urge, to break the spell, she held herself erect, keeping her gaze locked with his. Time stopped. They were tangled in a trap of their own making.

Her body shook, trembled, trembled with anticipation, with passion, with fear. The message from The Tarot: act with confidence. She was a free spirit, a dreamer, a lover. The last two buttons undone, she shrugged the blouse from her shoulders, and let it fall to the floor. Clad only in a peach-colored bra, no panties, peach-colored thigh-high stockings, and her shoes, she stood before him. Stepping out of the shoes, she took one step toward the bed. Her hands reached behind her, unfastened her bra and let it fall to the floor as she took a second step. Her foot on the edge of the bed, she slowly rolled her stocking down her leg, tugged it off, dropped it to the floor. Her other foot on the edge of the bed, she repeated the process.

Matthew's breathing had hitched then grown ragged as he watched her strip.

In that moment she wasn't worried about what he saw; whether he was disgusted by her forty-year old body because she knew with a certainty that he wanted her with a passion that took her breath away. A siren's smile on her lips, she lifted the covers and saw how eager he was—for her. With an innate feminine confidence in her power as a woman, she slipped under the covers and into his waiting arms.

36   DENNIS AND CHANGES

Diana drove the car into their assigned parking slot and rested her head on hands that still gripped the steering wheel. The meeting today with Dennis and his attorney had left her drained, distressed, and too tired to cry. And so she sat, the engine running, her mind numb.

A tap on the window.

Matthew.

With the engine still running, he was stymied when he tried to open the car door. Her neck barely held her head up but with effort she managed to move, to turn the engine off, unlock the door before slumping back against the seat, eyes closed.

"Diana?" he asked concern in his voice.

His arm brushed the front of her jacket as he reached across and unbuckled her seat belt.

"Diana?" he repeated, his concern escalated to worry, anxiety—all for her.

How to respond? With a sigh she opened her eyes enough to see him squatting next to the car.

"I'm all right," she managed in a voice reeking of exhaustion.

"No."

It was so like him to contradict her. If not for the amount of energy to accomplish it, she'd have smiled. Seldom did Matthew confront her—contradicting her was another matter. And there was a difference. Her parents and Dennis confronted; Matthew just quietly disagreed.

Diana focused on her hands, relaxing the digits, removing them from the steering wheel, letting her hands fall into her lap. Matthew picked up her left hand, massaging first the palm and then, one-by-one, each finger. When he finished working on her right hand, he placed it gently back in her lap.

"Neck, please," she whispered and then sighed as one of his large, calloused hands went to work. Her head fell forward. The sensations his touch provoked surged through her body igniting an energy she thought was extinguished.

"Better?"

"Much better. Thank you," she said as she shifted toward him. He looked clean, not like he'd just gotten off a job site. "How did you find me?" *Was that what I want to ask?*

"Security called. Said you were sitting. Car still running. Not like you at all," he replied.

"No, not like me at all," she said shaking her head in quiet agreement.

"Ready to go in?"

Ready to go in, take a long hot shower, change into something comfortable, and go to bed. "Yes, but there are some things in the trunk to take in."

Matthew took the keys from the ignition, pocketing them. He popped the lever to open the trunk and looked inside.

"I'll get the cart."

It took Diana several minutes to get out of the car and gather her briefcase from the back seat. *Moving legs that feel like pillars of cement isn't easy.* By that time Matthew was back with the cart and had loaded the four boxes. One hand at the small of her back, he guided her toward the elevator while pushing the cart with the other.

Someone to lean on literally and figuratively—she had his support. Relaxing, she let Matthew efficiently take care of getting them into the elevator, to their floor and into the apartment. He guided her to her room, divesting her of briefcase and jacket along the way. As he rummaged through her closet, she started to take exception but her rebuke turned to a sigh when he pulled out her oldest pair of sweats and hung them on the hook in the bathroom.

"Do you need help? Can you manage the shower on your own?" he asked in a serious voice with no hint of playful or seductive in its tone or his manner.

"I can manage."

"Do you want me to call Lily? or Sophia?"

Tears glistened, she shook her head. Matthew Houston was the kindest, most considerate, loving man she'd ever known and she'd lost her heart to him. She shook her head again, walked into the bathroom and closed the door before she said anything else, before he guessed he had her heart, before she confessed she loved him.

Diana padded into the living room, her hair still damp, no makeup, wearing her oldest sweats; the color faded, a few stains and tattered cuffs a testament to how well-loved and used they were.

Matthew looked up from behind the breakfast bar as she entered the room, dishes spread out on the counter. Her stomach growled, reminding her it hadn't been fed since early this morning.

"Food," she crossed the room a smile on her face. "What do we have here?" she asked perusing bowls and plates containing fruit, vegetables, cheese, crackers, and dip. "A feast. Thank you, I'm starving."

"Help yourself."

Loading her plate with some of everything, she crossed the room and sat cross-legged on the couch. Behind her, she heard a rustling sound and a pop. When he appeared he carried a full plate for himself and two glasses of champagne.

"Are we celebrating?" she asked her brow quirked as she reached for a glass.

"No." He handed her a glass and gestured toward their plates. "We don't have wine. Champagne seemed like a better choice than beer."

She leaned over and kissed his cheek. "Thank you. I love champagne and it's a treat to have it for no real reason at all."

His jaw tensed when she kissed his cheek and she wondered why, but didn't ask. *Best to let it go.*

"You were later than I thought you'd be."

He sounded casual but she knew better. He'd been more serious, more tense since he'd found her in the car. And it was typical of him to comment, to offer an opening if she wanted to talk. *Do I?* His worry, concern, and wonder about what had happened swirled around her.

"Remember I'd asked Dennis for starts of some of the outside plants?" At his nod she continued. "He dug up and potted smaller bushes and brought them as well as those boxes," she said nodding in their direction. "I took the plants to Sophia's. It just took time to load everything up, drive over there and unload them. I'm sorry. I should have called. I wasn't thinking very clearly by the time the meeting was over."

He shifted away from her, stood, and walked toward the kitchen. A sliver of distress curled in her chest. *Why is he moving away?* And then he was back with the bottle of champagne. He filled their glasses and sat, next to her. The distressed curl relaxed. *He isn't leaving me.*

"Do you want to hear about the meeting?"

"Yes."

She hesitated.

He added, "Whatever you want to tell me."

"I'll tell you the whole story. Dennis and Mr. Harris greeted Ms. Lawford and me with smiles and handshakes. I was caught off guard in some ways and cautious because I didn't trust him."

"And now?"

"And now I'm not sure. I think his desire to have Bill in his life is strong enough that he won't attack me again. During the meeting he was very agreeable. Everything and more on my original list was there. He gave me potted plants when I'd only asked for starts.

"I was stunned when he not only agreed to the divorce but added he hoped I'd consider marriage counseling and try to work things out," she said, her tone cool and distant.

Matthew tensed as he said, "I can understand he'd still want you as his wife."

"I told him it was too late. I don't want to be his wife. Right now I don't want to be anyone's wife."

He didn't move but she sensed he was more distant, more withdrawn. *Is it my voice?* Pausing, she struggled to moderate her voice, to speak in a warmer tone.

"Anyway, he agreed to an uncontested divorce. He brought the documentation that the private investigator has been terminated as well as the pictures and negatives. They're in my briefcase if you want to see them." To her own ears, her voice sounded hollow; not warmer.

How much more should I tell him? He's withdrawing, protecting himself. I owe him the truth of what happened. "He wants, for Bill's sake, to be friends if I won't reconcile with him. He thought counseling would be helpful for us to find a way to be amiable, again for Bill's sake."

"Will you?"

"Be amiable? I'll make an effort. It serves no purpose to be antagonistic. I suppose we'll both attend Bill's graduation, marriage, that sort of thing but there's no reason for us to be together when Bill visits. And as for the counseling? No, I don't think so. If I can't manage to be amiable, then I'll get some counseling for myself. No, I don't see any need to be in counseling with him at all.

"I left the financial settlement to Ms. Lawford to work out. I'd already moved half of our joint bank accounts into my own accounts but there are investments, that sort of thing to divide up. And then there's the house. I don't want it but I'll get some of the equity or something." She turned to him, placed her hand on his arm, felt the muscles bunch. "It isn't that I don't think I deserve my fair share or anything like that. I gave Ms. Lawford carte blanc because I trust her to protect my interests. I'd rather not spend that much time with Dennis, to tell the truth."

His arm relaxed, his energy shifted, and he move toward her. "If I had a magic wand," she whispered. "I'd have this all over and done with and be on with the rest of my life."

Gathering her in his arms, he kissed her forehead, held her close.

Sighing she relaxed and melted into his warmth, the tension of the day lessening.

"Bed," his voice was husky. "I want to hold you in bed."

She leaned back.

He let her go.

"Okay," she said standing and holding out her hand.

His arm around her waist, they walked to her room where he took his shirt off, toed off his shoes, and reached down to tug off his socks. He stood before her, his heat radiating, encircling her. Slowly his hands slipped under her top and gently lifted it up and over her head. Tossing it aside, he pushed her pants down over her hips, bent and peeled them off. Picking her up, they dropped to the floor.

She reached behind her, pushed the covers aside. Was the quiver from the coolness of the sheets on her bare skin or because he followed her down, nudging her toward the middle of the bed to make room for him. Pulling the covers up, he settled her against him, spoon-fashioned. Although his arousal bumped against her buttocks, he gave her this time to be held, to be cherished. Her eyelids drifted close. Sleep overcame her.

What was that? Matthew was already out of bed and out of the bedroom. Diana struggled to wake from the deep sleep of exhaustion.

Voices. *Bill?*

It was almost eleven. *Bill? Something must be wrong.*

Scrambling out of bed, she grabbed her robe from the closet shrugging it on as she headed toward the bedroom door.

Bill is here talking to Matthew a mile-a-minute. Distracted by the sight of Matthew standing bare footed, bare chested, tousled hair, bristly chin—so handsome he took her breath away. *OMG,*

*Bill is here and he's seen us like this. How did he get in here?
What happened to security?*

"The guy remembered me from the other night and let me
come up because I had all these boxes for Mom."

"I see," Matthew replied in a tone that indicated he didn't.

"Mom, look what I brought?" He bent over one of the boxes,
pulled the top open, and gently lifted out something wrapped in
a towel. Reverently he removed the towel and held out the
bronze statue of the slim woman reaching up, her fingers
catching the stars. "When I saw Dennis tonight, you know, for
dinner. He was telling me he'd packed up everything you'd
wanted and given it to you. I couldn't believe you didn't have
this on your list." He set the statue on the table, his hand
caressing it as he did so. "I remember you raising your arms just
like this every time you passed her. Don't you remember that,
Mom?"

She nodded. A catch in her throat blocked her voice. *Yes, I
do remember that.* Bill dove into yet another box and pulled out
a fairy figurine. One he'd given her for her birthday a few years
ago. *I hadn't asked for them because Dennis had given me some
of them and I wanted nothing more from him.*

"Thank you." Tears filled her eyes as she choked out the
words.

"Don't cry, Mom," he said as he put the fairy figurine down
and came toward her.

She smiled, not her brightest, but a smile nonetheless. "Oh,
Bill, I don't have the words right now to tell you how much this
means to me. Thank you. You've filled my heart to overflowing
with joy."

Bill turned to Matthew. "She gets this way when she's really
happy: all sappy, crying, blubbering. It's so cool to do this to
her." He laughed.

She playfully batted him on the arm. Matthew handed her tissue. She blew her nose, tucked the tissue in her pocket, and hugged her amazing son. He hugged her back, holding her for longer than usual.

"She gets like this too," he called over his shoulder to Matthew. "But you probably know all this anyway."

She froze.

He felt it and stepped back. "What's wrong, Mom?"

She just stood there, her mouth hanging open.

"What? Did I do something?" he asked with genuine confusion on his face.

Her son had no idea how those few words affected her and she was glad he didn't. *I'm not ready to share my feelings about my relationship with Matthew. It's too soon and they're too scary.*

"Your Mom's had a long, tiring day," Matthew said. "How about talking more tomorrow?" he added guiding Bill toward the door.

Being so vulnerable, so totally exposed overwhelmed her and she grasped the back of the couch to keep from sinking to the floor.

"Is it because of what I said about you knowing her? If it is, I don't know why she'd be upset. I think it's great—"

"Bill," Matthew's voice was firm, "whatever you think is going on between your mother and me, stop." He held up his hand. "If there *is* something going on between your mother and me, it's between us."

Transfixed she saw him reach out to Bill and lay his hand on her son's shoulder. In a softened voice he said, "And should there ever be something between us; it's your mother's place to inform you."

Bill turned back toward her. "I'm sorry if I got out of line, Mom. Really, I didn't mean anything."

"I know. I'm just tired." She tried to smile but her face was numb. The tears of joy that glimmered in her eyes a few minutes ago were gone. "I'll see you tomorrow?"

"Plan on dinner. Here. Tomorrow. Just you." Matthew stood by the door.

"I'll come by around three, Mom. That way we can spend some time together before Matt gets home and we have dinner. Okay?"

She nodded and he was gone.

The door shut, the dead bolt turned.

Silence.

When she turned toward the foyer, Matthew stood there, watching her.

"Do you want to be alone?"

She shook her head.

In seconds he was next to her, swooping her up, carrying her back to her room, and dropping her unceremoniously on the bed.

"What?" Her mouth opened in shock, outrage.

"Snap out of it." His tone was harsh.

"I—" She started, clutched her robe and struggled to sit up.

"Don't Diana," he bent over her, his serious face inches away. "Don't lie to yourself or to me. It's one thing if you don't want to acknowledge what we have with your son." He straightened and plowed fingers through his hair. "But don't deny you have feelings for me or that I have them for you."

Sitting on the edge of the bed, he stroked her hair back from her face; let his fingers trail down her neck and rest in the hollow. "We don't have to name them." He pulled her close, his breath ruffled her hair. "Just don't lie to yourself."

37   Sorting Things Out

The next day Bill did come early and they had a long talk about many things including her relationship with Matthew. She'd known at the time her son had not meant anything by his comments, just trying to jokingly reassure her he was okay with whatever she and Matthew did. However, his glowing opinion of Matthew had been tarnished by what had happened last night.

Once Matthew was home, he and Bill spent time out on the balcony while she finished putting the final touches on dinner. Her curiosity pricked, she openly watched them talk and shake hands obviously coming to some agreement before standing shoulder to shoulder, each with his right foot resting on the bottom railing, each with his arms on the upper looking out over the part of Fremont that made up their view. By the time she called them in to dinner the easy camaraderie and banter was back. Because she knew the conversation was about her, she doubted either of them would tell her what they'd talked about.

Diana stood in the lobby of the airport surrounded by a mix of people who'd come to see Bill and Charlie off. Memories of their two weeks together crowded her mind. Laughter, male laughter to be exact broke through her reverie. Jackson, Charlie, Bill, Matthew and Daniel's heads were thrown back, mouths agape in belly-deep laughter. Since none of the women were laughing, it must have been a male thing. Bill looked so relaxed and happy. *I'll miss him more than ever.*

Dennis chose not to come most likely because Bill had asked him not to. He still called Dennis by his first name but was now talking to and willing to spend time with his dad. Dennis may have made up some ground but he still had a lot of work to do.

Too soon the young men (she'd finally decided to refer to Bill and Charlie as young men) were off through security, striding down the concourse toward their respective flights. Looking over at Lily, she caught her eye, and smiled. Not really a bright smile, but as they had sorted out over their lunch this past week, their relationships with their sons were better than they had hoped for a year ago.

Jackson approached his wife, slipped his arm around her waist, and leaned down to whisper something in her ear. She nodded, briefly leaned into him, before straightening.

"Jackson put a pot of spaghetti sauce on before we left. Any of you who can come on such short notice are invited to show up between now and five o'clock when the master," Lily flashed a saucy grin and winked at her husband, "says it will be ready. There's nothing to bring; just yourselves and an appetite."

The scent of lime, the heat, the energy she associated with Matthew encircled her before his hand rested at the small of her back.

"What do you want to do?"

What she wanted to do was twitch her nose and have everything packed and moved back to the little house; the discussion she knew she had to have with Matthew over; and her life firmly on a new track. "I'm fine with going over there or not. We both enjoy Jackson's spaghetti but we do have food at the apartment and can easily make dinner ourselves."

His hand slowly stroked her lower back up, down, back, forth almost but not quite a circle. It didn't ease the dread lodged in the pit of her stomach when thinking of that conversation: the one about their relationship and where it was going; what would happen when they no longer shared the apartment. Officially they needed to move out by the fifteenth. Since it was the third, they had twelve days. However, with Dennis having called off his investigators and cooperating with the divorce, there was no reason she couldn't move back earlier; no reason except for the dark-haired, green-eyed, lover extraordinaire, working his magic on her body in the middle of the airport.

"Let's go have spaghetti," she said, looking over her shoulder.

"If that's what you want."

"Right now it is what I want. I think Logan and Hunter will be there and probably Sophia and Gabriella. I'll be able to keep myself distracted," she said her voice trailing off at the flash of heat, desire in his eyes. If she and Matthew went home, thoughts of Bill would be squelched for quite some time. The flush rose through her body, her cheeks a rosy color. His lips tilted, amusement reflected in his eyes. She staunched the urge to reach out and touch him in any way, closed her eyes for a fraction of a second and turned away. Turned back to the safety of her friends who were already starting to move off.

"Count on us," she called after Lily who acknowledged she'd heard with a wave of her hand.

Diana was grateful last night for the deserted hallway. By the time they reached the apartment door, her unbuttoned blouse was pulled from her slacks, her hair disheveled from his roughened hands, and her lips swollen from his kisses. There was something heady about the intensity of his love-making—he'd turned to her twice before dawn.

Now in the shower, he held her with the water pounding down, his arms wrapped around her, his cheek resting against her head. Slowly their breathing eased. His hands began to caress her back and then stopped. He raised his head, his hands moving to her arms before he shifted and space appeared between them.

She looked up and was astounded to see desire flickering in the depths of his eyes as he smiled, leaned toward her, and gently brushed he lips with his.

"Close your eyes," he softly ordered.

She did.

"Hold still," he whispered as he nibbled on her ear. His hands no longer touched her but his lips trailed soft kisses over her face. The washcloth glided along her wet skin as he soaped her. He was very thorough, having her lift her legs so he could wash her feet, even between her toes. At one point, knees weak, she came close to falling when he started washing her hair, and massaging her neck and scalp. Once he'd touched, soaped, and rinsed every inch of her, he kissed her: a long drugging kiss that left her clinging to him.

Turning the water off, he stepped away to grab a towel. He guided her toward the vanity, stood behind her, and watched in the mirror as he moved the towel across her body and tousled her hair until it was damp.

Every inch of her skin was relaxed and aware—sated with their loving through the night - aroused and yet not. The thought to give back to him what he'd given to her: kisses across his chest, nip his nipples, caress his penis quashed when he stepped away.

Taking her robe off the hook in the bathroom, he slipped it around her shoulders and tied it at her waist. Another one of those long, drugging kisses left her dazed and wanting followed.

"I'll start breakfast," he said giving her a peck on the cheek.

Spellbound she watched his bare buttocks, his long legs move as he strode away—grace in motion. Minutes after he was gone, she was still standing there lost in a fog of sensual satiation.

The practical part of her mind could think, knew she hadn't moved, knew she needed to get dressed, needed to talk to Matthew, needed to sort things out. The dreamer part didn't want to move, get dressed, much less talk to Matthew and sort things out.

The sound of him moving around in the kitchen, the smell of bacon and coffee permeated her room. Slowly she moved to the closet choosing an older pair of sweats: no stains, no frayed cuffs but certainly well-worn. In front of the bathroom mirror, she started her make-up routine. Mascara wand halfway to her eyes, she stopped. *Why would I put makeup on now? He's seen me stripped bare in every sense of the words.*

Looking closely, she peered at her reflection. *What is different? The fine lines fanning out from the corners of my eyes, the slightly deeper lines etched around my mouth? I don't see any gray hair but then I don't expect to. Neither of my parents had a gray hair until in their late sixties.*

Taking off the robe, she hung it on the hook, and turned back to look in the mirror. With a critical eye she studied her body, turning this way and that. *For forty I don't look too bad. I'm still a size eight. A gift of smaller breasts is no bad sagging.* Turning away she pulled on her sweat's bottoms. Moving into the bedroom, she got a bra from the dresser putting it on before adding the sweatshirt.

Still barefoot, she stood before her altar, raised her arms in prayer, and let the words come into her mind. *I am a beloved child of The Universe and The Universe protects and guides me as does The Tarot.* Lowering her arms, she remained in front of her sacred space. *Not so long ago my view of myself, my body in particular, was negative. I how Matthew would see me and how others would see me when we're together. We've been lovers for nine passionate, glorious days and he still sees me as desirable, beautiful, sexy, intelligent. Maybe I really am.*

The Tarot's message was to resist her instinct, to follow her dreams with confidence, to look to the future.

The Future. Head bowed as emotions spiked. *I want the next eleven days with Matthew. I want to feel safe, cherished, respected, cared about - to feel my body on fire. If I am selfish to want more time with him, so be it.*

At a soft knock she turned to see Matthew standing at the bedroom door, his look expectant.

"Hungry?"

"I'm famished," she smiled and walked toward him. "I smell bacon. Did you fix eggs?"

"French toast."

She rose on her toes, pressed a quick kiss to his lips and slipped past him.

Breakfast was a quiet affair. They both ate with relish, feeding bodies that had been depleted with a night of loving. Because Matthew had cooked, she cleaned up the kitchen taking stock of what was in the refrigerator. Tonight was her night to fix for dinner. They had the fixing for a tossed green salad but not much else. She pulled out two steaks from the freezer and set them in the refrigerator to thaw.

Matthew was on the couch, surfing through channels on the television.

What am I going to do? Pick up a book and sit beside him? Return to my room? Go into the office and work? If I start a conversation, what will I say?

The television clicked off. Matthew rummaged through the magazines on the coffee table, picked one up, and begin to leaf through it.

Every instinct told her to go into her office and get some work done. Every instinct told her to protect herself. Every instinct told her to pack up and leave now.

She started to walk out of the kitchen area but stopped.

"Matthew, would you like your coffee refilled?"

"Sure," he glanced over his shoulder at her, smiled and held up his cup.

Taking his cup, she returned to the kitchen and filled it, very glad he drank it black. She shook so hard she sloshed the coffee all over the counter; the idea of adding sugar and cream daunting. Her own glass of tonic in her other hand, she returned to the couch. *Wish there was a tonic to inspire courage.*

"Thanks." He took the cup from her outstretched hand without really looking at her, brought it to his lips and sipped before he rested it on his knee and turned another page.

"When you have a moment," she began in her most professional voice and stopped. *This isn't how I want to sound.* "I mean, there is something I'd like to talk over with you when you have the time." *That's better, more inviting.*

It was so slight she might have missed it, but she was watching him so intently she saw the shudder. *What is that all about?*

He tossed the magazine on the table.

Concentrating on what she wanted to say, she was initially confused when he didn't turn toward her. His face, reflected in the blank screen of the television, wasn't clear enough to see the look in his eyes. *Why did he look fatigued, defeated? What's happened?*

"What's wrong?" She laid her hand on his shoulder. He him flinch. "Matthew, please, tell me what's wrong."

"Just say what you have to say, Diana. Just say it."

She'd never heard him sound so weary, despondent.

"It can wait," she heard herself say in an effort to comfort him.

"No, just say it; get it over with."

She hesitated. "If you're sure."

He nodded.

"I know I talked about moving back to the little house this weekend, you know, after Bill left; but I've been thinking. The apartment is available until the fifteenth." He hadn't moved, hadn't turned to her, hadn't said anything. She thought his breathing more labored, as if he were carrying a heavy load.

The urge to stop, run into her bedroom and shut the door surged. *What's going on right now?* Closing her eyes, remembering the words of The Tarot to do the opposite of her instincts, she wrapped her arms around her middle, and said the words that could bring her great pleasure or unbearable pain.

"If it's all right with you, I'd like to stay until the fifteenth."

38 Until April 15

Arms wrapped tight around her waist, Diana waited, statue-like. Waited for what seemed an excruciatingly long time for Matthew to do something: to speak, to move, to show he cared. Tears welled in her eyes, drops peeking over the edge, sliding down her cheeks. Her stomach clenched, roiling with nausea. *I need to leave, get to my room. I'm going to be sick.*

A part of her frozen, frozen in grief, frozen in panic: an odd combination. Another part of her angry: angry at herself and angry at Matthew. At herself for being so stupid to show him how much she cared about him. At him for making her feel cherished and then turn away from her when she reached out. A jumble of words tumbled in her mind, a jumble of emotions created chaos in her body.

Matthew moved to a crouch in front of her, his arms outstretched. His hands gently rubbing up and down her arms freed her from her paralysis.

"How dare you!" she shouted jerking free of him. "How dare you!" She batted at his hands.

"Diana? What's wrong?" Matthew rose and stepped back. "Diana?" His voice was calm, quiet, his brow and shoulders raised, his hands palms up. "Help me here, Diana. I don't know what I've done to have you so angry with me. Please, tell me so I can fix it."

"There's nothing to fix. You-you... ." The tears flowed in earnest now, she gulped air but still her legs would not move, would not stiffen so she could stand, would not carry her away. She sat, spine rigid, arms wrapped around her waist, holding herself tight to keep from breaking apart, breaking into a pile of broken pieces right in front of him.

"Diana. I'm sorry." He looked contrite, anxious.

"What are you apologizing for?" She hated hearing the derision, the challenge in her voice but couldn't seem to stop. *Why don't I just stand up and walk away?* In the past she would have because it was an effective way of protecting herself: from her parents' endless criticism and Dennis' infidelity. But here she was, instead of leaving she remained facing this man who'd become so important to her she'd jumped into the void, risked her inner self.

Finally she managed to stand: righteously upright. Even knowing she hurt only herself by her posturing didn't help, didn't stop it.

Trust. I am a Beloved Child of The Universe. Her prayer to The Universe was to protect her; to keep her safe; to be with her. *Now is the time to trust The Universe will once more be with me, guide and protect me, keep me safe from myself maybe more than from Matthew.*

Release. Just let go. Her breath whooshed out. She dragged it back, deep, fully into her body. Her shoulders relaxed a fraction;

her breathing hitched but she let it out and breathed back in. Now that the tension was leaving her body, exhaustion threatened to bring her to her knees. *If I don't sit I'll fall down. Here or in my room?*

Lose. Diana brushed the wetness from her face with the sleeve of her top; took another deep breath, lifted her chin. *If there is any hope for us at all, I must stay.*

Backbone. Now is the time to rely upon it. She took the few steps back to the couch and perched on the edge.

Matthew sat, not in his usual slouch but more focused, more at attention, showing he was present in all ways.

The silence enveloped them. Taking a few moments, she sorted her thoughts so she was coherent when she spoke.

Matthew fidgeted and spoke first.

She almost smiled as it was so like him, facing things head on.

"I don't know what I did, Diana," he said, his voice calm, his face showing strain, his eyes troubled.

"You didn't do anything." Right then she felt like a prim and proper old woman. Haggard, tear-stained face, mussed hair, no make-up, hands fisted in her lap, almost falling off the couch she sat so close to the edge.

"You said "How dare you" to me. I don't understand what that was about?" Again his voice was one of reason; almost dispassionate except she could see how tightly he controlled himself, his emotions.

She couldn't answer him directly. And actually cringed at the idea of telling him how much his love-making last night and this morning had meant. *I don't know what he'd do, what he'd say.*

"I mentioned staying here until the fifteenth if that was all right with you. You didn't answer." There she said it again. It was scary but not as terrifying as it had been the first time.

He's talking to me and I'm not listening. She interrupted. "Matthew, please start over with whatever you were saying. I'm afraid I missed the beginning."

How different this is. He isn't sighing in an exaggerated manner or making some disparaging remark about my intelligence or attention span. I'm drifting again. He stopped talking. *Did he know when I drifted off?*

"Do you have any idea how long I've been in love with you?" His fingers caressed her lips as he slightly shook his head. "I don't think you do. I don't think you have a clue how I felt about you a year ago; how drawn I felt to you; how much I fought my attraction to you.

"I knew you were married: wedding ring." He grinned that quirky lop-sided one she loved. "I wouldn't put a move on you but I wanted to." His intense gaze captured her, held her prisoner. "Do you know I used to dream about you? Dream about unwrapping you, like a precious gift? Dream about making love to you all night?"

He isn't even embarrassed, talking about his feelings for me, his attraction, his desire. Her skin flushed with heat as he talked. *Will I ever be as comfortable with my body, with our love-making, with our relationship as Matthew?*

A slight smile quirked his lips. *I wonder what my expression looks like?*

He'd stopped talking and looked so serious. "You took me by surprise." His eyes darkened with a look she knew very well. "My best dream coming true and yet not. You only talked about until the fifteenth. I want you for the rest of my life. I guess I was trying to sort out what to say. No, that's not right. More like how to say I want you far longer than until the fifteenth."

Her breathing constricted again. *How does he do that? Take my breath away—so open in sharing his hopes and dreams about us.* Words stuck in her throat, unshed tears glistened. Ruthlessly she quashed them. Now was not the time to give in to tears. Balanced on the edge of the couch, rigid with tension, she balanced remaining silent with speech.

"I-I-I don't know about longer. I-I-I'm-well, that is to say, I'd like a little more time. You know. Until the fifteenth. And then. Well, I-I-I haven't let myself think beyond that."

"Until the fifteenth then." He sighed such a deep heart-felt sigh it touched her heart. "I'm going to be honest here, Diana. You may not like to hear this but I've got to say it."

She braced herself, elation and fear battling in her stomach.

"I'm not giving up. I'm going to use this time to convince you that we are right together."

She smiled. Not the smile of a siren; a rather wobbly one instead. A wobbly smile that meant she would not fight him on this.

He reached for her.

She willingly sought the comfort of his arms. As they closed around her that sense of rightness, of place; that this was where she belonged engulfed her. This time she relaxed with it. *Trust, release, let go.* Her instincts screamed for her to leave but they were soon drowned out by the only sound in her ear: Matthew's heart.

39 AFTER APRIL 15

A routine of sorts developed. Matthew left for work each morning; Diana remained at home, breathless from his parting kiss. Her consulting business was slowly growing. Referrals from former students added contracts with two more companies for personnel services. Smaller companies and start-ups were her main customers: too cash poor to have a formal personnel department but recognizing the need for one.

Ms. Lawford kept in touch with her regarding the divorce proceedings.

The remaining days were flying by.

One evening Matthew took her to see his house. Everything she'd known about it paled to the reality of stately Victorian building.

"How far behind are you?" she asked.

"Not much," he replied as he sketched out his ideas for renovating the kitchen.

"When did you last work on it?" she pried.

"Stop, just stop, Diana. It's a big project made up of little ones. And because it's over a hundred years old, it will always have something or another that needs work."

"It's lovely," she said her hand on the newel post at the bottom of the staircase.

"It'd been badly neglected when it came on the market. Original owners had passed it on to family who didn't care about it. If it broke, it stayed broke. But, they didn't destroy anything: lots of original plasterwork on the ceilings. All the woodwork is original, he said pointing out the details as they toured the house.

The quality of his renovation work in the master bedrooms, bathrooms, and living and dining rooms was creating a real showcase. He called it 'sweat equity'. She saw it as much more.

Upstairs he'd eliminated smaller rooms making two master suites and three additional bedrooms. At this time, the main floor consisted of a large living room, formal dining room, a music room off the foyer just perfect for a home office and a fifties kitchen. Matthew had already knocked out a couple of walls, and as he explained his plan, she could envision the gourmet kitchen and great room beyond.

She wasn't surprised when Jackson and Daniel's names were mentioned. Jackson was an architect and Daniel had finished restoring his old Victorian. Listening to Matthew talk about his plans as well as showing her the work he'd done was interesting and informative. *How many people know how much time it takes to scrape off one hundred years of paint? I do.*

Once the tour was over, he swept her up in his arms and carried her into his master bedroom. Carefully laying her on the bed, he made slow sweet love to her.

"Move here," he said. "Love you, want you here."

Surprise and terror warred—terror won out.

"I need to move back to the little house. I need more time."

He didn't argue, didn't say anything more but he did hold her tight against him until they dressed and returned to the apartment. Those last few days before the fifteenth, although they were still lovers, out of bed he seemed distant.

Matthew took off from work early on the fifteenth and together they packed their belongings having declined offers to help from The Circle, Jackson and Daniel.

Since they'd agreed to move her to the little house first and then go on to his, Matthew's things were the first items to be loaded on the truck. He came through the door with the cart for another load: her office. He looked strained and even though he hadn't brought it up again, she knew how much he wanted her to move in with him.

But to act on that? Nausea threatened every time she allowed the thought to settle in her mind. Quelling this bout, she continued to set the smaller boxes on top of the larger ones he'd stacked on the cart. As he left with the last load, Diana grabbed her suitcases and took a last look around the apartment that had been a place of refuge, of healing, of discovery before she lifted her chin and strode out the door.

"Thank you, Matthew," Diana said as she slumped against the door frame. "I really do appreciate your helping me like this."

"No problem."

"I'll be right behind you to help unload," she offered.

"Not necessary."

His withdrawal, the loss of his warmth, his energy, his focus hit hard. *So this is what my life will be like without him.*

"If you don't feel up to coming back here for dinner, I'll bring it over." Another offering.

"No."

He ran a hand through already disheveled hair and scrubbed the back of his neck, his other hand shoved in a back pocket.

"Matthew," she said and took a step closer. "Please let me help you."

He locked eyes with her; his emerald green gaze fierce. His mouth twisted in a wry grimace. "You really have no idea, do you? How hard this is," he said anguish in his words.

"I have a hard time wrapping my mind around the fact that you want me at all," she replied.

"Hell, Diana. What do I have to do?" he said, his voice rose in frustration.

"There isn't anything for you to do, Matthew. This isn't about you. It's about me figuring out who I am in this new part of my life. I'm not Dennis's wife. I'm not Bill's mother in the same way I've been for nineteen years. I just need some time to sort this out for myself, that's all. Can you give me a little more time?"

Tears welled but she held them back. The bile of panic spiked and a desperate need to go to him, to pull him into her arms drew her to him.

"I don't want to lose you, Matthew," she whispered the words as she wrapped her arms around herself. *Maybe I never had him to lose.* As she looked at his still tortured expression, she pushed that thought aside. Taking one step toward him, her arms now hanging at her sides, she took another step and yet another until she pressed against him. Her arms wrapped around his neck as she rose on her toes.

"Let's get you unpacked, fed, and tucked into bed for the night," she whispered in his ear as she nibbled on its lobe. She pressed against him more firmly, let her fingers roam through his thick dark hair, used her body to entice, to coax him to let her come with him.

She felt his capitulation as his body relaxed, his arms enclosed around her, his chin rested on her head.

"What am I going to do with you?" He tilted her chin, lowered his head, and kissed her.

"Stay with me tonight? Or let me stay with you?"

"I can do that. But what about tomorrow?" He held her head pressed against his chest.

His heart beat: thump, thump, thump—strong beats in a dependable rhythm so like him. A strong and dependable man, but so much more: generous, kind, caring, protective, and loving both physically and emotionally. He cared about her, wanted her, desired her.

A part of her was still confused as to why she hadn't decided to move in with him. She'd gone so far as to talk to Sophia and Lily whose counsel was to follow her instincts. The Tarot's was to do the opposite. On some level it was important to take this time to sort things out, to be certain this was the right path for her; this was the right time for her; that her highest good would be served.

"Tomorrow you'll go to work and I'll go to my appointments. Tomorrow night we'll decide what we'll do about dinner and whether or not we spend the night together. We are here, Matthew. Right here now. Don't push me away today because I don't know about tomorrow."

His body shifted, pulled away and he sighed.

"Let's go then."

"I'll be right behind you. I'm going to get a few things from the freezer and fix you dinner tonight."

"Nope. We'll get take-out of some kind. My kitchen needs work."

"Mexican and beer from a bottle?" she asked. So light, so young, she was floating on air. Impulsively she gave him a saucy grin. "I'll be a minute. I need to get my nightgown, robe, and slippers."

He laughed, a genuine full-bodied laugh. Tension melted as the first sounds rippled past her. He reached out, lifted her off her feet and he crushed her to him.

"No need," he whispered as he nuzzled her neck. "No need at all."

40   DIVORCED

The champagne cork popped and the bubbly spilled out, coursing down the bottle, frothing across Jackson's hands. He deftly poured it into the four flutes on the counter, passed the glasses around and raised his in a toast.

Four hands held the four glasses, clinking them together. Jackson looked at the three women facing him: Lily, Sophia, and Diana. "To the future; may it hold all of your heart's desires."

"Why Jackson, what a lovely toast," Lily leaned over and kissed his cheek.

Diana sipped her champagne and accepted the congratulations of the others. Ms. Lawford had spearheaded the divorce negotiations once Dennis had dropped his objections. All Diana had done was show up, read the papers, and sign where indicated. It was the last day of April and that morning the judge had signed the papers granting the uncontested divorce. No longer was she Dennis' wife, no longer was she married. She was free.

Except for the few weeks I lived in the little house, I've never lived alone. It's surreal. Her mind functioned on another plane, separate from her body, as if she were an observer, detached or maybe suspended. *Strange because I know I'm real, know I'm here, can feel the effervescence of the champagne on my tongue.*

Ahead of her? Experiencing life living on her own. *Not really a true test because Matthew and I spend most nights together at either his place or the little house.* She stopped for a moment in her meandering thoughts. *I still think of the house as "the little house", not "my house" or even "Lily's house". It's unsettling to have no place I call my own.*

As she tuned back in to her friends, a knock on the front door sounded. Matthew strode into the room.

"She's a free woman, Houston," Jackson called out, his jovial chuckle hanging in the air.

Matthew stopped in front of her, a look of relief and hope on his face. He reached for her hands, bowed his head and rested his forehead against hers.

"Done?" he whispered.

"Yes."

"Good." He dropped her hands, his arms slipping to encompass her.

That feeling of rightness enveloped her and she relaxed against his strong body, letting him bear her weight. He held her with such gentleness, as if she was made of the finest most fragile crystal.

Silence. Expectant gazes bored through the rightness.

"Champagne?" she asked, her words muffled against his shirt. "To celebrate?"

"Sure." Matthew dropped his arms and stepped back accepting the glass of champagne Lily held out.

"Would you like a water chaser?" Jackson asked. "And, I've got beer in the frig if you'd prefer."

"Water and then a beer would be great," Matthew moved around the kitchen island next to Jackson.

Knowing it wasn't wise to stand there in front of everyone wrapped in Matthew's arms didn't erase the wave of loss, of loneliness that crashed over her when he stepped away.

Sophia took her hand. "Why don't we sit in the living room and have another glass of champagne?"

Diana glanced in the direction of the fireplace and saw Lily already arranging the ice bucket and newly opened bottle on the table in front of the couch. Her glass was refilled as soon as she sat down.

"Our own toasts," Lily began, "although I do think Jackson's was excellent."

"He's come a long way in the past year," Sophia commented, "and all for the love of you, my dear."

"He didn't come as far as it might appear. He was much more in tune with the spirits of places and things than he admitted." Lily grinned and glanced toward the kitchen.

Sophia lifted her glass and touched the other two, smiling as she looked directly at Diana.

"May you find true joy in your future. May you know with a soul-deep certainty that you are loved. May you believe in the reality of your worth."

Lily shifted forward on her chair to clink her glass with Sophia's and then Diana's. She held Diana's gaze with her own, reached over and rested her free hand on Diana's knee.

"My concern is that in your fear, your disbelief, you will retreat into your head thereby abandoning your heart, and in the end be safe but alone. Therefore my prayer is that you find your way through the doubt and worry to the glory and the wonder of love. It is your right to have a man in your life, one who will hold you above all others; who will love you unconditionally; who will be loyal and faithful in all ways."

41 ELIZABETH

Beltane

Diana stood on Sophia's patio watching the scene before her. Jackson and Matthew, who had been invited last night, stood together watching as Logan directed Ashley's children in a Maypole dance around one of the supporting columns of the pergola. Since Lily and Elizabeth's marriages and men attending the Winter Solstice Ceremony in Ireland, it felt right to invite them to this Ceremony.

The dance came to an end. Applauding, Diana walked to the living altar of flowers surrounding a multi-hued green Victorian gazing ball. When they were gathered in a circle, arms raised to the sky, they invited the spirits of renewal to join them. One-by-one they called upon their own spirit guides or guardians to come into the circle.

The energy strengthened and golden light flooded through her, shimmered behind her now closed eyes, traveled from her bare feet through her body and out her crown chakra. All darkness banished replaced by gentle, glowing, golden light. Her body floated, suspended in this other illuminated realm.

She hummed, and then began softly singing one of her favorite songs, "Now I Walk In Beauty". The others joined her, their voices coming together in a kind of harmony of lighter and heavier tones. As the last note faded, Diana opened her eyes and witnessed the wonder on each woman's face. After eight years and with them all being so different, when they came together like this they shared a similar experience.

"Elizabeth," Gabriella whispered their missing member's name. "Do you feel it? When I focus on Elizabeth, something doesn't feel right."

Diana went within, focused on Elizabeth and felt discord. A glance around the circle told her everyone else did also.

Something was wrong with Elizabeth.

Once again they raised their arms in pray, calling upon The Universe, Great Spirit to watch over Elizabeth. Quietly they said the words that released their spirits, guides, and guardians and closed the circle.

"Let's call and see what's going on." Hunter spoke first. "If we all have the sense that something is amiss, something is."

As a group they filed into the house, got their cell phones, and turned them on. Diana turned when she heard Lily gasp.

"What's wrong?"

"I've a message from Michael," Lily was already punching the buttons to listen.

Diana saw tears come into Lily's eyes as she lowered the phone, pressed more buttons and then held the phone out so they could all hear Michael's voice coming to them from the speaker phone.

"She needs you." His voice broke with emotion.

Diana thought he might be crying.

"She lost—Dear God, she lost—"

He was struggling to tell them something was lost. At that instant she knew with a certainty what was confirmed by Michael's next words.

"The baby."

Jackson came to stand behind Lily, his hand resting gently on her shoulder. Matthew stood behind her, his hand on her waist.

What were they to do? What could they do? She knew the others were as stunned as she was. They all knew how much Elizabeth wanted to be a mother.

And on Beltane? A time when new life is beginning to sprout from the earth.

Without speaking they came together again, arms around each other, heads bowed as they sent healing prayers and streams of love to Elizabeth and Michael. As one they raised their heads and looked at each other, seeing sadness and determination mirrored in each other's eyes. Diana no longer wondered how or why; it just was.

"Who can go to her?" Sophia looked around at each of them. "I can take a week off."

"I've our Spring Recital coming up," Hunter's voice was bleak. "I don't see how I can go."

Each of them had a project or commitment that tied them to Fremont but each could go for a week.

"There is a way to do this," Lily spoke with determination. "I just know there's a way. We just have to find it."

"The Cauldron's funds would provide for our airfares," Sophia said. "We can always build it up again."

"I think we need to call Michael and see what has happened, how Elizabeth is, before we make any plans." Diana hoped she didn't sound too managing.

"I'll call Elizabeth," Gabriella volunteered.

"Since Michael called me, I'll call him back," Lily started walking away, her fingers flying over the keys of her phone as she made the call.

Diana turned to see Jackson and Matthew taking the younger children outside to play in the yard. Ashley looked dazed; Logan bewildered. Hunter pulled Logan into her arms, speaking in a low voice. Logan's shoulders sagged and she leaned into her mother's strength.

Sophia had already reached Ashley when the thought crossed Diana's mind she needed, actually wanted, to be doing something, anything rather than standing here, her arms dangling at her sides.

Drawn by an invisible force, she wandered toward the back bedroom, knowing it was where she needed to be. Stopping at the open door, she looked in and saw Gabby perched on the arm of the chair, hunched over, her arm wrapped around her middle, her phone to her ear, listening. She stepped inside. Three more steps and she was beside Gabby, her arm around her, pulling her against her, offering Gabby support as she listened to Elizabeth. Even with the phone to Gabby's ear, Diana heard Elizabeth's broken sobs.

Gabby shuddered.

Diana tapped Gabriella's shoulder and when Gabby looked up she mouthed. "I can talk to her." Relief flooded Gabby's eyes.

"Elizabeth," Gabby interrupted. "D is here. I'm going to hand the phone to her now, E. I'm still here. And, you know I love you."

Diana took the phone from Gabby's outstretched hand. Her mind had already recalled her own experiences with miscarriages. She'd had three. She prayed Elizabeth would not know this pain more than this one time.

"I love you, Elizabeth," she said and hoped her voice sounded kind, supportive. "Do you want to tell me what happened, or do you need to talk about something else right now?"

"I-I-I don-don-don't know why?" Elizabeth was hysterically gulping air as she tried to talk.

Diana's own tears brimmed but remained unshed as she listened to Elizabeth's broken voice try to make sense of senselessness. Asking unanswerable questions was part of the process but after a few minutes it was time to interrupt Elizabeth's teary rambling.

"Elizabeth. This is one of those times when there is no answer and you only hurt yourself trying to find one." She paused briefly to breathe deeply before going on. "This is one of those times when you must let go, release in order to heal."

"But it isn't fair," Elizabeth screamed at her. "I wanted this baby so bad," her voice now that of a small child. She hiccupped. "I'd be a good mother," she whispered.

"Yes, you will be a good mother," Diana affirmed. "And I have every reason to believe, I have faith you will be a mother when the time is right."

"Why wasn't it right now?" Some of the hysteria had eased but Diana could hear the pain of a broken heart in those words.

"Remember, love, we put our trust in the Goddess, in The Universe to guide and protect us. To know what will serve our highest good. I only know when I miscarried, I felt a bone-deep grief, a grief I've never felt before or since."

"You lost a baby?" Elizabeth whispered.

"Three."

"Oh, D. I never knew. How did you survive?"

"It was long before I had all of you in my life, so not very well for a few years. I had Bill and that helped. Dennis was working long hours to get ahead in the company. I felt very alone. But, time passed and, as I said, I had Bill. I managed.

"You, E, have all of us and a wonderful husband who is, I believe, talking to Lily right now. He's very worried about you."

"I know. I've been a bit hysterical about it." A wave of fresh tears followed.

"What is it, Elizabeth. Tell me what you're thinking right now."

"It-It-It's the b-b-beginning of t-t-the racing s-s-season. He c-c-can't do h-h-his job be-be-because of m-m-me. What if he hates me?" she blurted out.

"I can assure you, he does not hate you." Diana spoke in a firm voice hoping to break through Elizabeth's fears. "He loves you, E. He is worried about you."

"But he shouldn't spend so much time with me," she whispered. "He—" her words were lost in another spate of tears.

"Elizabeth, one of us will be there in a day or two. Can you hang on until someone gets there?"

"You're coming? All of you?"

Diana heard the hope in her voice.

"No, not all of us at once, but we're going to set something up so you're not alone." She noticed movement in the corner of her eye and looked up to see Lily in the doorway. She looked drained.

"Michael?" She heard Elizabeth's voice and realized she was not talking to her but to her husband who must have walked into whichever room she was in. "Diana." He must have wanted to know who she was talking to. She put her hand over the mouthpiece. "Where are things?" she asked Lily.

"We think it best if she comes here for a few weeks. Michael was scheduled to fly out tonight as he has a horse running in the Kentucky Derby. I told him to bring Elizabeth if at all possible and at least one of us would meet them in Louisville and bring her back here. He'll come out as often as he can for as long as he can. When the Triple Crown is over in June, we'll see where things are. At least we'll be in summer and have more flexible schedules."

"Diana?" Elizabeth's plaintive tone called her back to the phone.

"Yes, dear?"

"I'm coming with Michael. We leave tonight and I'll be there tomorrow. He talked to Lily." Her words were hesitant and sounded like a little girl's.

"We'll see you tomorrow, then." Diana mentally flipped through her schedule. "Remember, E. We love you very much. Do you feel it?"

"I know you all love me."

"It's time to hold on to the love you have in your life, Elizabeth. Michael loves you, we love you. Hold on to that love. It will see you through this."

42 HEALING

Diana and Lily flew to Louisville that night and met Michael and Elizabeth at the airport the next morning. After teary farewells and many assurances that Michael would be contacted immediately should anything go wrong, they waved good-bye as he drove off in his rental car. She was exhausted by the time they landed back in Fremont and grateful to see Gabriella and Hunter as they came through security. Gabby and Hunter took Elizabeth into their arms while Lily and she got her luggage.

A cobbled together plan was in place. She and Lily would continue on with Gabby, Hunter, and Elizabeth to the Murphy's' Fremont house. Sophia would bring Ashley, who was even now cooking dinner. Logan would stay with Ashley's children. Everyone agreed now was not the time to have the children around Elizabeth. Hunter had a class to teach so she would leave soon after everyone was dropped off at the house. The easiest piece and a blessing was with Gabby living at the Murphy house, Elizabeth would not be alone.

Diana and Lily traded off, keeping a close eye on Elizabeth and filling the others in on the details. If anyone was concerned, they'd first call Lily or Diana who would then contact Michael. While it added an extra layer of communication, both Lily and Diana believed it better than to have Michael called unnecessarily. Elizabeth was on an emotional see-saw. Michael didn't need to be on it as well. Of course they would call him if Elizabeth's emotional health tipped beyond the expected see-saw.

Dinner was a quiet affair. Sophia coaxed Elizabeth into eating most of her meal. It helped Ashley had fixed two of her favorites, Chicken Paprikas and Gulyas, a Hungarian beef and vegetable soup. Sophia brought her decadent chocolate cake as well as a tin of her peanut butter chocolate chip cookies two more of Elizabeth's favorites.

In the living room, they traded off with someone always on the couch next to Elizabeth, holding her hand.

"How did you ever survive the pain?" Elizabeth asked in a whisper when Diana was sitting next to her.

"I was fortunate. I had Bill. I had to get up every day and tend to him. It helped me get through." She paused to wipe away the tears slipping down Elizabeth's drawn cheeks. "You have Michael and us," she gestured to the other women as she spoke quietly. "You are not alone through this, E."

"I don't know what I did. You know?" Elizabeth said, looking at her, pain and uncertainty in her eyes.

"Do you think you did something and that's why the miscarriage?"

Elizabeth nodded her head and buried it in her hands. Her shoulders shook from her sobs.

Sophia came and sat on her other side, her arm around Elizabeth's shoulders. "What do you think you did?"

Did Elizabeth hear the compassion in Sophia's quiet voice?

"I-I-I don't kn-kn-know." Elizabeth wailed. "I m-m-must have done som-som-something. Why would t-t-this have hap-hap-happened?"

Sophia pulled Elizabeth closer into her arms and said words similar to Diana's earlier ones about trust. Trust in the Goddess, Spirit, The Universe. Elizabeth pulled away, her anger showing in her tightly drawn lips, fury blazing from her eyes, Diana was not surprised.

"The Goddess had no right to take my baby away from me!" Elizabeth shouted, getting to her feet. "No right at all! That was My. Baby."

"Ya know, E," Ashley's quiet voice interrupted Elizabeth's tirade, "if any one of us could make this different, we'd already have done it. Ya do know that, now, don't you?" She rose from her chair and crossed to where Elizabeth stood.

Elizabeth nodded and started to speak.

Ashley stopped her, her fingers on Elizabeth's lips. "Ya know we love you, that we'd do anything we could to take this pain from your heart." She waited until Elizabeth nodded before dropping her hand to Elizabeth's shoulder, lightly resting it there as she continued.

"Do ya also know that each and every one of us has been in a place like yours? Where our faith has been tested? Where we've wondered what we've done to have this happen to us? Think about it, E. Ya know each of us well. Ya know what we've faced. Look around at us. What do ya see?" She paused until she saw Elizabeth looking around the room. "Six women who've been where you are, some of us more than once, who've survived and live good lives."

Ashley stood tall and strong in front of Elizabeth, maintaining eye-contact even when Elizabeth tried to bow her head in what looked like an attempt to avoid it. Caring and compassionate, yet Ashley still confronted her younger circle sister; urged her to see the truth in front of her.

My own faith has been tested in these last four months. But Ashley is right. I am stronger because of it. I am more certain of my own worth. I have more self-respect in all areas of my life.

Her mind drifted to the first years of her marriage. *Dennis had affairs even early on and my first miscarriage was much like Elizabeth's. I felt so much anger, so much guilt. Bill was my salvation.* A soft smile on her face, other memories flickered. *Dennis caring, showing concern for me, flowers, coming home right after work. He brought take-out or fixed something simple— for a week. We did have some good times. What would I have done, how would I have regained my equilibrium without a week of Dennis' care and more importantly, Bill?*

The ringing of the phone broke into her thoughts. Ashley still stood with Elizabeth, her arms now around her, holding her. Gabby rose to answer it, returning moments later, mouthing "Michael".

"E? It's Michael." Gabby stood next to her friend, phone in hand, waiting for Elizabeth to turn and take the phone.

Elizabeth shook her head and turned away.

Lily leapt up, grabbed the phone from Gabby, and strode toward the front door, closing it softly behind her.

Diana knew Lily was doing "damage control" with Michael, trying to explain to him in a way that did not increase his own distress, why his wife would not talk to him.

Gabby stood there, stunned, her mouth agape.

Sophia now stood with Ashley in front of Elizabeth.

Diana remained seated having consigned herself to a back-up role. *In some ways, there's no point in talking to her because she's not far enough through her grief to hear what anyone of us are saying.* Silence was also Elizabeth's enemy, silence drew her deeper into the depths of darkness that came with the loss of a loved one. Even though Elizabeth was only a few months along, she and Michael had loved this baby with all their hearts.

Lily appeared in the doorway and motioned for her to step outside. Diana rose and made her way to the front door, closing it behind her.

"I was able to talk him out of getting on the next plane. Do you think that wise?" The door was barely closed before Lily started recounting the conversation. "He is fraught with worry about her to such a degree I'm worried about him."

"Perhaps we need to be more pro-active, call him every morning with an update, and again during the day? Do you think that would help ease his mind?" Diana slipped into her professional problem-solving mode a strength she and Lily shared.

Lily nodded. "Great idea. Its times like this I'm grateful for some of my life's experiences. I had one miscarriage and I remember how devastating it was. Hopefully I convinced Michael this was not about him, but about a process E has to go through.

"He argued at first because he feels this loss so deeply himself. But in the end, he agreed to stay where he was, do the best job he could, and call you or me to see how she is doing. But I like your idea, D. Calling him first. What times work best for you?"

Diana smiled. Lily was well past her initial hesitation about her conversation with Michael. "I'll call him in the morning and then let you know how he's doing. We'll have our planners with us then and we can work out the schedule. Let's go talk to Gabby and see how she feels being here alone with E tonight. If she's willing to sleep in the same room with her, I think that would be best, but I don't know what her schedule is tomorrow."

Diana and Lily returned to the house and pulled Gabby aside. Gabby had already decided to stay home from work tomorrow and had no qualms about staying close to Elizabeth during the night. They agreed Gabby would call Diana first thing in the morning rather than have Diana call for an update.

Diana took Elizabeth in her arms, held her close, matched her breathing to hers and then slowly changed her breathing to a calmer pace, inwardly pleased when Elizabeth's body followed her lead. She stepped back as the other women came to stand in a circle around their youngest member. Words were not necessary as they held her in their midst and focused on her healing.

With Elizabeth back in Fremont under such difficult circumstances, Diana's daily routine changed. Her day started with a call from Gabby, followed by a call to Michael, and then another call to Lily to bring her up-to-date and to decide who would call Michael next.

Her day also included time with Matthew, who either stopped by during the day or after work. He now had a few items of clothing, a razor and a toothbrush at the little house and she had the same at his. Most nights they spent together at one place or the other. And even with what was going on with Elizabeth, that hadn't changed.

With the support The Circle provided, Elizabeth moved from the state of crisis she'd initially been in to the point where she talked directly to Michael. Lily had convinced him to keep the conversations focused on the upcoming races, things going on at the barns, etc. Gabby reported that Elizabeth actually smiled while listening to Michael during a recent conversation.

With all seven of them in Fremont for now, they were getting together several times a week. They'd gotten Elizabeth out of the house to see Sophia's garden, over to Lily's for a spaghetti feed and Jackson's homemade ice cream and out for a day trip to the ocean. The day trip to the beach included the men and children. "The men" now included Jackson, Matthew and Daniel, who everyone could see was in love with Ashley's children.

Lily and Jackson traveled with Elizabeth to see Michael and to watch the Preakness. At first, Elizabeth appeared to perk up and be more herself. But by the end of the second day, she withdrew. Lily reported how hard it was to see Michael's conflict and how glad she was Jackson was there. He'd been a rock for Michael to lean on. "I don't know exactly what they talked about," she'd shared with Diana. "But after they'd been off by themselves for a time, Michael seemed better."

Sometime during the four weeks that had now passed, it struck her that she was not dealing with all of this by herself. *Every day Matthew asks how I am, holds me and tells me how wonderful I am. Every night he makes love to me with his body, filling me with ecstasy. I've always handled the crises in my own life and my circle sisters on my own.* A sense of wonder infused her as she recalled various events of the last month. *With Matthew by my side; how much easier it all is.*

It was the first of June and they were gathered at the Murphy's house; Summer Solstice a mere three weeks away. Solstice had always been a major ceremonial celebration for them, but now it was also Lily and Jackson's anniversary. Diana watched Lily flit around the living room rearranging things so everyone could sit in a circle on the floor. Once everyone was smudged and prayers to open the circle had been said, they began.

"If there are no objections," Lily spoke rapidly, "I'd like to go first." No objections voiced, she plunged in. "Jackson and I've done a lot of talking because this Solstice will be our first anniversary." She paused and took the time to gaze at each woman. "We want it to be something special." She shifted, raised her eyes toward the ceiling, muttering words Diana couldn't hear.

Her attention back in the circle, she smiled, leaned forward and said, "Let me try this again."

"Without each and every one of you in my life, I would not be married to the most wonderful man in the world. Both Jackson and I are cognizant of that reality; that without the gifts each of you gave me or us at some point during our "times of struggle", we would not be celebrating this day in our lives. We feel so blessed to have one another. I must say I never knew marriage could be like this: so safe, so loving, so—well, suffice it to say, I'm very, very happy.

"So, we are suggesting, well, actually it was Jackson's suggestion, that we all celebrate Solstice together. You know, like we did Winter Solstice. Elizabeth," Lily turned to look directly at the younger woman, "did an excellent job of setting that up and including the men. Actually, that is what Jackson means by 'celebrating Solstice together'." She turned to Diana, "Do you think Matthew will come? He seemed okay with Beltane."

"I'll talk to him tonight," Diana said. Memories of their talk surfaced. Matthew had had some questions for her that night. The words of the ceremony hadn't bothered him in the least. However, the part when they knew something was wrong with Elizabeth had.

"Are you a witch?" he'd asked in that calm assessing way he had.

"No, I'm not a witch," she'd replied before adding their practice of casting a circle was a Wicca tradition.

"Is that why you do everything in a circle instead of another shape?"

"In the old traditions the people used the sun, the moon, the seasons to understand their world. The concept of The Wheel of Life is very old."

Because he wanted to understand her beliefs more, she'd answer all his questions as best she could while packing a tote for the trip to Louisville. *What was most challenging for him was my adding to each answer that this was how I saw it and it wasn't necessarily how other women did.*

And, because Jackson, Daniel and Michael would be there, she expected Matthew to say "yes".

Lily straightened, the talking stone still cradled in her hands. "I just wanted to put that out there before we got to talking about what we wanted to do. You know, to make sure the idea of the men joining us was discussed." She placed the stone on the altar cloth.

"Before we go further, while men have attended two Ceremonies, this discussion is about making it 'the rule' rather than 'the exception'." Sophia picked up the stone, looking around the circle as she waited for comments. While they would remain a sacred women's circle, adding men to their major ceremonies would alter, in a fundamental way, how they saw themselves as well as what they did. The silence stretched.

Diana held her hand out and Sophia handed her the stone. "Another way to look at this——" she started and stopped, wanting to make sure what she said was not misunderstood.

"Did anyone feel this didn't work during Winter Solstice? That to continue this practice of including men in our major ceremonies would be a betrayal of who we are and what we stand for?” Diana looked around at the faces of the other women, knowing Lily would keep a neutral face to hide her feelings. *And Lily and Jackson will go along with whatever is decided, planning their wedding anniversary celebration around The Circle's Solstice Ceremony. Michael here for Summer Solstice will be healing for Elizabeth and to be honest, Matthew celebrating the beginning of summer with me in this way will be special.*

Elizabeth's hand reached for the talking stone. A surge of hope flowed as she placed the stone in E's out-stretched hand. Elizabeth rolled the stone in the palms of her hands, turning it over and over before speaking.

“I would welcome the men to our Summer Solstice Ceremony and plan to invite them again to this year's Winter Solstice Ceremony.”

The room was quiet. Diana observed the women who had yet to speak seem to go within, perhaps searching their hearts for their right answer.

Elizabeth sat tall and still, no longer tumbling the stone in her hand. “I gather from the silence there is acceptance that we will make this change,” Elizabeth's soft voice was clear and strong.

Heads nodded and Elizabeth continued to talk.

“However, this decision is too important to be made with silence. In some ways it's like our decision to create The Golden Cauldron and use our gifts commercially. We must, for it to work, speak out. I want to hear every voice. No one can be silent on this.”

Elizabeth queried each woman as to whether she supported this change. When it was her turn, Diana's face was solemn as she said, “yes”.

The Universe, Spirit, the Goddess was with them this evening. They witnessed Elizabeth's turning from the darkness of grief toward the light as she stepped forward to claim a place for Michael and the other men in their spiritual practice. Something major was about to happen. What it was or how it would affect her long-term? Only time would tell. But somewhere deep within her, she knew having Matthew with her when she raised her arms in prayer on Summer Solstice would be the beginning.

43 SUMMER SOLSTICE AND THE SHADOW OF DENNIS

Peace of mind eluded Diana as she stood in Sophia's backyard resplendent in its early summer beauty preparing for their Summer Solstice Ceremony. The rose scented air was a reminder of the tension, the discord between Matthew and her.

The reason?

The large bouquet of flowers taking up most of her dining room table. One would have to be blind to miss them.

And Matthew was not blind.

Of course he'd commented on them. And, embarrassed, she was defensive and snappish. "Why?" She'd asked herself that over and over.

Why was she embarrassed to have a large bouquet of fresh flowers on her table?

Why was she defensive?

Why did she snap at him?

She frowned at the answer: Dennis. They weren't the first flowers he'd sent, but they were certainly the largest. In addition, a bottle of champagne was in her refrigerator and two large boxes of chocolates were tucked away in her office. She'd planned on bringing them today, to share with everyone, but after seeing Matthew's reaction to the flowers, she decided "no". Since he was here, he'd see them and she didn't want to see the look on his face or answer any questions.

It had all started Memorial Day when Dennis began his campaign to win her back. At least that's what she thought it was about—winning her back. That morning when she woke up an American Flag was in the flag holder on the porch. She knew it was from him because they always hung the flag first thing in the morning on Memorial Day.

Matthew commented and she let him believe she'd been up earlier and put it up.

Since then something came every day: cards, flowers, chocolates.

No, he didn't call her, but when she got the gift, she called him.

To thank him.

Manners.

It was either the phone call or a thank you note and she really didn't want to write to him, not that she wanted to talk to him on the phone but that just seemed quicker, simpler. Pick up the phone, call, a few words of thanks then hang up. It was much easier than getting out paper, envelope, pen a note, seal, address, get stamp and mail.

Even though she'd told him to stop, the cards, candy and flowers arrived daily like clockwork much as they had when he'd wooed and won her in the past. Back then she'd wanted him so badly, it hadn't taken much.

Now? She admitted it was flattering, and he knew her well enough: knew her taste in chocolate and flowers. The cards were beautiful also. She loved the work of Melissa Harris, Jody Bergsma, Susan Sedon Boulet and Josephine Wall and found it hard to, well, if she were honest, impossible to throw out the beautiful cards.

If truth be told, and she wanted at least to be truthful with herself, she was curious about how determined Dennis was to get her back. While a part of her knew it would never work out, the other part that had been starved for so many years for his attention was relishing, reveling in every offering. Because that's what the flowers, cards, and chocolate were—offerings to her. In her own spiritual practice she made offerings of tobacco, salt, petals, incense, prayers as ways to connect to the sacred. It wasn't a live goat on an altar as in days of yore but it was still an offering.

Shaking her head to dispel these wayward thoughts, she smiled at Matthew. No answering smile, just a nod of acknowledgement. Her awareness of him intensified, her skin tingling with his touch although he stood ten feet away, now with his back to her.

"I need a few minutes," she heard her voice from a distance, as if coming from someone else.

"Please." The other women broke from the circle. Nodding in acquiescence to her request, they turned toward each other, voices too soft for her to hear. Purpose infused her steps as she strode toward Matthew, took his hand, rose on her toes and whispered in his ear, "Come with me, please."

He did.

She drew him back into the house and into the bedroom she'd used when she'd first left Dennis. A fitting place for this conversation. She closed the door behind them.

Matthew stood before her, hands stuffed in his back pockets, rocking toe to heel, toe to heel. To hide her nervousness, she moved to the window and closed it, blocking out the chatter of the others.

"I know you're upset with me," she began in her professional voice. *That's not the tone I need to use here.* She cleared her throat.

"We try to be honest with each other, Matthew." *This is not going well.* She met his gaze, dark with emotion, stood firm and maintained eye contact with him.

"I'm sorry you're angry that Dennis has been sending me flowers and that I've kept them rather than tossing them in the compost bin." She lifted her chin a fraction, refusing to look away as she tried to make things right between them. In a way she could understand why he was upset. She was "his" and the idea that another man would send her gifts rubbed raw. But Dennis wasn't just "another man", he was her ex-husband and they had a twenty-year plus history. "I have asked him to stop."

"So, the other flowers?" She shivered at the sound of betrayal in his voice.

"Yes."

"And you just accept them? You don't refuse them?" He glowered at her.

He was very angry with her.

"They've always just been on the porch when I got home." *I don't know if I have the courage to tell him about the daily cards and the chocolate if he's this angry and upset over flowers.*

"Hell, Diana. What do you think you're doing? Do you think I'm jealous? Well if you do, you're wrong. I'm pissed!" he was almost shouting at her. "Damn it, this is the man who beat you, who threatened you, who terrorized you. How you can have anything from him in your house is—" He shook his head and turned away.

For a moment it looked like he was going to leave. His head bowed, a hand raked through his hair, his shoulders slumped.

"They're so beautiful and my favorites," she said in a tear-stained voice.

"Is that all it takes to win you back? A bouquet of your favorite flowers?" he asked in defeat.

He reached for the door.

Her heart stopped, her lungs faltered, her brain whirled in panic. She was going to lose him—lose him forever.

"Please don't leave me," she whispered. Relief weakened her knees when she saw his body deflate as air left his lungs. She reached for him, her hands on his back warmed from the heat of his body through his chambray shirt.

"Please, Matthew. I'll tell him again. I'll call the florist, tell them I refuse any further arrangements from him. I'll take them to a nursing home or ask Lily to give them to her clients, if any more come." The words rushed, tumbled out. *How had I forgotten the beating, the threats, the intimidation, the years of infidelity? What is wrong with me?*

He turned and hope leapt in her heart as he gathered her into his arms and held her close.

She burrowed and breathed in the fresh lime scent of him, let his heat infuse her body and melted into him. Feelings of safety, of being cherished flooded her senses. His fingers under her chin, the pressure to look up. As she did his lips claimed hers and she slid her hands up, around his neck, slipped her fingers through his hair, pressed against him. There was a recklessness in his kiss, a primitive claiming, something to bind her to him. Welcoming those feelings, arousal coursed through her body.

When they pulled away from each other, their breathing labored and their cheeks flushed, the discord was gone. She wrapped an arm around his waist; he draped his around her shoulder pulling her against his side.

"Need a minute. Get control back," he grunted.

His breathing slowed. She took a deep breath and matched her inhales and exhales with his wondering if he was as afraid of losing her as she was of losing him; or if it was only his incredulity that she'd accept anything from Dennis. Reaching for the door, she opened it, and stepped into the hall. "They're waiting for us."

The circle was complete. All seven of them stood, arms raised in prayer, calling in their spirit guides, guardians and animal spirits who wished to participate in this Summer Solstice Ceremony. The living circle they'd stood around at Beltane was lush, the green Victorian gazing ball gone, a red one in its place. They'd added personal items to the altar as well as rose quartz for love, obsidian for protection and grounding, a Mexican pottery sun propped against the gazing ball's stand in the West to light the void. A bowl of fresh fruit sat in the South, a symbol of summer's bounty. Each had a small bag of rose petals to toss in the air during the ceremony. The men and children also had bags of rose petals, the Goddess's flower this time of year.

While the Talking Circle was an important part of their meetings, they'd decided to separate it from the Ceremony. They'd met before the Winter Solstice Ceremony and skipped it altogether at Beltane. What felt right, because they wanted the men and children in attendance today, was to meet again tomorrow.

Diana stood in the circle, Elizabeth directly across from her. E looked so much better: color in her cheeks, life showing in her eyes. She wasn't back to her normal sparkly self, but she was no longer the desolate being she'd been at Beltane. *Having Michael here helps.*

During their last talking circle, Elizabeth had filled them in on the Retreat Center's summer programs. Next week she'd return to Ireland. After the Fourth of July, a couple of weeks away, Sophia, Ashley, her children, and Logan would travel. *What a blessing for the children and Ashley too. It seems her marriage is more challenging right now so the time away will be good. Maybe Art will see what a treasure he has in his family if they are gone for a month.*

Bringing her attention back to the Ceremony, she quickly picked up where they were. Singing, her bailiwick. As they sung the familiar words to "The River She is Flowing" and "She Is Waiting", the feminine voices soared with joy.

As one they raised their arms, said the prayers to release the spirits who had come to this Ceremony and closed the circle.

Taking pouches of petals from pockets or belts, they turned, opened them and tossed rose petals into the air. A smile turned into a grin as the soft peach colors of Peace caught in Matthew's dark brown hair. The men and children joined in with their supply of rose petals and the air filled with swirling colors that too soon fell to the ground. As they walked, their bare-feet crushing the velvety softness, the scent of countless rose petals wafted through the air.

Her eyes again found Matthew, the desire in his eyes brought a blush to her face, heat bursting through her body. Aware he watched her every move, aware of the ardor in his eyes, she ambled toward him, taking great pleasure when his lips parted and his breathing stuttered. Raising her arms, she slipped them around his neck, pulled his head to hers and kissed him. His arms banded around her, tugging the last fraction of an inch until there was nothing to separate them.

"Matthew loves D. D loves Matthew." The sing-song words broke through the sensual haze creating space between them. Ashley's children made a circle around them, singing the taunting lyrics. Calling her children to her side, Ashley said in her soft accented voice that sounded more musical than stern, "Now, ya leave those two alone, do ya hear?"

Ashley repeat the question until, Diana supposed, she'd gotten an agreement from each of them. Matthew's hold on her loosened. Her face, pink with embarrassment, took on a rosy hue when she looked up and saw him grinning. Unable to keep that connection, she looked away.

He does love me. Not only has he said the words but he shows me every day in so many ways, little ways that to some might not mean anything, but to me mean everything.

Matthew may love me, but do I dare I love him?

44 FIREWORKS AND A PHONE CALL

The remainder of the day Diana observed Jackson and Lily as well as Michael and Elizabeth. Both men loved their wives and were utterly faithful. *Maybe Dennis does love me as much as he says he does but serial affairs are not what I want in a marriage.* Old doubts about how long Matthew would desire her surfaced. *If he put me aside, especially for a younger woman, I'd-I'd be-I'd be devastated.*

Grateful Lily had time for lunch the next day, Diana parked near her friend at the restaurant to facilitate the transfer of the flowers and candy to Lily's car.

"Give them to whoever will enjoy them," Diana said as the last of Dennis' gifts left her possession. That morning she'd spent a little time looking at the cards, noting the ones whose pictures or message touched her before burning them in the fireplace.

After their food was served, she dared to ask Lily the question she didn't want to ask The Tarot.

"How did you know Jackson loved you?" she said hoping Lily wouldn't notice the slight quiver or her twisting her napkin in her lap.

But, of course she did. Her brow arched, a look of interest flashed in her eyes before her face assumed a neutrality more conducive to Diana's comfort. *Yes, Lily does know me very well.*

"Well, he told me he did at one point." Lily smiled fondly. "But I'm assuming you are asking about how I knew in other ways."

Diana nodded, resisted the urge to take a sip of water and worked on stilling her nervous hands.

"It was the little things he did. Well, and the not so little things that went against his grain, so to speak. You know when he sat with me evenings on end, week after week, sorting out our relationship? That was huge. No man had ever done that with me and I know it was as painful for him at times as it was for me. And then, when I stopped to pay attention there were all the little things: remembering my favorite food, fixing my favorite ice cream, bringing me flowers, chocolate, asking about my day and then really listening to what I said. There was the time he'd just gotten home from a trip and I had to go out on a medical emergency with a client. He was exhausted but he came with me; waited in the ER lobby for me on a busy Friday night."

She stopped, took a bite of her salad, chewed and swallowed before taking a sip of her tea. "Does that help?"

"Yes, I suppose it does." Diana shook her head as many of the things on Lily's list were being done by both Dennis and Matthew. "I was just wondering how early in your relationship with Jackson you knew there was something worth fighting for or worth figuring things out for. There were certainly times when you were brought to your knees, Lily. It wasn't easy by any means."

"No, it wasn't easy but it could have been easier. I truly was my own worst enemy at times. I let my fear of what might happen, what could happen almost destroy what Jackson and I have now.

"I know you haven't asked me for advice, D, but I'm giving it to you anyway. Learn from both Elizabeth and me; learn to go within and trust your source; learn to face your fears realistically. Don't let a chance at bliss pass you by because you are afraid of what might be."

Diana smiled in recognition of those wise words from her friend. It was true both Lily and Elizabeth had almost lost what they had now because of fear. Lily's fear was based in her lack of trust in herself. Elizabeth's fear was about losing the people most dear to her. And Diana recognized her own fear: being cast aside, not being good enough, being left behind for someone better.

The next two weeks passed quickly. Dennis had not given up although he had changed tactics. Instead of cards there were now daily phone calls. If she didn't answer, he left voice mail messages. He'd also involved Bill in sending her emails with messages from him recognizing she might delete one directly from him without opening it. Instead of flowers, she'd found fruit baskets on her door step and last week a young woman with a note saying she'd been paid to clean the house. She liked to think it would have been just as easy to turn her away even if she'd not spent the evening before scrubbing the place herself.

Dennis's messages were about the good times in their marriage. He'd dredged up the vacation to Disneyland when Bill was seven; the weekends they'd gone to the coast and beach-combed; the times they'd sat together at Bill's games, cheering his team on; the neighborhood barbeques; and from the earlier years, all the Fourth of Julys, Thanksgivings, Christmases, New Years, and Valentine's Days. She steeled herself to skip to the end of the message and delete it. But she heard enough to become immersed in memories from her past: memories of the good times in her marriage to Dennis or after Bill's birth as a family.

The Fourth of July everyone gathered at the Murphys' house because it had the best view of the fireworks. Jackson, Lily, Sophia, Ashley and her children, Daniel, Hunter and Logan, and Gabriella gathered on the back deck to watch the spectacle.

Matthew seemed a bit on edge, nervous, not at all like himself. A couple of times she saw Jackson and Daniel give him, what looked like to her, an encouraging nod. When she saw a knowing look pass between her circle sisters she knew something was going on.

The fireworks were spectacular, their "oohs" and "aahs" punctuated by several "wows" and "awesomes". Matthew stood slightly behind her, one arm firmly around her waist, his free hand stroking her arm, toying with her fingers. He cleared his throat, shifted as if to bend down. In the background she heard a phone ring, it sounded like her cell phone. *Let it ring.* She leaned into his strong body, feeling relaxed and cherished.

"Diana," he whispered in her ear the feel of his breath created a warm, tingling sensation in her toes that rapidly spread upward. He tugged on her, pulled her away from the others who still stood on the deck looking out at the twinkling lights of the city.

"Diana," his whisper was more urgent and she turned in his arms, looked up at his face. So much more than desire was on his face, in his eyes: love shining because of her. Her breath caught in her throat.

"D, D, D." The little voice was accompanied by tugging on her pants. "D, it's a hospital man for you."

She tore her gaze from Matthew's to look down at Ashley's youngest holding her cell phone out to her.

"It's a doctor person, D. He said it's impordant."

One hand still in Matthew's, Diana took the phone, dread quelled the warm tingling feelings, a sense of foreboding filled her.

"This is Diana Pettybone."

"I'm Doctor Weatherby at Fremont General. We have a Dennis Pettybone in our Emergency Room and you are listed as his emergency contact. He's unconscious and we need permission to run tests and treat him. How soon can you be here?"

Stunned, she stood paralyzed not quite comprehending the doctor's words: Dennis unconscious; her name as his Emergency Contact. In her befuddled state she remembered he was on her contact sheet at the hospital and at the doctors.

Fireworks popped and whizzed, banged and screeched—there were no "oohs" and "aahs"—it was eerily quiet.

"What happened?" Lily's soft voice brought her back from her musing.

"Dennis is at Fremont General, unconscious. I'm the only one listed as an emergency contact and they need me to come." Frozen, she was immobile, unable to move, to think, to act.

Lily took the phone from her and began talking to the doctor.

"I'll come with you," Lily's words were ones she hadn't wanted to hear because they meant she had to go. She turned to say something to Matthew, saw the stark desolation etched on his face, the deep wound in his eyes.

What was there to say?

Lily took her arm and they walked away.

45   Dennis and Memories

When she and Lily walked into the frantic ER, they were waiting for her. Immediately, she was taken back to see Dennis who was conscious but groggy and confused. He'd been crossing the street when hit by a motorcycle, tossed in the air and landed hard hitting his head in the process. Something similar had happened to Lily and images of that ordeal flashed through her mind. *He knows who I am, a good sign as far as Dr. Weatherby was concerned. I'm not so sure.*

He clung to her, holding her hand in a tight grip, unwilling to let her go until the doctor finally convinced him he must so she could sign papers. Once free, she signed and then fled the room, eager to be gone.

"Diannaa!"

She stopped when she heard Dennis cry out for her.

"Please."

She hesitated to turn back at his plea.

What do I risk by turning back?

Matthew might understand why I came and signed papers, consented to treatment, but can he understand if I stay? Her stomach churned, she was going to vomit right here in the ER.

"I'm going to call Bill and let him know what's happened," she said and continued out of the cubicle. *I need time: time to think, time to decide what to do.* Out in the lobby, she got her cell phone out to call Bill and saw Lily. Together they stepped outside. Lily stood beside her as she called Bill, woke him up with the news his father had been seriously injured. Lily stiffened as she described the accident to her son. Remembering Lily's own encounter with a truck, Diana hoped her friend didn't have nightmares.

"He's conscious now and recognizes me, which Dr. Weatherby says is a good sign. He has a concussion and they'll be doing tests to determine if there's further injury to his brain. If you have a pen and paper, Bill, I'll give you the hospital phone number so you can call and check on him yourself, maybe even talk to him."

In the space of a minute, as Bill was writing the number down, an orderly appeared urging her to come back inside.

What's happening? She handed the phone to Lily to finish the call and hurried after him.

As soon as she entered the ER itself, she heard him. Calling for her, fear and agitation in his voice. Security stood outside his cubicle. Dr. Weatherby hurried forward, his tense expression relaxing when he recognized her.

"Glad we found you. Hope he'll calm when he sees you haven't left. He can't get up right now. We don't want to give him a sedative because of the head injury nor do we want to have to restrain him. Either option could cause complications."

Diana nodded, knowing she had to stay; if not for Dennis, then for Bill and maybe for herself.

"Please, if you could ask Lily Hughes to come back, I'll go right in."

At the doctor's nod, Diana marched into the cubicle, stopping at the foot of the bed.

"Knock it off, Dennis. If you want me to stay you need to behave," she said in her most parental tone, hoping it was strong enough and that he would heed her.

"I want you here with me, Diana," he said in a little-boy-about-to-cry voice. "Please don't leave me alone," his voice trembled from pain and fear.

She knew herself and while she did not bring home every stray dog or hurt bird, she was compassionate and could not walk away from him right now. *If Matthew is the right man for me, he'll understand.* Staying at the foot of the bed, she spoke calmly to Dennis explaining he would only make things worse if he tried to get up or fought them, encouraging him to be cooperative, reminding him of what a great team player he was.

Lily came in and spent a few minutes in encouraging conversation with Dennis before stepping to the door. Diana followed remaining in Dennis's sight. She lowered her voice and Lily followed suit so Dennis couldn't make out their words.

"I have to stay with him for now—at least until they complete the tests and they know the extent of his injuries. Right now all they know is he has a severe concussion so sedation is a risky option. He's calm if I'm here and agitated, almost combative when I'm not." Head bowed, her shoulders sagged under the weight of the moment, of the reality of the decision she'd made.

"Do you want me to talk to Matthew?"

Diana raised her head at Lily's question, a ray of hope filtered through her darkness.

"Yes, would you, please?"

A glance at her friend and she dared to ask the question to confirm her suspicions. There'd been something about how he'd looked when he'd turned toward her, how he looked as she'd turned away.

"He was going to propose tonight, wasn't he?"

Lily nodded, a wobbly smile on her face, tears glittered in her eyes. "It was all planned. We were beginning to drift towards the farthest corner of the railing, leaving just the two of you on the other section of deck, the lights of Fremont and the fireworks creating a fairyland backdrop. So romantic." She sighed. "I'll talk to him and I'll talk to Jackson. Between the two of us, we'll do what we can. I can understand your dilemma, D. I'll do my best to help Matthew see it too."

They hugged; a long comforting hug that must sustain her for hours.

An orderly came to take Dennis to X-ray and she walked beside the gurney, extracting a promise from Dennis to behave. Her threat to leave if he didn't cooperate worked.

Dennis had a broken collar bone and a torn rotator cuff in addition to the severe concussion. He faced several days in the hospital and a long recovery. The rotator cuff would require surgery and take months to properly heal.

Over the next three days, Diana remained at the hospital. They brought a cot in for her to sleep and allowed her to use the shower in his room. Lily brought by a change of clothes when she and Sophia dropped off her car.

Why did she stay? Initially Dennis wasn't always lucid but when he was if she wasn't next to him, he raised a ruckus. Never knowing when he'd awake kept her there. Dr. Weatherby impressed upon her the importance of him remaining calm so further injury was not sustained.

The next day Dennis was more lucid but still upset if she wasn't in the room when he woke. By midday, it was obvious not only was he fearful about his future, he wanted her in it. Tangential meanderings through their past, he talked about many things. Diana reminisced with him about different life events they'd shared. What twisted in her heart and her stomach was his continual apologizing for his infidelity, promising that if she gave him a second chance he'd prove to her he'd changed.

It was so tempting, being there with him, helping him eat, sit, move, listening to him apologize, hearing his words of respect, love, the promise that what they'd had at the beginning would be recaptured and a good life built upon their new foundation.

On the second day, she found herself talking with him about plans to renovate the kitchen and master bathroom.

The third day he was able to get up and move around on his own although he couldn't be left alone because of the short term memory loss and confusion that was normal for a severe concussion.

The discharge planner had stopped by to discuss his released from the hospital, his care needs, etc. He would need someone with him 24/7 until the effects of the concussion were minimized to the point he would be safe if alone.

She was at a crossroads.

Am I going to move back to the house and take care of Dennis?

Am I going to stay my course?

And if I choose to stay my course, will Matthew be with me or have I lost him forever?

Not once had she heard from him. Her two calls with carefully worded voice messages hadn't been returned. Jackson and Lily had talked to him but Lily only shrugged when she'd asked her friend about the outcome.

What am I going to do? Time was running out and a decision loomed in her near future.

Dennis was talking to her, rubbing his thumb in the palm of her hand in a seductive pattern.

When had that happened? Why hadn't I noticed?

She startled and tugged her hand from his. His confusion showed in his eyes, the frown on his forehead and the quirk of his mouth.

She stood and took a step back.

He was able to get up from the bed on his own and moved to do so.

Picking up her purse, she moved toward the door, getting to it before he made it out of bed. She turned, pasted on what she hoped would be a bright smile and infused a jovial tone in her voice.

"Dennis, I'm going home to take a hot shower. I need a bit of a break from this place." She rattled on, "I'm sure you can understand because I know you are chafing at the bit to get out of here." With a wave of her hand and "I'll be back," tossed over her shoulder, she strode out the door.

He followed her, down the hall, to the elevator, begging her not to leave him, pleading for her to come back.

"I promise, Dennis. I promise I will be back. I really have to check on things at home."

"When?" he whined.

"I can't say exactly. I've mail and email to check, things to do around the house."

A nurse, who had followed Dennis distracted him as soon as the elevator doors opened, giving Diana time to step in and push the ground floor button. When the door closed, she staggered as relief swamped through her and grabbed the side rail to keep from falling.

Thankful she'd had the foresight to have Lily and Sophia bring her car so she had a way to get home, she sat, her head resting against the headrest. Conflicting emotions flooded her, battling in her brain and body—euphoria and nausea.

What am I going to do?

The Tarot has helped me through difficult times—will it help me now?

46 THE CELTIC CROSS SPREAD

Once home, Diana took a long, hot shower and dressed in sweats. *Maybe we could be a family again,* flickered through her mind several times as she fixed a tonic, sorted through mail and checked her emails.

Dennis had been so grateful I'd been there and stayed. He'd thanked me over and over. And, he'd apologized over and over for his past infidelity. Bill and Dennis now talked easily during his twice a day phone calls—maybe?

Tears welled at the memory of the look of concentration, of hope on his face when he looked into her eyes and listed why he loved her. She'd waited so long to hear those words, for him to see her in that way, to love her how she wanted to be loved. He'd reminded her of the good times in their marriage. *Maybe it's enough of a foundation to build a future together. Maybe we can be a family again.*

Those thoughts she pushed from her mind as she smudged the house, herself and the cards. Sitting on the couch, she drew the deck from its Harlequin patterned red and gold silk bag and shuffled.

"Which direction do I go? Toward Dennis or toward Matthew." That didn't feel right, it wasn't the question. What was? *I want to know with a certainty that I'm the only woman in his life...whoever he is.*

At the time she'd got the cards, she'd also picked up her Journal. She opened it

Show me the Way forward to find a life of joy, love, respect, caring, compassion where I am cherished, valued for who I am and safe.

She shuffled the cards three times, repeating her question as she cut the cards and dealt the Celtic Cross spread. "Show. Me. The. Way" whispered from her lips as she laid the cards in the familiar pattern.

First card = Present Position: Eight of Pentacles

Second card = Immediate Influences: The Hermit

Third card = Goal/Destiny: Six of Swords

Fourth card = Distant Past: Five of Wands

Sixth card = Future Influences: Ten of Swords

The next four cards lined up one above the other to the right were left face down so she wouldn't be distracted by them. In her Journal she diagramed the layout filling in the cards she'd drawn before she wrote:

In my present position I need to pay attention to details as errors or sloppiness may be my undoing --- (Dennis and the emergency contact); hard work will be satisfying and successful; I need to apply myself and work smart --- (I've got some ideas to build my business but in addition I need to be clear on the details and apply myself if I want a joyful life where I am cherished, valued, and safe.

Immediate Influences: The Hermit --- search for answers to life's problems! I need to withdraw (take this time now?). Peace and quiet (here in the little house).Take advice from others (maybe ask others to come by?). Someone who will defend, inspire, and protect me (role Matthew has played). Follow my heart, not the crowd.

Goal/Destiny: Six of Swords. I've had this card before. Problems! Overwhelmed by crisis; unable to cope with day-to-day problems; energy drain (definitely the last three days with Dennis). Future is better than the present...things will work out. (Thankfully!)

Card four = Distant Past: The Five of Wands. Caution. (Yes, that's me) --- as I read this card it speaks to the problems in the early part of this year, leaving Dennis, hiding in the apartment, etc. as well as the last fifteen years of my marriage. Now in the distant past? It's only been a little over six months since I made the decision to leave Dennis and had to deal with the drama and chaos of those first three months. But it does feels like it all happened much farther back in time.

Card five = Recent Past: King of Wands certainly describes Dennis at his best. His wooing of me --- handsome, strong, charismatic man over forty, takes action, gets results. He has been very creative in reminding me of the good times in our marriage...and there were more of them than I'd remembered on my own. Yesterday when he had Bill call me on my cell phone and then asked me to put it on speaker phone — I never saw that coming — but he used that to his advantage engaging Bill in his favorite memories growing up. I thought I heard hope in Bill's voice—maybe not.

Card six = Future Influence: Ten of Wands reversed. I'm not facing problems and they won't go away on their own. I need courage to overcome them. I need to get out of my intellectual rut, open myself to new ideas — look for ways to stretch my imagination. The answer to my problem is in me. A part of me hates this message — the answer is in me. Another part believes the answer is always in me. Why can't I see this answer clearly if I already know it?

Her Journal now closed, Diana paused. There were references to both Dennis and Matthew in the spread at this point. And there was a message of hope. Hope her problems could be solved, hope she could have the life she dreamed of. On a sigh, she reached for Card seven, turned it over, and opened her Journal.

Card seven = The Questioner: Ten of Cups (another recurring card). I'm entering a period of peace and contentment. I have supportive family (Bill likes Matthew but yesterday he seemed hopeful Dennis and I would reconcile.

Diana stopped, closed her Journal her finger keeping the place. *I think he'll be okay with whatever I decide. At least I hope so.*

Reopening her Journal she continued.

Great friends and a special love relationship —. Commitments made and kept; joy and happiness; forgiveness and reconciliation. I have all the material possessions I need.

She stopped again this time surveying what she saw from her place on the couch. While the furniture came with the house, her personal touches in the stones, figures, plants, and artwork were scattered around the room. The office held all of her business related items and should she need it, there was still room for more. *I do have every material thing I need.* The idea she could make a life without either Dennis or Matthew flickered through her mind and took root. *If that is my choice, I know I can do it.*

Card Eight = Environmental Factors: Ace of Wands. Anything is possible. It's a good time to begin a new project; personal power and intellect is at a high point. I'm to tap into my creativity. I've high energy and enthusiasm. It is a good time to start a family; fertility is assured – a warm, wonderful family life.

Diana put her pen down, closed the Journal, stood and padded into the kitchen. *I need something strong to drink after reading that card.* She got out the ingredients for one of her organic tonics, pumping an extra measure into her glass, her mind awhirl as she mixed everything together and sipped.

When was my last menses? We used protection but there were two times when the condom broke. Don't panic. Finish reading the cards and then you can try to figure things out.

But the last clear memory of her monthly flow was when she was in Italy. Shaken, she set the glass of tonic on the counter. *That was before we'd been intimate—lovers.*

A deep, cleansing breath, and then another. *Better.* She picked up the glass of tonic and returned to the couch. Journal in hand, she turned over the next card.

Card nine = Inner Emotions: Knight of Cups.

A male under forty, romantic and calm natured. Taken aback, she stopped reading and leaned back on the couch. *This reading is more than I can deal with.* She laughed as she scanned the layout. *No, I can deal with it. The cards are clear that while I will have problems, I have the ability, the support of others to overcome them.*

She picked up her pen and wrote:

Male under forty; romantic and calm natured; matches decisions with his heart; thinks carefully before acting and speaking. Sensitive to others – well-educated, idealistic, persuasive. Possible invitation or proposition. In love he is considerate and generous.

And he was in the process of asking me to marry him when I dashed out to Dennis. Oh how I must have hurt him. And after all he's done for me? He is generous, considerate, calm and loving. What if I can't make it up to him? What if he can't forgive me?

A thought struck her that maybe the Questioner Card, the Ten of Cups, was about her finding a way to reconcile with

Matthew, to find a way for him to forgive her rather than her being the one who forgives. She turned back to the spread, turned the last card over and gasped as she grabbed her Journal and pen.

Card ten = Final Results: The High Priestess.

The card portrayed a woman whose arms were raised just as she and her circle sisters did when they prayed. Carefully she read the words on the card before she placed it back at the top of the line and prepared to write in her Journal.

Inner peace and strength. You will be pre-occupied. A passive reaction is best. Remain calm and sure of the outcome. The answers are already inside you; tap into your gut feelings.

Diana sat in silence; her Journal closed resting in hands now limp in her lap. The need to get up, to check to see if she was pregnant waned. A bone-deep lethargy overcame her. She tucked her feet up on the couch, closed her eyes, and let herself drift into the void. Her mind floated as she felt wrapped in a cocoon of peace.

47   HER CHOICE

Diana woke, her neck stiff, her left shoulder, arm and hand asleep. Sitting up she rubbed her neck with her right hand while she shook her left to banish the sharp tingles prickling her skin. Slowly she leaned forward, gathered the cards together and tapped them gently into place before slipping them into the silk bag. With her Journal and pen, she took the cards into the office and put them away.

She considered getting her planner and figuring out her last menses.

She thought about going to the store for a pregnancy test kit.

Instead she returned to the couch, curled up in a corner and closed her eyes, going inward, into a place of peace and quiet, into a place connected to her soul.

I know what I want: love, respect, joy, happiness, to be cherished, to be valued, to be safe. Can I trust that Dennis has changed enough to really have a chance for us to build the life I want? She pondered the time she'd just spent with him, the efforts he'd made to win her back. He was contrite; maybe even ashamed of what he'd done to her, realizing her value once she left. *I believed him when he says he loves me. But can I trust him?*

In her quiet place, where answers waited, she evaluated what she knew and compared it to what she wanted her future life to be. *Could Dennis be the one I can build that life with? Yes, if I'm honest with myself, I think he can.*

A deep cleansing breath quieted her mind. An image of Matthew formed in her mind: tall, handsome, strong, virile. *He loves me.* Just the thought of his love and sensuous warmth settled in her abdomen. *Should I choose Matthew because I crave his touch? Is there more than blinding passion between us?*

"Yes," she admitted out loud. "There is much more. While it's true I love being in his arms, I also love just being with him, sitting next to him while he watches sports on the television; listening to his deep voice reverberate through me when he is on the phone with a client or one of his crew.

We've had long talks about the future, what we each wanted to do with our lives. He had no desire to be a construction tycoon, to build a large company—wanting instead a hands-on kind of business where he could pound a nail, lift a board, turn a screw.

A memory of her helping him paint a room in his house brought out a smile. At the end, she'd as much paint on her as she'd put on the wall. They'd laughed about her clumsiness with a paint roller or brush—no feelings of embarrassment, just the joy of being with him.

"You paint with abandon," Matthew'd said swiping a splatter of paint from her nose.

And that was how she'd felt—pushing the roller up, down, crisscross, it making no difference how she did it as long as the wall got covered. It was one of the most freeing times of her life.

How telling is that memory? Painting a wall with a roller—freeing?

Clarity struck with a blinding light.

Freedom wasn't even one of the things on her list of what she wanted in a marriage, but with that memory she knew in her heart it was high on her list. *Having that kind of freedom, that sense of abandon will not happen with Dennis.*

Diana sat on the couch, quiet in contemplation. The Ten of Wands appeared in her inner vision with a message for her. *You have problems you aren't facing.* Retrieving her Journal, she read the entry. The words "new ideas" seemed brighter on the page but that didn't seem quite right. The idea she needed new ways of seeing things did.

When looking at her problem one way, she could see a future together with Dennis—they'd be a family again.

But looked at another way, she saw his emotional manipulation—the cards, chocolates, flowers, the instigating of emails and phone calls through Bill—as an emotional assault: to manipulate her to his way of thinking, to his way of doing. If they reconciled in the end it would be more about him, what he wanted. Dennis might love her and she was convinced he'd never hit her again. But the reality was her life would revert to revolving around him.

She'd changed and was perfectly content with the quiet companionship and the sensuality of her relationship with Matthew. And with him she experienced freedom, she was cherished, she was valued; she'd have it all. Standing, she paced and thought about what she needed to do to be with Matthew. He'd never talked about wanting children but she'd noticed how good he was with Ashley's little ones and Charlie, Logan and Bill.

First things first: I need to see him, to talk to him, explain—apologize. I haven't forgotten I might be pregnant. I just need to talk to him first. His decision needs to be based on his feelings for me, not because I'm pregnant. If I even am.

Upstairs, Diana grabbed a change of clothes tucking them into a cloth bag. Downstairs she added her cell phone charger and planner. Snatching her phone off the computer table, she flipped it open and keyed in Lily's number as she started toward the door.

Lily answered on the second ring.

"Hi D, what's going on?"

Because she'd kept in touch with Lily, she didn't have to go into a lengthy explanation of the last three days.

"I'm going to see Matthew after I stop at the hospital to see Dennis. I'm going to ask a huge favor, Lily."

"Ask away."

"I'm telling Dennis I'm not going to reconcile with him. I know he's afraid of what he faces once he's out of the hospital. My favor is: will you help him figure things out?" The silence on the line seemed to go on forever. Breath trapped in her lungs, her throat seized as anxiety clenched every inch of her body.

"So, you've decided you want Matthew in your life rather than Dennis?"

"Dennis will always be in my life, Lily. He's Bill's father. We can be on friendly terms but I don't want to be with him for the rest of my life. I want to see if I can have a life with Matthew. If he still wants me, that is. I know you and Jackson talked to him but you said all he did was listen. And then nothing. I've not heard from him at all, even though I've left a couple of messages. I know I've hurt him more deeply than perhaps I even realize." She stopped. "I'm babbling. I don't know exactly what I need to do but... ."

"I'll meet you at the hospital and stay with Dennis after you've said what you need to. Are you on your way now?" Lily's voice was matter-of-fact.

Tears streamed down her face as she nodded before it dawned on her that Lily couldn't see her. "Yes," she muffled through her tears.

"I'll catch up with you in the lobby and we'll go up together."

"Okay," she whispered, reaching for something to dry her eyes, to blow her nose.

The dial tone in her ear.

Lily had hung up. Grabbing a box of tissue, she headed for her car.

It wasn't a surprise to see Sophia when she arrived: just in case she needed to talk to someone after she talked to Dennis.

And she did. Needed to talk, to be held, to be assured she'd done the right thing.

His face had crumpled, tears fell down his cheeks, he looked devastated as she told him she would not be returning to him.

"Marry me, Diana," he begged. "I don't expect you to just live with me.

"Whatever you want, it's yours," he'd said adding a list of things including the remodeled kitchen and master bath.

But still she'd turned him down.

Lily had stepped in then, diverting Dennis so she could slip away.

Walk away from him.

Leave him behind.

Sobbing in Sophia's arms, she admitted she felt so bad for him; even after the way he'd treated her it was still hard to walk away.

In time her sobs quieted and she raised her head, the growing wad of tissue pressed to her still watering eyes. She must look a mess but if she didn't go to Matthew right now, her courage would fail her and she might never go.

Standing on shaky legs, she stumbled before her knees stabilized her so she walked straight. Sophia accompanied her through the drizzling rain to her car, assured her she'd be home and up if she needed her, gave her a long comforting, supportive hug and let her go.

Diana slid behind the wheel of her car, fastened her seat belt, backed out of the parking space and drove off to her destiny.

48 HIS CHOICE

He was home. His truck was in the driveway. Lights from the house wavered through the rain-spattered windshield.

Twice now she'd turned the engine on and started to drive away, twice she'd stopped. Her fear he would turn her away overpowering, she rested her head on hands that had a white-knuckled grip on the steering wheel.

He will either turn me away or he won't. If I don't go to the door, I'll never know if he can forgive me, if we can have a life together.

The Tarot said she had what she needed inside her; she needed to follow her heart. Since Winter Solstice she had drawn upon depths of courage she didn't know she had.

"Now or never," she muttered to herself as she got out of the car and hurried through the now driving rain toward the front door. Stopping at the bottom of the stairs, she took a deep breath, straightened her spine and drew on that courage.

I can do this and I will survive if he turns me away. The mantra in her mind, she slowly but steadily climbed the steps to the house and knocked on the door.

Maybe he isn't home. I don't hear anything. She half-turned to leave before catching herself and turning back. Knocking louder, she fumbled and found the doorbell. Pushed it. The chimes resounded deep in the house.

A thin pane of glass separated them.

He on his side of the door, a frown creasing his forehead, his expression blank.

She on her side, not moving, hands at her sides.

He didn't move.

Her shoulders sagged. *He's going to turn me away; leave me on the doorstep.* The urge to turn away, run down the steps and drive off to save herself from the disgrace of him not even opening the door and telling her to go away was strong. Instead she remained like a statue, bedraggled from the rain, drinking in the sight of him dressed in jeans and a t-shirt, bare feet, stubble darkening his jaw, tousled hair.

He looked tired, almost haggard.

A refection in the glass showed her face streaked with tears, her hair a mess, her clothes rumpled and damp.

What did I do to him when I went to Dennis?

More tears streaked down her cheeks. The pain was more than she could endure. *I have to go.* Her gut clenched with emotions, her head pounded with stress.

She steeled herself to turn away, walk down the stairs to her car and drive away. *To where? The little house or maybe Sophia's or maybe Sophia would come to the little house.* She willed her legs to move, to carry her away from the pain.

The door opened.

He didn't asked her in, but at least now there was a chance to tell him what she wanted and hope he wanted it to.

She opened her mouth but no words came out. Standing on the porch, crying quietly, wanting him so badly—but the words would not come.

He stood aside and gestured for her to enter. Willing her numb legs to move, she stumbled across the threshold and grasped the back of a nearby chair to keep from falling. His fresh lime scent a torture.

She turned to face him. He stood in the open doorway warily watching her.

The urge to fling herself into his arms swelled. With effort she stifled the impulse. Instead, she took one of those deep steadying breaths and hoped her voice would work.

"I'm so very sorry, Matthew. I don't really have words other than that because there aren't any. At the very least, I should have stayed long enough to talk to you about what had happened and why I thought I needed to go." She held her hands clasped in front of her, knuckles white as she fought for control, she ached to touch him to be touched by him. If that was ever to happen again, she owed him the truth.

"Dennis was hit by a motorcycle, sustained a severe concussion, a broken collarbone and a torn rotator cuff. He's still in the hospital but now beyond danger from the concussion enough he can have pain medication. Lily's with him and will help him figure things out. You know, his discharge, rehabilitation, those sorts of things. I—" she paused looking for any sign he even heard her, was listening to her. Intense emerald green eyes bore into her.

"You know Dennis has wanted to reconcile, to remarry." She looked him straight in the eye. "I told him "no". I told him I loved you and if you would still have me, you were who I wanted to spend my life with.

"So, I'm asking you, Matthew Houston. Will you marry me? Will you spend the rest of your life with me? Will you love me?"

Her breath caught in her lungs as his arms banded around her, pressed her against his long length. She struggled to turn her face, to raise it so her mouth could find his.

A hand slid across her back, up to her shoulder and around to cup her chin. Gently he raised her head and kissed her at first hesitantly and then more ravenously.

Picking her up, Matthew carried her up the stairs to his room, laid her on his bed, stood back and watched her.

"I'm getting the bed wet," she said squirming upright to take her jacket off.

A noise downstairs. They'd left the front door open.

"Stay." He pointed at her as he uttered the single word. And he was gone. She heard his voice, someone else's, and then his steps on the stairs, the hall, and he was back at the door.

"One of my crew. Sent away. When?" The last word was muffled as he stripped his shirt from his body.

"When what?" Her body tingled with awareness as the desire for her shone in his eyes and in the taut lines of his body.

"Wedding." He was crawling up the bed toward her, his jeans now unbuttoned, his penis pressing against the open placket.

The fierceness of her desire for him seized her and she clutched the bedcovers.

"Lammas, the first day of August." His hands tugged her soaked shoes off, pulled her pants down over her hips. She raised her hands to unbutton her blouse but he pushed her hands away.

"Mine." She watched in fascination as he worked diligently on the row of buttons, unclasped her front closure bra, and slowly pulled the fabric away as if he were unwrapping a sought after present.

She was the High Priestess, being worshipped by this man; at peace in her response to him and assured of the outcome. Her arms wrapped around his neck and pulled him down to her. She reveled in the feel of his hard body against her, the evidence of his desire pulsing against her thigh, the heat of him enveloping her as her senses filled. He claimed her with his hands, lips and eventually his whole body. She welcomed him in every way she knew how, wanting him to know how much she loved him, desired him.

There was still the issue of whether she was pregnant or not, but she pushed that aside and let the passion grow between them until it consumed them in a fiery blaze and she saw the Universe expand behind her closed eyes.

49   THE WEDDING

Lammas, the pagan holiday that celebrates the beginning of the harvest season: halfway between Summer Solstice and Fall Equinox. In some traditions it is the time to think about hopes and fears, but not Diana. She had faced her worst fears and now faced her future with a hope that blinded her with its brightness. While she had told him they'd marry on Lammas before they'd made love, afterward she'd had a serious conversation about the possibility of being pregnant. He'd known when the condoms had broken so it wasn't the surprise she'd thought it might be. What had surprised her was he'd charged out to an all-night drugstore for the home pregnancy test. When it came back positive, he was thrilled.

Lammas, the time to be protectors and nurturers of what we've planted—full partners with the Goddess and God; or in her personal tradition, The Universe.

Sophia had offered her house but she and Matthew decided to wed in his yard. It meant hours of toil to bring everything up to snuff as the flower beds were in need of a serious weeding and bushes were over-grown. He hired a landscape company to come in and do the work. His focus was to finish the kitchen.

Diana stood under an arbor of climbing flowers, their scent wafting through the breeze. A fountain's water played in the background. Her circle sisters had preceded her down the aisle and she'd asked Giovanni to escort her. He'd been delighted because of the friendship they'd formed during her time in Italy. She'd talked it over with Bill but together they decided against him doing it. Dennis had not come to terms with her refusal much less her decision to marry another. They hoped having Giovanni escort her would allow Bill to maintain the closeness he had rebuilt with his father.

The simple and short ceremony was performed by a judge Lily knew. In less than ten minutes she was Matthew's wife, a simple gold ring on her finger, a matching one on his.

A soft smile bloomed as she looked around the garden. Matthew had planted a living sacred circle after talking to Sophia. In the center was a Victorian gazing ball: gold to represent the season of harvest. Other colored balls were stored in a shed hidden behind well- manicured shrubs so she could change them according to season.

Ashley and her children did not travel to Ireland and Sophia's trip was short because of her sick friend. Logan and Gabriella had. They, along with Elizabeth and Michael, arrived a few days ago.

Daniel was playing with Ashley's children. Did she see longing in Ashley's eyes? Perhaps not, but her gratitude for the time he spent with her children was clear.

And as she watched, Elizabeth reached up and caressed her husband's cheek. Finally making peace with her miscarriage, she looked forward to getting pregnant again. Her doctor had advised she wait twelve weeks before trying to conceive and the twelve weeks were up. She and Michael were almost combusting right there in front of everyone.

Giovanni was pestering Gabriella who was doing her best to ignore him by staying close to Hunter, Logan, Lily and Jackson. The latter two were still so in love. Would she and Matthew be able to weather the trials of life? *We've already faced our fair share of trials but as a married couple there will be more. Everyone has them.* Her gaze flitted across the people who'd come to witness their marriage: Bill, her circle sisters, Matthew's crews and their families, friends like Daniel and Giovanni.

Lammas, a time to nurture and protect what has been planted. Her gaze sought Matthew who was engaged in conversation with Daniel and Jackson. He turned, his gaze rested on her abdomen before glancing up, smiling as she caught his eye. She nodded in acknowledgement of the current flowing between them as she pressed her hand to the slight swell: another child of The Universe would make its entrance into this world sometime after Winter Solstice.

New Release Mailing List:

You have just finished the third book in The Sacred Women's Circle series. Be the first to learn about future releases, any pre-release pricing or sales and special events by signing up for my mailing list at http://eepurl.com/NWgIH

For More Information on The Sacred Women's Circle series check out:

My website: www.JudithAshleyRomance.com
My blog: www.JudithAshleyRomance.blogspot.com

A request:

If you enjoyed *Diana*, please consider telling your friends and family and writing a review on Amazon and Goodreads. Goodreads reviews are important because Barnes and Noble, Kobo, and other places use them to help their readers find books they'll love.

ABOUT Judith

Judith, in her real life, has been a part of sacred women's circles for over twenty years and knows first-hand how important spirituality is when dealing with life's challenges.

Her imagination has always been active and through books she's been a princess res-cued from the tower by the handsome knight, a missionary in India, explorer in the Amazon jungle, a priestess of the Goddess, and a nun to name a few. She's lived with people from all walks of life including different tribes of indig-enous people on five continents in tents, wood cabins, igloos, castles, mansions, high-rise apartments, penthouses, dungeons, basements, and cottages.

Then one day in Judith's real life, the stories that make up The Sacred Women's Circle series flooded through her in daydreams, lucid dreams, and conversations so real at times she wondered about her sanity. It was a compelling experience! An experience that was a catalyst to starting her journey to tell these stories and see them published.

Judith's prayer for you:

Each and every day of your life may you find joy, may you see beauty, may you experience wonder, and may you know you are unconditionally loved.

For more books from the heart in fiction and non-fiction please visit Windtree Press

http://windtreepress.com